I0647819

Changeling Press LLC

ChangelingPress.com

Axel/Ryder Duet
A Hounds of Hell MC Romance
Jamie Targaet

Axel/Ryder Duet
A Hounds of Hell MC Romance
Jamie Targaet

All rights reserved.
Copyright ©2025 Jamie Targaet

ISBN: 978-1-60521-936-3

Publisher:
Changeling Press LLC
315 N. Centre St.
Martinsburg, WV 25404
ChangelingPress.com

Printed in the U.S.A.

Editor: Treva Harte
Cover Artist: Bryan Keller

The individual stories in this anthology have been previously released in E-Book format.

Table of Contents

Axel (Hounds of Hell MC 3)
A Hounds of Hell MC Romance
Jamie Targaet

Sadie -- I finally found the courage to escape my abusive boyfriend. But I didn't make it far, landing in a small Virginia town called Mercy. There will be no mercy for me if my ex finds me. Thanks to Axel, the gorgeous biker who towed my car to his garage, I have a place to stay and a job at the town's greenhouse. I also have the hope that I might have a second chance at love one day, with Axel.

Axel -- When I got called to tow a broken-down car to my garage, I found the beaten and battered angel who owns it on the run from the devil. Here in Mercy, with me, she's healing and learning to live again. When her ex figures out Sadie's here, even his mob ties can't protect him from me. His entire mob family can't take back what's mine and there's going to be hell to pay when they try.

Chapter One

Sadie

Sadie Downing's hands shook as she carefully wiped the blood from her face with a washcloth. Her eye hurt, the flesh around it swollen and bruised. It would be black by morning. Her nose still bled, and she was pretty sure it was broken. The split in her lower lip wasn't new, but Bobby's fist had reopened the wound tonight.

Catching sight of herself in the long mirror on the bathroom door, the tears came on. It even hurt to cry. She looked like a shell of herself in the reflection, rail thin in just Bobby's T-shirt. Her arms and legs were littered with more bruises. Bobby's spend dried on her thighs.

Oh yes, because immediately after the yelling turned to hitting, his anger would fade. Once she started to cry and cower he'd gaze down at her like she was a broken bird, rendered flightless by his cruel hands.

Bobby would pick her up then, cradle her like she was precious to him while she cried, lost in confusion. Then sex would follow. When she cried out, he mistook her pain for passion. By that point, she'd been grateful he'd never seemed to care that she really wasn't participating.

When did everything go wrong tonight? Her mind replayed the moments before Bobby got angry. What had she done? What had she said that set him off? She'd been so careful.

Sadie had hoped that they could celebrate the promotion Bobby was certain he was getting at his job. She'd dressed up, made his favorite dinner. It was supposed to have been a good night. And she needed one with all the fights they'd been having lately.

Blinking back tears, she crept back into the bedroom they shared. Bobby was sprawled across the bed, snoring as he always did. As carefully and as silently as she could, she grabbed her bathrobe from the foot of the bed. Pulling it on, she headed for the kitchen.

The dinner she'd spent hours on splattered the walls, appliances, and floor. Broken plates and serving dishes also littered the floor so she was careful where she stepped. As quietly as she could, she pulled a trash bag from under the counter. She'd need to clean up the mess before she could go to sleep.

The problem was that she just didn't want to clean it up.

"I can't do this anymore," she whispered in that quiet space. "I can't."

Her heart flew as anxiety bled into fear. She had two choices. She could clean it up and things would go on as they always had. Or she could leave it. But she'd pay for that once he walked into the kitchen in the morning.

Well, she had another option, didn't she? But *could* she run? Could she get away from Bobby and never return?

He'll kill you, her inner voice started chanting. *Bobby will kill you and no one will ever know.*

And if she stayed? Did she really want to live like this? Was she really willing to stick around until he managed to get her pregnant? Once that happened, trying to leave would be ten times worse.

Was she willing to stick around until Bobby killed her? It was a fear that sometimes kept her up at night. Normally, that fear would be her motivation for cleaning up the mess in the kitchen.

Desperation rose, pushing her to go back to that bedroom where he still snored. The clothes she'd worn earlier to clean up the house were in the hamper, and it was easy to grab those. With those clothes in hand and her shoes, she fled to the laundry room and got dressed as quickly as she could. Her coat and shoes were in the hall closet and that just left her with two other items she needed. Her wallet and her car keys. He'd destroyed her phone months ago.

The trick to keeping anything from Bobby was hiding it in ordinary places where he wouldn't think to look. Her wallet was still there, buried in a bag of potting soil she kept in the garage. There was nothing in her checking account, but she had a credit card with no balance. She had a $5,000 credit line there. It wouldn't get her far, but it was something.

Then there was the matter of her car keys. Bobby hid them months ago. She'd searched for weeks before she found them, hidden in a toolbox he never really used. Hope swelled in her chest when she found them still there.

Tightening her coat around her aching body, Sadie gazed at her car in the shadows of the garage, a twenty-year-old sedan that hadn't been driven in months. Would it start? Did it have any gas?

Swallowing hard, Sadie had to make a decision. Either she stayed and her future days would be as brutal as today had been. Or she needed to leave.

And so many things could go wrong here. What if the car didn't start? What if it was low on gas? What if the sound of starting the engine or the garage door going up woke him?

Summoning her courage, Sadie's fingers tightened around the keys. She was going to do this and once she started, she couldn't back down. After hitting the garage door button on the wall, she frantically unlocked the door of her older car. Her heart pounded in her ears as she jumped in, started the engine.

Sadie could have cried when the car started. A quick glance at the gas gauge showed she had just under half a tank.

"Thank you," she said tearfully to whatever guardian angel was watching over her, watching the garage door slowly rise.

The second she thought the car would clear the door, she hit the accelerator and didn't look back.

* * *

Axel

It was a cold February morning. Alexander Harper had just sat down with his first cup of coffee when his phone hummed in his pocket. When he pulled it out and looked at the screen, he saw the call was from Cowboy Pete's, a local gas station just off the interstate.

"This is Axel," he said, using the road name he'd been given by Razor when he'd been a prospect.

"Hey, hon. How are you?" He recognized Elsie Damron's voice. She'd worked at the gas station since he was a kid.

"Cold," he said. "What can I do for you today?"

"A young lady stopped for gas a little while ago," Elsie explained. "She filled it up but now her car won't start."

"You give her bad gas?" Axel asked, grinning.

"No," Elsie said. "Well, I hope not. There's smoke rolling out from under the hood. Looks like it's overheating to me. Can you come take a look at it?"

"Yeah." Axel knew the quiet morning was too

good to be true. Putting the call on speaker, he placed his phone on his desk, grabbing a tie from his desk drawer to pull his hair back from his face. "Did you already call Tyler? I appreciate the business, but it would be a lot closer, and cheaper, to tow it to his place."

"Yeah, I know," Elsie said, her voice dropping to a loud stage whisper. "But I think you would be better for this particular situation."

"Okay, I'll head that way," he told her. "What's she driving?"

"He's going to come get you," Elsie said to someone there with her. To Axel, she said, "Yeah, it's an older sedan. A Lincoln, I think. What model year is your car?"

Axel couldn't make out what the other person said.

"It's a 2002 model," Elsie told him.

"Give me thirty minutes," Axel said, ending the call.

Taking his coffee with him, Axel headed back into the shop. His twin brother Ryder was working on an SUV brought in yesterday. Ryder looked up when he saw Axel approach.

"Where you off to?" Ryder asked.

"Got to tow someone in," Axel told him. "I'll be back."

When Axel reached Cowboy Pete's with the tow truck, there were several cars there. They had a halfway decent grill inside the station, and it was a popular breakfast stop for town regulars and travelers alike. He pulled into the lot and parked, heading in to have Elsie point out the lady and her car.

Elsie grinned when she saw him at the counter. "Thanks for coming, hon. She's a couple of spaces down from where you parked. The black Lincoln."

"You bet," he told her, spotting the Lincoln in the window behind the counter where the older lady stood.

"Axel?" Elsie called as he headed for the door.

"Yeah?"

"If I can do anything for her, you let me know, okay?" And the kind older woman meant it.

"Will do," he told her, curious now about what he was walking into.

The black Lincoln that now parked just three spaces to the right of him with no cars parked in between. It looked like someone was sitting in the driver's seat. Walking up to the car, Axel tapped on the driver's window. The lady jumped in the seat, startled. Axel saw a flash of red curls before she peered up at him through the window.

The young woman's left eye was black and swollen almost shut. Her nose was swollen and bruised, her lip split. Someone had beat the fuck out of this little lady. Slowly, she opened the door and got out of her car. Her careful movements told him her face wasn't the only thing that hurt her this morning. Axel stepped back to give her room as she closed the door and leaned back against it.

The way she wrapped her arms protectively around herself and the fear in her green-eyed gaze had him pausing. Now he knew why Elsie called their garage. Tyler wasn't a bad guy, but he was gruff and lacking in most social niceties. The young woman before him looked like she'd been through hell and was expecting more. "Hi there," Axel said. "Elsie called me to come look at your car. What's going on?"

"It overheated I think," she said quietly. "It was okay for a couple of hours. But then it heated up and started smoking. I stopped to let it cool off the first time. Then I stopped here to get gas and let it cool off again. But when I tried to restart it this time, it wouldn't."

"Pop the hood for me?" Axel asked.

She scrambled back into the driver's seat, searching for the hood latch. Just when he was about to offer to do it for her, she found it. Axel lifted the hood and removed the radiator cap. Walking back around to where she sat behind the wheel with the driver-side door open, he said, "Try starting it."

It did start but looking into the radiator, he saw the coolant start to bubble up like a milkshake. Walking back toward her, he saw white smoke coming out of the tailpipe in the rear. Well, that wasn't good news. "Turn it off," he told her.

She did as he said, climbing back out of the car.

"Yeah, that's a blown head gasket," Axel explained. "The smoke coming out of the back is coolant getting into your exhaust system. It's not supposed to do that."

"Can you fix it?" she asked. "H-how long will it take?"

"I can fix it," he said. "How long it will take depends on a couple of things. I need to find a replacement for the head gasket and if there's any damage to the engine, we might need parts for that too. Once we have the parts we need, I can have it fixed in two or three days."

Axel could tell that wasn't the answer she was hoping to get. It was probably a good idea to get all the bad news out at once. "It's also going to be expensive," Axel told her. "You're probably looking at two to three thousand dollars to fix it."

Those big green eyes were getting shiny with

tears and Axel felt a tiny bit of panic creeping in. He was no damn good with tears. Never had been. He had to find some way to make the situation the little lady was in less terrible.

"Where are you headed?" he asked. "Do you have any friends or family we can call who can come help you out?"

Dropping her gaze, she shook her head.

"Where are you heading?" Axel tried again.

She shrugged for an answer.

"Do you know if your insurance covers towing?" he asked. If nothing else, it looked like he was going to be towing her back to his garage.

She shook her head. Pretty red curls swung with her movements.

"Do you have your insurance information in the car? We could call," he offered.

"I don't have it," she told him.

Didn't have a destination. Didn't have insurance information. What the hell was the situation here? When he gave her the cost of towing the car, she reached into the pocket of her coat, pulled out a credit card, and handed it to him. It was brand new and shiny. Axel doubted it had ever been used. "Thank you," he said. "I'm going to run this, and we'll be on our way."

She scrambled back into her car like a scared mouse. Axel shook his head as he headed back to his tow truck, reaching in to get the card reader they used for payments. The name on the card was Sadie Downing.

What the hell had happened to Sadie?

The transaction went through, which surprised him. He walked back to her car, tapping on the window to return her card. Again, she scrambled out of her car, looking around nervously.

Axel just had to ask. "Are you okay? The local hospital is on the way back to the garage."

"I'm fine," she said a little too quickly.

"Okay." He would leave it at that. "Why don't you go ahead and climb in the tow truck? I'll get your car hooked up and we'll get going."

"Thank you," she said, quickly making a beeline for the truck and climbing into the cab.

It didn't take Axel long to hook up her car and get them on the road. Sadie, if that was her name, huddled quietly in the far corner of the cabin with her head leaning on the window. While he normally appreciated the silence, just now it was awkward. He really wanted to ask her what happened. Who did that to her face?

One thing was pretty certain. She was on the run, and she was afraid. Looking at her, he understood why.

When they made it back to the garage, Axel raced around the front of the truck before she could climb out. He helped her down, watching her wince at the movements. Just how bad was she hurt? Would she be okay? Could he talk her into going to the ER?

"We have a lounge in the garage," Axel explained. "It's not a lot. A couch, some old magazines, and a TV. But it's warm." Leading her past the offices to that lounge, Axel moved slowly, matching his pace to hers. He watched her take a seat on the ancient leather couch in the lounge. Her gaze met his. There were shadows behind the one green eye that was still open.

"There's no one we can call for you, Sadie?" He had to try again. Since there was no odd reaction to him using her name, he was guessing that was legit.

Sadie shook her head. "Are there hotels here in town?"

They had a couple near the interstate exits -- older hotels that had seen better days and it wasn't uncommon for hookers and drug dealers to work out of them. Axel didn't like the idea of her being there alone in the state she was in.

"Let me think about that," he told her. "In the meantime, I'll get under the hood and see what we're looking at."

"Okay," she said. "Thank you."

"Would you like some coffee?" It was the one thing he had on hand to offer her.

Shaking her head, she reached for the remote on the battered coffee table in front of her and turned on the TV. It was something. Leaving her there, he went back to her car, backed it into a garage bay, and started the diagnostics. The codes confirmed what he already knew. In addition to the blown head gasket, there was some damage to the engine, though it wasn't as bad as it could have been.

Well, hell. The car could be fixed. Could the little lady in his lounge be fixed?

When Axel returned to the lounge sometime later, he found Sadie lying on the sofa, fast asleep and curled up on her side in a ball. He didn't want to wake her up because, from the looks of her, she needed the rest.

Blowing out a sigh, Axel stood in the doorway, trying to wrap his mind around the situation. The young woman wasn't his problem. Yeah, he was sorry she was beat up and needed work on her car. Axel reminded himself that his job was fixing her car and getting her back on the road. That was it. That was where *his* responsibility ended.

As he moved closer, Axel's gaze moved over her still form, mostly hidden by the enormous winter coat she wore. She was a natural redhead, her face pale as milk with just a sprinkling of freckles. Her long lashes were a darker shade, a delicate fan resting on her cheek, at least on the eye that wasn't swollen shut.

She looked so small lying there. Whoever did that to her was likely the bastard she was running from. Axel had been through her car. There were no bags or suitcases. He didn't even find a purse. Did she have a license? Because she didn't have a vehicle registration or insurance information in her glove box.

Blowing out a breath, he headed to the office. He'd need to call around and find the parts he needed. Axel knew how to fix the old Lincoln she was driving. He just had no idea how to fix what was happening with the young woman sleeping in his lounge.

* * *

Bobby

"Fucking little whore," Bobby Bianchi muttered under his breath.

Yeah, he'd had quite a bit to drink last night, but he'd been celebrating. A man deserved to celebrate things going well in his life. Going well for a change. Tony had made him a lieutenant yesterday, permitted him to put together his own squad. Bobby was moving up through the ranks of the family. It was a big fucking deal.

The fact that Sadie was *not* in bed late with him? That wasn't unusual unless he told her to do otherwise. Her ass needed to be up doing things. It was her job. Once he was up, the house needed to be clean, or her ass needed to be in the process of cleaning it.

But that wasn't what he found as he marched

from the bathroom to the kitchen. As he took in the mess she'd left in his kitchen, he scrubbed a hand over his mouth.

It took him a minute to remember what had happened exactly. She knew he was celebrating, and she had a nice meal waiting for him when he got home. But she'd pissed him off as she often did, and he couldn't remember exactly how this time. The ungrateful little bitch he allowed to live in his home had fucked up *something*. That he'd gotten mad had been all her fault.

And she knew to have everything cleaned up before he got out of bed, and she hadn't. Broken dishes littered the floor, old food splattered everywhere. Why the hell was the mess still there?

Where was she?

Bobby marched through the house, ready to beat the shit out of her when he found her. But she was nowhere to be found. She wasn't in the bathroom or downstairs fooling with the laundry. The living room and dining rooms were empty and none of her things seemed to be out of place. What the fuck was going on?

As he headed for the garage, he was already shaking his head. She couldn't be *that* dumb, could she? Her old car had sat there in his garage for months, taking up space. She didn't even have the keys. He made sure of that.

But his suspicions were confirmed when he stormed into the quiet space of the garage, staring at the space where her old Lincoln usually sat. It was gone and apparently, so was she.

"Fuck!" he shouted.

Bobby ran back into the house, the wall clock telling him it was just after nine in the morning. When had she left? Where the hell had she gone? He didn't allow her to have a phone. She didn't talk to anyone unless it was in his presence. The bitch didn't have friends or family to speak of.

Fuck, this is bad.

Christopher answered the phone quickly. Bobby started shouting the minute "hey" was out of his friend's mouth, needing him to get his ass over there right fucking now.

"You want me to help look for her?" Christopher asked.

"Yeah," Bobby said. "So, get your ass over here. I just got fucking promoted. If word gets out that I can't even manage my girlfriend, it could be bad news for me. Bad news for me is bad news for *you*."

"Okay, yeah," Christopher said. "On my way."

Bobby really hadn't thought Sadie had it in her to try and fuck with him. He was sure she knew better. But sure enough, he'd been wrong. When he found her, she would regret her choices.

Chapter Two

Sadie

When Sadie awoke, sharp panic had her scrambling to sit up. Had Bobby found her? Was he going to turn up any minute and drag her back to the house that had been her prison for the last several months? Would he kill her?

This time Sadie had really done it. She'd left, made it out of Bobby's house, and made it all the way to this small Virginia town. She hadn't expected to make it that far. But Bobby wouldn't just let her go. In his mind, she belonged to him. He *would* come for her.

With her heart racing in her chest, her mind struggled to recall how she got to this dingy little lounge. Her car had overheated on the interstate, just after she reached Virginia. She'd been lucky to make it to a gas station. The nice lady there had called the garage and the mechanic had brought her here to fix her car. Exhausted by that point, she kind of remembered the guy who towed her in telling her that it would cost a couple thousand dollars to fix the car at *least*. It was also going to take a few days.

She hadn't intended to fall asleep, and it left her feeling disoriented. The old leather couch she'd been sleeping on was surprisingly comfortable. The news was on TV, the screen telling her it was just after three in the afternoon. She couldn't really hear the broadcast over the sounds of machinery in the garage beyond. All she knew was that she'd been asleep for a few hours.

What was she going to do?

Sadie had fled Bobby's house with the clothes on her back, her wallet, and her car. The credit card she kept for emergencies was all she had at the moment, and she didn't think Bobby knew she even had it. Did she really want to max it out to fix her Lincoln? If she was going to survive this, Sadie needed to disappear. She'd need money to live on until she could figure things out.

The bathroom was just outside the lounge. When she washed her hands, she looked into the small mirror over the sink. Tears threatened to come on as she looked at her reflection, realizing she didn't even recognize herself anymore. She looked like someone had tied her to the back bumper of a car and dragged her down the road for a couple of miles. And Bobby, the man who claimed to love her more than anything or anyone else, had done that to her.

Bobby had taken everything from her: her freedom, her dignity, her happiness. As she stared at the eye that was swollen shut and the vivid bruises that covered much of her face, real terror crept in.

Bobby *would* kill her when he found her. He'd told her so many times that he'd kill her if she ever tried to leave him. He'd promised to kill anyone who tried to help her. And she believed him. She knew he would do just that.

Trying to get her breathing under control, Sadie leaned back against the bathroom door. What she needed now was a place to hide, to heal. The guy who had towed her car here had asked if there was anyone she could call. She didn't lie to him when she told him there wasn't. It sucked being alone, but she was also grateful for that. She didn't have to worry about him hunting down family or friends to get to her. It was the only small advantage she had.

It was hard to push thoughts through the panic, but she had to try. When Bobby came looking for her, he'd describe her as a redhead who was badly beaten up. Either of those things would be easy for people to remember, even in passing. And Sadie didn't want any harm to come to some innocent person who was just trying to help her.

No, she needed to limit the number of people who saw her until she could heal up. She'd need to do something with her hair too.

Thoughts of what she needed to do ran through her mind as she fought to keep her fear at bay. Stepping out of the bathroom, Sadie ran right into someone hard. When she glanced up to see the man who brought her here -- she didn't get his name earlier -- he reached out to try and steady her. She flinched away from his touch.

"I'm sorry," he said quietly.

She darted around him and returned to the lounge, and he followed her. In the fluorescent lights overhead, she got a better look at him. He was older than her, probably somewhere in his mid to late thirties, and tall with wide shoulders. The black leather jacket he wore with jeans was a shade lighter than the boots he wore. His dark hair was pulled back from his face in a small ponytail. He was actually nice looking with high cheekbones and a square jaw. His blue eyes were kind, reflecting pity as his gaze moved over her.

"Are you sure you don't want to go to the ER?" he asked again.

Sadie nodded. That was the last place she could go right now, and she couldn't remember the last time she'd had medical insurance.

"If you change your mind, let me know," he said. "I've been calling around to try and find a new head gasket for your car and --"

"Have you started working on my car?" Sadie cut him off.

"Not yet," he replied. "I need the parts first and -_"

"Can we *not* fix it?" she asked slowly, not liking the way her voice shook. She knew the man probably thought she was crazy as she watched confusion bleed into his expression. "I mean... I'm glad to pay you for anything you've done to this point but..."

"If you're not planning to fix it, what are you going to do?" he asked.

Sadie shook her head at herself. She couldn't answer his question. Not right now.

"I'm not going to fix it *right now*," she said, hoping that sounded better. "I was thinking once I find a place to stay and maybe get back on my feet, I could fix it later?"

After a moment, he shrugged. "Okay. It's your choice. The thing is, you'll need to keep it somewhere while you're getting everything figured out."

She hadn't thought of that. What *would* she do with it? If it was out in the open, and if Bobby saw it, he would come after whoever had it. Even if they were just letting her park it.

Her mind was spinning, fear not helping that process. She took a seat on the couch where she'd slept.

"I'm sorry," she told him. None of this was his problem.

"You don't have anything to apologize to me for," he told her. "I'm Axel, by the way."

Sadie nodded, keeping an eye on him as he sat next to her on the couch. The patch on his jacket caught her eye, a wolf's face wreathed in flames. Red and orange lettering spelled out "Hounds of Hell."

"I could... pay you to store it for me until I find a place if that's something you do," she said, trying to keep calm. Maybe they could cover it up.

Axel's elbows rested on his knees. Slowly, he shook his head.

"If you can't, it's okay," she added quickly, realizing just how dependent she was right now on this man's kindness and patience. And he didn't owe her anything.

"I can keep it here for a little while," Axel said. "My brother and a friend of ours own the garage here. I won't charge you anything. I'd like to help. I know it's not my business but... you look like you've really been through something."

Oh, she had. And while she appreciated that he was trying to help her, the sincerity in his face had her blinking back tears. "Thank you," she told him. "Let me know what else I owe you and..."

Axel shook his head. "When was the last time you ate?"

Sadie remembered the nice dinner she'd spent a few hours on yesterday to celebrate Bobby's promotion. Were the remnants of it still splattered on the walls and floor of his kitchen?

"Yesterday," she managed to say.

"There's a decent diner across the street. I could run over and get you something." Axel must have read her reluctance in her expression. He followed that with a quick, "I have to eat too. Anything you can't eat or don't like?"

Sadie shook her head.

Just like that, she was alone again in the lounge. Her gaze was trained on the TV, but she wasn't really watching it. Her mind was a jumble of panicked thoughts that she really couldn't control as she waited.

The sound of steps outside the lounge had her freezing on the couch. A man walked by the open lounge door before coming back to peer in. It startled her because, for a moment, she thought Axel was back. The man who now stood staring at her from the hall had the exact same face as Axel. But he was wearing a red hoodie, his hair was cut short, and he had a short beard.

"Hi there," he said to her. "Have you been... helped?"

Sadie swallowed hard, nodding.

"Have you seen a guy that looks just like me?" he asked, his tone kind.

She nodded. "He went to the diner across the street."

"Thank you," he said and hurried off, leaving her to her anxiety as she waited.

* * *

Axel

Axel jumped a little when a hand clamped over his shoulder from behind. He was waiting at the diner's counter for his order, surprised it was as busy as it was considering it was a couple of hours before the dinner rush. Turning, he found his twin standing behind him.

"Who the hell is that woman?" Ryder asked, jerking a thumb in the direction of their garage.

Axel blew out an exhale. "She owns that Lincoln I towed in this morning," he explained. "The blown head gasket?"

"What happened to her *face*?" Ryder asked. "Has she been to the hospital?"

"She won't go to the hospital," Axel told him. "I offered."

Ryder nodded, thinking about it for a moment. "She running from somewhere?"

"Most likely," Axel told him. "She's too scared to

say much. I'm getting us something to eat. I'll see if I can get her to talk to me."

"Might be best not to get involved," his brother said. "Just fix up her car and send her on her way. We have enough shit to deal with right now."

Axel knew he was probably right. He'd called around to find parts and like he told her, he could probably have everything fixed in a few days.

Ryder could read him like a book. "What?"

"She fell asleep while I was calling around," he said. "Now she's saying she doesn't want to fix it right now. She's asking us to hang onto it until she can get back on her feet."

Ryder rolled his eyes. "No. That's even worse. She goes off and whoever did that to her face shows up here raising hell. We don't need that."

They really didn't. They'd had all the trouble with Cottonmouths and Razor's daughter Jade last summer. Then they'd had to deal with Snow's old lady's ex a few weeks back at Christmas. It would be nice for things to get back to something like normal. At least for a little while.

Still, Axel wasn't ready to just throw the little redhead in their garage to the wolves just yet. Yeah, he knew she was on the run. Whoever did that to her face might do much worse if they found her. It wasn't their problem, but Axel knew he'd sleep a lot better if he did something to help her.

"Fuck, I know that look," Ryder grumbled.

His brother did indeed. Axel was going to help Sadie. It was just the right thing to do.

Shaking his head, his brother said, "Leave me out of it."

"Okay," Axel told him, watching him march off.

His order was ready five minutes later. The wind

was picking up, blowing dark clouds across the cold winter sky. Axel made it back to the garage before it started raining, finding her just where he left her in the lounge. He'd gotten them burgers and fries with soda. Almost as soon as he started handing her things, her stomach growled loudly.

"Thank you," she said.

He could have kicked himself watching her try to eat the burger with that split lip. Blowing out an exhale, he said, "Shit, I'm sorry. That's bound to hurt."

Sadie shook her head quickly. "It's not bad."

"Yeah, well, they're usually pretty generous with the salt on those fries too so…"

She nodded and for a few moments, they ate in silence.

"You say you don't have anyone we can call," he said. "What about places that are familiar to you? Places you've lived before?"

The panic in her one good eye shut that down. Okay, those were places someone might go looking for her.

"Is this a husband or boyfriend?" Axel asked.

At first, he wasn't sure she was going to answer. But after a moment, she said, "Boyfriend."

Well, that was something. She wasn't legally tied to the fucker anyway. A friend of his from high school had just gone through a horrible divorce. Maisy had been lucky she had a place to go, with her brother and his wife. His friend hadn't had to deal with it alone.

That's what they needed here. He would have offered to let her stay with him and Ryder, but his twin could be a dick sometimes and had already let him know he didn't think getting involved with this little lady was a good idea. That and Ryder loved bringing home a club slut now and then. Axel really didn't want to explain that to their guest.

Besides, the house he shared with his brother was back in the sticks, a good fifteen minutes outside of Mercy. It would be better for her to stay in town. The cops could get to her quickly. If she had to run, Mercy wasn't far from the interstate. They had a couple of hotels in town, but Axel wouldn't feel right about having her stay at either of them. Not when you had drug deals and such running out of them at night.

That was when the idea came to him.

Liza Austin and her husband lived in Mercy. They ran a greenhouse next to their home, and it was within walking distance from the garage. Once in a while, Liza rented out a room in her house though it had been a little while since she had. Her husband had some health troubles back in the fall. She could probably use some help around the house or greenhouse since she was caring for her husband too.

Sadie would probably be safe there. The Austins were good people.

"I have an idea," Axel said, having just finished off his burger. "There's a really nice couple here in town and they sometimes rent out rooms in their house to help make ends meet. We should see if they have a room to rent for you."

She hadn't made much progress on her burger. Her hands shook as she set it down, using a napkin to wipe her mouth and dab at that injured lip. She wasn't protesting yet.

"Yeah, the Austins," he went on. "An older couple. You can walk to their place from here. Liza's husband has had some health issues in the last few months and just maybe she could use a hand around the house or at their business."

Sadie swallowed hard. "Their business?"

"Yeah, they own a greenhouse here in Mercy," he explained. "That greenhouse has probably been here longer than I have."

Something shifted in her expression, so slight he almost missed it. Was that a flicker of hope in her one good eye?

"A greenhouse?" she repeated.

Axel nodded. "It's a nice one. They sell trees and shrubs and starter plants for gardens. I don't go over there much. I can kill a plant by looking at it. But if you have a green thumb or like that sort of thing..."

Maybe she did. She seemed interested. But she wasn't saying anything.

"Want to go visit them in a few minutes?" he offered. "After you've had a chance to eat."

Sadie sighed. "I don't know... What in the world are they going to think when they see... me?"

Axel caught her gaze. "We all need a little help from time to time. I'm sure they have too. Maybe you guys can help each other."

After a long moment, she asked, "Why are *you* trying to help me?"

"Because you look like you need help," he said. "Because where I'm from, a man who would lay hands on a woman the way this so-called boyfriend did you is a piece of shit. Where I'm from, we don't tolerate that."

His heart squeezed in his chest to see that single tear slide from the corner of her green eye.

"It's just..." Now she wiped away that tear with her napkin. "The couple you mentioned sound like nice people. I'd love to see their greenhouse. But... I don't want to cause them any trouble. Especially if the husband has health problems. You know?"

"You're not going to cause them any trouble,"

Axel said.

"You don't know that."

She had a point. She didn't mean her personally but if that son-of-a-bitch found her... That's what had her worried.

"I should probably mention that the sheriff's department is just a block away from Liza's house," Axel explained. "And what the law can't handle? Well, sometimes we deal with that."

Her gaze moved to the patch on his jacket. Now she was getting it. But he didn't want to scare her by talking about the Hounds. There was time for that later.

"Just go with me to talk to Liza," he said. "Will you do that?"

After a moment, her gaze dropped. She picked her burger back up. "Okay."

Chapter Three

Sadie

The rain was cold as Sadie followed Axel to the nursery he'd been talking about. Since she'd pulled the hood of her coat over her head, she didn't get a good look at the nursery. She kept her head down against the rain as he knocked on the door of a lovely white shop in the heart of Mercy.

An older lady answered the door, her blue eyes friendly as she motioned Axel and Sadie into the small office building.

"Axel, how are you?" the lady asked in a heavy Southern accent as she closed the door. "Who's your friend?"

Nerves were getting the better of Sadie as the woman's gaze moved to her. To be polite, Sadie lowered her hood. The woman's smile faded as her eyes widened in surprise.

"Sadie, this is Liza Austin," Axel introduced them. "Liza, this is Sadie."

"It's nice to meet you." Liza's smile returned though there was concern in her expression now. "What can I do for you today?"

"Well," Axel jumped in and Sadie was grateful he did. "Sadie here had some car trouble on the road this morning. It looks like she's going to be staying with us in Mercy for a little while until she can get back on her feet. I was wondering if you were still renting out space at the moment?"

Liza's expression was really concerned now. "She was in a car accident? Child, why aren't you in the hospital?"

"She wasn't in an accident," Axel said meaningfully. "The injuries are from something else."

The woman's brows knit, and Sadie couldn't blame her for her confusion.

"I left my boyfriend," Sadie admitted. If the woman was going to let Sadie into her life in any way, she deserved to know the truth up front. "I'm looking for a place to stay. I don't have a lot, but I can pay rent, or I can help you out in exchange, earn my keep."

The confusion was gone in an instant, the woman's full attention on Sadie now. "I have a place where you can stay," Liza told her. "And I could use some help right now. If nothing else, here in the house. But if you happen to have a green thumb, I can always use help with the business."

"I studied horticulture in college," Sadie said. "Hoping to finish that degree one day. I'd love to help with the greenhouse."

Axel's expression was one of surprise while Liza just smiled.

"That's perfect then," the woman said. "Axel, go get her things and bring them on over here. I need to get Sadie settled in."

Axel looked to her, and she shook her head.

"I don't have any things for him to go get," Sadie told them. "The car is all I have right now."

They exchanged a look while Sadie stood there, embarrassed. What they must think of her.

"I do have to get back," Axel told them. To Sadie, he said, "If you need anything, it's just a short walk. I'll stop by tomorrow and see how you're doing, okay?"

"Thank you," Sadie told him and she meant it. "I appreciate everything."

As she watched him go back out the door, her heart sank just a little. Axel seemed like one of those rare good guys she always heard about. Maybe they did exist after all. On top of it, he was gorgeous in a rugged sort of way. And wasn't it just her luck that she'd met him when she was beaten to a pulp and at the lowest point of her life? What would it have been like to have met him another time?

"What was your name again?" Liza asked.

"I'm Sadie Downing," she said, extending her hand.

Liza Austin shook it firmly. Her white hair was as curly as her own, tied back in a ponytail with a blue bandana covering her head. She wore a heavy cable sweater with jeans and the gentle lines around her eyes deepened when she smiled.

"Well, this really is good timing for us," Liza said. "My husband had back surgery a few weeks ago and I could use some help. If you do a good job, well, you can stay as long as you like. Room and board."

Sadie was grateful. She didn't want anyone's pity. And keeping busy would help her fight back the fear that Bobby could show up any minute and finally end her.

"Let's show you around," Liza told her.

Sadie's gaze swept around the tidy office with its soft yellow lighting and well-kept plants all around. It was warm and welcoming.

"This is our business office," Liza told her. "The greenhouse is right out back."

It was a short dash from the back door of the office building to the enormous greenhouse behind it. Sadie had been expecting it to be nice. But nice didn't do it justice.

The greenhouse stood tall and proud, its glass panes streaked with rain. It was a grand structure, with a peaked roof that rose high into the sky and intricate metalwork that decorated the windows and doors. Vines and flowers crept up the sides of the building, lending a touch of natural beauty to the already stunning structure.

Sadie followed Liza inside, enjoying the rush of warm, humid air that carried the scent of blooming flowers and vegetables. The greenhouse was filled with rows upon rows of plants, each one beautiful and healthy. She hadn't realized just how much she had missed growing and nurturing plants, enjoying the peace it offered.

"This is beautiful," Sadie told her.

Liza's smile was proud. "I know. It's fully insulated and solar. I had a climate control system put in place a couple of years back. It cost me an arm and a leg but with it, I can pretty much grow any crops I want all year round. Anyway, our house is behind this, and we have a few of acres of land I use for planting spring to fall."

"I don't think I've ever worked in a greenhouse this well-kept," Sadie admitted. "I'm just hoping I can do a good enough job."

"I'm sure you'll do just fine," Liza said. "Once you're healed up a little. Right now, let's take care of you."

Out of habit, Sadie was already shaking her head in denial. "I'm fine, really. I just --"

Liza held up a hand like a crossing guard, cutting her off. "You're not with him anymore. You're with me. And I'm thinking maybe a nice hot shower or warm bath. We'll get some dinner in you and then you can tuck in and catch up on some sleep."

The woman's candor knocked down the last of her defenses. Sadie burst into tears. Liza pulled her into a hug.

"Hush, now," Liza's voice was gentle. "Things are going to get better. You'll see."

Easing back Sadie swiped at her tears with the back of her hand. "He's going to be looking for me... I appreciate your help so much but if he showed up and did anything..."

"Hon, the sheriff's office is just a block over," Liza said, not seeming concerned. "And Axel? Well, he's one of the Hounds. If this boyfriend of yours shows up and tries anything, believe me, they can handle him."

"What are the Hounds?" Sadie had to ask.

"Motorcycle gang," Liza replied. "They've had a club here for years. They're not bad guys or anything. But no one crosses them for a reason. If you have Axel as a friend, you're well looked after."

A motorcycle gang? Was his brother a member too?

"Come on," Liza told her. "You're dead on your feet. Let's get you in the house."

* * *

Axel

When Axel got back to the garage, he found his brother and Hero waiting for him. And he wasn't entirely surprised.

"Where is she?" Ryder asked, hands shoved in the pockets of his jeans.

"She's going to be staying with Liza Austin," Axel told him. When the tension eased in his twin's face, Axel could have laughed. "You thought I was bringing her to *our* place?"

Ryder shrugged. "I figured it was a possibility."

Even Hero cut his brother a look.

"With you bringing home club sluts a few times a week?" Axel snorted. "No. She's been through enough."

"What *has* she been through?" Hero asked. "What did she tell you?"

"Honestly, not a lot," Axel said. "She's running from a boyfriend, the one who did that to her face, and she's scared to death. She got out with the clothes on her back and that car. I haven't even seen her with a phone."

"He might not have let her have a phone," Hero said.

Axel nodded, not letting himself stop and consider that. "Maybe that's actually good because without a phone, he can't track her location unless the car's tagged in some way."

He made a mental note to go back through the Lincoln and look for any tracking devices. He could also pull Snow in to look behind him. Snow, the club VP, was also the Hounds' tech guy.

"We still need to be smart about this," Hero told them. "If we're putting the car up for her until she figures out what she wants to do, we don't need to be obvious about it."

"I was thinking about taking it out to our place," Axel said. "We've got room in the garage since dumbass here crashed his Jeep."

Ryder flipped him off. He knew he was a dumbass. He'd spent a small fortune on the loaded Jeep only to crash it one night six months later when he was drunk off his ass.

"We'll keep it there and I'll throw a tarp over it too," he continued. "Once I'm sure there's no bugs on it."

"That should work," Hero said, seeming satisfied. "Hope things get better for her."

"Same," Ryder said. "Taking her to Liza was a good idea."

Axel thought so too. Once Sadie admitted to Liza what actually happened, the older lady went into full protective mode. It made him happy that Sadie was staying with her, especially too since she seemed really interested in the Austins' greenhouse.

"Make sure you let Razor know about this too," Hero said before heading back for the office.

"Will do," Axel replied.

But as he got back to work, he wasn't able to take his mind off the girl who found herself stranded in Mercy today.

* * *

Sadie

"Good morning," a friendly voice said as Sadie just opened her eyes.

The sun was shining brightly through the tall windows of the bedroom, the warm beams lighting up the room. And the bedroom where she'd slept was already pretty and inviting. She must have fallen asleep as soon as her head hit the pillow because she didn't remember much about the room from last night.

Now, as her gaze swept across it, she saw it was lovely, all in shades of cream and cornflower blue. The frilly curtains that framed the windows matched the duvet she was huddled under. The bed frame and nightstand were antiques made of gorgeous dark wood. The entire vibe of the room was calm, peaceful.

She'd almost forgotten what that feeling was like.

"I just realized I didn't bring you any fresh towels." Liza said, bright-eyed, with a small stack of towels in her arms and what looked like the clothes she'd been wearing on top. "And if you need more, just ask."

"Thank you," Sadie muttered, more grateful than

she could ever express.

Slowly, she tried to sit up. Everything hurt so much more this morning. Liza's eyes widened as she dropped the towels and clothes on the foot of the bed and hustled around to help her. Arranging pillows behind her back, Liza had her comfortable fast. The flannel pajamas Liza loaned her were warm and covered her up, which was a good thing. If the poor woman saw how colorful the rest of her was, she'd be more upset and concerned than she already was.

"Are you sure we can't get someone to look at you?" Liza asked. "My doctor is right here in town and he's a really nice guy."

Sadie shook her head. "I'll be fine."

"You know legally he can't tell anyone you're a patient, right?" Liza asked. "If that's what you're worried about."

She *was* worried about it. Anyone who tried to help might *think* they weren't allowed to say anything. But Bobby worked for a dangerous crime family in New Jersey and none of them worried about legalities. It's why she had to be careful. If someone got hurt because of her, like Liza or Axel, she'd never be able to live with it.

"I'm okay," Sadie said, trying to be reassuring. She could tell she missed it by a mile. "What time is it?" she asked Liza, trying to redirect the conversation.

The older woman pushed up her sleeve to see the smart watch she wore. "It's almost noon."

Old panic welled up in her. How could she have slept so long? What was she going to do now? Wait for Bobby to show up?

And he would show up.

"You didn't even make it out of there with your phone, did you?" Liza asked.

"He… wouldn't let me have a phone," Sadie replied.

The woman's jaw tightened as anger bled into her expression. "Hon, you don't need anyone to give you permission to do anything. Do you know that? I am so sorry about what happened to you. I really am."

"It's not your fault," she told her.

"It's not yours either. That's the point." The woman shook her head. "Can I help you get in the bath? Or I can bring up something for you to eat."

The woman's kindness just wasn't something she was prepared for. Tears stung the backs of her eyes as she considered how lucky she was to be there with someone like her. And it had been Axel who brought her there, taking her to someone he knew and trusted.

"I'll be able to get in the shower," Sadie said. "I'll come down. You've already done so much for me."

"It's no problem," Liza told her, looking like she still had plenty to say. "I've got to make my husband lunch anyway. Come down when you're ready."

"Thank you."

It was no small effort for her to pull herself out of the bed once Liza left. Everything hurt. When she made it to the bathroom and stripped off to get in the shower, she caught her reflection in the long mirror on the back of the bathroom door. Vivid bruises painted her skin in sharp purple, black, and green. The worst ones covered her ribs and laced up her back. The one around her left kidney really hurt. Bobby had kicked her there hard more than once.

Once she was dressed after her shower, Sadie made her way down the stairs, finding the kitchen by following the sounds of activity. An older man sat eating at the table in the cheery room and Liza smiled when she noticed her.

"Henry," Liza said to her husband, a thin older man with a full head of white hair and a friendly smile, "this is Sadie. Sadie, this is my husband, Henry."

The man did his best not to stare at her as she sat across the table from him, but he didn't succeed. Wincing, he shook his head.

"I sure am sorry for whatever happened to you," Henry said after a moment, turning his attention back to the other half of the sandwich on his plate.

"Me too," Sadie said.

"Liza here tells me you might know something about working with plants," he went on. "That true?"

Sadie nodded. "Yes, sir. I've always enjoyed gardening."

"She's studying horticulture in college," Liza added, placing a plate with a sandwich and chips in front of her.

Henry smiled. "I guess so. She lit right up when you said that. What did you think of the greenhouse?"

"It's amazing," Sadie told them. "I'm really looking forward to working in there."

"Good," Henry said. "Because there's a lot to do and with me out of commission for a while yet with my back. Maybe with your help we can stay on schedule with everything."

It was all she wanted. To be useful and doing something she sincerely enjoyed. "Thank you for letting me stay with you." Just maybe there was hope after all. "I'll work hard."

"I think you will," Liza told her, joining them at the table with her own lunch.

"Where are you from?" Henry asked, earning a look from his wife.

"It's okay," Sadie said. "I'm originally from New Brunswick, New Jersey. I've lived there most of my life anyway. I went to school at Rutgers for a while."

"When did you stop going?" Henry asked.

"Not long after I met him." She didn't want to say his name. "I made it through the first two years. I'm hoping I can finish at some point."

"You will," Liza told her. "You might want to transfer somewhere else, but I wouldn't think that would be hard."

Liza had that right. If Sadie never set foot in New Jersey ever again, she'd be fine with that.

"I take you don't have anyone who can help you," Henry said after a moment.

Sadie shook her head. Her mother had been young when she had her, telling Sadie she'd been an accident. Her father had never really been in the picture and her mother had floated from one relationship to the next most of the time Sadie had lived with her. Almost as soon as Sadie left for college, her mother found someone she was serious about and married him. They now had two little kids and a nice house in Newark. Sadie went to stay with them over the holidays after her freshman year. The visit had been uncomfortable, and her stepfather almost seemed to resent her. Her mother only talked to Sadie one more time after that, letting Sadie know the rest of the family was going to Europe for the summer. Her mother had really been saying, "We don't want you to come back," without saying the words. Sadie just let it go.

Not long after that, she met Bobby, and he'd ripped her world apart. The fact that her mother had no idea where she was or what had happened to her only made the betrayal that much worse.

"Well, if she did, Henry, she'd be there, wouldn't she?" Liza shook her head. "Have you ever been here in Mercy before?"

"I don't think I've even heard of it," Sadie replied.

"It's a great town." Liza's pride came through in her words. "I've always lived here. It's not big, but it doesn't need to be. We have everything we need, and there's a lot of good people. I hope you like it here."

Sadie nodded. She hadn't seen much of Mercy so far but when Liza said there were a lot of good people? That rang true. The couple she was eating lunch with had been nothing but generous. And there was Axel. He said he'd stop by and check on her today. It had been kind of him to say that, but she wasn't about to count on him. The poor man had found himself in the middle of a mess. He'd done the best he could to help, but he didn't owe her anything.

That didn't stop her from hoping she'd see him again. The idea that he was in a motorcycle gang was intriguing, even though she knew she had no business being interested in that. Or in him. Bobby was part of the mob and look how *that* turned out.

Still, Axel wasn't Bobby.

Wanting to steer the conversation in a different direction, Sadie asked, "So what is your planting schedule like for this year?" It was the right question to ask. The couple excitedly told her about their plans for the year while she ate her lunch.

Chapter Four

Axel

"Here we fucking go," Snow said from the other side of the Lincoln.

Axel slid out from under the sedan just as Snow walked around to him. He held up what looked like a small black box. One side was just a magnet, which held it to the vehicle. The other side showed a small green light.

"Are you fucking kidding me?" Axel asked.

Snow raked a hand through the white strands of his hair. "Yeah, it sure as fuck looks like a tracking device."

When Axel climbed to his feet, his mind was spinning. The car had been in their garage for the last twenty-four hours or so. The son-of-a-bitch who'd beaten up Sadie could be there any time now. He could already be there. *Fuck*.

"We need to call a meeting," Snow said. "Right fucking now."

Axel and Snow got to the clubhouse in about ten minutes. Razor, their club prez, was waiting when they got there. Hero and Ryder pulled into the lot separately five minutes later.

Apparently, Snow had told Razor some of what had gone on yesterday with Sadie. Axel filled him in on the rest. You could have heard a pin drop in the meeting room once he'd finished talking.

"I say we smash the fucker," Ryder said. "The device doesn't work anymore. Takes care of the problem."

Razor shook his head. "They've probably already got a location. We take out the device, they're coming here for sure."

"What else can we do?" his twin asked.

"Someone needs to drive it on out of Mercy," Razor said. "Make it look like she kept on going."

"They're still going to come here," Axel pointed out.

"Not right away," Razor said. "They won't backtrack until they have trouble finding her. It buys us some time." Razor looked at each of them in turn, the last one being Axel. "It needs to keep moving," Razor went on. "The sooner the better."

"Who's taking it?" Snow asked, sitting across the table from Axel.

"I'm staying right here," Axel said. "If we're wrong and someone shows up here looking for Sadie, I'm not leaving her unprotected."

He didn't miss the look Hero cut Razor.

"I thought you might say that." Their prez turned his gaze on Ryder. "How about you?"

Ryder shrugged. "As long as I can make it fun. And we're not overloaded at the garage right now. Where am I going?"

"How about Biloxi?" Razor offered. "I owe our brothers down there some guns. You can deliver them for me."

Ryder's grin was sly. "Works for me. I've got a couple of little sweeties I'd like to visit there."

Axel bet he did. His twin had "little sweeties" in a lot of places.

"What do you want me to do with the device?" Ryder asked.

"What is he driving down there?" Snow asked.

"My pickup truck," Ryder answered.

"*Our* pickup truck," Axel clarified. But if it kept Sadie safe, he'd live with it.

"Whatever," Razor said. "Go get that truck and

bring it back here to the clubhouse. I'll get you the guns; Snow will place the device on your truck. You're going to head for Gulfport first. You're going to get rid of the device in the Gulf of Mexico. Be quick about it. Then you can make the delivery to Biloxi and do whatever else you want while you're there."

Axel's gaze locked with his twin's and he nodded. It sounded like a solid plan to him.

"I'm on it," Ryder said to end the meeting.

Axel followed him outside. "Hey, thank you for doing this."

Ryder mounted his Harley. "You bet. Just let me know if something goes south so I can get my ass back up here. Okay?"

"Yep." Axel gave his brother a hug, watched as he started up and headed back to their house for the truck.

Snow drove Axel back to the garage and Sadie was on his mind the entire time. Since he told her and Liza that he'd stop by and check on her today while he had a minute, he decided to do just that. It was still cold but sunny today, so he headed for the Austins' on foot, reaching the office building in no time at all.

Liza smiled to find him at her door. "Hey, Axel."

"How is she?" he asked, hoping her friendly greeting meant everything was going well.

"She *looks* worse," Liza told him. "But I couldn't get her to take it easy today. She's in the greenhouse."

"Is it okay if I go visit with her?"

Liza waved him away, chuckling. "You don't need my permission. She'll be happy to see you."

Knowing his way around, Axel headed for the back door as Liza headed toward her counter to continue her paperwork. He stopped.

"Thank you for taking her in," he said. "I mean

it. I owe you one."

Liza's smile was knowing. "You don't owe me anything. Besides, she does know what she's doing with plants. I'm kind of hoping she'll stay. Good help is hard to find."

That made him happy. And sure enough, he found Sadie in the warmth of the greenhouse. Glossy red curls hid her face from him as she worked at what looked like planting seeds in a planting tray. She wore the same clothes, only clean now, and he made a mental note of that.

"Hi, Sadie," he said quietly, trying not to scare her.

She jumped a little anyway, but the tension eased and her shoulders lowered after a moment. When she looked up, he couldn't help wincing. Axel had been in big ass bar fights before and came out looking better than she did right now. Moving slowly, he joined her near the center of the greenhouse. He made a point of not standing too close to her.

"How are you feeling today?" he asked. That seemed like a safe question.

"I'm okay," she told him. "It feels better having something to do."

Axel understood. He'd never been one to stay in bed to recover from anything unless he just couldn't fucking move. It also told him that she, like him, was used to taking a beating and getting back to work the next day. But the reasons were very different. How long had she lived with the bastard?

Her calm demeanor had him dreading what he was about to tell her. But he had to. She deserved to know what was going on.

"Sadie, I went over your car," he started slowly. "Snow helped me. He's our tech guy. We found a tracking device."

Sadie kept working at planting the seeds but now her hands were shaking. "He's going to find me?"

When she didn't stop working, he carefully caught her hands in his. Patiently, he waited until her gaze met his. "There's a chance he will find you," Axel explained. "But probably not today."

Her left eye *was* swollen shut today. That split lower lip trembled. "What do you mean?"

"My club, the Hounds, called a meeting," he said. "Our prez was worried that if we just destroyed it outright, he'd come right here. So, my brother is going to drive the device away from here and get rid of it. It will buy us some time. It will look like you kept moving on."

Sadie took a deep, calming breath, slowly released it. Hesitantly, she pulled her hands from his grasp.

"When he doesn't find you," Axel went on, "yeah, he might backtrack and end up here. If he does, we'll deal with him."

Nodding, she dropped her gaze. "He'll find me, Axel."

With gentle fingers, he tipped her chin back up, making her look at him. "Maybe. But just because he finds you doesn't mean you're his."

Shying away from his touch, she moved back from the tray she'd been working with. He watched her curl in on herself.

"What if he gets your brother?" she whispered. "What if he does start here? He could hurt you or Liza or her husband Henry."

"Even if he came here today, he couldn't find you that easily," Axel said. "You're safe here with Liza. You're close to the police. And you have us. And I'm going to tow your car over to my place, cover it with a tarp. It won't even be here in town to find."

Tears spilled from her right eye. "What if he figures it out? What if you got hurt or…"

He couldn't take it anymore. Axel carefully wrapped his arms around her, wishing he could absorb the blows for her. She just cried into his chest, shaking like a leaf.

"Sadie, it's okay," he whispered. "I'm not going to let anything happen to you."

"You don't even know me." Her voice was muffled into his chest.

"I know I want to help you," he said, smoothing his hands over her back.

"You don't understand," she said, holding onto him now. "Bobby is…"

So, the bastard was Bobby, huh?

When she didn't say anything else, Axel eased back from her, trying to get her to look at him. "What? What about Bobby?"

When she looked at him, more tears came on. "I d-didn't tell you yesterday… Bobby… See, Bobby isn't a good man. He, ah, he's part of a mob family."

The last couple of words were so quiet that he almost didn't hear them. But he wanted to make sure he heard that right. "He's part of what?" he asked gently.

"He's part of… a mob family," she told him. "Has been ever since I've known him. He *kills* people, Axel."

Mob? Interesting. "I'll keep that in mind." Axel meant it to be reassuring.

Confusion bled into her expression. "You're not… worried?"

"I'm part of a family too," he explained, careful

to keep his voice calm. "There are some who would tell you we're bad men."

"Your motorcycle gang?"

He nodded. "Some of us probably are bad men, Angel. But my brothers here in town? My brothers have my back, and I have theirs. And no one threatens us or those we decide to protect. Not without paying a price."

"Why would you protect me?" she asked meaningfully. "Why?"

His heart sped up at her question. "Sometimes you don't need a why," he said. "Sometimes you just know the right thing to do when you see it."

Swiping at her tears with her hands, she shook her head. "I don't know how I'll repay you or Liza. But I'll find a way. I will."

Putting a careful hand on her shoulder, Axel tried to pull her out of her head. "If one day you want to repay this," he said, "I'll tell you what someone once told me. Find someone to help. You'll know when the time is right. They won't have anything to offer you but that's how it's done. You can just tell them what I'm telling you now."

Sadie looked confused and he knew she was scared. But he'd keep an eye out for Bobby, and he do his damnedest to keep her safe.

"Is there anything I can bring you?" he asked. "Anything at all."

She sighed. "You've done so much for me already. You… have no idea. I never thought I'd make it this far," she told him. "I wouldn't have made it this far without your help."

Axel didn't know what to do with that. He wasn't good at playing the hero, and besides, that role in the club was already taken. Still, he smiled at her before he headed back to the garage.

"Is it okay if I come check on you tomorrow?" he asked.

"Yes," she said quickly. Catching herself, he saw the section of her face that wasn't bruised darken in color. And wasn't that something? No one could blush like a ginger. He hoped it was the start of better times in her life.

* * *

Sadie

"I'm heading to the pharmacy to get Henry's pain meds," Liza said from the doorway of her bedroom.

Sadie had just finished putting herself together for the day, wearing the long-sleeved T-shirt from Axel's garage with her jeans. She'd been staying with the Austins for just over a week.

"Okay," she said. "Want me to just pick up where I left off yesterday? With the bean plants?"

"That would be just fine," Liza said. "Can I get you anything while I'm out?"

It wasn't the first time she'd thought of it. Liza was going out and the pharmacy would have what she wanted. So, she told Liza there was something she could get for her.

After dinner, Sadie returned to her room, picking up the bag Liza brought her back from the pharmacy that morning. She smiled at the boxed hair dye kit, admiring Liza's cleverness in selecting the shade. If her own hair color were a few shades darker, it would be the rich brown with auburn highlights that the model wore on the box.

Every day was a little better for her. The fear that Bobby could show up? That never really left. But Liza kept her plenty busy in the greenhouse. It was the first day of March and they wouldn't be able to plant gardens for a couple more months. But with everything Liza grew and tended in the greenhouse, there was an unending number of things to do. And she wanted to keep busy. So busy she wouldn't have a lot of time to worry. So tired she'd fall asleep when her head hit the pillow.

She had another distraction, although anticipating Axel's visits every day wasn't something she *should* be doing. A relationship with the wrong guy had taken everything from her. It could have cost her life. But every day Axel showed up, bringing them lunch from the diner across from the garage. Every day they chatted in the greenhouse over that lunch, and they were fast becoming friends.

Sadie couldn't remember the last time she'd had anything to look forward to. Axel probably didn't even know how much he brightened her day with just a smile. And it was one gorgeous smile.

Heading into the bathroom, she got to work on her hair, hoping the kit would change the color enough. The face in the mirror was still discolored, but it was a little better each day. In another week, she might even look something like her old self. When she stripped off to get in the shower to wash the dye out and clean up, she stopped to look herself over in the mirror on the bathroom door. She'd gained a little weight. Little wonder because Liza was a wonderful cook. Before Bobby, she'd had a nice figure. Maybe she'd get that back too.

Sadie usually let her hair air dry and as it did, she saw that the dye had really darkened it and it was a pretty color. She just didn't like it as much as her own. But it wasn't as eye-catching. Now she just looked like another brunette. And that was good.

Axel's words played often in her head. Bobby wouldn't start with Mercy. When he did arrive in Mercy, and he would, she wouldn't be easy to find. Well, she could help them out and help herself, right? Her car was hidden at Axel's house. Her hair was darker now. The police were close to Liza's house. She had Axel and the Hounds -- even though she didn't know a lot about the motorcycle gang he belonged to.

And Axel didn't scare her.

But just because he finds you doesn't mean you're his.

The words played over and over in her mind every night before she fell asleep. For so long, she'd allowed Bobby to convince her that she was pathetic. That she was *nothing*. He treated her like his property and then told her she was worthless to him. When she heard those vicious words over and over, she started believing it.

Then Axel came along and told her that even if Bobby found her, she wasn't his. The thought made her heart feel lighter, better.

She must have been worth something. Axel was helping her. So were Liza and Henry.

The next morning after breakfast, Sadie went to work in the greenhouse, and it was a warm day for March. More people were walking about in Mercy and a couple of older women came to look around. That wasn't new. There'd been a few people most days who came to look at plants for gifts or were already planning their gardens for the year. These two ladies? Well, they were a little more curious.

"You've got a new worker, Liza." The lady with her short gray hair pointed Sadie out. "When did she start working for you?"

Liza smiled, never missed a beat. "That's Angel,"

she said.

She felt her face warm at that. Angel was a little nickname Axel called her sometimes. She didn't realize Liza knew that, but it made her smile that she used it.

"Her parents are good friends of mine. She's looking to do this for a living and when she moved here, I gave her a job. She's really good help. I'm hoping she'll want to stay on after Henry heals up."

All three women smiled at her. "I'll bet she is good help," the lady said.

"How is Henry?" the other lady asked.

And just like that, the panic was gone. Liza knew Sadie worried Bobby would show up one day. Her quick work to conceal Sadie's identity meant a lot. After a few moments, the ladies made their purchases and went on their way. Once they were gone, Liza made a beeline for her.

"You heard all that, right?" Liza asked.

"Yes. Thank you," Sadie said. "I really appreciate your help."

"My story's okay with you?" she asked.

Sadie nodded, wondering what color she was turning under her new dark hair, but Liza was smiling.

The older lady laughed. "You still blush like a redhead. But your hair looks nice. It's a pretty color."

"It is," Sadie told her. "It will just take some getting used to."

"Maybe you won't have to worry about it for long," Liza told her.

Her heart squeezed in her chest at that thought. Maybe one day she wouldn't have to worry about Bobby, and she could just be herself. Maybe she could be someone worthwhile.

Liza and Axel thought she was worth something. It was a start.

Chapter Five

Sadie had been reading for an hour or so after dinner when Liza tapped on her bedroom door.

"Sadie, Axel's here to see you," she called.

Her heart skipped a beat, breaking her out of today's doldrums. Axel had shown up to have lunch with her every day since she came to Mercy except today. Yeah, she knew they were just friends, and he wasn't obligated to her for anything. Hell, seeing her every day for two weeks was a lot. She wasn't proud to admit it, but his absence today had taken away her happy thoughts.

"I'll be right there," Sadie called back.

Darting into the bathroom, she did a quick check of her hair, her teeth. Liza had brought her a cute green sweater from the town's thrift shop. Grabbing it from the closet, she stripped off the T-shirt she wore today and put it on. And with that, she decided she looked decent enough to head down.

There was no sign of Liza or Henry when she made her way down the stairs. Just Axel waiting at the bottom, smiling when he spotted her. And those smiles of his messed with her head *and* her heart.

"Hi," she said when she reached him.

"Hey," Axel said. "Got a few minutes to talk?"

Sadie nodded, following him into the living room. She appreciated him coming by since she didn't see him at lunch but when they sat together on the couch, she sensed this was more than that just a casual visit. Something was up and anxiety was creeping in.

"I'm sorry I didn't make it by today," he said. "I had to deal with something that needed immediate attention."

She understood. "I'm surprised that hasn't

happened before now with your work at the garage."

Axel shook his head. "No, it wasn't a garage thing."

Now her anxiety was gaining strength. Was it motorcycle gang thing?

He must have realized her panic was rising and smiled. "No, everything is okay, Angel. I just wanted to let you know Ryder made it back in town today."

Sadie let out a sigh of relief. They had already done so much for her; she didn't feel right asking about that trip, though she'd wanted to. She didn't want to seem ungrateful.

"Was everything okay?" she asked.

"Fine." He waved her concern away. "We have friends where he went. He decided to visit with them a while and leave me with all the work."

She laughed with him, but she wasn't completely convinced all was well. "He didn't run into any trouble?"

"Not at all," Axel said. "Just maybe we won't ever hear anything out of Bobby."

She certainly hoped not. But she knew she wasn't that lucky.

"And you haven't been in contact with anyone from that time in your life," he said. "Right?"

"I really don't have anyone to contact even if I wanted to." It was the truth.

"I was thinking about that," Axel said. "Now Liza insisted on paying for the entire thing herself, and she's hard to bargain with, but we finally made a deal."

They bought her something?

Reaching into the pocket of his jacket, he pulled out a small rectangular box. She recognized the logo on the top of it. They got her a smartphone?

Sadie just stared, astonished for a moment. "You got me a phone?"

"Yeah," he said, handing it to her. "It's not a top-shelf iPhone or anything but it's a good one."

She didn't know what to say. She hadn't had a phone for almost a year and her last one had been on the cheap side. Before Bobby decided she didn't need a phone, he always went out of his way to find hers and break them when he was angry.

"I don't need anything fancy," she told him. "I don't need one at all."

"Well, Liza and I talked about that," Axel said. "Maybe you do. Just in case something should happen, and I'm not saying that I think something will, but with that, you have a way to reach help if you need it."

"Thank you so much," she said, pulling the top off the box to reveal the small black device inside. "I'll thank Liza too."

"Snow helped me pick it out," he went on. "You'll meet him at some point. He suggested maybe creating all new accounts, just to be safe."

That wouldn't be a problem. She had a couple of friends at college, but Bobby had cut her off from them and everyone else. What were the odds that they even remembered her?

"I think he's right on making new accounts." Putting the top on the box, she set it on the coffee table in front of them. "I'll be careful."

"That's it?" he asked, grinning.

She smiled back though she wasn't sure she understood what he was getting at.

"You're not going to ask me for my number?" Axel asked, his grin getting wider. Before she could say anything, he said, "My number is already in there. Liza's too."

She managed to hold his gaze this time. "I'm glad."

"Yeah?"

Sadie nodded.

"Since I have your number now," Axel said, "can I call you or text you?"

"When? Later in the day works for me. I have a standing lunch date with this guy every day," Sadie teased. "But he stood me up today."

"I guess someone needs to tell him to step up his game, huh?" Axel's smile faded.

"Well, he just missed one day," Sadie told him, not moving when he leaned closer.

Axel moved slowly, leaning into her with his gaze on her lips. It was sweet and romantic. Everything she wasn't used to and never had before. All she could do was try and be patient with her heart flying in her chest.

When his lips brushed against hers, it was soft and seeking. A light, tender dance that was over too soon even while she knew he had to be as nervous as she was. He didn't try to touch her outside of that kiss.

His deep sigh filled the quiet space as they sat there together. Axel didn't seem to be asking for more.

"Hey, I know that you're not in a place where you're remotely ready to think about another relationship but..." Axel took his time, like he wanted to be careful with his words. "If it's okay, I'd like to keep hanging out."

Tears stung the backs of her eyes. He wasn't wrong in realizing where she was in things. But she'd been trying to ready herself for a time when he was looking to be with someone before she was ready -- if she ever would be again. It really hit her today, the first day he wasn't there at lunch. What happened when he wanted to move on but she didn't. *Couldn't.*

"I'd love to keep hanging out," she told him. "I just... I don't want to end up disappointing you."

"How would you do that?" he asked. "I promise I don't have any expectations. I'm happy to just take each day as it comes."

"Really? You don't expect anything at all?"

Axel shook his head. "Ryder's my identical twin but as people, we're night and day. Ryder's a good guy. He's my brother. I love him. But he's perfectly happy with a different girl every night of the week. It was the biggest reason I didn't just have you stay with us. I didn't want you seeing that."

Sadie just listened because they talked every day but usually not about his brother.

"We inherited the house when our folks were gone," he went on. "I don't think either of us are willing to move out because it would feel like giving the other one the house and land. Neither of us is willing to do that."

"So, you have land," she said. "Like a farm?"

He nodded. "Like that. I mean, altogether, we have thirty acres out there and a lot of it is just woods. But there's about ten acres around the house that's all cleared... Sometimes I think it would be nice to just build a second house out there and separate a little." He chuckled then. "It will probably be me. He wouldn't have time between sneaking off to visit friends and chasing girls."

"You could build your own house," she said. "Keep a garden. It would be nice."

"Yeah, it would," Axel said. "Plus, I wouldn't have to be embarrassed by my shithead brother. I could have people out there."

"I'm grateful that he took the... tracker away for

me," Sadie said.

"Yeah." Stretching, Axel rose from the couch, and she quickly did the same. "I am too. See? He can be useful once in a while."

Pulling her in for a quick hug, he blew out an exhale. "I'm going to head back home. I *will* see you tomorrow."

Sadie wasn't sure she liked the way her heart skipped a beat at that news. It didn't help that she liked the way he hugged her with his entire being. She liked to bask in that whenever the opportunity presented itself.

Standing in the doorway, she watched him walk out into the crisp, early spring evening. He waved as he mounted his bike. It roared to life and took him down the road, leaving her wondering what it was like to ride a bike. What did his family's home and land look like?

Once she couldn't see the lights of his bike anymore, she closed the main door and locked it.

Back upstairs in her room, she took the phone out of the box. As she expected, it had a charger with it, so she plugged it in. She placed it on her bedside table to charge while she showered and got ready for bed. When she came out of the bathroom, she had her first text on the phone, and she smiled to know it was him.

Axel: I'm home. Sleep well, Angel.

It took a minute. It felt like an age since she'd texted someone. She replied with *Goodnight*.

She was still smiling when she got in bed.

* * *

Axel

"You bringing the girlfriend?" Ryder asked as they worked at cleaning up around the garage.

Axel stopped sweeping the floor for a moment. "What?"

"What's her name? Angel?" his brother asked. "Is she coming Saturday night?"

Axel grinned. Angel. It was his nickname for her, but Liza started calling her that to further protect her identity and now, that's what everyone called her. It was clever. He liked it.

It was the end of June and Saturday night they were throwing a party at the clubhouse to celebrate some brothers visiting from Lexington, Kentucky. Honestly, he'd thought about asking Sadie to come with him. They hadn't talked a lot about his life as part of the Hounds, so he wasn't sure she'd want to go. And he was torn about asking her.

Sadie was safe from his brother, who would normally be his only concern in bringing a date to the party. Ryder had managed to steal a date or two from him over the years. The members here in Mercy would behave themselves with Sadie, and the prospects wouldn't approach her unless they wanted an ass kicking. But their Kentucky brothers might be a challenge and his Sadie was a beautiful young woman.

If he were being completely honest with himself, it was more of a challenge for him. They weren't in a relationship technically, but that didn't mean he was above good old-fashioned jealousy. He truly wasn't. Axel could and would wait for his girl to come around, and she *would* be with him.

Did that mean he'd put up with *any* form of competition? Absolutely fucking not.

"Probably not," Axel told him and got back to sweeping. "I haven't really even mentioned it to her."

"You think it bothers her you're in a biker club?"

"No, I don't think so," Axel said.

"Ever hear anything out of her shithead ex?" Ryder asked.

Axel tried to always be ready, but so far, there'd been no sign of Bobby and nothing suspicious. On one hand, Axel was happy. It had been four months since Sadie came to Mercy and as the weeks passed, she seemed less and less worried about Bobby. Oh, he wasn't forgotten. Axel had proof of that every time they went anywhere in town, which wasn't often. She was always looking around, over her shoulder. He knew it wasn't a doubt in his ability to keep her safe so much as it was just that lurking fear that the fucker could show up any time and ruin her new life.

"Not so far," he told Ryder. "And it's a little early to call her my *girlfriend*. We're friends."

"But you want her to be." Ryder knew him better than anyone, not even pausing as he worked on cleaning the glass windows that separated the lounge from the main work area. "You see her every day."

Yeah, Axel *wanted* her to be his. He thought they might be headed in that direction. *Slowly.*

No. She *would* be his. And no one would ever hurt her ever again.

"Maybe so," Axel said.

The sound of conversation in the work area had them looking up to see Jade, Hero's old lady. And she wasn't alone. Was that Sadie?

Jade stopped by often to see Hero, but it was the first time Sadie had been to the garage since the day she arrived with her overheated car. That was different. He made his way out there with Hero right behind him.

Jade shook Sadie's hand. "I'm Jade. I'm with Hero."

"Angel," Sadie introduced herself.

"You're Liza's new helper at the nursery, right?" Jade asked.

His girl nodded, the chestnut curls of her hair bobbing with her movements. And it was lovely, but he still missed her natural red hair.

"And you're friends with Axel?" Jade went on.

Axel cut her a look, like that would do any good. Hero swept Jade into a quick hug as he reached Sadie.

"You're bringing her to the party Saturday night, right?" Jade asked him.

Axel hadn't even told her about it which made it awkward, and it only took a beat for Jade to realize that.

"I haven't mentioned it just yet," Axel told her. "But I definitely will."

Jade did look sorry for the misstep. Hero, a master of conversation, stepped in right on time. "What are you doing here?" he asked Jade.

"I need you to look at the right front tire," she told him.

Hero rolled his eyes, following her out of the garage. That left him there with Sadie.

"Come on." Axel motioned for her to follow him to the office. When they made it, he gave her a quick hug.

"Jade seems really nice," she said. That and the way she stood let him know that he needed to explain about Saturday.

"Hey," he said. "Yeah, the club is having a party Saturday night at the clubhouse. I was still trying to decide whether or not I should ask you to go. And it caught up with me, huh?"

She visibly relaxed at his explanation. "It's the Hounds?"

Axel nodded. "Including some brothers from

Kentucky."

He took a seat behind the desk and after a moment, she sat in one of the chairs on the other side. Axel reminded himself that she was young. Too young to have been through half the shit she'd been through so far. Sadie was in her early twenties still and he was on the wrong side of thirty.

"I guess I've kind of kept you away from the Hounds," he said, "and that part of my life to this point. But I need you to understand that it's not because I'm ashamed of you or ashamed of *them*. The Hounds are a rough crowd, Angel. You've met my brother and Hero. They're decent guys and so are the rest of them. I guess I just didn't want to throw you into that world and have it scare you away from me."

Those gorgeous green eyes widened, the small smile forming on her lips.

"The parties we have at the clubhouse are wild," he explained. "You have wall-to-wall bikers drinking, acting stupid, fighting sometimes. You've got members like me and my brother already in. You have prospects who want to be and do stupid shit trying to be impressive. And there's women there too."

That got her attention.

"There's always a number of young women, like yourself," he went on. "They're like the prospects in a way. They're there trying to find a biker willing to make them their old lady, you know. Some call them club sluts and plenty take advantage of what they're offering. I have in the past. My brother does every damn party. Sometimes things going on during the party aren't that subtle."

He didn't know what to think of the expression she wore so he hurried on.

"Not all the women around us are like that or

ever even were that," he explained. "You just met Jade. Her father is our club's prez. She never knew him growing up. Her mother died early, and her grandmother raised her right here in Mercy, and she wouldn't allow Razor anywhere near Jade. She had her reasons, I suppose. But once her grandmother passed, she found her way back to Mercy after college. She found Hero. They're happy."

A little of the tension eased.

"Snow, who you've seen here a couple of times, is our VP. He got involved with the owner of Whisk and Whimsey, the bakery here in town. Emily had never been involved in our world either. You'd like her. And they seem happy."

"Okay," she said slowly. "So, do Jade or Emily go to these parties? Or --"

"Jade usually shows up but she doesn't stay long," Axel said. "It's not her scene, but she goes for Hero and her dad. Hero usually doesn't stay long after she goes. And this is the first one we've thrown since last summer. Emily is probably asking the same questions you are. She might not even show up."

Sadie was still processing everything, but he wanted to put all his cards on the table.

"Look, the only reason I hadn't said something is because I didn't want you to think I was hiding anything or hiding you. I don't know if that's something you'll ever want to go to but…"

"I understand," she said. "You've done so much for me, Axel. It's just… It made me realize something. I don't want you to give up anything in your life for me. You don't owe me anything. If you normally go, you should be able… to do what you normally do."

Darting around the desk, Axel took a knee next to her.

"Angel, I do mostly go to those parties," he said. "I used to hook up with a club sl -- girl, once in a great while. It's not something that I ever needed."

Was that relief flashing in her green eyes?

"I know we're just friends," he admitted. "And after everything you've been through, I sure as shit don't want to put any pressure on you at all. But I'd be lying if I said I wasn't hoping one day that we could be more."

That color flooding her beautiful face fucked with his body and heart. It had his heart squeezing in his chest, had him hard as a rock. Sadie's smile had his hopes soaring.

"I know what I've been through," she told him. "I just don't want it to define the rest of my life either."

Axel was so proud of her. She was strong. She'd survive this.

"Okay, with that in mind," he said slowly, "would you like to go to the party with me Saturday? We don't have to be there long at all. And if you'd rather not, that's okay too."

Taking a deep breath, Sadie said, "I'd like to go."

"Then we'll go," he told her, leaning in for what he only meant to be a kiss to seal the deal.

But no. The kiss started out slowly, a light dance of his lips against hers. After a moment, her breath was coming as fast as his. Her little hands slid up his arms, found their way into his hair. When she opened for him, it was all he could do to keep his hands off her, to keep himself from hauling her off and dragging her to his bed.

When he managed to break that kiss, she was shaking. But he didn't think now that it was all fear. The thought had his libido growing fangs.

"I didn't ask," Axel said, trying to catch his

breath. "What are you doing here?"

"I just wanted to visit you for a change," she told him, smiling.

Brushing a kiss on her forehead, he said, "I'm so glad you did. Want to go eat lunch in the diner?"

"Yeah," she told him.

It was a good day.

Chapter Six

Sadie

Austins' Nursery and Greenhouse closed at midday each Saturday and all day Sunday. It was just after two in the afternoon on Saturday and she and Liza got everything done until Monday.

It shouldn't have been awkward for her to let Liza know she wouldn't be home for dinner, but it absolutely was.

Liza saw her coming. "What's on your mind?" she asked, smiling. "You've been antsy all damn morning."

"I know," Sadie said. "Sorry. I, ah, I just wanted to let you know I'm, ah, I'm going out tonight. I won't be here for dinner."

The older lady's smile didn't move. "Is this a date?"

Yes.

"No." She didn't even sound convincing to herself. "Axel invited me to a party tonight. And we won't be out long."

Now Liza was chuckling. "Angel, I'm not your mother," she said. "You don't need my permission to go anywhere."

"I know," she said quickly. "But you've been so kind to give me a place to stay and I --"

"I really haven't given you anything," Liza replied. "You work your butt off for me. I'd call us mostly even."

That stopped her cold. It meant a lot that her employer, her *friend*, saw things that way. Sadie never wanted to be anyone's charity case. And after what happened to her with Bobby, she never wanted to be totally reliant on anyone else ever again.

"So, are you going to the party at the Hounds' clubhouse?" Liza asked.

Sadie nodded. "Axel asked me if I wanted to go and I told him I'd try. I... really don't know what I'm in for."

"Well, you're going with Axel and he's not going to let anything happen to you," Liza said. "So don't worry."

"Okay."

"Have you met Hero or Jade?" she asked.

Sadie nodded.

"Okay, good," Liza told her. "If something happens and you get separated from Axel, although I can't imagine he'd let that happen, find Jade and stay with her."

"I can do that," she said. "And he said we didn't have to stay long."

"Yeah, well, they can be rowdy events," Liza said. "He probably told you that. But I have to tell you, I'm proud of you for going tonight. It's a step in the right direction. And I think you'll have fun."

"I have no idea what to wear though," Sadie admitted. She'd gathered a few things into a simple wardrobe since she'd been living with the Austins, but she didn't have a lot.

"Well, jeans will be just fine," Liza said. "But it would be nice for you to find something to wear that you like and feel good in. Come with me."

She didn't know what Liza had in mind until she led her to the office, pulling her purse from the locker she kept behind the counter. Quick as anything, she held out a few folded bills to Sadie. It added up to a hundred dollars.

"Oh, no, I couldn't," Sadie said.

"You could and you will," Liza told her. "I'm not

giving you anything. You work hard for me. Take that and find something you'll feel pretty in."

Shopping? She must have had a look of panic on her face because after a moment, Liza smiled. "I'll go with you if you want me to."

Sadie shook her head at herself. She was a grown woman, and she shouldn't need someone to go with her wherever she went. And she already had gotten so much from Liza. The woman and her husband, and Axel, had literally saved her life.

"I-Il be okay." Sadie just wished she was as confident as she was trying to sound. "Thank you."

Sadie was okay half an hour later when she walked into Carmen's, a little clothing shop next to Mercy's pharmacy. She didn't need much. A new top of some sort would be good and some new shoes. She'd been wearing the same beat-up sneakers she'd worn most days when she still lived at Bobby's. It would be good to get other shoes and get rid of the reminder.

The shop had a lot of nice items and in no time, she found a top that she thought would work and a cute pair of ankle boots. Looking both ways, she darted back across the street, a short walk away from the Austins.

"You got the time?"

The sound of that Jersey accent in that deep voice had her freezing the moment she stepped onto the sidewalk. Slowly, she turned to find a heavy-set man with thinning black hair and blacker eyes looking her over and waiting for an answer. The man leaned against his dark blue car with his hands in his pockets, looked to be waiting for someone.

Her hand shook as she fished her phone out of her jeans pocket. "It's 3:45," she told him.

The man winked at her. "Thanks, doll."

When he went back to just gazing around, Sadie blew out a sigh of relief. Racing back to Liza's house, up to her room, she didn't feel like she could breathe until that door was closed behind her.

She was safe.

Was she going to live the rest of her life like this? Afraid that any stranger she ran across was someone Bobby sent? If she was going to think like that, she might as well go back to Bobby.

Sadie had a nice life in Mercy, surrounded by nice people. Okay, she didn't know many people, but it was something.

She got ready for the party, dressed in the bright blue top she bought. With her jeans and the new boots, Sadie thought she looked pretty good. She'd gained weight since living with Liza and she had curves again. She missed her own hair color, but the chestnut brown was growing on her, framing her face in a wild riot of curls.

The tap at her door had her turning to see Liza standing there. "Before Axel gets here, I wanted to give you this." Liza handed her a small container of pepper spray. "You shouldn't have to use that, but if something *does* happen, give them a face full."

Sadie nodded before hugging Liza.

"Try to have fun," Liza said. "Axel's good people. Ryder? Well, maybe one day."

Laughing, Sadie knew Axel would agree with that assessment of his twin brother.

"The clubhouse is on the edge of town and not really in walking distance," Liza told her. "If anything goes sideways, call me. I'll come get you." Shaking her head, Liza laughed. "I told you earlier that I'm not your mom. But I sound like one, huh?"

"Thank you," Sadie said. She'd take it.

Axel arrived to pick her up, chatting with Liza and Henry when she came down the stairs. He winked at her when she walked into the living room.

"You look amazing," he told her. "Are you ready?"

"I think so," Sadie said.

"Have a good time," Liza called to her as she followed Axel out the front door. Her pepper spray was tucked into the small cross-body bag she wore and so far, the new shoes felt comfortable enough.

When Axel led her to the huge Harley parked by the sidewalk, Sadie stopped. Two helmets hung off the back.

"We're riding on that?"

"Have you ever ridden?" he asked.

Sadie shook her head.

"I can go grab the truck if you want me to." His expression was sincere.

He was a member of a biker gang. It would probably look better if they arrived on that. Her heart raced as she considered it.

"Okay, I'll try." She didn't sound so confident.

He grinned. "It's maybe a five-minute ride. Not long."

Axel shrugged out of the denim jacket he wore, the Hounds insignia on it, and handed it to her. She pulled it on, enjoying the warmth and the fact that it smelled like him. He helped her with the helmet next, making sure it was secure. The finishing touch was a pair of sunglasses that were slightly too big for her face but would protect her eyes.

When he mounted the bike, he did it slowly, motioning her over. "Hop on."

Scared as she was, being pressed up behind him

when she climbed on wasn't bad at all. She wrapped her arms around him, feeling hard muscle beneath the thin T-shirt he wore. That wasn't bad either.

"Ease up a little, Angel." Axel laughed. "I want you to hang on but don't compress my ribs."

That had her laughing too as she did just that, and the bike roared to life beneath her. They were off and he kept the speed down, which helped make it less terrifying. She closed her eyes at first, grateful for his jacket because the air they punched through was chilly. After a couple of minutes, she opened her eyes, watching the road and everything they drove past in a new way.

She'd just gotten used to the ride when they arrived, pulling into the parking lot of what looked like an old office building. A sea of bikes were parked around it and music blared from the building. A handful of bikers and a couple of women stood outside the front door, smoking.

Axel helped her off the bike, and she removed the helmet and sunglasses and handed them back to him. As warm as the early summer evening was, she probably didn't need to wear the jacket, but she kept it on, fluffing her hair a little. She let Axel take her hand, leading her into the party. As they passed the group smoking, she saw the man who had asked for the time in town earlier. He winked at her the same way as she walked by.

Didn't Axel tell her that the guests the Hounds had were from Kentucky?

"There he is!" Snow pulled Axel into a hug as they made their way into the gathering area just inside the door. People were dancing to music, and smoke laced with the smell of weed floated in the air all around them.

Snow peeking around Axel. "You brought Angel." The white-haired biker smiled at her. "Welcome. Have you met my Emmy?"

Sadie shook her head. She didn't let go of Axel's hand as they followed Snow through the crowd to a small table where Hero and Jade sat with a petite blonde who was dressed for a garden party, not a biker's party. But when they approached the table, a smile lit up her face.

"You must be Angel," the blonde said.

Snow leaned down to press a kiss to her head. "Angel, this is Emmy. My old lady."

"Emily," she said, shaking her head. "It's nice to finally meet you."

"It's good to meet you too." Sadie grabbed the last seat at their table. Axel stayed right behind her chair, chatting Snow up.

It was loud in that smoky room. Jade passed her a bottle of beer, opening it for her.

"Axel said your father is the club prez here?" she asked Jade who laughed and nodded.

"Guilty," Jade said. "He's a great guy. I really didn't get to know him until about a year ago. Long story, but yeah…"

It was nice sitting there and talking with the other two women. Both were as kind as they were gorgeous and Jade in particular had everyone laughing, telling tales about the rough and tough bikers partying all around them. Most of them Sadie hadn't even seen before. Some were dancing in the middle of the floor with women in super short skirts and way more makeup than she'd ever worn. Some of them crowded around a pool table while others drank and talked loudly.

When Hero stood up to talk with Axel and Snow,

Emily elbowed Jade. "Will you hold the table? I've got to go to the bathroom."

"You know where it is?" Sadie asked. "I'll go with you."

She stopped to tell Axel where she was off to and he nodded, watching her follow Emily to wherever the bathroom was. When she came back out, she heard shouting. A couple of younger men were swearing at each other, and it looked like a fight was going to break out. And even worse, she lost track of Emily.

"Fuck you, asshole!" one of them yelled, shoving the one with jet-black hair until he staggered back.

"You really want to do this?" The black-haired biker took a swing at his enemy, missing him.

Panic bloomed in her chest when the shoving started in the crowd around her and someone crashed into her, causing her to stumble backwards. She would have fallen except for someone caught her.

A deep voice by her ear asked, "Are you okay?"

When Sadie nodded, the man behind her, with a hand still on her shoulder, started shouting at the ones fighting. And it didn't take long for things to quiet down after the booming of that voice.

The fighter with black hair looked to the man behind her, embarrassed. "Sorry, Razor," he mumbled.

The other biker in the almost fight was Ryder who was obviously already drunk off his ass. With his trademark smirk, he stumbled over to them, pulling someone behind him. The young woman with bright red hair kept him from falling over, all the while laughing with her red painted lips. Her clothes were skin-tight and her sleek boots had four-inch heels.

Snuggling up to Ryder, the woman with hair that looked just like her natural color tried to look contrite.

"Sorry, Razor," she said clearly flirting with the

older man. "I'll get him tucked into bed. I'll come back and tell you how he's doing."

"I'm good." Razor waved them away.

When Sadie turned and looked up, she stood facing the club prez, a handsome older man who was tall and lanky. Jade had her father's sharp eyes but that was it. His features were defined, his long hair gray, and he had the devil's smile. She knew she must have been staring up at him like a moron.

"Are you Angel?" Razor asked.

All she could do was nod.

"You've met Ryder, right?"

Oh, she had. "Yes."

"You picked the right brother," he said with a wink. With a hand at her back, he steered her back in the right direction. Axel looked relieved when they reached him. "Found your Angel, brother."

"Thanks, man," Axel said. "Was that my brother trying to start shit?"

"It was," Razor told him. "One of the girls has him."

"Sorry," Axel said.

Making it back to the table, Sadie was happy to talk with Jade and Emily over another beer. Emily's bakery sounded amazing, and Jade worked for the school system helping with special needs kids. Jade was from Mercy, but like Sadie, Emily wasn't. Between the two of them, she felt like she knew a little more about the town.

And it had been how long since she'd been able to talk to other people? Have friends?

Three beers in and she was warm, enjoying herself. But the party around them was getting rowdy again. When Emily caught Snow's attention and let him know she wanted to go, Axel came up behind

Sadie.

"You ready to go too?" he asked close to her ear.

"I think so," she told him.

Making it outside, it took them a couple of minutes to spot Axel's bike in the crowded parking lot. But they managed. When she climbed on this time, it was better. Maybe because it wasn't new. Maybe because she had a beer or two.

"You made it two hours," Axel told her, helping her with the helmet. "Did you know that?"

"No." She'd enjoyed herself and time had flown. She couldn't help but grin at him. "I really like Jade and Emily."

He nodded. "I don't know Emily that well but Jade's great. I'm pretty sure Emily is too to put up with Snow."

"I like Razor too," she admitted.

Axel smiled at her over his shoulder, and he was so gorgeous to her in that moment. It had her heart fluttering in her chest like a schoolgirl. She couldn't remember the last time she'd felt like that.

"Where do you want to go now?" he asked.

"Where else could we go?" Yeah, she still had a good beer buzz. It was so nice not to be riddled with fear and worry. She couldn't remember the last time she'd had that.

"I have an idea," he told her before pulling on his own helmet and starting the bike.

The ride headed out of Mercy, down an old country road. Sadie felt alive watching the shadows and lights race by as they moved. The hum of the bike between her legs was making her feel things she wasn't sure she'd ever feel again. Pressed into the muscled wall of Axel's back, she just enjoyed the intimacy of that contact.

He stopped at what looked like an old boat dock, sitting at the edge of a peaceful lake.

"It's private property," he explained. "Our uncle owns it, but he's older and doesn't get out a lot."

Not far from the dock was an old stone path. Axel got them off the bike and pointed it out to her.

"Want to take a walk?" he asked.

At her nod, he took her hand and led her down that path and into a wooded area that she found so pretty with the starry sky overhead. It was cooler in the woods with the sound of rushing water nearby and a chorus of crickets all around them.

The moon was almost full and hung high overhead, reflecting off the water. When Axel tugged on her hand, she saw he was towing her toward a pretty gazebo at the edge of the water. She couldn't help smiling. The entire scene was lovely and no one else was around. The only houses were in the distance on the other side of the lake. The light shining from their windows made for a charming scene.

Taking in a deep breath, Sadie smiled. The random flash of a firefly lit up the nighttime landscape. The beautiful scene around them was an unexpected surprise.

Turning to her, Axel swept her into the circle of his arms. With the tips of his fingers at her chin, he tipped up her face until her gaze was on him. His kiss was gentle, seeking.

"Beautiful," he whispered, holding her.

"Yes, it is." She smiled up at him, her arms winding around his neck.

"I meant you." Axel laughed.

When she kissed him, just because she could, he didn't stop her. This kiss escalated, had him holding her tighter. His body was warm and solid against hers.

Lost in this enchanting moment, her fingers clutched his hair and she pressed herself against him with a need that she didn't recognize at first. How long had it been since she felt desire?

Nervous as she was, with Axel it felt easy. She trusted him. He felt so good in her arms.

Sadie's growing desire was all the motivation he needed. When Axel hauled her against him, reclaiming her lips in a scorching kiss that had her struggling to breathe, Sadie went with it. Her heart hammered against his as his hands slowly roamed over her. He carefully pulled his cut off her and draped it over the wooden railing of the gazebo. She didn't really think about it when her hands reached for the hem of his T-shirt, trying to push it up.

When he grabbed the back of that too-small T-shirt and pulled it off, she broke the kiss to look. His upper body was gorgeous, even in the dark. His wide, muscular chest was littered with tattoos and a dusting of dark chest hair. She spotted smaller, fainter marks too which were probably scars. It was hard to tell in the dim light. She got her hands on his chest because she had to, letting him kiss her as he wanted.

When Axel sank down, she let him pull her down there with him. Axel rolled her under him, his shirt a barrier between her and the wooden floor of the gazebo. His kisses blazed over her lips, down her neck.

When his hands found the hem of her shirt, she froze. That had him lifting his head to meet her gaze.

"We okay here?"

Sadie swallowed nervously.

"Sorry, I got carried away," he told her. "*Sorry.*"

Carefully, and so slowly, Axel slid his hands beneath her top, his fingers skimming over her ribs and back. She had scars aplenty, but they weren't visible at the moment. She wasn't on display, and right now, she was comfortable with things. Maybe that was his intention.

And she felt nice, lying there in the gazebo and kissing Axel. It was the most excitement she'd had in so long. She wasn't going to let her ex take that away from her too. Yes, she was scarred. But she didn't want to think about them or the man who put them on her.

With a determined sigh, Sadie reached up to hook a hand around Axel's neck, pulling him down to her for a kiss.

"Make me forget," she whispered against his lips. "Make me feel *good*."

There was hesitation in Axel's face, but after a moment, he kissed her back, keeping his weight off her. His lips blazed a path over her jaw to her neck, teasing the soft flesh there as his rough hands smoothed over her bra. "You're beautiful, Sadie," he whispered in her ear, making her shiver. She loved the sound of her name on his lips.

Arching her back, she made it easy for him to unhook her bra. When he got his hands under it, Sadie was gasping beneath him. Her hands slid into the thick dark locks of his long hair, clutching there as his fingers delicately played with one nipple, teasing it into an aching little peak.

Currents of pleasure flowed through her bloodstream as she writhed beneath him, enjoying his attention. When he gave her other breast the same treatment, she hooked a thigh over his hips and nudged up into him. She could feel the heated length of him beneath the denim and she wanted that. She wanted everything. How long had it been since she felt anything like that?

Axel chuckled, lifting his head. His hands went

to the front of her jeans.

"I'm going to take care of you, darlin'," he crooned. "But you have to promise me something. Anything you don't like, tell me. I stop. No questions asked."

He meant what he said, sincerity in his face and voice. The jeans she wore were button-fly and he dropped gentle kisses on the soft flesh of her tummy as he undid each, making her shiver. Making her forget everything but him.

It amazed her how a guy his size was able to pull her jeans down as carefully as he did, because they were pretty snug. But he managed it, his hands soft whispers over her skin as he explored her. There were scars littering her legs too, but he couldn't see them. She could pretend she was beautiful, perfect for him. Axel just looked at her like she *was* perfect. It almost broke her.

Axel dropped more kisses over the tops of her thighs, over the light pink panties she wore. The way his hands worshipped her left her breathless. He was so careful when he pulled her panties down and hooked one of her legs over his shoulder. Her heart started racing. She couldn't even remember the last time a guy had gone down on her. Bobby never had.

Oh, God. Axel played her like a long-neglected instrument. At first, it was awkward for her. Within a few seconds, the sheer pleasure of it pulled her out of her head, had her writhing on the gazebo floor. Desperate for the teasing touches of his lips and tongue, Sadie's hands gripped in his hair. Her hips rolled, seeking more.

The man knew what he was doing. He traced circles around her clit with his fingers and tongue until she was begging him for more. For *anything*. When he started working a finger into her, it hurt a little because it had been months since anyone had touched her. It didn't hurt for long. Axel's touch was seeking and careful. He made her crave and ache, finding a space inside her that lit up her entire body like electricity. When he used his mouth on her clit and added a second finger, he sent Sadie flying.

The orgasm shook her like a rag doll, left her panting and dazed beneath him as he worked at pushing down his own jeans. She tried to be patient when he'd fished the condom packet from his pocket, when he had it out of the foil and rolled it on in record time. Her world spun when he rolled them, ending with him on his back and her straddling his slim hips.

Sadie saw his cock was swollen and ready, up against his belly. She wanted *that*.

Axel was panting beneath her. "You going to stare at it, darlin'? Or do you want to hop on?"

He didn't have to ask twice. Taking him in hand, she stroked him before holding him up to her entrance. It was rare that she'd ever gotten to be on top and it only pushed her excitement higher.

She sank down on him, and he let her take him at her own pace. He was bigger than she was used to, splitting her open as her pussy swallowed him. The stretch and burn only made her want more. His hands at her hips were careful. He felt so good and solid beneath her. Steady.

When Axel was buried in her as far as he could go, she sucked in a breath and let her body adjust. Her inner walls were stretching around him.

She moved on him, rotating her hips to enjoy how he hit all those hidden places inside her and damn, he felt good. Planting her hands on his chest, she held herself up. His heartbeat was a steady drum against her palm. His eyes drank her in as she fucked him, gazing up at her like she was beautiful.

Tears stung the backs of her eyes as she rode him. How long had it been since anyone made her feel worthwhile? Worth something?

"How's that feel?" he asked, his voice whiskey deep.

"Good," she managed. And oh, it really did.

He filled her up in a way that brought a slight twinge of pain. It didn't take long for her to feel ripples of pleasure pulsing through her veins, pushing her toward the high they both sought. Axel moved his hips with her, pushing up into her and driving her crazy.

All it took was for him to move one hand between them, his fingers teasing her clit with a finesse she would have appreciated if she'd had time. Sadie cried out as she came and Axel kept the pressure up, fucking her as she held on. She squeezed him rhythmically with her pussy walls, weeping around his cock as he kept driving into her.

Before she could collapse, he rolled them again. She liked being under him, appreciated the care he took. His grip on her tightened and his thrusts gained in speed and strength. His lips blazed a trail over her neck as he fucked her, taking her breath away as they pushed each other closer to the edge.

Sadie wrapped herself around him as he pounded into her, hanging on. Release rode her as hard and fast as he was. When she came, the world spun around her. Axel reached his end a beat later, his strangled cry booming among the chorus of peaceful night sounds, pumping into her until he was spent.

As they stayed there, holding each other and struggling to catch their breath, she wished she didn't have to leave this small bit of happiness.

Chapter Seven

Axel

The sound of his cell phone pulled Axel out of heavy sleep. He grabbed it from his bedside table on the third or fourth chime without looking at the screen.

"Good morning," he drawled, hoping it was Sadie.

"Where are you?" It was Razor. And he knew that tone. Something was wrong.

"I'm here at the house," he said. "What's up?"

Razor's deep sigh had anxiety creeping in.

"Axel... something happened last night," Razor said slowly. "Your brother hooked up with that cute little redhead and apparently went home with her."

Okay, that wasn't surprising. More often than not Ryder brought them back to the house they shared. But when Axel returned home last night from a wonderful evening with his Angel, there was no indication his brother had been there or brought a date back with him.

"Some fellas broke into her place while they were there," Razor went on. "They messed them both up. The girl is dead and Ryder..."

"Ryder's what?" Axel shot straight up in bed. Was his brother alive? Who attacked them?

"He's in the hospital," Razor told him. "Critical. We're not sure he's going to pull through."

"I'm on my way," Axel said, already grabbing clothes.

"We'll meet you there," Razor said.

Axel scrambled to get dressed, hopped on his bike. He took the roads faster than he should have with thoughts of his twin in the hospital, possibly dying, playing on a loop in his brain.

So many questions raced through his mind. *What the fuck happened*? Who the hell broke into that woman's place and attacked them? Why? Ryder had always been more interested in fucking girls than picking fights. He didn't know of anyone Ryder would have pissed off that badly.

Did that mean the target was the girl? According to Razor *she* was dead.

Had it been a rival gang like the Cottonmouths? Was the girl someone's old lady and she was stepping out on him? It couldn't have been any of their visiting brothers from Kentucky, right? The thoughts preying on his mind didn't let up until he got to the hospital parking lot. Axel was off the bike, hustling into the lobby where Razor and Snow were waiting for him.

"Where is he?" Axel asked, panicked. "Is someone with him?"

Razor was already moving. "Hero's up there."

The elevator ride seemed to take forever, and Axel's heart pounded so loudly he was sure his brothers could hear it. Once they were off the elevator, it was the first door to the right and Hero left so he could go in. The sight that greeted him left him cold. His twin lay on the hospital bed, looking pale and lifeless. Axel's heart felt like it would beat out of his chest as he approached that bed where his brother was hooked up to tubes and machines. The only obvious injury was an ugly cut and bruise on his left temple.

It was so quiet in that room with the ominous mystery of whatever happened looming over them. The only sound was the machinery, probably keeping his brother alive. Marching out, he followed his brothers to the waiting room down the hall.

"What the hell happened?" Axel asked, as soon as they reached the lounge.

Hero stopped under the muted flatscreen TV that was mounted on the wall above him.

Axel shook his head, scared and pissed off. "Who did this?"

Hero's expression was grave, he looked to Razor.

"That's what we're trying to figure out," Razor told him. "Snow and I already did some checking around. All our visiting brothers from Kentucky are all accounted for last night. Hell, all of them passed out in the clubhouse, to be honest."

"What's his condition?" Axel asked.

"They were shot," Hero said quietly. "It looked like they were in the middle of, ah… Whoever did this, shot Ryder in the back three times. Nicked his lung, took out his right kidney. Barely missed his liver. The sheriff thinks they knocked him out of the way after that, probably where the head injury came from. Looks like he hit the corner of her nightstand and got knocked unconscious. It's a nasty concussion."

"He's unconscious," Axel said.

"He was on the table for several hours," Hero explained. "Hasn't been back from surgery long. Hopefully, he'll wake up here in a while."

Axel sure as fuck hoped so. "And the woman?"

"A couple of those shots went through him into her," Razor said. "They said it looked like once they knocked Ryder off her they shot her in the face. High caliber weapon."

"Did *you* find them?" Axel wanted to know.

Razor's hand felt heavy on his shoulder. "No. Sheriff Sawyer came and found me early this morning. That woman lived over on Elm. It was sometime up in the morning… Two or three o'clock? The neighbors heard the shots and called the police. One of the neighbors told the sheriff he saw two men drive off from her place, spinning wheels."

That got Axel's attention. "They saw who did it?"

"They saw what looked like two men in the dark driving off in a car," Razor told him.

No bikes? So, it probably wasn't a rival gang. And the woman was the one they were after...

Axel's next thought froze him to the spot. The woman he saw all over his brother at the party last night had red hair. Red, curly hair like Sadie's. She was comparable in size to his Angel too.

And his Angel had told him her ex, Bobby, was in the mob...

Axel felt sick. "Fuck. Fuck!"

Razor moved his hand as Axel began to pace. "I'm sorry, brother."

Scrubbing a hand over his face, Axel stopped. Trying to control his anger, his gaze met that of their prez. "I have terrible feeling about what may have happened, Razor," he said, fighting back rage to get the words out. "Fuck!"

"What do you mean --"

Razor held up a hand to cut Snow off. "Say it."

Blowing out an exhale, Axel looked at each of his brothers in turn. "I didn't get a close look at the woman with my brother at the party. I never pay attention to any of them anyway. He has a different one every week. But from what I remember, she had curly red hair and she's close in size to my Angel."

Patiently, they waited for him to continue.

"When she came here to Mercy," he explained, "especially that first day, she was fucking terrified. It took a little while to get her talking about it. I mean, fuck. You saw her, Hero. He beat the living daylights out of her."

Hero nodded.

"When she did talk about it, and it wasn't much, she told me that her ex, Bobby, scared her so bad because he worked in a mob family."

"Explains the tracker in her car," Razor offered.

"It does," Axel went on. "The neighbors didn't see men leave that house on bikes. They said they were in a car, right? They just broke in there, shot them up, and left? It just might be a mob hit. Ole Bobby sent someone down here to kill the ex who got away from him. And you know it wasn't him because he would have known that was the wrong woman."

"Son of a bitch," Razor said. After a moment, their prez scrubbed a hand through the long gray locks of his hair. "Sounds plausible. It's been what? Four months since Ryder took that tracker to Mississippi, right?"

"About that," Axel said.

"Then it went just like I thought," Razor said. "They followed the last location of that tracker to whatever swamp he dropped it in and have probably been working backwards from there."

"It brought them here." Axel felt panic welling up inside. "And it's only a matter of time before they figure out they killed the wrong woman. Hell, they might know already. What the fuck do we do now?"

"We're going to have to be careful whatever we do," Snow warned. "One of ours took a hit. The sheriff knows we'll be looking for payback, and they'll try to shut us down if they think we're going to make a move. They'll be watching."

"Right," Razor said. "Plus, we need to keep Ryder safe because he ain't dead. Once they figure that out, they'll make sure he can't talk to cover their asses. That also puts a target on your back, Axel."

It did because few people could tell them apart.

His blood ran cold to think that fucker or his minions were here in town to kill his girl. Bobby Fuckface had already done enough to her. She'd been lucky she got away from him alive. And now the fucker wanted her dead?

It wasn't going to fucking happen. They'd have to get through *him* and they'd have better luck fighting the devil himself. If anything happened to his Angel *or* his fucking brother, they'd wish for something as sweet as hell.

"I need to get Sadie out of town," Axel told them. "I'll take her and hide her in my house."

Razor shook his head. "Best to leave her exactly where she is."

What? "Leave her where she is?" It was too risky. "Why the hell would I do that? I need to get her out of sight."

"Axel, by now they'd been in town a couple of days," Razor said. "She can't disappear now with them watching."

Fuck. "If they figure her out, that's a target on her, Liza, and Henry." Axel couldn't do that to them.

"We'll just have to keep a close eye on them," Razor said. "We need to let them know what's going on and plan from there. That's what you and me are going to do. Snow, you and Hero organize a protection detail. And I don't want just any fucking prospect on this. We have to shit Tiffany cufflinks here. If it's obvious, they'll find her. It's over."

"What do we do if we spot *them*?" Snow asked.

"Stay on them until we can deal with them discreetly," Razor told them. "Everyone good on the plan?"

"I'd like to stay with Ryder for a little bit," Axel

said.

"You two head on," Razor told Hero and Snow. To Axel, he said, "I'll stay right here. Go see your brother."

* * *

Sadie

Angel, I'm heading over to see you. I'll be there in five.

Sadie read the text from Axel and smiled. After last night, she wanted to see him too.

The party had been fun, at least the couple of hours she'd been there, especially talking to Jade and Emily. But what happened next was better. They'd made love and the memory left her feeling warm, desirable. She hadn't completely undressed but Axel could read her. He paid attention to how she was, what she was okay with. Sadie didn't know there were men who were capable of that.

Axel had made her beautiful. She hadn't wanted the night to end. It had been so sweet the way he'd delivered her back to Liza's front door like he was returning her to her parents. The kiss there under the warm summer moon had been sweet, full of promise and hope.

She was still smiling when he arrived at the house.

Axel wasn't smiling. Something was wrong.

"Are you okay?" she asked, fighting back anxiety as he followed her to the living room. He didn't answer.

"Axel?" she asked, worried now at the grim expression he wore.

Blowing out an exhale, he pulled her into his arms and held her for a long moment. Sadie held him too, wondering what had him like this.

Easing back, Axel's gaze met hers. "Where are Liza and Henry?"

"Henry will be back down in a minute," she explained. "And Liza's folding laundry." *Why did he need to see them?*

"Everything is okay," Axel told her, looking her in the eye. "But we all need to talk."

It was back in an instant. All the fear and anxiety that she had been able to suppress for a little while. Her hands shook as she left the safe circle of Axel's arms and walked to the laundry to find Liza. It only took about five minutes for everyone to gather in the living room, but it felt like an eternity for her. What was happening?

It had to be Bobby.

Henry took the recliner where he usually sat, and Liza joined her on the couch. Only Axel remained standing, and if he didn't tell them what exactly was happening soon, she would fall apart.

"Look," Axel said, looking like he was trying to think of how he wanted to say what he'd come there to say. "I took Sadie to the party at the Hounds clubhouse last night. I brought her home and headed back for my house."

He cut her a quick glance. Well, he hadn't *just* brought her home after the party…

"Ryder was there and he did what he does," he explained. "He found himself a date and he left the party with her."

Liza nodded, smiling. Ryder's reputation was no secret.

Only Henry sat listening with concern bleeding into his expression.

"It's all over the news," Axel told them. "My

brother went home with the young woman he was with. She lives here in town and... Two men broke in her house while they were there. Ryder was shot three times and has a concussion. We don't know if he's going to make it. The woman is dead."

The memory flashed in her mind from the party. Ryder getting scolded by Razor for nearly getting into a fight in the clubhouse, the cute redhead laughing by his side. Fear hit her hard as she reached her conclusion, and she felt terror take root in her body. The woman's hair was about the same shade as her natural red and it was curly like hers.

"We don't know anything for sure but," Axel went on, "I think your ex might be behind this, Angel."

Sadie was thinking the same thing. The tears came on fast, her heart racing in her chest. It was just what she feared. Bobby and his men were here. She'd put Liza and Henry in danger. Ryder's brother could die. The other woman with red hair was dead.

It was all her fault.

"I am so sorry," Sadie struggled to speak. "I'm --"

"No." Liza stopped her and wrapped an arm around her shaking form. "Angel, this isn't your fault."

"It is," she said, barely hanging on. "I got... I got Ryder shot. What if he dies? What if something happens to you or Henry? I've got to leave. Now. It's the only way to keep you safe... I can..."

Axel took a knee in front of her, making her meet his gaze. "Darlin', breathe."

It was hard. She felt like she couldn't catch her breath. The edges of her vision were fading to black.

"Look at me," Axel said. "Look at me. Stay with me."

"She's having a panic attack," Liza whispered,

smoothing her hand over Sadie's back.

"Angel, none of this your fault," Axel told her firmly. "Let's get that straight. We just need to talk about how to handle this. Liza and Henry are involved too since you're living here. But no one here is blaming you for any of it. And you're not leaving. If Bobby or his people are loose in the town, they might just notice if you disappear, darlin'."

"That's right," Henry said. "But I do want to know how we're handling this. Sheriff Sawyer involved?"

Axel nodded. "The sheriff's department is all over this. Razor was heading there when we left the hospital to have a talk with them about what we believe is going on. I'm sure they'll be keeping an eye on this house. They'll help keep all three of you safe."

Henry looked happy with that answer.

"And if it's okay with you and Liza," Axel said, "I'll be staying here with you."

She didn't miss the quick communication between the couple. How quickly they agreed to it as opposed to throwing her out to the wolves, which they could have done to save themselves, had her fighting a new wave of tears.

"We've got plenty of room and I know that would make me feel better if you stayed," Liza said.

"Thank you," he told them both. "I'll try and make sure no one sees me coming or going after this."

"I'm sorry about your brother," Liza told him. "I hope he'll be okay."

"Me too," he told them.

"Henry, let me get you lunch, hon," Liza said, motioning her husband to follow her. Using his cane, and with Axel's help, he was up and slowly making his way to the kitchen.

Sadie's heart dropped. If someone broke in, Henry couldn't run away. He could be killed.

Now that they were alone, Axel moved to sit next to her on the couch. His arm felt good around her shaking form. He felt strong enough to hold her together. "Axel," she said. "I'm so sorry about Ryder."

He nodded, his expression grave.

"I'll understand if you need to be with him because he needs you too," she said.

His expression was grim, hard to read. "Don't worry about that right now. I just need you to be vigilant at all times. Anyone or anything you see that's out of the ordinary, you tell me."

She froze, remembering the man on the street the day she went shopping. His accent. The fact that he was at the party.

"What?"

"Oh, God," she told him, shaking her head at herself. "There was a man," she told him, shaking harder now. "Saturday. I went shopping at the store next to the pharmacy. When I came out, a man was there leaning against his car, and he asked what time it was. He... had a Jersey accent."

"Is that where you came from?" Axel asked. "Jersey?"

"Yes," she said. "I went to Rutgers. Bobby lives near there."

Axel sighed. "You haven't seen him again, have you? Or anyone else?"

"I did see him again," she explained, swiping at tears with her hands. "He -- he was on the porch at the party."

Axel's eyes widened. "At our clubhouse?"

She nodded.

"Fuck. Wait. If he was at our clubhouse, he'll

show up on the cameras."

"What?"

"I'll call Snow," he told her. "This is good news. Thank you, darlin'."

He should be doing anything but thanking her. All of them were in this situation because of her.

"Stop thinking whatever you're thinking," he said. "This isn't your fault. It's Bobby's. Remember that."

"I'm trying, but…" Sadie leaned against him. "If anything happens to you…"

"It won't, Angel," Axel told her. "We'll get through this."

Chapter Eight

Axel

By that evening, the news outlets updated the story of the woman's murder last night and released her name. Morgan Davis.

Here we go. Now that they had a name, it wouldn't take Sadie's ex and his goons long to figure out that they killed had the wrong woman. And they were going to figure out that in shooting Ryder, they'd signed their own death certificates. And God help them if his brother didn't make it.

Sadie sat at the table, looking every bit as terrified as she did the day she arrived in Mercy, beaten and scared. Axel hated it. He hated that all those weeks of seeing her smile as she got used to her new life were gone now. He was also pissed at the fact that an innocent woman was dead, and his brother was fighting for his life in the hospital. Axel hated this entire fucking situation.

And the really shitty part of it? They needed to keep someone with Ryder at the hospital at all times to protect him. And it couldn't be *him*. The last thing he needed was for someone to think Ryder had a miraculous recovery and follow him to the woman they were really looking for. He was so pissed about the entire situation he could barely keep it down.

"Hey." Snow hustled into the clubhouse where Axel waited. "Razor's right behind me."

Axel nodded, waiting for their prez before he said anything.

Razor strolled in, his gaze meeting Axel's. "What do you have?"

When Razor spotted Sadie sitting there with him, his eyes lit up in interest.

"Angel ran into a fellow in town Saturday with Jersey accent and a dark car," Axel told them. "Saw the same fellow at our party last night."

Razor cut his gaze to Sadie, very interested now. "Is that so?"

Sadie nodded, looking from Razor to Snow.

"Jersey?" Snow asked. "We didn't have any brothers from the Garden State at the party that I know of."

Axel nodded.

"And the ex and his mob buddies are from Jersey?" Razor asked his Angel.

"Yes," she said.

"So, we need to pull some security footage," Snow told them.

In five minutes flat, the four of them were crammed into the back office where Snow kept the security system complete with three monitors showing different views inside and outside the clubhouse. All were public areas, not private rooms.

"About when did you two arrive yesterday?" Snow asked them.

"Sevenish," Axel told him.

It gave Snow a jumping off point. He pulled up a list of files from yesterday, organized by different times.

"Where did you first see him?" Snow asked Sadie.

"On the porch," she said. "When we walked in, there was a small group of people smoking. He was out there with them."

Snow started pulling up files, carefully scrubbing through the footage while Sadie watched. When he got to the third file, she said, "Stop."

There on the screen Axel saw himself, Sadie's

hand in his as she followed him toward the door. There was a group of visitors there on the porch, just like she said. A couple of them looked like brothers from Kentucky. Sadie's green eyes carefully scanned the scene as Snow slowly scrubbed through the footage.

"That's him!" Sadie pointed to a balding man with dark hair. The fat fuck stood there talking to three of their brothers from Kentucky who wouldn't have known that he didn't belong there. The footage showed Axel and Sadie walking past them and into the party. As they all carefully watched the screen, Axel spotted the man later inside the clubhouse during the party. He didn't see him hovering anywhere near where Sadie sat with Emily and Jade.

The fucker *did* stay on Ryder's ass the entire time, the girl they'd mistaken for his Sadie hanging all over him for most of the evening. They didn't see anyone else in there with him that didn't seem to belong. They'd most likely used the one his girl saw as a scout.

"Angel, when did you first see this man?" Razor asked.

Just as she told Axel, she explained running out of the store and someone stopping her to ask what time it was.

"Did you feel like that man in any way had an interest in you?" Razor asked.

Sadie shook her head. "I don't think so."

"Was there anyone with him?"

"No," Sadie replied. "I didn't see anyone with him."

"Did you see him in a car?" Razor asked.

"I did. He was leaning on a dark blue sedan. I don't know what it was. It's like one of those old Cadillacs or something with a long front end and a long back end." Dropping her head, she said, "I should have paid better attention. I should have --"

"No," Axel cut her off, capturing her hand in his. "You did just fine. You gave us a place to start, Angel. We'll track this guy down and from there, we'll get this situation under control."

"Ryder's already been shot." Sadie said. "Any of you could get killed. I can't... I can't live with that."

"Hon, we *are* lucky to still have Ryder," Razor said. "But that isn't your fault. We weren't prepared, but we sure as fuck are now. We'll take care of it."

Tears gathered in those gorgeous green eyes as she looked from him to Razor and back. "I'm not worth it," she said so quietly they almost didn't hear it.

"Axel sure loves you," Razor told her, "so you *are* worth it. And yeah, you may have been part of the reason Ryder got shot. But if it makes you feel any better, you're not the only reason we're going to deal with these assholes."

Their prez was correct on all counts. Axel did love her and they would deal with it. He nodded when she looked to him. "Snow, make sure our visiting brothers have a look at this guy before they head back," Axel said. "Just to cover our bases."

Snow nodded.

"I feel like they won't know any more about him than we do," Razor said.

"I was thinking the same thing," Axel told him. "Who's with Ryder?"

"Beast and Rubble are there today," Razor told him. "With three prospects."

"What's the plan?" Snow asked them.

"I want all eyes wide fucking open," Razor told them. "And it's all hands on deck. We need to keep our brother covered at the hospital, make sure Angel is safe. We need to find that asshole." Razor pointed to the man Sadie saw, frozen on the middle monitor. "And anyone else who is with him. We'll deal with them, but we got to fly under the radar. Sawyer is going to be watching us."

When Sadie's gaze met Axel's in question, he said, "That's the sheriff."

"Liza and Henry okay with you staying there?" Razor asked.

"They are," Axel said. "Speaking of them, I'd probably better get her back."

"I'll be directing traffic," Razor told them, as he got ready to take Sadie home. "Put the word out to everyone to be monitoring. We're going to be fucking busy for a while."

"Will do," Axel told Razor. "Thank you."

* * *

Sadie

She checked her phone probably for the hundredth time since Axel took her back to Liza's house before heading out to do whatever Razor had him doing. Axel was going to be staying with them, right? Was he staying tonight? Was he okay?

Sadie knew she maybe needed to find a therapist or something. She knew she was carrying around a shit ton of emotional baggage with her. She was grateful that Axel was as patient as he was with her. *So far.* It was just so hard to get her mind to slow down. Worrying about what Bobby would do to her? Well, she was used to that. Worrying about what he might do to any of the people in her life now was new. Ryder could easily have died. She didn't want to think about what could happen to Liza or Henry or any of Axel's fellow Hounds.

The tap at her door had her jumping where she

sat on the edge of her bed. "Come in," she called.

She was surprised when Axel let himself into her room, shutting the door behind him. Sadie went to hug him, so happy to see him. It felt more like a tackle because she launched herself at him, just so relieved he was okay. His chuckle as he gave her a squeeze helped take the edge off her anxiety.

"I like the welcome, darlin'," Axel said, stealing a kiss.

"I'm just so glad to see you," she said. "I didn't know if something happened or…"

"Nothing new," he told her. "We've got eyes and ears everywhere, looking for that guy. If Razor's right, and he usually is, they won't wait too long to finish business."

Didn't that send a spike of fear through her heart?

"Don't start that," he said, leading her back to her bed and to sit with her. "All the worrying in the world isn't going to help."

On some level, she knew that. But there had been so many times when her worries were her only companions.

"Besides, we have a good plan in place," he told her, wrapping an arm around her shoulders. "With any luck, this will be over soon. You can take your name back, and your hair." Axel's smile had her heart hammering in her chest. "You won't have to live like this."

Sadie knew his words were meant to be reassuring, and they were. It was everything.

"It's not so bad," she said. "I've been happy here. I love working for Liza. She and Henry have been so good to me."

"They are the best," he said.

"And I like the name Angel," she admitted. "It's grown on me. It's a name you gave me. I'm not sure I'd even answer to my actual name at this point."

His smile widened at that.

"I really do want my hair back," she said with a smile.

"I think you're beautiful either way, Angel."

Axel kissed her then. It was slow, romantic. His hands were careful with her as they skimmed over her back while his lips danced with hers. Her heart raced in her chest as she allowed him to pull her closer. Her hands slid into the silky locks of his hair, loving the way it felt sliding through her fingers.

When Axel pushed her back onto the bed, Sadie froze.

Breaking the kiss, she said, "Oh, no. We couldn't."

Axel grinned down at her. "We can be quiet."

Oh, she *wanted* to.

"Liza will know," she told him, pretty sure she was right.

"Darlin', they knew what they were getting into when they said I could stay here. We're not teenagers," he said.

"I'll be eating breakfast with them first thing in the morning," she explained, feeling her face burn.

She wasn't trying to get out from under him and Axel's smile didn't move as he peeled off the cut he wore, dropping it onto the chair beside her bed. Then he reached over to turn off the lamp on her bedside table, leaving them in the shadows.

Sadie appreciated the gesture. She was still self-conscious about her scars. But maybe one day, she could learn to coexist with them. One day she could show them to someone else. Axel was only the third lover she'd ever had. But she'd opened her heart to him, hoping things would work out between them.

"Someone's thinking awfully hard," Axel teased her. "Are we okay here? Because if we're not, it's okay."

He never failed to amaze her. Having a man like him care what she thought or felt? It was *everything*.

"You told me not too long ago that you were interested in more," Sadie said, her mind scrambling for how to say what was on her mind. "I don't know if you meant *this* or..."

She felt his gaze move over her in the dark, his smile didn't move. "This is very *nice*," he told her. "But this isn't the only thing I wanted, Angel. I can get this *any time*. There are always girls lurking around the clubhouse. Ryder brings them back to our house every week. Don't get me wrong. I love being inside you but there are other things I'm interested in."

Her heart flew in her chest, his words sending it soaring. "Like what?" she asked.

"I'd like to wake up each morning, and see those fiery red curls across my pillow," Axel said quietly. "I'd like to take you out for a night of drinking and dancing. I want to see if I can talk you into going skinny-dipping in the river."

Sadie laughed with him. "You'll have to teach me how to swim first."

"I need to teach you a lot of things, darlin'." Axel lowered his head, and his lips blazed a path across to her jaw, to light up all the sensitive places along her neck. "Some self-defense. How to use guns."

While she was enjoying the way he layered kisses across her skin, she had to ask, "You'd teach me things like that?"

"Yes," he whispered against her skin, not really

stopping.

"You think I could learn any of that?" she asked.

"I know you can," he said, rolling them on her bed until he was on his back, and she was above him, a knee on each side of his hips.

His attention had her body humming. Just because she was there and she could, she ground her center down on him. When he moved with her, it took her breath away. He felt so warm and solid beneath her. When she ground down on that heated ridge again, the low moan she pulled from him had her thinking they *could* be quiet.

Sadie climbed off just long enough to work her way out of her jeans. Not missing a beat, Axel undid the front of his own, shoving them and his boxers down past his hips. With his swollen cock revealed, waiting on the flat plane of his abdomen, she reached for him, stroking him carefully with her hands before getting her mouth on him.

Axel's big hands were in her hair as she worked him with hands, lips, and tongue. He did pull off being quiet, the harsh rush of his breath the only sounds he made in the calm of her bedroom. He fought her for long minutes, the heated length of him filling her mouth as she hovered over him.

"Darlin'," he whispered breathlessly, "hop on... Please."

Peeling off her panties, Sadie straddled him, wincing at the creak of the bedspring as she moved.

"It's okay," he whispered. "We'll make it work."

Axel looked so desperate beneath her it made her grin. He rolled on a condom and grabbed her hips. She lined him up, putting him where she wanted him. And after a moment, they were moving together without making any conspicuous noises.

She loved the way his cock felt inside her, filling her up. She loved the steady beat of his heart beneath her palms, the way it kept time with her own as she slid up and down on him. It wasn't easy being quiet when he hit a space within her that felt like heaven, but she managed. When he slid a hand to where their bodies joined, his fingers found her clit. And his touch was magic, knowing just how to push her desire higher. With that insistent touch and the right movement of his hips, Axel sent her flying as release found her and sent the world spinning away.

Sadie ended up sprawled over him on her bed, her breath rushing along with his. It felt so good to be in his arms, to feel safe and loved, even if it was only for a little while.

"Where are you sleeping?" she asked.

"Liza gave me the room next to this one," Axel said. "Really not feeling like I have the energy to walk over there."

When she lifted her head to gaze at him, Axel smiled. "I'm a morning person. I'll be up and at 'em before you are."

It sounded good to her.

Chapter Nine

Axel

When his phone hummed in his pocket, Axel fished it out to see his brother's number on the screen. "Ryder?" he asked when he answered it.

"Hey, brother." Ryder sounded tired but it was him.

"Hey," Axel said. "How you feelin'?"

"Like hammered shit," Ryder said. "I've definitely felt better. They got me good."

They certainly had. "What are the docs saying?"

"Oh, there's going to be more surgeries," Ryder told him. "I lost a damn kidney."

"You're lucky to be alive," Axel said. "Who's there with you?"

"Beast is still here," Ryder replied. "Rubble had to get to work. I think Snow is coming up later today."

That was good. He appreciated his brothers helping them out. "What do you remember?"

There was a pause, a deep sigh. "I was plastered. Like usual. We left the party and headed over to her place. I was busy, you know. They shot me... I never saw them, brother. Never saw a damn thing."

"What about the woman? Morgan?" Axel thought that had been her name. "Did you know her before the party?"

"Yeah, I mean, we'd met," Ryder told him. "We hadn't fucked around until then. Why? You think an ex of hers did this?"

Fuck. How did he tell his brother what they were thinking happened? It was a risk in telling him because he didn't want Ryder to have anything against his Angel. And honestly, all the evidence pointed to people out to get her.

"No." It was the truth. "I'm thinking that this was someone out to get my Angel."

It got quiet and Axel was shaking his head at himself for even saying anything. Ryder needed to worry about getting better right now, not what happened.

"What?"

"Don't worry about it," Axel said. "Do you need anything?"

"No, no, no," Ryder cut in. "What do you mean that this had something to do with your girl?"

"Just what I said." Axel exhaled. "Remember the tracker Sadie's ex put on her car that you dropped off in Mississippi? Remember me telling you he's in the mob? It's looking like he might be making the rounds trying to find her."

"Huh."

"Think about it," Axel said. "That woman's neighbors saw two men running out of the house and jumping in a dark car. They weren't on bikes, man. It wasn't a rival gang. If they looked into the hits from that tracker, it would have taken them to the gas station and our garage. And you're from our garage, banging a girl who had hair just like Sadie's before she darkened it."

"Fuck," Ryder said. "When you put it like that…"

"I know."

"That's why I haven't seen you here, huh?"

"Yep," Axel told him. "But I'll do anything I can for you. You know that."

"I do." The sound of talking in his brother's hospital room filled the pause. "Doc's here to have a look at me. I'll talk to you later."

"Okay," Axel told him, wishing he could be there

to talk to the doctor about his brother's road to recovery.

Axel didn't realize that Hero had wandered into the office during the call.

"How is he?" Hero asked, leaning against the door frame.

"He's still here," Axel told him. "That's the most important thing."

"How's Angel?" Hero asked. "Jade really likes her."

That made him happy. He knew she'd fit in well with Jade and Emily. They would be friends for her, and she needed that.

"She's hanging in there," Axel told him. "Anyone see anything?"

"Not just yet," Hero said. "But we've got everyone on it. Razor told the prospects if any of them can get him intel on these pricks, he'd consider making them brothers."

Well, that was one way to motivate them.

"Hey, we'll be ready when they show up," Hero said. "And they *will* show up."

Axel knew they would. He wanted them to. He wanted Bobby Fuckface himself to come to town. He wanted to face the abusive motherfucker down and show him a small sample of what he put Sadie through. Bobby was *his*.

While Axel knew the Hounds could deal with Bobby and whoever else he sent or brought with him, he worried about how it would all impact his Angel. She was already blaming herself for Ryder.

"They will show up," Axel repeated. "The sooner the better."

* * *

Sadie

"Excuse me, Miss?"

Sadie froze at the sound of that familiar voice. The Jersey accent. Trying to get a hold of herself, she took a deep breath before looking up from the pothos plant she was repotting.

And she found just who she suspected. It was the same heavy-set man who'd asked for the time. The same one who had been at the Hounds party Saturday night.

And likely one of the men who'd shot Ryder and killed the woman he was with because she looked like her.

"Miss?"

You can do this. You have to.

Trying to brush the soil off her hands, she looked up, pretending she wasn't terrified and probably doing a poor job of it.

"Can I help you?" she asked.

The man in his nice suit with a huge gold chain hanging around his neck moved closer. The cologne he wore was overpowering, his teeth were artificially white. His dark eyes were small and mean.

Her heart lurched in fear to realize that she remembered the man. He worked for Bobby. He'd been to the house once or twice.

But he hadn't recognized her so far…

"Yeah," the man said. "Got a friend laid up in the hospital. I was wondering if you guys had a nice plant I could take to him. Make him feel better."

Make him feel better? *You're one of the men who shot him.*

"Of course," Sadie said, trying to add a little of the Southern accent everyone including Axel spoke with in Mercy. "Would you like to see what we have?"

Sadie led him into the greenhouse, showing him an entire row of small potted plants that would work for a hospital gift. Like it would matter. He didn't care about the gift. For all she knew, he was heading to the hospital to finish Ryder off.

"Thanks," the man said, walking around her to look at the plants she offered. Maybe ten seconds passed before he picked out a small fern, plucking it from the table and holding it up to her. "This one."

"Okay," she said. "That's just ten dollars."

The man nodded, handing it to her long enough to fish out his wallet. He exchanged a ten for the plant, studying it idly for a moment when she handed it back to him.

"What is this?" he asked.

Sadie shrugged a shoulder. "I know it's a fern. Maybe a Boston fern? Yeah, Liza could tell you."

"That's all right," he told her. "Thank you."

Fear glued her to the spot until he'd walked out of the greenhouse. Once he'd rounded the corner, Sadie dashed into Liza's house, into the first-floor bathroom. She was shaking so badly it was all she could do to pull her phone from her back pocket and tap the screen to call Axel.

"Hey, Angel," Axel said in an upbeat tone.

"Axel," she whispered. "He was here. That man from the party was just here. H-he just bought a plant -
-"

"Slow down," Axel's tone was all business now. "What?"

"The man from the party, on the camera, he just left the greenhouse," she said slowly. "He bought a plant. He s-said he had a friend in the hospital he was buying it for."

"Fuck," Axel huffed. "Thank you, Angel. I gotta

go."

"Be careful," she whispered.

"Always," he told her. "Call you as soon as I can."

And then he was gone. Ending the call, Sadie took a seat on the closed toilet until she was calm enough to head back to the greenhouse.

* * *

Bobby

When he got back to his house from the gym, he frowned as he pulled up in the driveway. Now usually at this point, he was smiling because he was trying to decide how he wanted his evening to go. As he used the remote to open the garage door, he would usually go over the options in his head. If he wanted a nice evening, he'd head into the house and find her. Normally, she was in the kitchen, dinner going, all dressed up the way he liked. She'd greet him with a smile, her little hands twisting in front of her. Those hands always gave her away. He knew she was somewhere between scared and eager to please him, and it was just what he wanted. He'd kept a few girls at his house over the years, but Sadie was the one he'd enjoyed the most.

As the garage door rose, the gaping hole where her Lincoln was usually parked jarred him out of his happy memory. It was a huge reminder that she took off in that Lincoln and left him. Nearly five months she'd been gone, and it left him angrier by the day. Pulling into his normal place in the garage, Bobby put it in park and killed the engine.

Bobby walked around the space where her car was parked even though it was no longer there and let himself in through the kitchen door as he always did. It was quiet as a tomb in there. No lights on. No smells of delicious food and honestly, Sadie had been a pretty good cook.

It was like she sucked the life out of the entire house when she left. It just felt hollow and cold. He stood there by the counter, taking in his kitchen. He didn't like it.

The mess he created that last night Sadie was there, celebrating his promotion in the ranks, stayed there for almost a month. The first couple of weeks he'd been so angry, so hell bound and determined that her ass would be back any minute and she was going to clean it her fucking self like she should have done that night. She should have just fucking cleaned it like usual and gotten into bed with him.

Sadie had fucking ruined everything. The dumb little bitch didn't realize that she had helped him celebrate his promotion in exactly the way he planned. He fucking loved it when she dressed up, her hair and makeup just so. She'd greeted him in that pretty dress, a dinner all ready behind her that he just knew she was so proud of…

Bobby had sacrificed the meal to get the response he wanted. He made up some shit to be angry about and he took that dinner and painted the kitchen with it. Her reaction was everything he wanted. Tears streamed from those pretty eyes, and she begged him - - God he loved when she fucking begged him! -- to understand that she just wanted to celebrate.

But the tears hadn't been enough. A couple of slaps across the face had her makeup streaking her pretty pale face in black. When that bottom lip quivered, and he'd split that the week before, he couldn't help himself. He popped her to open that wound back up because the blood was pretty spilling over that lip. When she trembled, she was so much easier to knock down. Bobby didn't ever kick her *that* hard. He wanted it to hurt, to keep her attention. He wanted to watch her body all weak as those colors bloomed and spread across her white skin like a macabre flower garden.

Bobby liked marking her up, enjoyed the physical manifestations of his ownership. She had to live with them all over her body, important reminders of who she was and who she belonged to.

By the time she was curled up on the floor, trying to protect herself, he'd drag her off to the bedroom for what he really wanted. When Sadie got to that point, fucking was exquisite. With black tears and blood all over her face, he loved to force himself into her mouth and choke her on his dick. Grabbing handfuls of those red curls, he'd fuck her face until she was breathless, until his come mixed with the blood from her lip. Something about the despair, the resignation left on her face made him so happy.

Then he'd fuck her a couple of times. Rough sex was his favorite, and that last night had been particularly special. He'd been so happy he'd even decided to take it easy on her for a couple of days. And what did she fucking do?

Scrubbing a hand through his sweaty hair, he stomped off to the bathroom to get a shower. He got the water hot, climbing in to clean up.

And there on the little basket she'd hung in the shower were more fucking reminders. Her shampoo that smelled like rain, her little pink razor. Bobby chuckled a little as he got under the spray, reaching for her shampoo and lathering his hair with it, thinking about that razor.

When they were just getting started, she used to

shave her body hairless, including her cute little pussy. When he told her he didn't want her to shave her little mound anymore, she'd been confused. Smarted off to him a little about how it was her body, and she liked the way it looked.

It was still, to this day, the hardest he'd ever gone on her and one of the first times he'd laid hands on her. It pissed him off so badly she was even questioning what he wanted. How he wanted her to look. It had been important to make her understand who was in charge and what happened to dumb little bitches when he didn't get what he wanted. She'd never shaved it again and Bobby grinned just thinking about it. It was covered in curls just a shade darker than what was on her head. A little red badge of ownership that he just loved to see.

Closing his eyes, he took in the scent of that shampoo and enjoyed the smell of it enveloping him in the steamy shower.

When he found her gone that next morning, he'd have been lying if he said he wasn't shocked. He totally fucking was. He didn't see that in her, his submissive little ginger. Hadn't seen that coming at all.

Hell, he hadn't even put that tracker on her car until a couple of months before she hightailed it out of there. He and his crew had busted out an electronics store. The owner got in bad money trouble with his boss. They'd had a few of those trackers in stock and he grabbed a couple, put them on his car and hers.

The first hit they'd gotten from the tracker on her car was in a town called Mercy, Virginia. She'd been there from early that morning until later the next day -- to sleep, he supposed. But then she was off again, making her way further south. All the way to somewhere in Bumfuck, Mississippi.

That was where his men started. It took the dumb fucks a couple of days to get to the last location the tracker had indicated. It took them to the water's edge, a view of the Gulf of Mexico from the shore. When Dennis called him to explain all this, Bobby had been dumbfounded. Of course, his guys reached the conclusion that she'd offed herself.

Maybe she'd shoved it off in that remote little stretch that made it look like she had?

But Bobby believed it too. For a couple of days. He didn't think taking herself off the board was something she was even capable of. Maybe she had. She'd left him after all, and he never thought she'd do that either. And he knew she wouldn't have been aware or even thought of a tracker being in her car.

His guys hung out a few days, watched and asked around. No one saw anyone matching Sadie's description. There had been no choice but to call his men back. Especially since he was trying really hard not to have it seem like he couldn't control his woman. Bobby had just about convinced himself she was gone three weeks later.

He'd forgotten he had an appointment to get the oil changed in his car. He almost made Dennis do it, but he dragged his ass out and headed for the garage. While he waited for them to service his car, something occurred to him.

Bobby hadn't been able to get back home fast enough. Pulling up the data from the tracker, he looked at the locations it gave him from the time she left his house. The first location was a gas station off I-77 in Mercy, that small rural town in Virginia. But there was a second location in the same town, and it turned out to be a garage.

They'd found no sign of Sadie in Mississippi.

Had her car broken down? Had it needed parts? Could it be that Sadie sold the car to someone and then it disappeared somewhere in Mississippi? Had someone found the tracker?

Something told him Sadie might still be in Mercy.

Bobby sent Dennis and Paulie down to Mercy to see what they could find. He put Pat and Dom on finding out if anyone from that garage had called around to find parts for Sadie's Lincoln. Bobby got a bingo on both. Dom found a junkyard an hour away from Mercy that had parts for her Lincoln. Dennis and Paulie scoped out the garage, found no sign of Sadie or her car. Until Friday. He got a call from an excited sounding Dennis telling him that one of the garage owners had a cute little red-haired girlfriend that matched Sadie's description. Bobby gave the order -- waste both of them. That bitch wasn't going to leave him and go off for a happy fucking ending. It didn't work that way. Not in his world.

Once he was out of the shower, he still had no word from Dennis. He'd asked for confirmation that it was Sadie they took out. But after checking his phone? Nothing. Taking a seat on the edge of his bed, he Googled local news outlets around Mercy and found a couple of TV stations. He didn't see any mention on the first one. The second station's website reported a woman in Mercy had been murdered and the man with her was in critical condition.

They'd left the guy alive. That was fucking sloppy.

When he saw the image of the woman who'd been killed, it was all Bobby could do not to throw his phone through the wall. The young woman was young, pretty, with the right curly red hair. They gave her name as Morgan Davis and that wasn't a surprise. If Sadie was still out there, and he believed she was, it would make sense for her to be using an alias. But the woman in the fucking picture wasn't Sadie. And Dennis had seen the real Sadie a time or two. How could he have mistaken the woman in the photos for Sadie?

Fuck this.

Bobby had no intention of letting that little bitch run around out there and make a fool out of him. He's warned her if she ever left him he'd find her and kill her. And he'd kill anyone helping her. Bobby kept his fucking promises.

Bobby decided to take care of this himself. He was heading down to Mercy, Virginia first thing in the morning.

Chapter Ten

Axel

"Axel, where are you?" Razor's voice was loud when he answered the phone.

"Just reached the hospital," he said. He parked his bike and headed for the main entrance.

"What are you doing?" his prez asked, his tone sharp.

"I'm not letting that fucker up in that hospital kill my brother," Axel told him, riding the high he had going from fear and adrenaline. Restless energy coursed through his body, had him ready to fight whatever would keep his brother safe.

"We're not either," Razor said. "But I want you to stay out of sight."

"What?"

"Stay out of sight, Goddamn it!" Razor shouted. "You want to help? Head up to your brother's room and guard him. But hide your face."

Fuck. Axel knew he was right. If the fuckers realized Ryder had an identical twin, it could make things worse for them or create confusion.

"Will do," Axel grumbled.

"We'll deal with it," Razor said. "We've got you, brother." Razor meant it.

"Thanks, man." Axel tucked his phone back into his pocket with shaking hands before hustling into the hospital. When the elevator reached the ground floor, the doors opened, and Snow marched out.

"We got this," Snow told him, dashing off the way Axel came.

When Axel reached the top floor, his brother's room was the first door on the left. Ryder's eyes widened as he watched him race into the room.

"Someone going to fucking tell me what's going on?" Ryder asked, looking way too pale and small in that bed. The side of his face was colored in bruises, a thick line of stitches running along his temple.

That stopped Axel cold. Ryder hadn't been awake very long and it was hard to see him in that hospital bed. Normally, his brother was the rowdy one -- usually drunk, with a different girl each night.

"My girl ran into a guy in town Saturday with a Jersey accent," Axel explained. "Same guy showed up at our party Saturday. From the security footage, looks like he spent most of his time there following you and Morgan around. Today, the guy from the party bought a plant at Liza's greenhouse. Said he was bringing it to see a friend here. I'm guessing he meant you. Angel called us as soon as he left."

That got his twin's attention. "One of the sumbitches who shot me? Is coming here?"

Axel nodded. "Most likely."

"What are you doing up here, Brother?" Ryder asked, frowning.

"Someone has to stay with your dumb ass," Axel told him. "They can't take a chance of you identifying them. You still being alive and all."

Ryder shook his head. "If what you and Snow say is true, they're coming here. They're *here*. Don't you want to shut that shit down? Especially if they're after Angel?"

Yeah, he really fucking did. "I can't leave you here," Axel told him. "Unprotected. You know that."

"I'll be okay," Ryder told him.

"How?" Axel wanted to know. "You going to fight them off in the state you're in?"

The tap had him turning to see the door. Mercy's newest deputy smiled from the doorway. Margot

Donner was tall and slender in her uniform but still very pretty in an unconventional way. Her dark auburn hair was pulled back from a slender face. She had enormous brown eyes and a nice smile. She'd been friends with Ryder since high school. It was quite possible that she was the only woman outside of their mother to have a relationship with him where he *didn't* fuck her.

"What's he grumbling about now?" Margot asked Axel, turning that smile on him.

Sending up a small prayer of gratitude for her timing, Axel smiled back. "Everything. See if you can't straighten him out, huh?"

"Will do," she told him, grabbing a chair and pulling it to his brother's bedside. She seemed so calm. Was she unaware of the situation they were in? Or was she so calm because she was playing down what she knew?

"I'll be back," Axel told him, leaving them to it and trusting that if something happened, Margot had it. Axel was pretty sure Margot had had a crush on Ryder since they were high school seniors.

Closing the door behind them, Axel headed back the way he came. He just had to figure out how to help under the circumstances. When he reached the lobby, he took a look around. When he didn't see anyone or anything out of place, he moved closer to the main hospital entrance, trying to linger out of sight.

It took a minute, but he spotted Snow in a lower level of the parking lot. He walked slowly down the hill. Razor was out there somewhere too with Hero, Beast, Rubble, some prospects. Where the fuck was the man from the camera footage?

As if he conjured him by thought, Axel spotted the fucker, walking slowly up the hill carrying that plant. The man looked heavier than he had on the camera, his gait slow and steady. The hot summer sun winked off his shiny forehead as he drew closer, had him sweating in his shiny, gray suit.

Well, fuck. What was Axel going to do? What was Razor going to do? Were they just going to let him roll up into the hospital for Ryder? He knew Razor wasn't dealing him in on the plan because he couldn't be a part of it. But Axel really hated being out of the loop.

Axel was just about to move when someone marched into the fat fuck's path with purpose, knocking the plant out of his hand. Hero stood a head taller than the man they suspected was here for Sadie, not budging when the man's gaze moved from the plant up to meet his brother's. Yeah, he couldn't make out what they were saying from his spot just inside the hospital entrance, but Axel could tell from the tension of their body language just how that conversation was going.

After a moment, the smaller man's face darkened in anger, and he began shouting at Hero who looked to be yelling back. It was drawing the attention of the various visitors and valets milling around the front of the hospital.

When a heavy hand clamped on Axel's shoulder, he jumped where he stood. Sheriff Sawyer walked around him, the older man's gaze meeting his. Now Margot's appearance was making sense.

Sheriff Randy Sawyer had been Mercy's sheriff since he and Ryder were children. The man was tall as Hero and fit for a guy who had to be somewhere in his sixties. Axel couldn't recall ever seeing the man smile. His face was stern with heavy lines, battle scars from years of dealing with shady people and even shadier happenings in their town. Bushy salt and pepper eyebrows framed cool, assessing dark eyes and his mouth was pressed into a thin line.

"I know it's your brother," the sheriff said. "But you need to let us handle it. Call Razor off."

Axel didn't miss the sheriff's meaning, didn't react or say anything. As he watched, Sheriff Sawyer marched out to where the two men were having it out in the parking lot. By this point, Razor was walking up the hill toward them and he spotted Snow not far away. He knew there were other brothers out there too.

After a moment, the man Sadie identified stomped off angrily and all of them watched as made his way down the hill. *Good.* His brothers would get the details on his car -- make, model, and plates. Once the fucker left, Sheriff Sawyer, Hero, and Razor walked back into the hospital, heading straight for Axel.

Razor rolled his eyes. "You were supposed to stay with your brother."

Axel followed them as they walked by him. "Someone's up there with him right now," he told his prez in a low voice.

The sheriff led them into a small, empty conference room not far from the entrance. Angrily, he closed the door.

"What the hell is going on?" the sheriff demanded, looking at each one in turn.

"We're just keeping an eye on one of our own," Razor said.

Sheriff Sawyer looked from Razor to Axel. "You think that man had something to do with what happened to Ryder and Ms. Davis?"

It wasn't like they had a lot of choice. After a long moment, Razor nodded curtly.

"Look, I want to deal with this case and bring in the perpetrators every bit as much as you do," Sawyer told them.

"I doubt that," Axel told him.

The sheriff's brows rose. Razor cut him a look.

"You have any proof that man was involved in the murder?" Sawyer asked them. "Because if you do, hand it over."

Razor shook his head. And he was right. Yeah, they had that man in their video footage at their party. Did they have solid proof he was the one who broke into Morgan Davis's house and killed her? Shot Ryder? No.

"Stay out of it," the sheriff warned them. "All of you. I know one of the victims was one of yours. But your brotherhood doesn't give you permission to circumvent the law. You need to let us handle this."

It was a tense moment with the sheriff and their prez staring each other down but it ended with Sawyer walking around them, back out of the room. Once he was gone, Axel exhaled.

"What did he say?" Axel asked Hero. "What happened?"

With hands on his hips, Hero shook his head. "The fucker played dumb the entire time. Said he was visiting an old friend who was sick here in the hospital. The more I tried to trip him up, the louder he got. Probably wasn't the best idea to engage him like that."

"We didn't really have a fucking choice," Razor told them. "By the way, is *anyone* up there with Ryder?"

"Margot showed up right after me," Axel explained. "She's up there now."

"Fuck." Razor sighed. "Yeah, we need to think up something else. Sawyer is going to be up our ass if we aren't more careful with this thing."

"Or he'll beat us to them," Axel said. "And I

really want to deal with these assholes myself."

Nodding, Razor said, "You'll get that."

"We know now what the fucker is driving," Razor said. "That helps. Didn't see anyone else with him."

"How are we going to keep Ryder safe here?" Axel wanted to know.

"That's not a bad question," Hero said. "If he were better off, we could pull him out of here."

Axel's gaze met Razor's.

"Maybe we should pull him out anyway," Razor told them. "I hate to do it and risk his recovery but Sawyer's going to be watching this place like a hawk now. It's a public place so he can do that. But if we take Ryder back to the clubhouse, we're just a couple of miles away. Something starts to go wrong; we can get him back here."

And they could all guard him at the clubhouse. Axel didn't like jeopardizing his brother's well-being either. But his life was also in danger if he stayed at the hospital. If his fellow Hounds could help him keep Ryder safe, he could stay with his Angel and guard her.

"When do you want to do this?" Hero asked their prez.

"Tonight," he told them. "Late, late tonight. There are fewer staff. Probably will need you to come with us for this, Axel, you being his closest relative."

Axel could do that. He'd just have to be careful going to and from Liza Austin's house. And he didn't want to leave Angel or the Austins unguarded.

"Okay, but someone needs to keep an eye on the Austin place while I'm gone," Axel told them.

"We'll put someone on that," Razor told him. "Okay, back here at midnight. I'll let you know who is coming to watch the Austin place while you're out."

"Thank you," he told them.

* * *

Sadie

After dinner, Sadie retreated to her room. Thankfully, it had been a busy day and she hoped that Liza bought her excuse of just being tired as the reason she disappeared into her room early.

Her nerves were shot from the man coming to the nursery today. Bobby's men were here in Mercy now, looking for her. They were too close to finding her. She tried reading, but her mind rejected the words on the page until she gave up. She went into the bathroom, covered the roots of her hair that had grown out. Taking her time in the shower once that was done, Sadie was losing to fear and frustration at the entire situation. *What was she going to do?*

It had only been an hour or so after she called Axel that she heard back from him. Yes, the man came to the hospital, but they cut him off before he could do any harm. Apparently, the sheriff also showed up. It was encouraging because maybe they were all really close to catching these men before they could do more harm. Maybe soon it would all be over, and she could continue living here in Mercy with her friends, and her job. And Axel...

The darker corners of her mind reminded her that the men were still here for a reason. They had to know they killed the wrong woman by now. What would Bobby do about it? Send more men? Come to Virginia himself?

Late at night, the panic was hard to fight off. If it would save anyone here in Mercy who had been so kind to her from harm, maybe she should just find those men and let them kill her or take her to Bobby. No one here deserved to be shot like Ryder or killed just for trying to be good people. Just for trying to help someone who escaped from a horrible situation.

Maybe she should run away from Mercy, get started in a new place. She began to dress before thinking harder.

But she had proved she could survive after Bobby. Granted, she had a lot of help. And what made her heart feel like an aching open wound was the thought that she liked it here in Mercy. It had become her home. Axel had become her home.

A summer rain had started, the scent of it drifting in through the window by her bed. Turning off the light, she stretched out on her bed, trying to concentrate on the sound of the rain hitting the roof. She would have given anything to be able to shut out all the thoughts and fears that plagued her.

When someone's weight on the bed behind her pulled her out of sleep, she startled awake. Sitting up with a gasp, she found Axel sitting next to her on the bed, pulling her into his arms.

"I'm sorry," he whispered into her hair. "I didn't mean to scare you."

"I know." Sadie held him for all she was worth. "I'm just happy you're here."

They stayed that way for a long moment. It felt so good, just being held in the shadows of her bedroom with the sound of rain all around them. For a moment, she could forget everything else. For a moment, she was safe and loved.

Axel smelled good. She buried her face in his hair, pressing a kiss to the soft skin of his neck.

"How is Ryder?" she asked, continuing to chain kisses over his skin.

Axel's hold on her tightened, his hands starting to explore her.

"He's fine, darlin'," Axel said. "Yeah, that guy showed up, but he never even made it in the hospital."

"Did you stay with him while all that was going on?"

Shifting on the bed, Axel picked her up and placed her on his lap. The feel of him hot and hard beneath her was definitely pushing those lingering fears out of her mind. He was warm, solid. She wrapped herself back around him.

Axel eased back so he could meet her gaze. "That was originally the plan but a friend of his is a deputy sheriff now and she stayed with him while everything was going on."

He explained how everything went with the confrontation between the guy and Hero, the sheriff's warning.

Fears were trying to push their way back in. "Do you think the sheriff can handle it?" she asked.

His expression took on a somber note. "Darlin', if that guy pulled out in front of me at an intersection or knocked over my bike, yeah, maybe the sheriff's department could handle it. But this is serious, and lives are on the line. I'm not putting my trust in Sawyer and his people. It's not the way of our club. We're not going to sit on our asses and wait for the sheriff to do his thing. They shot my brother and that demands an answer. And we ain't letting anyone answer for us."

It sounded like something Bobby would say, without the insults. The mob and Axel's club were both outside of the law. She didn't know a lot about either, but it sounded like they had similar ways of dealing with things. If someone had attacked Bobby and his men, revenge would be swift and brutal. The Hounds might just handle things the same way.

Bobby and Axel couldn't have been more different otherwise. Where Bobby allowed all the rage he harvested from his violent world to bleed into his personal life, Axel seemed to mostly have control of it. She'd never really even seen him upset. Imagining Axel moved to violence was something she struggled to envision.

"We're going to take Ryder out of the hospital," he said. "We can't protect him there and now we know Sheriff Sawyer is watching closely."

"Is that safe for Ryder?" she asked. "Considering his injuries?"

Axel sighed. "Probably not, but we don't really have a choice. They can't take a chance that he saw something or could identify them. We'll take him to the clubhouse and most of the Hounds will stay there with him."

"What about you?" she asked, noticing he said *most* of the Hounds.

"I'm staying with you," Axel said, stealing a kiss. "I have to keep you safe too." More kisses, his arms tightened around her. "I will personally make sure that asshole never fucking ever hurts you again."

His words seared themselves onto her heart as he captured her lips with his own in a heated kiss. Her heart sped up as he poured so much emotion into that kiss, soft promises made with his lips and hands. Axel was careful with her when he rolled her under him, moving down her body to pluck at her jeans, to work the tighten denim down along with her panties. There was an impatience in him today that she'd never witnessed before.

Axel dropped hot kisses over her tummy, over the red curls of her mound. When his hands pressed her thighs apart, they were trembling. All she could do was watch as he situated himself between her thighs, pressing hot insistent kisses along the tender skin leading up to her apex.

Sadie thought she might pass out. Axel apparently did nothing halfway. When he got his mouth on her, the loud gasp that escaped her had him grinning. Then he doubled down, daring her to make a sound. He kissed her pussy like it was her mouth at first. Long, deep, slow kisses that had her moving restlessly in his grasp.

When his fingers slid around her lower lips, pulling them back to reveal her clit, all she could do was watch. When his tongue slid around that sensitive pearl, Sadie was covering her mouth with a hand. Axel teased her clit with so much finesse while one finger slid around her opening with such a light touch it had her shivering. When it slid into her, searching out the places inside that made her tremble, his tongue continued to focus on her clit with a tenacity that left her breathless.

Waves of sensation rose quickly, hitting her with a speed and strength she wasn't prepared for. While Axel stayed right there, giving her no relief as his mouth and fingers worked her, Sadie twisted in pleasure, trying to keep quiet. Axel didn't let up, and the orgasm was drawn out, bleeding into another one. It wasn't long until she used the heel of her shaking hand to carefully push him away, shaking her head and struggling to breathe.

Axel grinned at her with her juices shining off his lips. Reaching up, his hand wrapped around the back of her neck and pulled her in for a lusty kiss. She tasted her own excitement from his mouth, kissing him back as much as she could while her orgasm shook her to her core.

"You like that?" he whispered in her ear.

"Yes," she said as he carefully gripped her hips and pulled her down the bed, beneath him.

Then he was stripping off with a quiet speed that was impressive. His T-shirt flew off the side of the bed. Yanking open his jeans, he pushed them down past his hips and took himself in hand. "I hope you're ready," he whispered even as he climbed back over her. Situating himself between her thighs, he rolled on a condom and pressed into her, sliding easily considering how wet he had her. When he slid home inside her, he stopped, his eyes closing. Axel was trembling.

"I've been thinking about this all day," he whispered. "About you."

Sadie loved how he gave her a moment to adjust. Wrapping herself around him, she enjoyed the feeling of being surrounded by him. His weight, the smell of him, the gentle push as he began to move inside her. Where Bobby had pounded her roughly, like they were in a porno, Axel made her feel loved, special.

His careful hands didn't grab, twist, or hurt. They smoothed over her skin like it was a sacred privilege to touch her. His cock was larger than Bobby's and he could have made it hurt, pumping into her as mindlessly as her former lover had. But Axel's movements were careful, slow until he needed to push them into release, like he was savoring the feel of her, their union. As he moved within her, Axel enticed her with kisses, with murmured encouragements like "You feel like heaven" or "You're so good for me, baby."

When he slipped a hand between their bodies, the gentle pad of his finger on her clit, she writhed under him. She circled her hips, wanting more of everything. Her nails dug into his back, her heels nudging at the backs of his thighs to go faster, harder. When release caught up with her, she buried her face in the damp wall of his chest to scream as she shattered.

"So beautiful when you come for me," Axel whispered against her lips. Claiming her mouth for a searing kiss, his thrusts quickened. Her pussy walls were still quivering around him as he chased his own end. When his hold tightened on her, Axel lost himself in her, ending with a low growl muffled by her hair as her breath rushed with his.

They stayed there wrapped up in each other for long moments on Sadie's bed, a soft beam of moonlight across them was the only light in the room. Axel rolled onto his back and took her with him, holding her. He was unusually quiet as his fingers traced small circles over the skin of her shoulder and back.

Something was wrong. Why was he so quiet? "Axel?" she asked. "Are you okay?"

"Yeah, Angel. I am... I hate to do this, but I've got to leave here in a few minutes. Won't be gone long. Promise. We're going to meet around midnight at the hospital, take Ryder out."

Sadie didn't understand. "Why do it in the middle of the night?"

"It's less fuss that way," Axel told her, carefully sitting up. "He got shot. They're going to try and talk us out of signing him out AMA, but there aren't as many people on staff at night. Less people will know."

Sitting up with him, Sadie pulled her shirt down to cover her naked lower half. "Will he be safe?"

"Safer than if we leave him there. They'll try to kill him. At least at the clubhouse, if the worst happens, we're not far from the hospital. We got someone to help us out if we really need them. Hopefully, we'll deal with this situation quickly and get him back up there." Axel pulled up his jeans, fished his T-shirt off the floor. "I won't be gone long, Angel. I promise."

"Okay." Her voice sounded high and thin to her own ears.

That stopped Axel and he placed his hand over hers. "Look, I know you're scared. But we'll get through this. And once we have, you can keep right on living here in Mercy. Happy. Free. Loved. Doesn't that sound good? Call if anything seems off. I'm not going to let him take you back."

Sadie shook her head. "I'm not worried about me, Axel. If anything happens to you --"

He cut her off with a kiss, soft and patient there in the dark. "Nothing is going to happen to me," he whispered. "Try to get some sleep. I'll be back before you wake up in the morning."

As she watched him finish dressing and head out to meet the others at the hospital, she sent up every prayer she knew that it would be just as he said.

Chapter Eleven

Bobby

It was close to midnight when he reached the gas station in a little town called Mercy where Sadie had first stopped on that cold February day when she left him. It wasn't much better than a hole in the road with its outdated gas pumps and aging brick store that had seen better days. The newest thing on the store was a sign announcing a new grill had opened up inside: "Coming 2019."

Bobby grinned as he parked his sedan in the parking lot and sat there for a minute, watching the two people running the gas station milling around inside. Dennis told him it was open 24/7 and it was just his luck a lady named Elsie, the very woman he wanted to talk to, was working tonight.

No other patrons were there at the moment, so Bobby headed for the front doors. When he walked into the brightly lit store, he saw the grill wasn't open yet, so there were no customers, only the other employee with Elsie. The man looked to be somewhere on the wrong side of sixty and a strong wind would blow him over. Didn't look like much of a challenge.

"Can I help you?" the woman behind the counter asked.

Bobby smiled at her. "Yeah, I'm here to see Elsie."

The older woman had a lined face. There were heavy strands of white in hair she had pulled back in a ponytail. Behind the counter, she was higher up. Bobby was willing to bet if she was standing next to him, she'd barely be five feet tall.

"That's me," she said without preamble. "What can I do for you?"

"How good is your memory, Elsie?" he asked.

Oh, the look that earned him had him chuckling. "I mean no offense," he told her. "I just need you to think really hard about a young lady who came through here back in February."

The woman was still looking at him like he was stupid, with her arms folded across her chest. "We have a lot of people come through here every day. What makes you think I remember half of them?"

"Oh, you'll remember this one," he told her. Pulling out his phone, he quickly scrolled to the picture of Sadie, sitting at the table with him one night at dinner, all dressed up. It was his favorite picture. "Recognize her?"

Elsie squinted at the picture on his phone, and he moved it even closer, wanting her to get a really good look. After a moment, she shook her head. "Nothing springs to mind," she told him curtly.

Tucking his phone away, Bobby nodded. "Okay. To be fair, she didn't look like *that* when you saw her. She was driving an older black Lincoln that day and she probably looked a little beat up."

Something flashed in her expression. *There it is.* Bobby knew she would remember.

"Let's say I did remember something," Elsie said. "What do *you* want with her?"

"I'm family. We've been looking for her for weeks."

"Family, huh?" Elsie didn't look convinced.

"Yes." Bobby did his best to sound sincere. "We haven't heard a word from her since then. When we couldn't find her with any of her friends or that asshole boyfriend of hers, well, we had to resort to tracing her steps."

That took a little of that judgment out of Elsie's

expression. All she had to do was tell him what she knew. That was all. But it was really pissing him off that she was stonewalling him.

"Why do you think she stopped here?" Elsie asked. "You asked if I remembered her."

"Sir?"

Bobby turned around to see the wiry little old man stood behind him, doing his best to meet his gaze.

"I think you should leave the store," the old man said. "If you ain't going to buy nothing, you best move on."

It was all he could do not to laugh. Turning back to Elsie, he asked, "Is that right?"

"That's right," she said. "Or I'm calling the cops."

Pulling his Sig Sauer from its holster, he turned and put a bullet in the old man's brain. When he turned back to Elsie, all that "tough country woman" sass had faded from her demeanor. Now she watched him with wide, terrified eyes.

"Tell me about that morning," Bobby demanded, holding the handgun at his side. "Now."

"S-she stopped by early that morning," Elsie said. "Her car was overheating."

"What else?" Bobby demanded.

"I c-called a local garage," Elsie explained. "To tow her car and take a look at it. That's all. I never saw her again."

"Which local garage was that?"

"*Three Guys Garage*," she said, her gaze moving nervously from Bobby to her dead friend and the blood on the floor behind him.

It matched the intel he was given. Bobby shook his head. "See? That wasn't hard, was it? All you had to do was answer the fucking questions and you could have just continued on with your Green Acres, farm-living, bumpkin, fucking life."

He shot Elsie right between the eyes, marching back out of the store to his car. He wasn't going to waste his time stopping by the garage tonight. One Randall Harper, or Ryder, as he was called, was in the hospital in Mercy. While the redhead he'd been caught fucking by his men wasn't Sadie, he worked at *Three Guys Garage*. It was almost a sure thing he knew *something* about Sadie.

* * *

Axel

The nurse stood there for the longest moment with her mouth agape. "Excuse me?"

"We're here to take my brother home," Axel repeated.

After she stared at him for another second, she shook her head. "That's not in your brother's best interests. Considering the seriousness of his injuries, he needs to stay here."

"It's a risk we're just going to have to take," Axel told her. He knew this wasn't going to be easy, but with the people who shot Ryder still around and Sadie all by herself back at the Austins', he very much wanted to extract his brother before the shit hit the fan. "We're taking him home."

"Is this about insurance or finances? We have people in the business office that can review options with you tomorrow morning if you'll just --"

"Look, it's not money. It's not a lack of confidence in anyone here. But I *have* to take him out of here. And I'm going to take him out of here. Make it happen."

The nurse frowned now. "You'll need to speak

with the doctor," she tried. "He's not back on until seven tomorrow morning."

"No, I really don't need to speak with the doctor," Axel told her. "Now we can do this the easy way or the hard way. Which will it be?"

"I'll... I'll be right back," she told him, hustling off with the other younger nurse watching her go with a confused look.

Rushing into his brother's room, Axel found Ryder awake.

"What's going on?" Ryder asked.

Guilt hit Axel hard then. His twin looked like he lost a fight with a steamroller. He was pale, thin, and frail. The bruises from where he hit his head had spread over damn near half his face. What if they took him out of the hospital and he got worse? Or died? How was he going to live with that?

"We came to take you out of here, brother," Axel told him. "But maybe we shouldn't. How are you feeling?"

Ryder's gaze was assessing. "Someone coming here to get me?"

Axel nodded. "Let me ask you something. Did you know Margot was coming yesterday?"

"Yeah," he said. "I guess she found out what happened to me through her job. She texted a few minutes before you got here to let me know she was coming."

Razor was right. The sheriff brought her because he knew she and Ryder were friends.

"The sheriff's office is watching us," Axel told him. "And we can't trust them to help keep you safe here."

After a minute, Ryder shrugged. "Do I get to at least go back to the house?"

"No," Axel told him. "The house is thirty minutes away from the hospital. If something starts going downhill, the hospital is five minutes from the clubhouse."

"Fuck," Ryder muttered.

"I'm sorry, man," Axel said just as Snow walked in the door. "Maybe we should just try and stick it out here. I don't want to take a chance of something happening to you. I really don't."

Snow stopped at his side, folding his arms across his chest.

"Axel's right," Razor said, walking into the room. "It should be your choice."

Ryder looked at each of them in turn. "There's a really cute blonde nurse on the morning shift though. She's got a great ass and --"

"*Pffff,*" Razor cut him off. "If you're thinking like that, you'll live. Let's get him dressed, Axel."

Grabbing the duffel bag he left by the door, Axel pulled out fresh clothes for his twin, a loose T-shirt and pajama pants. Getting all the wires and needles out of him took care and enough time for the nurses to return with a tall, thin doctor who looked like he hadn't slept in a while.

"I'm Dr. Taylor," he said after taking in the scene before him. "I'm hearing that you're here to take Mr. Harper out of the hospital."

"That's right." Razor stepped up, staring the doctor down. "We need to sign something? Get it ready."

"Can we at least review why this isn't a good idea?" the doctor asked.

"Pretty sure we're aware of that," Razor told him. "But taking our brother out of this hospital is something we have to do."

"Then can I ask why?" Dr. Taylor was persistent, stepping closer to their prez like that was going to make a difference.

"No, you may not," Razor told him.

"Sheriff Sawyer has deputies checking in each shift," the doctor went on. "I'm pretty sure it's because Mr. Harper is here."

"I'm pretty sure you're right," Razor said. "Next shift, let them know he's checked out."

"They are here to protect him from whatever happened that night." The doctor shook his head. "Is that what this is about?"

Razor stared him down. "What do you think? No offense, doc, but you should be grateful. If the men coming for him find him here, he's dead and some of your people could get hurt. We're doing you a favor. Now if you need something signed to cover your ass, have it ready before we leave."

The doctor shook his head, muttering something to the nurse as he marched out. With one last look of disapproval, the nurse followed him.

Axel got his brother dressed, wincing at his injuries as he did, and those were the ones not covered by all his bandages. By the time they had him dressed, the younger nurse returned with a wheelchair. She had a folder in her hand and her expression was apologetic.

"I'll need Mr. Harper himself to sign this," she said, approaching the bed where he sat with his brother. She handed the folder to Ryder, pulling a pen from her pocket to give him that too. "It's an AMA form. It's a waiver saying that you're leaving against medical advice and the hospital isn't responsible for the impact on your health as a result."

Even though he looked like a mile of rough road, Ryder winked at the cute young woman in her dark blue scrubs. "You got it."

As Ryder read over the form, she gathered his meds from the bedside table, going over how and when to give them to the patient. Within ten minutes they were ready to go, the nurse lingering.

Razor cut her a look. "Is there anything else?"

"I'm required to push the wheelchair to the main entrance," she explained, looking like she wanted to be anywhere else.

"Hey," Ryder told her, giving her his trademark grin. "It's okay. You can. But we have reason to believe the ones who shot me up might be coming here looking for me. So as soon as we get to the front, head back up here fast as you can, okay? And if you see anything off, go ahead and call the sheriff. Okay, darlin'?"

Axel was hard put not to laugh at the way the nurse blushed, nodding her agreement. Bad as Ryder looked at the moment, he could still charm them.

And it went just that way. The minute they got out the door, Ryder nodded to the nurse who nearly sprinted back into the hospital. Hero drove up fast in what looked like Jade's SUV and they moved like a SWAT team, getting Ryder loaded in the back.

Once they reached the clubhouse, Axel sighed in relief. Ryder would be a lot safer. It was a load off his mind.

After they got his brother settled, he needed to get back to his Angel.

* * *

Sadie

The first rays of sun were lighting up the sky when Sadie woke up. She just didn't want to get up. Not when Axel was warm, his solid form wrapped around her in sleep. She knew he had to have been tired. It had been after two in the morning when she fell asleep so she knew he had returned late. Stretching as much as she could in his octopus hold, she took a minute to enjoy being held by him. She felt safe with Axel and that was precious to her. It was something she never expected to feel again after living with Bobby. No way she'd ever take it for granted.

After a few minutes, she stretched again. When Axel stretched behind her, she knew he was waking up.

"Good morning, beautiful," he whispered, pressing a kiss just under her ear.

"Good morning." Turning in his arms to face him, she had to ask, "Is Ryder at the clubhouse?"

Axel hadn't even opened his eyes yet. "He is," he said. "Razor, Snow, and Hero are staying with him. Other brothers are there. Prospects. They're looking after him."

That was good news. It was a relief even though she knew Axel would be worried because of his injuries. Hopefully at the clubhouse, his brother was beyond Bobby's reach.

"Was the hospital okay with it?" she asked.

"Doesn't matter if they were or not," he said, brushing a kiss on her forehead. "We got him out. Like Razor pointed out, it's for the best. They show up at the hospital to finish him off, other people could get hurt."

That had her shivering. The last thing she wanted was anyone else getting hurt because of her. It was bad enough Ryder had been shot and a young woman lost her life. How would she ever face him? Would he be willing to accept her as his brother's girlfriend considering that?

"Stop," Axel said, his gaze on her now. "I don't know what's circling around in that beautiful brain of yours but stop."

He'd guessed correctly. "Still, it's my fault Ryder got hurt," she whispered.

"We've been over this," he said. "It's not. We make enemies all the time in the club. We're used to it. Much of that is over money, transactions. Things that don't really matter in the end." Smoothing her hair back from her face, he sighed. "You matter. Your safety and your life matter to me. And what matters to me matters to my brothers. That's just the way it is. Okay?"

She knew she was staring at him like a crazy person, but she couldn't recall the last time someone had sheltered her, made her feel part of something. She wanted to be with Axel and part of his life in Mercy. She loved her life. But the same fears crept in. The whispers telling her not to get too attached. It was only a matter of time before Bobby showed up. And if he let her live, her life would be even worse than it was before.

"Let me ask you something." Axel's deep voice broke into her thoughts. "How did you end up with that guy? I mean... Do you have any family or friends who could have helped you?"

Sadie had managed to avoid that question so many times since she met Axel. Every time he let her. But guilt pushed her to answer this time. When she considered everything the man had been through to give her her life back, the sacrifices he and his club had made for her, she knew she owed him some explanation.

"I have family," she said quietly. "My parents divorced when I was two. By the time I was ten, I really didn't see my father anymore. Mom had an endless string of loser boyfriends after that, but eventually she remarried, had a couple more kids. She just… she couldn't be alone."

Axel shook his head. "She wasn't alone. She had you. So, you have siblings?"

"A half-sister named Zelda," she replied. "I'm not sure what her little brother's name is. They're kids. I've only been around them once."

"They still around?" he asked.

"Yeah." Sadie dreaded the next part. But she'd come this far. She wasn't going to chicken out now.

"Did they know?" Axel asked. "Or did they notice that they hadn't heard from you in a while?"

"Mom? Well, I did manage to call her one day from the house. I found my phone and charged it. I just got her voicemail, over and over."

"Did she call you back?" he asked.

"I don't know." Tears stung the backs of her eyes. "He checked the call log when he got home. He was furious. He smashed my phone with a hammer."

"Are you serious?" he asked as she blinked back tears. "He took your phone and hit it? Jesus. I'll bet smashing your phone wasn't the only thing that happened."

Axel had no idea how right he was.

Propping his head up on an elbow, Axel's gaze on her was angry. "I need you to understand something. What he did was fucking *wrong*. Keeping you a prisoner in that house?"

Sadie let the tears come then.

"The worst part is what he did to your mind, Angel," he whispered. "All the awful shit he did to you and all the while he conditioned you to think you had it coming. That you *deserved* such awful behavior. You never deserved a second of it. I hope you know that."

That's what she *wanted* to believe. But it had been so long since she'd been confident in her own head.

"You deserve so much," he told her, leaning down to kiss her slow and sweet. "You deserve to be happy."

Sadie nodded. "I've been happy. Here in Mercy. I will never be able to repay you or Liza or Henry for saving me. And that's what you all did. You literally saved my life."

"I'm glad you're happy," Axel said. "All I want is for you to be happy here in Mercy with me."

Swiping at her tears, she smiled, hoping to lighten the mood. "Jade introduced me to Beast as your old lady."

Axel's smile widened at that. "Did she now?" Pulling her closer, he playfully squeezed her. "What did *you* think of that?"

"I'm not entirely sure I know what it means," Sadie admitted. "But she's Hero's old lady and they look happy together. So... I think I like that."

"I love that." Axel claimed her mouth with a slow, careful kiss. He took his time, the emotion he poured into that kiss sweeping all the doubts and fears from her mind. When he ended the kiss, he blew out an exhale. "As much as I want to stay here and start something, I need to get to the garage. Get started."

Sadie wished he could stay too. "How are you guys going to keep the garage going in this mess?"

The emotion that flashed in his blue-gray eyes got her attention. In an instant it was gone, and he kissed her forehead again.

"We'll be fine," he said before sitting up and stretching on the other side of the bed. "Try not to worry about anything, Angel. Can you do that for me?"

"I can," she told him, watching him make his way into the bathroom for a shower without gazing back at her. Sadie was all too afraid she knew why.

If Bobby's men, or even Bobby himself, were here in Mercy to get her, they weren't going anywhere until they found her. That probably meant checking out places where she had been, and they had to know that she'd been at Axel's garage. Her car had been there more than 24 hours before they sent Ryder to Mississippi with the tracker they found on it. Axel knew that too. He *wanted* Bobby to find him there.

Sadie knew Axel was strong and that he had his entire MC to back him up. But he'd never met Bobby. Bobby had the devil's temper, and he didn't fight fair. And he didn't stop until he got what he wanted.

More tears came and she fought to control them. She couldn't think like that. She knew Bobby wanted her dead. And if that's what it took to protect Axel or those who'd sheltered her here in Mercy, it was a price she would willingly pay.

Chapter Twelve

Axel

"Hey."

Axel and Hero both looked up from the day's schedule. Neither of them had been there more than ten minutes. It wasn't a huge surprise to see their prez standing in the doorway. From the grim expression on Razor's face, Axel could tell something was up. What now?

Closing the office door, Razor walked over to the desk.

"Is Ryder okay?" Axel had to ask. Hero told him his brother was okay this morning when he left the clubhouse but...

"Ryder's fine," Razor said abruptly. "Sheriff Sawyer stopped by to talk. He tried to get you on the phone when he saw you weren't home. You must've turned it off."

While Axel enjoyed a moment's relief, Hero asked, "What did he want?"

"He brought bad news," Razor told them. "Someone went into Cowboy Pete's overnight, shot both Elsie Damron and Clyde Donner. They're both dead."

"What?" Hero asked, the same shock Axel felt reflected on his brother's face. He, Hero, and Ryder had gone to high school with Margot Donner who was now a deputy. Clyde was her father. She'd be wrecked.

"Who did it?" Axel asked. "Do they have him?"

Razor shook his head. "No one else was there at the time. Pete got there, he and the sheriff went through the cameras. I can't say I recognized the guy they had on camera who pulled the trigger. It was so blurry you couldn't make much of it out. But the cameras outside caught his license plates. The car's registered to a guy in New Jersey named Robert Bianchi. I'm thinking that's probably Bobby."

Axel knew it was. Bobby Fuckface himself was here in Mercy and Axel let his fury rise. *Good.* He *wanted* the fucker here. He wanted to take him out. Slowly, painfully. His Angel was happy here in Mercy, but she was always looking over her shoulder. She always would as long as Bobby still breathed air. Axel was going to remedy that situation.

"The sheriff have anything else to say?" Hero asked.

"Yeah," Razor replied. "He wants us to sit tight." Their prez did air quotes around "sit tight."

"Well, hell," Hero muttered.

"The man himself is here," Razor told them. "Might want to consider moving Angel to the clubhouse with your brother. At least until this shit is over."

"That's a good idea," Axel said.

She'd go if he told her to. She'd do anything to protect Liza and Henry. Axel also had to consider that Bobby and his goons killed the wrong girl Saturday night, and damn near killed his brother. It just might be the reason Bobby came himself. *He* would be able to spot Sadie, even with her dark hair. If she stayed out in the open, it was just a matter of time before he found her.

Axel would personally dispatch any mob fucker including Bobby himself that tried to take her away from him. It was a fucking guarantee.

Rising from the chair behind the desk, Axel knew he needed to move her. *Now.* "Brother, will you hold the garage so I can get Angel to the clubhouse?" he asked Hero.

"Of course," Hero told them.

"I'll keep eyes on you until you get her there," Razor told him. "Move fast."

He didn't have to tell Axel twice.

* * *

Sadie

It was hot in the greenhouse as she worked to get the pruning done. She'd been so absorbed in her work that it startled her when she finally noticed Axel standing over her. After a moment, she smiled, relieved to see him.

"Hey." Putting down her pruning shears, she turned to give him a hug.

But Axel was stiff in her arms. When she eased back to gaze up at his face, his smile was tight and there were shadows behind his eyes. Something was wrong.

"Angel, I need you to stay at the clubhouse for a little while," he explained. "Can you do that for me?"

"What's happened?" Sadie asked, her heart racing.

"Let's get you a bag packed and get you over there," he said quickly. "Then I'll tell you everything. Promise."

Oh, it was bad if he needed her to go to the clubhouse *right now*. Her heart started racing, her old friend fear putting a cold hand on her shoulder, there as always. And if it was bad, well, she was all too afraid that she knew what that meant.

"H-he's here, isn't he?" she asked, already starting to tremble.

"Angel." Axel's tone was pleading, "Please. Is Liza around? We'll just let her know, get what you need, and I need to get you over there."

Bobby was in Mercy.

Panic made her struggle to breathe as the edges of her vision were fading to black. She moved on autopilot, allowing Axel to guide her from the greenhouse and into Liza's kitchen where the woman herself worked at unloading her dishwasher. Her friendly smile faded as she took in the two of them.

"Is everything okay?" Liza asked.

"I need to take Angel to the clubhouse for a few days, Liza," Axel said in a rush. "I'm really sorry for stealing her. But I'll have her back to you as soon as I can."

"Okay," Liza said, coming up to give her a tight hug. The contact grounded Sadie, pulled her back out of her fear. "Do whatever you need to do. Just keep her safe."

"I-I'm sorry," Sadie told her, blinking back tears.

"You don't have anything to be sorry for," Liza told her, smiling. "Honey, Henry and I think of you as our family now. You are. I trust Axel to keep you safe. And when all this is over, you'll just come right back here. Okay?"

"I love you," Sadie told her, feeling her heart cracking in her chest.

What if Bobby already knew where she was? What if he hurt Liza and Henry just to hurt her? She'd never forgive herself.

"I love you too," Liza said, giving her a squeeze before letting her go. "Go on with Axel now."

"Should they come with us?" Sadie asked Axel. "What if they already know I'm here?"

"We'll be fine," Liza told her. "Don't worry about us."

With the efficiency of a SWAT team, they had her bag packed and Axel guided her out to his truck, driving her to the clubhouse.

She watched the greenhouse fade into the distance in the side mirror, trying to get her mind to slow down. She hoped she got to return to the greenhouse and work again with Liza. More than that, she hoped no one got hurt because of her. As scared as she'd always been of Bobby and what he would do, it wasn't nearly as bad when she knew she was the only one who was going to face the consequences.

Knowing so many people she cared about could now possibly be caught in Bobby's web had her terrified. Would they be able to stop him before he did more harm than he had already?

Axel carried her bag as he hustled her into the clubhouse. A couple of the prospects were cleaning up as they walked in. Sadie just focused on breathing as Axel led her down a hallway and finally to a door in the back. When Axel opened the door, she saw a room that probably had once been an office. Now it was a bedroom with a large bed against one wall, a dresser against another wall, and a desk across from all that with a desktop computer and a huge monitor.

"My room here at the clubhouse," he explained. "Full members get a room here so if we party too hard or need a place to go…" Shutting the door behind him, Axel motioned for her to sit on the edge of the bed. Grabbing the chair at his desk, he dragged it over to sit in front of her, taking her cold hands in his.

"What happened?" she begged him. "Tell me."

"Angel, is his name Robert Bianchi?" Axel asked slowly.

Oh, God. It was him. He's here!

Sadie didn't even have to answer that question. Her reaction alone confirmed the answer.

"Darlin', he went to Cowboy Pete's overnight,"

Axel said. "He shot and killed two people there. They got his plates on camera. That's how I had his name."

"The woman who helped me?" Sadie was shaking. "Was she one of them?"

Axel nodded, dropping his head. "Yeah. He shot Elsie and a man who's the father of a friend of ours."

"I'm so sorry," Sadie told him, trying to pull her hands free from his. Needing to move, to pace. She felt like she was suffocating. Bobby killed that woman. Just for helping her. *Just like he promised.*

Axel didn't let go, keeping her anchored there with him. "Breathe, Angel," he whispered. "You look like you're about to pass out."

"I can't!" Pulling free of him, Sadie darted away from the bed, pacing back and forth as chants of *It's all your fault* preyed on her mind. "It's my fault she's dead, Axel. My fault your friend's father is dead... D-don't you see?"

Axel was up in a beat, putting himself right in her path and wrapping his arms around her. She just let it go, sobbing against his strong, solid body. She should never have left. She should never have stayed in Mercy. More people would die. Her fault. *All her fault.*

"Stop," he whispered into her hair. "This isn't on you. This is what he wants you to think. If he can make you think you're a bad person and all the evil shit he does is *because* you're a bad person, he keeps you under control. That's all."

"How can you say that?" She wanted to know. "Ryder was shot because of me. What if something happens to him? What if --"

"No," Axel cut her off. "Stop. None of this is your fault. No one is blaming you for any of it. Okay?"

Axel just held her there in the quiet of the room.

He let her cry, which was something she needed. His heartbeat was a steady cadence, trying to entice the erratic beat of her own to slow down, match his.

"Angel, he's here," Axel said, "but he's not going to get to you. I need you to understand that. And we're going to try and keep everyone else safe too. The sheriff is on this. We're on this. Just please, try not to worry."

He was asking for the impossible and he knew that. Axel steered them back to the bed, urging her to sit down. Kneeling in front of her, he said, "Ryder's next door if you want to check on him. Razor is sticking around and so is Beast and Rubble, okay?"

Numbly, Sadie nodded.

"If you turn left out of the door, you'll run into the kitchen," he went on. "The prospects stocked the kitchen since we might be here a while. Help yourself."

She knew Axel had to leave. He had the garage and whatever they were doing to find Bobby. It was a selfish thought but at Liza's at least there had been plenty to do. She had little time to think about the past or worry about the future there. Unless she found something to do here, she was as good as trapped in her own mind.

"Please don't leave the clubhouse, okay?" Axel pleaded. "I need to know you're here and you're safe."

"I'll stay," she whispered.

"I won't be too late getting back here," Axel said. "Call me if you need anything."

With a quick kiss, Axel left her there in his room. Sadie sat there for a long time, sending up every prayer she knew that Axel would come back to her safe and unharmed.

* * *

Bobby

"Look, boss," Dennis told him again with feeling, "I honestly thought it was *her*. She had the red hair and she was the right age and height and all. She was with the guy who runs that garage. It had to be her, right?"

Bobby should have known better than to send Dennis to Mercy to check things out. Dennis had sworn to him that he would be like a bloodhound, and he'd track Sadie down for him.

Yeah, the only thing the fat little coward in front of him would be able to trace the scent of was a pizza or calzone. The guy's entire demeanor, from his greasy thinning hair, to his round middle, to the ugly, scuffed shoes he wore screamed "sloth." It spoke volumes about the guy with his beady little brown eyes. He was a good talker but couldn't walk the walk.

That wasn't something Bobby needed with his new promotion. He was moving up in the ranks in the family. And the men he surrounded himself with were a reflection of how he ran things. Dennis would make a very poor impression on his way up. It just helped him make his mind up on the best course of action.

Bobby shook his head. "You're a fucking moron. You know that? It's not like picking up the wrong can of soup at the grocery store, Dennis. You killed another woman and almost killed the guy from the garage. You're lucky he's still alive because I'd be willing to bet that Ryder the redneck biker knows a little something about where my Sadie is."

Dennis had been working for him for just over a year and knew him. Dennis was already sweating bullets.

"We'll find her, boss," Dennis pleaded. "Vinny and Gabe? They're keeping an eye on everything here in town. If she's here or ran through here, we'll find her."

"You know who else is all over this fucking town, Dennis?" Bobby asked. "The fucking cops. That's who. We can't afford any more stupid fucking mistakes. You might have just fucked up everything already."

"Hey, please," Dennis tried. "I'll make it up to you. I will. And if you can just send me a picture of your girl. Yeah. That way we could make sure we know it's her. There won't be no more mistakes. I swear to you on the lives of my kids."

"Your step-kids, you mean?" Bobby shook his head. Pulling out his phone, he scrolled until he found the picture of her he'd shown in the gas station.

Dennis had seen it before he left for Mercy. But this time as he looked at it, he did a double take. His dark eyes widened.

Bobby grinned. *Dennis had seen her.*

"I know where she is," Dennis told him, hope lighting up his face. "She has her hair dark now, but she's been working over there at that greenhouse in town. Yeah, she sold me a plant to take to that garage guy in the hospital."

"When?" Bobby asked.

"Yesterday, boss."

Sadie *was* here. Probably had been the entire time.

It was late and Bobby could go pay that greenhouse a visit, but they likely wouldn't be back to work there until tomorrow morning. That was good enough. Especially since he now knew Sadie was here in town.

Bobby just wanted to see her one last time. To keep the promise he made to her. He'd told her if she left him, he'd kill her. He *meant* that. Now that Dennis and the other two had royally fucked things up here, he wasn't so sure about taking out any more uninvolved people. He had to worry about the law enough doing his fucking job. He didn't need to be wasting more people off to the side. He already shot and killed the two at the gas station. That could catch up with him one day. "Where's Vinny and Gabe?" Bobby asked, watching relief flood his man's face.

"They're right here in town," Dennis told him. "Want me to get them on the phone?"

Bobby nodded, pulling the wire out of his pocket. He watched Dennis struggle to pull his phone from his slacks pocket. It took nothing to loop the wire around Dennis's neck, hold onto him until the fat bastard couldn't breathe anymore and gave up the struggle to form a huge heap on the floor of his hotel room.

"Hello?" a voice called up from Dennis's smartphone on the carpeted floor.

Bobby scooped up the phone. "Vinny? It's Bobby."

"Hey, boss," Vinny replied. "Whatcha need?"

"I need you to get over here to my hotel," he explained. "I'll text the address. I need a little help with something tonight."

"You got it," Vinny said quickly. "We'll be right there."

"Thanks."

He'd get his guys to dispose of Dennis. And tomorrow? There'd be no more bodies left to find except Sadie and anyone who helped her.

* * *

Axel

Axel made it back to the clubhouse later than he

expected. He'd kept the police scanner on in the garage the rest of the day, hoping that if some shit went down, he'd hear about it. He was especially waiting for them to show up at the hospital, thinking Ryder was still there. The assholes here for his Angel had murdered three people so far. People who had lived in Mercy all their lives. Tensions were high.

In the early afternoon, Axel called Razor to check in. Ryder was fine. His Angel apparently was deep cleaning the kitchen in the clubhouse. His prez had heard nothing from Bobby or any of his goons. The sheriff's department, considering Margot's father had been killed and she was one of theirs, was doubling down on the case. It wasn't just the Hounds keeping an ear to the ground, waiting for these assholes to surface.

And they were getting backed up on work. He and Hero kept their nose to the grindstone, getting through several projects while Razor hung out at the clubhouse and Snow and Beast kept an eye on the town today. It was eerily quiet. It felt like the calm before the storm. And the storm *was* coming.

As he secured his bike, Axel kept an eye out, looking for anything or anyone out of place. Everything seemed fine.

He found Sadie asleep in the middle of his bed. The fact that she was wearing the same clothes from earlier told him she hadn't intended to go to sleep for the night. Still, he was glad she was sleeping. He knew she was beside herself worrying about the entire situation.

And it pissed him off so much that Bobby had programmed her that way. Made everything her fault. *Fucker.*

Darting back out into the hall, he tapped on the next door. When his twin called *yeah*, Axel went in to check on him. Ryder didn't look a lot better. But somehow, he didn't think his physical injuries were the only things plaguing his brother, going by the look on his face.

"How are you feeling?" Axel asked, sitting on the edge of his bed.

"Like hammered shit," Ryder said. "The pain meds are helping but... I'm thinking I've got a long recovery ahead of me."

Axel nodded. Unfortunately, Ryder was probably right.

"Did you hear the latest?" Axel asked, having an idea of what might be on his brother's mind.

"About Elsie Damron and Clyde Donner?" Ryder nodded. "I left Margot a couple of messages. Haven't heard back from her."

It was exactly what Axel suspected. Ryder was worried about Margot.

"She'll get back to you when she can," Axel told him. There was no way in hell she wouldn't. She'd had a thing for Ryder since high school. Everyone but his dumb ass knew it too.

"Just hope she's okay," Ryder admitted, taking Axel a little off guard with the feeling he put in those words.

"Losing Clyde is horrible," he said. "But she'll be okay in time."

There was something more there. He just couldn't tell what. Ryder shifted uncomfortably on the bed and Axel helped him, propping a couple of pillows behind him to make him comfortable.

"Margot hinted about going with me to the party Saturday night," Ryder explained. "And I blew her off. She was giving me the business about not wanting the club to know I was best friends with the new deputy in town. And what did I do? I took some chick I barely knew to that party. Why did I do that? If I'd taken Margot, maybe Morgan wouldn't have gotten killed. I probably wouldn't have gotten shot."

"You don't know that for sure," Axel said. He couldn't recall ever hearing his brother having doubts like this. Especially when it came to women.

Margot had tried to get him to take her to their party, huh? Maybe she was tired of waiting.

"Try not to worry about it," Axel said finally, not really knowing what to tell him.

"How can I not?" Ryder shook his head. "I can't even be there for her. Her father just got shot like a dog in the gas station where he works and I'm laid up here. I can't do anything for her. And it's my own damn fault."

Ryder was really struggling with the situation. Axel's heart went out to him.

"You might not be able to be up and around, but you can still be there for her," Axel said. "She'll be in touch. Talk to her. She's going to need a friend."

"I've been a pretty fucking awful friend," Ryder told him. "How's Angel? Razor said she cleaned the hell out of the kitchen."

"Must have," Axel said with a laugh. "She's out cold next door. Which is a good thing, I guess. I know she's about to worry herself sick."

Ryder studied him for a long moment, the bruises around his one eye still looked painful. "You really care about her, don't you?"

Axel couldn't help the smile that thought brought on. "Yeah, I really do."

"I'm starting to think you're the smart one out of the two of us," Ryder said. "Really."

"How strong are those pain meds?" Axel asked

with a wink.

"No, brother, I mean that," Ryder told him. "Neither of you were looking when you met Angel. And I was proud of you trying to help someone like that. I really was. But just watching what you two have develop? Well, I have regrets."

"Regrets?"

"Your way of living brought you a good woman," Ryder explained. "Yeah, some mob assholes are trying to kill her and maybe us. But still. You're happy, brother."

Axel was.

"My way of living got my ass shot," Ryder told him. "And, as a result, I can't be there for one of the few people who ever cared about me. It sucks."

All this was new. Had being shot made his twin think about things? Did he finally realize the best woman for him had been there all along in Margot?

"You'll get better," Axel told him. "You'll get another chance at it." Rising from his seat, Axel headed for the door, ready to climb into bed.

"Axel." Ryder caught him before he made it out the door.

Axel turned back to his brother. "Yeah?"

"If that sumbitch really is in town," Ryder said, "take him down. Make it hurt."

"Brother, it will be my pleasure," Axel said. "Count on it."

Chapter Thirteen

Sadie

It was dark when she woke up and she realized she'd fallen asleep in her clothes. She'd just meant to take a nap after cleaning the kitchen. Now it was dark, Axel was curled around her in bed, and the screen of her phone said it was just short of three in the morning.

"You okay?" Axel's voice was rough from sleep.

"As much as I can be," she answered, snuggling back into him.

"I heard the kitchen here in the clubhouse has never been cleaner."

Sadie heard the smile in his voice. "I had to have something to keep my mind occupied," she said. "That or I was going to go crazy."

"Did you visit with Ryder today?" Axel asked.

Guilt clawed at her, but she had to be honest. "No. I wouldn't… know what to say. Would I tell him that I'm sorry my crazy ex shot him?"

Axel chuckled in the dark behind her. "He's as lost in his head as you are yours and he doesn't blame you for anything."

"He should," she said.

"Darlin', none of this is your fault," Axel said again. "Ryder believes the same thing we do."

"Did anything else happen today?"

"No," he replied. "Not that I heard."

They lay there for a few minutes, and it was quiet. For a moment, she thought maybe Axel had dozed off. But when his hands moved carefully over her back, she sighed at how good his touch felt.

"The minute you woke up, your body went all tense," he said. "You need to find a way to manage the stress, baby. It's not good for you and we don't know how long this is going to drag on."

"Axel, I'm so afraid," she admitted. "Please do what you can to protect Liza and Henry."

"Angel, I will," he said. His arms tightened around her. "It was part of the reason I brought you here. That takes them out of the equation."

"Do you really think so?" she asked, her voice sounding small to her own ears.

"I do." Axel pressed a kiss into her hair. "Angel, he's after *you*. And you're here with us. We'll deal with him and anyone he wants to bring with him."

He sounded so certain, so confident. Her heart wanted to believe every word he said, to be hopeful about the future. Her mind dragged her back down into the old familiar pool of fear and anxiety. "What's going to happen now?" she asked, not entirely sure she wanted to hear the answer to that.

"We wait," he said, his hands skimming over her hips now. "And I don't think we'll be waiting too long."

"You don't?"

"Darlin', your ex sent his goons here and they killed a woman they thought was you and shot up my brother," Axel said. "Then he showed up himself and shot two more people in cold blood in the last twenty-four hours. He needs to wrap this up and fast before the law catches up to him on all that. He can't afford to hang out long."

"You think he's going to figure out I'm here?" Her mind wouldn't stop. "And just face off against all of you?"

"Probably not," Axel told her. "But we're not going to worry about that right now, okay?"

How could she not worry? How could he tell her something like that and expect her to let it go for the rest of the night?

In a flurry of movement on the bed, Sadie was rolled onto her back and Axel moved over her. She reached for him, her fingers finding his warm flesh. He only wore his boxers, his skin so warm and solid under her hands.

"Can I have you, darlin'?" he whispered before claiming her mouth in a demanding kiss.

Well, when he did it like that...

Sadie went with it, enjoying his kisses and the soft touches of his hands. Without breaking the kiss, they worked off her jeans and socks. She was all too eager to peel off her panties. His attention had them soaked. When his hands went for the hem of her top, she froze, just like she always did. But instead of moving on as they always did, Axel's movements came to a stop.

"Angel," he asked softly. "What is it you're afraid I'm gonna see?"

Sadie knew he'd ask one day. And he'd seen the smaller scars that littered her body. He never asked about them. He just accepted that they were part of her. She didn't know if she was brave enough to go there now. With a deep sigh, she sat up on the bed and reached over to turn on the lamp next to the bed. Axel sat up with her, the bedding pooling in his lap as he squinted in the light.

With shaking hands, Sadie pulled the top off over her head. Sweeping the dark locks of her hair over her left shoulder, she turned her back to him so he could see for himself. Her entire body shook as she waited for him to look his fill, to react to what he saw.

The gentle touch of his fingertip as he traced the word crudely carved into the back of her shoulder threatened to break her. Sadie would never forget the day Bobby carved his name into her back with the knife he always carried.

She hadn't lived with him long and at the time, she hadn't realized she was his hostage, not his girlfriend. When she questioned him, and she didn't even remember now what she'd questioned him about, he'd dragged her back to the bedroom by her hair and shoved her face down on the bed. She'd thought he had other intentions -- and he did force himself on her after he was done with the knife, but he'd held her down, kicking and screaming, carving his name into her skin with a blade he hadn't even think about sterilizing.

Bobby hadn't been even a little remorseful. He told her she was a little bitch and now the world would know who she belonged to. She'd cried in the shower later, trying to clean it the best she could. But of course it became infected, enough that it made her sick for a week. By the end of that week, she thought maybe the infection would spread, poison her blood and kill her. At the time, she probably would have welcomed death.

Sadie wasn't sure what reaction she expected from Axel. When he leaned forward, pressing his lips to the hideous collection of scars, she released the breath she hadn't realized she'd been holding.

"I get it now," he whispered.

"It's so awful," she said. "I'm sorry."

"It's part of you," Axel said softly. "And *you* are beautiful. All of you."

She was looking at him now. "How can you say that?"

"Darlin', if you haven't figured it out yet, I'm in love with you," he said, "I'm not sure how to break it to you."

"How?" Sadie swallowed hard. "That's never

going to heal... or go away. How could you love me
when that... reminder is always going to be there?"

Axel kissed her scars again. "Because it's still
part of you, Sadie. And when you love someone, you
love everything about them."

The tears came on, but she didn't care. Turning
back to him, she wrapped her arms around his neck,
kissing him like her life depended on it. He let her,
keeping his hands on her thighs.

"I love you too," she said softly, running her
fingers through his hair. She pressed another soft kiss
to his gorgeous mouth. He coaxed her into continuing
it a moment longer. Axel's breath came fast. She
ground herself down against him, pulling a deep moan
from him.

"I'm never going to hurt you, Angel," Axel
managed to say, willing her to believe him.

"I know," she whispered, pressing kisses over his
face.

Axel's hand tightened on her thigh, his touch
firmer. "I'm never going to let anyone else hurt you."

"I believe you." Sadie pressed kisses to his neck,
nipping at his earlobe. She grinned when his hips
bucked up under her.

"Good." Axel took her breath away when his
mouth claimed hers in a scorching kiss.

Sadie didn't, couldn't, deny him anything. When
his tongue teased the seam of her lips, she let him in.
The deep sound of his moan as his mouth explored
hers was a sinful vibration that ran through her veins
like lightning. Her hands found their way back to his
hair and settled there. She gasped as he pressed
himself between her thighs, his hands exploring every
inch of her exposed beneath him.

Axel's mouth scorched a path down over her

jaw, down the sensitive column of her throat. His teeth nipped at the flesh where neck and shoulder met, and she shuddered beneath him as he marked her possessively.

She gasped to feel his hands gliding up over her ribs, one gently curling around the breast he wasn't consuming with his mouth and tongue in a way that had her writhing helplessly beneath him.

"I'm yours," Sadie whispered, fighting for breath.

He moaned again, a deep rumble with her nipple in his mouth and it had her squeezing her thighs around his slender hips in desperation. His other hand slid down between them, slid into her folds, and Sadie gasped beneath him. He pulled back to gaze down at her, his beautiful blue eyes filled with so much emotion as his fingers kept moving, so gentle as they slid from her clit to her weeping entrance and back up.

"You're so soft and wet," he whispered in her ear before teasing the shell of it with his tongue. "All for me."

"Yes." Her back arched as a single finger slid into her entrance, his touch was so careful, searching.

"You're so beautiful," Axel whispered, sliding in a second finger. He continued to work his fingers into her, stretching her and searching until he rubbed against a space inside her that drew a sharp cry, lit up her entire body.

"Right there?" He pressed into the same spot gently while she sucked in her breath. If not for his weight on her, she would have shot off the bed.

He smiled -- it was beautiful -- as he continued to take her apart with his fingers. Sadie held on for dear life, fighting for air. The third pass he made over the space inside her, she lost the world for a moment, caught up in a wave of pleasure and intensity that she hadn't experienced before. Release left her gasping and wrecked.

When she came back to herself, Axel was still above her, still watching.

"I love the sounds you're making," he said, sucking the fingers that had just been teasing her into his mouth and moaning as if it were some delicacy he was tasting.

Chuckling as her face went up in flames, Axel pulled her hands from his hair and pressed her hands over her head until she could feel the smooth metal bars of the headboard.

"Grab onto the bars," he said sternly, "and don't let go until I say."

Sadie's hands shook as they found the slender bars. He watched to make sure she did as he requested.

"You gonna be a good girl for me?" Axel asked, his expression serious.

She didn't want to make him unhappy. Especially if he could make her feel like *that* again. "Yes," she promised.

"Good." Axel claimed her mouth in a deep kiss that left her breathless, wanting more. But then that sinful mouth was moving down over her throat, her chest. He stopped to lave each nipple with that talented tongue, making each one diamond hard and achy.

When his mouth was moving down to her stomach, it took everything she had to hang onto those bars. She wanted to sink her hands back into his hair, hang onto him, something.

When he reached her pussy, he gazed up at her with smoldering blue eyes. "You still holding on for me?"

Sadie nodded, her grip tightening as if to prove her point.

His rough hands slid up the inside of her thighs, his touch whisper soft, spreading her open. Axel breathed her in, his eyes closing. Her thighs trembled beneath his hands. His fingers stroked her, soothed her.

"Shhhh. I'm going to make this so good for you, Angel. Do you want that?"

"Yes," she managed.

The first flick of his tongue against her clit and her hips shot up. One of his hands slid up to her tummy. The next lick, she realized he was holding her down. And then Axel devoured her. There was just no other way to explain it. He was using his tongue on her in ways that couldn't be legal. He brought her off again, and she was well on her way to another when she started begging him to stop.

"I… can't," she pleaded, realizing that the more she fought to hang on to the bars, the more she fought against his command over her body, the more he seemed to like it. A low growl halted her from trying to use her legs to push away from him, and she was afraid to let go of the headboard.

"One more, baby," he whispered. "Yes, you can."

He was right. It was all she could do not to scream his name, feeling as if her entire being had been torn asunder.

Sadie wasn't completely aware of the first few moments following that orgasm. At some point, Axel had climbed back up her body, holding himself above her with one arm. He used his other hand to line himself up with her entrance and Sadie gasped as he began to push into her.

He was thick, stretching her as he pushed in

deeper with each strong thrust of his hips. He was long too, leaving her with a feeling of fullness she wondered if she'd ever get used to. When he finally bottomed out, he stopped to gaze into her eyes.

One hand gently traced the curve of her face. "You all right, Angel?"

Sadie nodded, but honestly, she was so beyond any experience she'd had to this point in her life that saying words was pretty much impossible. Axel had been so careful making love to her up to now. Now? She was just hoping she'd survive it.

A gentle thrust had her inner walls gripping him, trying to hold him inside.

"That feel good?" he whispered, repeating the motion.

"Yeah." It was more of a gasp than a word.

"Yeah?" Axel seemed in no particular hurry now as he moved gently in her, his eyes sliding closed. "So tight. You feel so fucking good... So good."

When his hand slid between them, his fingers gently teasing her clit, Sadie almost let go of the bars to swat his hand away. She was so sensitive now. Axel must have sensed her distress because he moved his hand, sliding it up her body and up her left arm.

"Let go. Put your hands in my hair, baby," he whispered in her ear, the seductive purr of his voice almost causing her to come again by itself. "Hold onto me."

Hold onto him she did with her arms, her legs. When she had a solid grip on him, he began pounding her into the mattress. Slowly he was losing control as her core began to tighten again, his thrusts hard and erratic. The rough groans pulled from his throat? That was a sound she loved as she held on, letting him lose himself in her body.

"Sadie!" With a desperate cry of her real name, he found his release, his arms tightening around her almost painfully as he thrust his way through it, pulsing inside her.

He collapsed but kept his weight off her, holding himself with his arms. He dropped his forehead to her chest, taking several ragged breaths. Sadie fought to breathe with him, still feeling tired but in a happy, sated way now.

"Thank you," she whispered, "for understanding about…"

Axel sighed. "There's a really good tattoo artist here in town named Deva."

"Okay." She wasn't sure how that came up next but listened.

"You should have her take a look at your shoulder," he said. "A cousin of ours used to cut when she was in high school, and she hated the scars when she was older. Deva used the scars to create beautiful tattoos for her."

The thought had never occurred to her. An opportunity to cover up what Bobby had done, to mask his ownership claim on her flesh with a beautiful image of her choosing? "I'd love that," she said. "I didn't know that was a thing."

Axel held her tighter. "Once all this is done, we'll schedule a consultation so she can take a look. I'm sure she'll have some ideas."

Sadie loved that idea. She loved being in Axel's arms. She loved living in Mercy.

Once again, her entire life was down to surviving Bobby. But now she wasn't alone. Now, she believed she actually had a chance.

* * *

Axel

He'd just finished dressing when he heard the tap at the door. Rushing to answer it so his Angel could keep on sleeping, he darted out to find Razor in the hallway. Razor motioned for him to follow him. And he did, arriving at the conference room where Snow, Beast, and Hero waited. If they were all gathered, something was up. *What was this happy horseshit?*

"Tell him, Snow," Razor began.

"A couple of fellas showed up at the hospital late last night," Snow said. "Looking for Ryder. One of the deputies was monitoring and I guess he scared them off. No one was hurt."

"That's good," Axel said. "It wasn't Margot, was it?"

"Considering that her father's dead from this mess and Ryder got shot, no," Snow told them. "And it's a good decision to keep her out of it."

Axel agreed with that.

"They could hit us at any time," Razor told them. "Three people are dead and Ryder's a mess. They've got the law on their heels so they can't afford to stay here in Mercy much longer."

It was exactly what he'd told Sadie early this morning.

"We've got some preparations to make here at the clubhouse," Razor told them. "And not much time. We need to get some weapons ready."

"I just feel like Bobby is too much of a fucking coward to hit us here," Axel said.

Razor nodded. "You could be right about that. But let's get a few things done and keep our eyes and ears open. We need to be ready either way."

Chapter Fourteen

Sadie

The rhythmic hum of her phone pulled her out of sleep. Looking around, Sadie saw she was alone in Axel's room and her phone was vibrating on the bedside table. Through sleepy eyes, she saw Liza's number on the screen. Snatching up the phone, she tapped the screen to answer.

"Liza," she said. "Is everything okay?"

It was quiet on the other end for a long moment. There were shuffling sounds in the background.

"Liza?"

"Hello, Sadie baby," a deep, familiar voice greeted her.

Bobby. Oh my God it's Bobby. He's on Liza's phone. Why does he have Liza's phone?

"Aren't you going to talk to me, baby?" he asked, his tone pure venom and sarcasm.

"Please," she started begging with her heart threatening to beat its way out of her chest. "Please don't hurt them."

"What did I always tell you?" Bobby sounded more like his normal angry self now. "You leave me? I kill you. I kill anyone who helps you. Remember?"

"I r-remember," she stammered. "But Liza and Henry just gave me a job. That's all. They didn't know --"

"Oh, I think they knew *something*," he said.

Knew? Past tense? Had he already hurt them? What was he going to do? Her mind scrambled and she struggled to breathe, trying to take everything in.

"I don't know where you're hiding," Bobby continued. "But if you want to keep anyone else from getting hurt, you need to come down here to the greenhouse. Really. Fucking. Fast."

She was already pulling on clothes, trying to find her shoes. She'd do anything to protect her friends.

"I will," she said, sounding out of breath.

"It's bad enough you got that other pretty little lady killed," Bobby went on. "You got those two little old folks at the gas station killed too."

While she was scrambling in fear, a small protest broke out in the back of her mind. *Not your fault*, a voice that sounded a lot like Axel chanted. *Not your fault.*

"And don't even think about trying to bring someone with you," he said. "I'll hurt your little biker friends too. We almost got that one from the garage. But come to find out, there are three of them that own that garage. They hiding with you? You fuck all three of them, baby?"

That stopped Sadie, and for the first time, fear and guilt weren't the only emotions running through her. A thread of anger was there too. The man had made her life hell for almost a year. She'd lived in fear ever since, even though she had people who cared about her now.

"I see a cop," he warned, "I'll put a bullet in each of their brains. You hear me?"

She heard him. "I'll be there in five minutes," she told him before ending the call.

Throwing her hair into a ponytail and shoving her phone in her pocket, she dashed out of Axel's room, sprinted from the clubhouse. Yeah, she was four blocks away from Liza's place, but she had so much adrenaline washing through her, she was power walking up the sidewalk. She thought she saw Jade on the other side of the street but didn't stop.

All she could do was hope that Liza and Henry

were unharmed. All she could do was go as fast as she could -- anything to protect her friends.

When she reached the greenhouse, she was fighting to breathe. But she didn't stop, even when she spotted the damage they'd done, with many of the panels of Liza's beautiful greenhouse smashed and broken. Had they thrown rocks through the walls?

She marched on until she found all of them, standing just outside the entrance. Four men surrounded Liza and her husband. Henry looked disheveled, his nose bleeding. His gaze met Sadie's and she mouthed *I'm sorry* to him.

Liza just looked terrified when she spotted her. And right in front of her, the nightmare himself. Bobby.

He was thinner than he had been the last time she saw him, and he wasn't as big as he was in her memories. He wasn't even as tall as Axel. But that cold, sardonic look was in his eyes as his gaze roamed over her. It lingered on her hair.

"There she is," Bobby said. "That darker hair looks like shit on you."

Once she'd been so eager to please him. First, because she thought she loved him. Later, to survive. Now, his words about her hair didn't hurt at all. She realized she didn't care what he thought.

"Let's talk about how this is going to go," Bobby said.

"You could just leave," she said then, keeping her chin up as she held his gaze.

That pissed him off. "Oh, I'm going to," he said as color crept up from the collar of his dress shirt. "But first, I'm going to deal with *you*."

Frustration bled on her fear, and it rushed to the surface.

"Deal with me then." Sadie's challenge didn't sound as confident as it did in her head, but she wasn't stopping now. "Kill me. And let's be done with this."

His expression was hard to read. She knew she'd caught him off guard, but it didn't take long for his anger to push down surprise.

"Just like that?" Bobby snorted out a laugh. "You must have grown some balls being a biker slut, huh?"

And that *really* pissed her off. Axel was the man she needed and loved. Bobby would never be half the man Axel was.

"I'd rather be a biker's slut than your *anything*," Sadie said.

Liza listened to their confrontation, nodding. Sadie didn't miss the note of pride in her expression when their eyes met.

"Look at you talking all tough," Bobby said with a smirk. "You're not going to be running that smart mouth long."

Rushing at her, Bobby captured a handful of her hair in his fist, yanking on it viciously. Pain bloomed in her scalp as Bobby dragged her toward the sleek black car parked in the small parking lot.

"Boss?" The man who spoke was tall and thin with a long scar running down the left side of his face. "Want me to waste these two?"

That sent a spike of fear through her. "Leave them alone," Sadie said even though she was wincing in Bobby's painful grip. "I'm going with you. They aren't going to say or do anything. Please!"

In the span of a heartbeat, the sound of approaching sirens reached her ears.

"Fuck," Bobby muttered, jerking open a rear door of the black sedan. "Did you fucking call the cops?" he demanded before he shoved her in the back of the car by her face.

"No," Sadie said even as she slid to the other side and tried to scramble out that door.

Bobby caught her by the arm and when she looked back at him, he punched her in the eye. The pain was searing, and it stopped her as the other three men sprinted to the car and jumped in. One climbed in the back with her and Bobby, sandwiching her in the middle.

The engine roared to life, and they were spinning rocks with how quickly they were backing out of the parking lot, flying up the road as the sound of sirens grew closer.

Sadie blew out a sigh of relief. Liza and Henry were still back there, still alive. Axel was still alive and safe. If Bobby had figured out Axel was her lover, he would have gone after him first. But her friends were alive. Axel was alive. Bobby would probably stop somewhere on the way back to New Jersey and put a bullet in her head and that would be that.

The people she cared about were going to be okay. As long as that was true, she could accept her fate.

I love you, Axel.

* * *

Axel

They'd just gotten back to the clubhouse, grabbing arms and ammo from Razor's house, when Hero's phone chimed. He answered and Axel could hear the panicked voice on the phone from where he stood.

"Baby, slow down," Hero told Jade. "What's going on?"

The voice droned on as a look of apprehension formed on his face. The phone call had Razor's undivided attention too.

"Liza and Henry okay?" Hero asked, looking at Axel.

Fuck. What was happening?

"Did you see what direction they went?" Hero asked as Razor pulled his phone out, scrolling on it quickly.

"We'll take care of it, baby," Hero told her. "Take care of the Austins for me."

"They used Liza and Henry to draw her out," Hero said to them after ending the call.

Fucking Bobby had his girl?

"And they have Angel," Hero confirmed.

Axel was running for the door when Razor stopped him, holding up his phone. He'd forgotten Snow had put a tracker on the phone he gave her. And he sure as fuck was grateful she had her phone on her. It was a small bit of hope.

"They're on 460," Razor said. "Go!"

Hero was on his heels as they ran back out to their bikes, hopping on and riding like hell.

It had been exactly what he'd feared. Bobby found a way to go around him to get her. And if they couldn't catch up, his Angel was gone.

No, he wouldn't accept that. Speeding up, he rode like hell toward 460. Axel was getting to his Angel. And he'd fuck up anyone who got in his way.

* * *

Sadie

She caught a flash of blue lights in the rearview mirror. It was a terrifying ride because they were going well over a hundred miles an hour and the squad cars were keeping up. Even Bobby, who normally would be taunting the hell out of her, was absorbed by the car chase.

Maybe Bobby wouldn't win after all. Crazy as the chase was, maybe they'd crash and die. Compared to what Bobby had in mind for her, it would be a better out. She'd much rather die in the car than get dragged back to Bobby's home for more torture before he killed her. She couldn't even think about Bobby's plans. The sheriff's department cars from Mercy were closing the gap. Maybe they'd save her?

"Fuck!" the driver shouted, pulling her attention to the road ahead of them. She was slung into the front seat hard when he slammed on the brakes, stunned by the impact.

More police, state police from the look of it, set up a roadblock on the narrow, two-lane road.

The driver and Bobby shouted at each other as the driver turned the wheel sharply, pulling into the grass off the road. There was nowhere to go. All around them was farmland. The driver kept going, tearing out the underside of the car as he drove over the uneven ground, hitting holes and rocks as he went.

Again, he slammed on the brakes, bringing them to a halt.

"Why you stopping?" Bobby shouted.

"It's a fucking creek!"

Rushing water and huge rocks snaked along the ground, cutting off their escape route.

"Drive fucking through it!" Bobby yelled.

"Can't, boss," the driver shouted back. "We'd never make it across that thing."

Punching the front seat in fury, Bobby was losing his mind. "Turn us sideways," Bobby said. "We can use the car for cover."

The man on the other side of her looked as uncertain about what was going on as she was. Once the driver had the car situated, he climbed out the door and she rushed to follow him. Grabbing her ponytail, Bobby pulled her back to him.

"Where do you think you're going?" he asked, getting in her face.

The small chance at survival she had gave her courage. She spat in his face and shoved him back as hard as she could, surprising him enough to make it out of the car.

Sadie just started running. Bobby or his men could shoot her, but she wouldn't make it easy for them. She didn't run in a straight line as she ran like hell for those woods, giving it her all as she fought for survival. Ignoring the pain in her face and scalp, Sadie ran. Shots rang out behind her, and she knew any of those shots could hit her, take her out. But she didn't stop, didn't slow down.

When she reached the edge of the woods, she felt a measure of relief. With the branches and roots of the trees all around, she did slow down. Hope swelled in her heart. Maybe she'd survive this. Maybe she'd see Axel again after all.

As if her thoughts conjured him, she heard the roar of motorcycle engines. Stopped behind a particularly wide oak tree, she saw Bobby's men in a shoot-out with the police, using their car as cover. Bobby was heading in her direction, and that had her on the move again. He was a football field away from her and she got a move on, staying along the edge of the trees.

When Sadie saw the large group of motorcycles, hope swelled. It was Axel and the Hounds. They came for her. *He* came for her. Happy tears gathered in her eyes as she kept moving. Now she ran in front of the trees, hoping Axel would see her.

He must have. As gunfire continued ripping at the peace of the country, Sadie watched three bikes leave the road. Her heart leapt as they raced in her direction. She was so caught up in watching them draw closer, she tripped and fell, giving Bobby an opportunity to catch up to her.

Bobby shoved her hard once she regained her footing, causing her to stumble and hit the ground again. While she was there, he kicked her in the ribs *hard* and then again. The sharp pain stole her breath, had tears stinging the backs of her eyes as she looked up at him, standing over her with his gun pointed at her face.

"You don't deserve to get off this easy, baby," Bobby told her. "But I'm fucking keeping my promise."

Squeezing her eyes shut, Sadie focused on Axel. Bobby was going to shoot her, and Axel would be forced to watch her die. All she could do was wait. And the shot rang out, the sound almost drowned out by the thunder of engines, so close now, but she felt nothing. When she opened her eyes, she saw Bobby holding his right arm, blood seeping from between his fingers. The gun still hung limply from that hand.

"Motherfucker!" Bobby screamed as the bike engines near her abruptly stopped.

More people stood over her where she sprawled on the ground. Axel's tense form moved to stand in front of her, facing off against Bobby. He also held a gun at this side.

Bobby just stared at him for a moment. "Well, you heal fast," Bobby told him, panting and keeping pressure on his arm.

"Wasn't *me* your goons shot up, *Bobby*," Axel said angrily. "It was my brother."

"And that's why you're out here?" Bobby looked incredulous. "Looking for payback?"

Axel turned his head just enough to look at Sadie from the corner of his eye.

"Oh, please." Bobby fake laughed. "You can't be here for that whore."

The shot had her flinching on the ground. Bobby dashed behind one of the trees behind him while Axel swore under his breath while the shooting continued on in the distance.

"You've got to be fucking kidding me," Bobby said from behind the tree. "You're putting yourself in this situation for my sloppy seconds?"

"I'm not the one who got his dumb ass in a 'situation,'" Axel pointed out. "But I'm going to get you out of it."

Bobby's laugh was a rough, humorless sound. "You think you got what it takes to take me out?"

"I know I do," Axel replied.

"Then let's be real men," Bobby called. "Shall we? No guns. You and me."

Axel snorted at that. With his good arm bleeding, Bobby knew he wouldn't be that good a shot.

"Fine by me," Axel said. "Come on out with the gun."

Bobby did that. He still held the gun in his right hand, his dominant hand. Now he wasn't trying to stop the bleeding from the same arm.

Sadie watched Bobby put his gun slowly on the ground while Axel did the same. Her fear rose as they stood there, measuring each other up with the symphony of gunfire down the road playing on. She knew Bobby was physically strong, even injured.

She sent up every prayer she knew that she wouldn't have to watch the man she loved die at

Bobby's hands.

The tension was palpable. The two men faced off, sweat shining on Bobby's face either from the wound or the hot summer sun overhead. A dark red stain spread across his shirt sleeve from where he'd been shot. Opposite him, Axel stood with his stance wide and ready.

Despite his injury, Bobby was the first to move. His eyes, cold and calculating, fixed on Axel, and it occurred to her then that they both had a foot in violent, unforgiving worlds. Bobby had bragged to her about all the years of dirty fights under his belt. With a sudden burst of energy, he lunged forward, his left arm swinging in a wide arc aimed directly at Axel's face.

Axel anticipated the move and dodged effortlessly, his movements fluid and precise. Not missing a beat, Axel launched his counterattack. His body coiled like a spring, he unleashed a swift uppercut aimed with precision at Bobby's chin. The connection was solid, a perfect strike that sent Bobby stumbling back. His dark eyes widened in shock and pain, his footing unsure. Bobby wasn't used to that; the bitter taste of vulnerability was foreign to him.

"How does it feel to have someone beat *you*?" Axel growled at him. "Huh?"

"Yeah?" Bobby said. "What did the vile little bitch tell you?"

Gritting his teeth, Bobby came back at him, mounting a fierce comeback. With a series of left-handed jabs, he aimed to overpower Axel, each punch thrown with more desperation than the last. But Axel blocked him every time, looking like a seasoned fighter. His movements were a blur, saying a lot about his unwavering focus and agility. Axel danced around

Bobby's attacks, a moving target that seemed scary in his ability to evade each strike.

"You should have left it alone, redneck," Bobby said. "You got no idea what you're getting into. There's a whole family behind me."

"Yeah? There's a family behind me too, asshole," Axel shot back.

Sadie flinched when someone grabbed her under the arms. Her hand curled around the soil she landed on as he hauled her up, pulling her back from the fight to safety. He must have read the fear in her face.

"Axel's got this," Hero whispered, his expression pure confidence.

It just was when her attention turned back to the fight that Axel spotted his moment. With a feint to the left, he drew Bobby's attention, creating just the opening he needed. Then, with all the force he could muster, Axel delivered a devastating right hook directly to Bobby's injured arm. The impact was catastrophic, a brutal reminder of Axel's power. Bobby's cry of agony echoed through the woods as he crumpled to the ground.

"Axel," a voice from behind them called.

Sadie turned to see Sheriff Sawyer approaching, Razor right behind him.

Standing over Bobby, Axel's breathing was heavy, his chest rising and falling with the exertion of the fight.

"Axel," Razor called this time. "Stand down."

Razor's voice got Axel's attention.

Bobby knew he'd been bested. It was quiet, the standoff between Bobby's men and the police over. Bobby had to realize he had only two possible outcomes -- death or jail. But he had one last moment while Axel was distracted. Reaching across the ground, his hand curled around the gun where'd he left it. With a shaking hand, he lifted it, pointed it at Axel.

Sadie just moved, running at Bobby. She threw the dirt she still held in her fist right in Bobby's face, before he could pull the trigger.

"Shit!" he yelled, dropping the gun to try and get the dirt and debris in his eyes out. "Stupid bitch!"

Strong arms closed around her, pulling her away from Bobby. The rush of Axel's breath rushed in her ear. "It's okay, darlin'," he whispered. "It's over... We got him."

Could that be true?

Razor motioned them back as the sheriff and one of his deputies took Bobby into custody. He glared at her the entire time, hate flashing in his eyes.

Sadie met his gaze, not looking away. She wasn't going to give him more of the only things he ever wanted from her, fear and humiliation. The sheriff talked quietly to Razor as the deputy walked Bobby slowly back to the road. At one point they looked at her. Razor nodded and the conversation ended quickly after that.

Razor walked over to them.

"We good?" Axel asked.

The older man nodded. "Yeah." Razor looked to her. "They'd like to talk to you in the next day or so about everything. That feel like something you could do?"

"Yes," she told him. She was shaking like a leaf but hope that she'd never had before made her stronger. "I will."

"Let's get back then," Razor told them.

Axel lingered with her behind the others as they headed for the road. "Are you okay?" he asked her, his sincerity messing with her considering she just watched him beat the shit out of Bobby.

"I am," she told him with her chin up. "Are *you* okay? Are you hurt?"

"I didn't feel a thing," he told her. "All I knew was that Bobby had you. And if anything happened to you..."

"It didn't," she said. "You saved me."

"I love you, Angel," he told her.

They reached the road, Axel mounted his bike and waited for her to climb on behind him. She surprised him with a kiss instead. A soft kiss. A promise of the future.

"I love you so much, Axel."

Epilogue

"Axel, where are we?" Sadie asked with a laugh.

He'd put a blindfold on her back at the garage --
well, it was a necktie but it worked -- and took her for a
drive. Then he led her out of the car, and they were
walking. The cool autumn sun was warm on her skin
as she walked along with him as best she could
without being able to see.

"Okay," he said, finally removing the tie so she
could take a look. It took a moment because the tie got
slightly tangled in her bright red curls.

They stood in front of a charming older
farmhouse. White with green shutters, it looked freshly
painted. Renewed in the middle of a large land area
with an old rotting barn behind it and a few old oak
and maple trees scattered around.

"Where are we?" she asked, looking around. "Is
this your house?"

"Yep," Axel told her. "I live here with Ryder. For
now."

"For now?" Sadie grinned. What was he up to?

Pointing across the land, she saw a wide-open
space that looked like it had just been cleared. The land
bordered a dense patch of woods, all lit up in shades of
red, orange, and gold. It was lovely.

"Remember when I told you that both of us lived
here because neither wanted to give the house up to
the other?"

"I do," she told him, loving the smile he wore.

"Well, I'm going to let Ryder buy me out," Axel
explained. "And that over there will be a good place to
build a home."

Sadie thought it was a beautiful area for a house.
She was happy for him. It couldn't have been an easy

decision. But the way he was looking at her... Her breath caught. There was something else.

"It *is* a good place to build a house," she said.

"Not a house, darlin', a *home*," he said. "I'd like for it to be a home, but it wouldn't be that without you."

Sadie's heart squeezed in her chest.

"And you can see there's plenty of land around it," he said. "You can have all the gardens you want to grow."

She couldn't keep the smile off her face. "I could."

"So, what do you think?"

The hope in his expression just about brought her to tears. Sadie threw herself into his arms, loving the man with every fiber of her being.

"I'd love to live here with you," she said. "Yes."

"Yes?" Axel's eyes were glossy with tears.

"Yes." Sadie meant it. "I love you."

Axel wrapped his arms around her, kissing her breathless for a long moment. Her heart was filled with gratitude and joy as she walked with him, hand in hand, to take a look at the land that would be their home.

She couldn't think of a single other thing she'd ever need or want.

Ryder (Hounds of Hell MC 4)
A Hounds of Hell MC Romance
Jamie Targaet

Margot -- I've loved Ryder since we were kids, but he's never been the type to stick with anyone for long. Being a deputy sheriff means I see the world differently -- by the law. He's the opposite. The Mafia took my father from me. When they return to threaten everything I care about, including Ryder, I realize the line between right and wrong isn't so clear. If we're going to survive this, I'll need Ryder's strength. Maybe this time, we'll face danger together.

Ryder -- Margot's been right in front of me for years, but I'm the guy who never sticks around. Commitment? Not for me. Now she's all I see. When the Mafia comes after the Hounds, everything is at stake. Margot's not just a deputy sheriff -- she's the woman I've always needed. The woman I love. I'll die before I let anything happen to her.

Chapter One

Margot

Margot Donner wasn't going to break. Not in front of her peers. Not in front of her boss, the man who'd been Mercy's sheriff since her high school days. *Not today.*

When he called her into his office first thing that morning and asked her to shut the door, she knew something was off. Sheriff Randy Sawyer was a good man, tall and imposing. The deep lines on his stern face could have been carved by moral integrity. He'd always reminded her of the sheriffs in the old 60s Westerns she used to watch with her grandmother, ones with frontier grit.

Pulling off his hat, the sheriff set it on the desk between them. His steady gaze, directed at her when she took a seat in the chair across from him, led her to know something was wrong. She'd seen that expression before when her boss had to deliver the worst possible news.

Oh, God. What's happened? Was Ryder okay?

"Donner," the sheriff said. "You worked off shift around seven last night, didn't you?"

Margot nodded. She worked that same shift every other Saturday.

"Did you go home after that?"

Now she was confused.

"I went to visit Ryder in the hospital," Margot told him. "It was probably around midnight before I left. It gave Dawson a little time to catch up on reports and it gave me an excuse to stay late with Ryder. Then I went home and went to bed. I'm sorry I missed your calls, sir."

With everything going on in the normally quiet

town of Mercy over the last few days, she couldn't remember checking her phone before she left her apartment.

"I drove over to your house too." Now Randy's expression was grave. "You must have been at the hospital. I guess you weren't listening to the news either."

"We turned off the TV in his room," she explained. Margot didn't want Randall Harper, Ryder to his club, to see news reports about the murder of Morgan Davis. He'd left with her from the party at the Hounds of Hell clubhouse last Saturday night. He'd gone home with the beautiful redhead and was in bed with her when someone broke into her home and shot them. The woman died while Ryder lost a kidney among his serious injuries. "I didn't want Ryder to see anything on the news that might upset him. You know?"

Margot already felt like the worst friend in the world. Just a week ago she'd teased him about shocking the shit out of his MC and bringing *her*, a deputy sheriff, to the Hounds' party. Playfully, she'd told him he might regret not taking her with him that fateful night. *Wishful thinking.*

But she certainly didn't hope for anything bad to happen to him or the girl he did take that night.

Ryder and Margot went way back, had been in the same class from kindergarten to high school graduation. She'd always been his friend. That's all she'd ever be to him apparently, despite the little flame of hope her heart had protected all these years.

Randy nodded. "I see."

"Is everything okay?" Margot finally asked.

The sheriff sighed. "No, Margot it's really not." His use of her first name froze her to the spot. "A man walked into Cowboy Pete's last night. He shot and killed two people. One of them... was your father."

Margot stared at him in a stunned silence. "What? My dad?"

Randy nodded, his expression the same mask he wore so many times to tell the families of crime victims the worst news. She just never thought she'd be on the receiving end of it. "I'm really sorry."

"A robbery?" she asked.

"No, it wasn't," Randy said. "We reviewed security footage and the man in the video appears to be there for other reasons. There's no audio so we don't know what was discussed."

No. This can't be real.

It took everything she had to hold herself together, to not give in to grief. How was her father dead? Why would someone shoot *him*? He'd worked at Cowboy Pete's for years and everyone in town knew Clyde Donner. Most liked him very much. Her father was a smaller, older man who didn't have much to say but he saw a lot. And he would literally help anyone in need.

Her heart cracked in her chest while numbness took hold of the rest of her. Her mind struggled to fully grasp what her boss would have her believe. She was *never* going to see her father again.

"Can I see him?" she asked.

Randy winced in a rare show of emotion, and caught himself a second later. How bad was it? In their line of work, they'd seen a lot.

"He was shot in the face," Randy said after a long pause. "It's your decision."

"I'd like to see him, please."

Nodding, the sheriff fished his phone out of his jacket pocket. "I'll text Gordy and let him know we're on our way."

Margot felt like she was on autopilot as she followed him out of the office. She knew her boss had no idea what else to say. The hospital was a short walk across the road and before she realized it, they'd reached the morgue. Old Gordon Barber waited like always, in his pristine white lab coat with tired gray eyes behind his glasses.

But this time the mortician was waiting for her. His practiced somber and respectful look this morning was for her. Margot swallowed hard, fighting to keep emotions at bay.

It wasn't real. Her father wasn't dead. He couldn't be. It wasn't him.

Four covered bodies lay on metal tables. Margot took a deep breath, steeling herself. Gordon led her and Randy to one of the tables against the wall. Everything was quiet. She'd been there before, just not playing the part of the heartbroken family member. With a shaking hand, she reached for the corner of the white sheet covering him, stained with blood where it covered his head.

"Margot, don't," Randy said. "Just look at his hands."

If the fucker shot him point blank in the face, was the man under the sheet really her father? What if they were wrong? She hated the way her heart lurched, terrified to even hope...

Quickly, she dropped that part of the sheet. Lifting the sheet further down, she revealed his left arm. She spotted the gold wedding ring he always wore on his ring finger, her mother's wedding ring. He'd worn it since she'd passed ten years before. His old-fashioned watch with its cracked face and stretchy metal band fit snug around his wrist like always.

"It's him," Margot said in a voice that sounded high and afraid. Just for a moment, she held his cold hand in hers. *It was real.*

Randy thanked the morgue assistant as he led them back out, explaining he would take care of her father until she made funeral arrangements. When the man walked away, she stood in the silence of the hallway at just after five in the morning. Her boss regarded her with kind eyes.

"I want you to take all the time you need," Randy told her. "I'm so sorry, Margot. Clyde was a good man."

"He was the best." Her voice didn't sound right to her own ears. She was still holding up. Yeah, she was shaking but she held the tears back. But she wouldn't be able to for much longer.

"Thank you," she mumbled, struggling to accept her current reality. "Can I ask you something?"

"Yes."

"Are these murders tied to Morgan Davis?" she wanted to know. *Did the sons-of-bitches who shot Ryder do this?*

"I don't have proof," Randy said. "Not right now. It's possible... I suspect it *is*."

Nodding, Margot was ready to return to her vehicle. She needed to make funeral arrangements. She'd need to deal with her parents' house. So many things to do...

"Margot," Randy said, causing her to pause and look back. "If you need anything, let us know. Okay?"

"Thank you," she whispered.

Her head didn't feel connected to the rest of her as she climbed into her SUV. For a long moment she sat, trying to wrap her head around everything. She didn't remember starting the engine or driving to her parents' house. The next thing she knew, she stood on the front porch of the house where she grew up.

So many memories flashed through her mind from just the porch. Waiting for the bus on her first day of school, having her prom date pick her up her senior year of high school. Her parents sitting together on the porch on sunny days. Once her mother passed, sometimes her father still sat in his chair on warm, sunny days.

Now he was gone too.

Unlocking the door, she let herself into her parents' home. Her father kept it just the way it had been when her mother was still living. Everything clean and gently worn. Everything in its place.

She stood in the quiet of the living room, taking in all the framed pictures of the three of them -- her, her mother and father -- and the happy life they'd led. They'd been a simple family. Sure, they struggled for money sometimes. But she'd been happy and loved.

The tears came, watering the pain blooming in her chest. Most of the happy photographs on the tables and walls were of her. Her with her parents, her with her friends. They'd been so proud of her when she'd finished college. At least her father had still been around to see her become Mercy's newest deputy sheriff.

But now she was alone. The realization brought on more tears. What was she going to do now?

Well, Margot still had friends she'd known since school. They'd gone to games and danced together as teenagers. They danced at bars and went on vacations in their twenties. Now? In their thirties, her friends were married with kids, living in nice homes.

And Margot?

There had been a couple of boyfriends. The first

one, Sam, had been a good guy. Her parents wanted her to marry him. When she finally ended the relationship, she didn't know which she hated more: letting down her parents or the young man she'd considered her best friend. But he'd never be more than a friend and making him believe otherwise for four years hurt her heart.

Corey with his pretty blue eyes and glossy blond curls had been an impulse boyfriend. She hadn't meant to have more than a one-night stand with him, but no one sent him that memo. They shared an apartment for six months and fought most of the time. The sex had been amazing, but the man had so many issues. When Margot's mother passed and she'd gone off to the police academy, the distance offered Corey the excuse he needed to bail out of the relationship. She hadn't been sorry.

Margot's first law enforcement job had been with the city police in the next county. She'd been homesick within a year. She worried about her father, now a widower. It took a couple of years before an opening in Mercy's sheriff's department was announced. The minute she learned of it, her application was in. When she got the job two months ago, she'd been elated.

Finally. *Finally.* Something good happened to her. She could be a deputy sheriff in her hometown, just like she always wanted. She could be closer to her father. She even found an apartment a couple of blocks away from the house where she grew up.

And there was Ryder.

Dropping heavily onto the sofa, Margot's mind spun from the shock.

What a horrible week.

She'd been patrolling on Saturday afternoon. Randy'd thought it would be funny to put her on patrol on the same night the Hounds of Hell threw a party. Her boss winked at her, told her if Ryder got into any trouble, she could enjoy taking him in. She'd laughed along with him, not bothered by the fact the sheriff knew of her damn-near lifelong crush on the handsome biker.

What bothered her was watching Ryder, as she had a thousand times, with another woman on his arm at the night of the party. Ryder dated so many women over the years she'd honestly lost count.

Margot had loved him the first time she saw him, when they'd started kindergarten. Later the first day of school, she learned Randall Harper had an identical twin named Alex. While they physically looked alike, that's where most of the resemblance ended. The differences between them became more obvious as they grew older. By high school, Randall flirted with all the pretty girls in the junior and senior classes. Always talking to different girls, going out with them to games and school dances.

Alex, on the other hand, was quiet and serious. He actually went to class and did well in school. Alex graduated with honors. While he went out with girls too, Margot could count on one hand how many. Alex wasn't anything like his playboy brother.

Margot cursed her own traitorous heart so many times. Why did she have to fall for Randall and not Alex? Why did her heart get stolen by the womanizer?

The twins always loved motorcycles. In their twenties, they'd fallen in with the Hounds of Hell. Instead of heading off to school like many of their friends, they stayed in Mercy. The girls Randall -- now he went by Ryder -- went around with were flashier and trashier. And just like in high school, he never settled on one.

Alex became Axel and remained the serious one. Axel got them jobs at a local mechanic's shop where they met Hero, another member of the Hounds around their age. When old Dusty Daniels died, the twins and Hero bought the garage and had successfully owned it since. The twins were good mechanics and Hero did bodywork for them too.

They'd just taken over ownership when her mother had been fatally injured in a car accident one night, driving home from her quilting club meeting. They'd towed what was left of her minivan to their garage. Margot went with her father to arrange for its disposal. Clyde went into the office while Margot lingered in the truck, shocked and shattered from the loss of her mother.

"You okay?" The deep voice had broken into her thoughts all those years ago, pulling her out of her grief. In wonder she found her crush of many years peering at her through the open window of her father's truck, his gaze kind. At first, she thought it must be Axel but after a moment, she realized it was Ryder.

Margot remembered the sheer panic of the moment. She didn't think Ryder ever noticed her.

"I'm fine." Her voice choked with tears. Clearing her throat, she tried again. "I'm fine."

She expected Ryder to move along then. Instead, with hands on his hips, he stepped back from the truck. "We have sodas in the lounge. Come have one."

On instinct, Margot opened the door and climbed out of the truck. She couldn't have looked worse. She'd thrown on sweats and a baggy sweatshirt to go out with her father rather than be alone with her grief. Her hair was pulled back in a half-assed ponytail, her face scrubbed clean. It helped to realize Ryder would never look at her like he did all the other young women who came and went so easily from his life.

Why would he? Ryder even then had been fiercely handsome. Yes, he and Axel were identical twins. Even so, there was a wildness to Ryder that Axel didn't have. It was in the cocky way he walked -- and he had a nice ass with thick thighs any girl would want to ride. Ryder was broad-shouldered with long, muscular arms, already littered with tattoos at that point, peeking out from the too-tight T-shirts he wore beneath his cut. It was in the way the thick, dark waves of his hair stuck up at odd angles most of the time, making her want to run her fingers through it and mess it up more. It was in the hard planes of his face, the strong line of his jaw. His eyes were a darker blue like a stormy ocean, hard most of the time. When he was pissed, that steely-eyed look would freeze most to the spot. When he turned it on a girl he wanted... well...

Margot had seen that look and how women reacted, but it had never been directed at her.

She followed him to the garage's lounge. The worn leather couch was surprisingly comfortable. A small mini fridge sat next to the flat screen TV and Ryder walked to it, pulling out two plastic bottles of soda.

"Hope this is all right," he muttered, handing her a root beer.

Margot nodded, scrambling from the unexpected loss and oddly, the opportunity to talk to her one true crush.

"I'm sorry about your mother," Ryder told her, taking a seat next to her and twisting the cap off the plastic bottle he held.

His kind words sent a fresh spike of pain through her heart. None of it seemed real. Her mother's absence didn't make any sense.

Margot shook her head. "I keep hoping I'll wake up any minute," she said, "and be relieved it was all a dream. Mom's going to be there, like she always is…"

Ryder took a drink, quietly listening. Margot hadn't known how to handle uncomfortable silences back then. She'd rambled on to fill the void.

"What am I supposed to do now?" she asked.

"I wish I had some great wisdom to offer here," Ryder said softly. "But I really don't. If you ever discover the answer to that, I'm hoping you'll share it with me."

Margot remembered meeting his gaze. Pain had flashed in his gorgeous eyes.

"You probably remember our father died of a heart attack when me and Axel were high school freshmen," he explained. "Just dropped dead. We did our best to take care of our mother. But she didn't do so well. She lived to see us graduate. I think that's what she was waiting for, to make sure we'd make it to adulthood. Once she was pretty sure our dumb asses could survive as adults, well…"

She hadn't been sure what to make of that and didn't want to ask. But she also didn't want it to seem like she didn't care. She'd probably never get a chance to talk to the object of her unrequited love ever again.

"Do you want to talk about what happened then?" Margot asked.

Ryder swallowed hard, his gaze on the bottle of root beer in his hands. "She'd had a real bad time that summer," he explained. "I'd come in all hours of the night, partying with my friends. She never slept, always watching TV. No emotion, just that blank face like she was waiting on something or someone to give her a reason to stay."

Her heart started pounding in dread. The whole story had never fully been told in town.

"I found her on the floor at three in the morning in early fall that year," Ryder told her. "Day after our eighteenth birthday. She, ah…" His throat worked as he swallowed, took a deep breath. "She took herself off the board. She had some old pain pills left from breaking her arm a couple of years before. She swallowed all of them and I guess…"

"I'm so sorry," Margot said. She couldn't even imagine what *that* had been like. Her mother died in an accident; she hadn't wanted to leave her family. His mother didn't want to be there anymore, family or not.

Ryder nodded slowly. "I've been asking myself since that day 'What am I supposed to do now?' I guess I'm still trying to figure it out."

His mother had passed away a few years before that conversation on the old leather couch. But his eyes became glossy as he talked. The loss still haunted him.

The sudden loss of her mother took a long time to navigate and there were days she still wished she could call her mom, ask for advice. Her father had always been there for her, without fail. Neither of them had been the same after her mother died, but Clyde had always been a steady presence. She still hung out with him once a week on her nights off. One week, she'd come over to the house, and he'd make the fried bologna sandwiches she'd loved since childhood. The next week, she took him out to eat at the diner her parents loved.

And now, Clyde was gone too. The tears were hot and thick, blurring her vision and choking her sobs. The sounds of her sorrow echoed in the house where she grew up. Empty now, hollow like she felt inside. *What am I supposed to do next?*

Her phone vibrated in the pocket of her uniform pants. With a shaking hand, she fished it out of her pocket to read the text notification on the screen. Three text messages from Ryder, the first one around three that morning, the latest one a minute ago.

Ryder: *Margot, I just heard about Clyde. I'm so sorry.*

Through her tears, she managed to send a broken heart emoji back to him.

It wasn't a minute later that he wrote back.

Ryder: *I'd come to you if I weren't laid up right now. You know that. Come visit me if you want to talk.*

Swiping at her tears with her fingers, she typed a message back, grateful to hear from him. She smiled through her misery.

Margot: *I'll stop by the hospital later. I could use someone to talk to.*

Ryder: *I'm at the clubhouse.*

What? Before she could type out a text demanding to know why, she knew the reason. The men who'd shot Ryder and killed her father were at large. And Ryder hadn't died. They'd come for him because they couldn't take a chance that he'd seen something. The Hounds had pulled him out of the hospital to protect him. As worried as she was about his recovery, she agreed with the Hounds on this one.

Margot: *The Hounds are never going to let a deputy into the clubhouse.* She added a wink emoji.

Ryder: *Probably not. But Razor wouldn't have a problem with YOU coming to the clubhouse.*

Margot understood the distinction he made.

Margot: *Then I'll be by tomorrow.*

Ryder was her friend. That's all he'd ever be to her. But right now, he was all she had.

Chapter Two

Ryder

The next day Ryder smiled to read the text from Margot Donner.

Margot: *If you still think Razor is okay with it, I'll come see you later today.*

They'd become close after her mother's death. She was the only woman he'd ever kept as a friend for years and never fucked. Yeah, she was a cop, but she was one of his favorite people.

"What are you grinning about?" Beast asked, shifting pillows behind Ryder's back.

Ryder wasn't admitting to shit. He had a reputation to maintain. "Just waiting to hear Axel got these fuckers," Ryder told him, groaning as the bigger biker hauled him up into a sitting position on the bed.

"That's it, huh?" Beast went over to the desk in Ryder's room at the clubhouse, lifted off a tray that held his lunch.

Beast's dark-eyed gaze was filled with humor. His muscular friend, with his wild fringe of dark hair, towered over Ryder in the bed. Once he situated the tray in front of Ryder, his beefy arms folded across the wide expanse of his chest. The face of the dark wolf inked on his friend's forearm drew his attention with its sinister gaze.

"Maybe," Ryder said, steadying the tray on his lap, shaking his head. His MC brothers were still feeding him soup and applesauce. "Can I get something solid?"

Beast shook his head. "Nah, you need to heal up."

Ryder snorted. "I'm full of fucking holes. I'm surprised this shit isn't running right out of me the minute I eat it."

The chime of Beast's phone had him fishing his device out of his pocket. "Yep?"

The deep voice on the other end of the phone sounded like Hero.

Ryder tried hard to listen -- he knew his twin brother was handling things, especially with his girl in danger. Still irked him greatly that he couldn't be there to fight at Axel's side. To have his back. That had always been the deal between them. To always have each other's back.

As Beast listened to whatever Hero said, Ryder let his head fall back against the pillows with a deep sigh. Alex, now Axel, had been born first by seven minutes. A fact his twin had never thrown in his face, never used at all. And Axel certainly earned the part of the older brother even though they were identical. Axel could be counted on when Ryder needed him. If he was hung over from a night of partying, Axel let him stay home and took up the slack at work. When he got himself into the occasional fight, Axel tipped the scales if he'd underestimated the other guy. Or came to bail him out.

Ryder also had spent years watching his brother earn everyone's respect. His brother and Hero made all the business decisions for the garage. When it came to dirty jobs the club needed doing, Axel was among the first approached. Cool-headed and calculating, Axel didn't miss a damn thing.

Ryder didn't command the same respect. He wasn't *disrespected*. And he got important jobs from the club. Okay, maybe Ryder wasn't as cool and calculated as his twin. But he was a good shot, a damn good fighter with any weapon or hand-to-hand combat. And when crazy was called for? He could do crazy all day long.

Yes, Ryder was a ladies' man. Axel took comfort from the occasional sweet butt although not to the extent Ryder did. He liked the ladies and didn't limit himself to the ones who came to every party fishing for a Hound to claim her as his old lady. He liked his women fast and flashy, like his bikes. Ryder appreciated a nice ride.

Unlike his bikes, he never stayed with any woman more than a few weeks. "Love" was amazing the first few weeks. But as attachment tried to take hold, Ryder felt himself being strangled by those thin vines of commitment.

"It's done," Beast told him, ending the call. "Sounds like a fucking free-for-all. Sheriff Sawyer got to the Mafia guys first, then once our guys got there, Axel beat the shit out of his girl's ex. Probably the same fucker who shot you and killed Elsie and Clyde over at Cowboy Pete's."

Ryder smiled. He knew Axel would deal with it.

"The guy dead?" Ryder asked, bracing for regret. It would have been nice to put down the guy who shot him full of holes -- or gave the order -- himself.

"Nah," Beast told him. "Sawyer took him in."

That could spell trouble down the road.

"At least Axel's old lady is a little safer," the other biker told him as he wandered out of his room. "Until they let him out."

Axel's old lady.

Everyone called her Angel but if he remembered rightly, her name was Sadie. *Was* she his twin's old lady?

Yeah, the way it started out, Ryder'd assumed she was some sort of pity thing his brother had taken on. But weeks went by after she decided to hide in

Mercy, and his brother stayed close to her all that time. By the time her ex and his men found her, yeah, he had to admit they'd felt like a couple. The young woman looked at his brother like a knight in shining armor. That wasn't anything new. Ryder had seen that before. His brother had a soft spot for women and kids.

It wasn't until the party Saturday night when Axel brought her to the clubhouse that it hit Ryder. The way his twin looked at *her*. Damn. He should have noticed before. His brother had found love, and he knew next to nothing about the woman except she'd been horribly abused by her ex and looked at his brother like he hung the fucking moon.

Shouldn't he know something about his brother's girl? If she was in Axel's life, she'd be in his too. Hell, they'd brought her to the clubhouse a couple of days ago to keep her safe. Ryder heard her hustling around beyond his door. She never popped in to check on him though.

Lying still with the pain bleeding vividly into his awareness, Ryder reached for his pain meds, taking a double dose now that he knew his brother was safe. His brother had saved his girl and beat the fucking bad guy. Axel had to be feeling pretty good about things about now.

Ryder tried to shift on the bed to make himself comfortable, willing the pills to take the pain away sooner rather than later.

He and Axel couldn't have been further apart in life right now. His brother was the conquering hero, setting things right for his girl and his dumbass twin brother. Ryder went home with a girl, and she got shot in the face, killed. Ryder got shot with her, providing the enemy with a weak board in the fence. They had to take him out of the hospital to keep him safe from the

Mafia until Axel resolved it. Didn't that make *him* a useless pile of shit?

Before his eyes slid shut, his gaze fell on his phone. He realized he'd never answered Margot, and he wanted to before he crashed. Lifting the phone in his shaking hand, he read back over the conversation.

Margot: *If you still think Razor is okay with it, I'll come see you later today.*

Ryder smiled at the wink emoji at the end of the sentence. Margot wasn't in the best place either right now, but she was trying even though her father had been killed.

And his twin had avenged that too. It made his heart squeeze in his chest. It should have been *him* to make that right. If he hadn't gone home with the redhead that night... He couldn't have said he remembered her name if he hadn't heard it on the news.

Margot had hinted at him that he should have taken *her* to the party. Why hadn't he? They would have had a good time, played pool, drank beer. They wouldn't have ended up in bed together. But just maybe Morgan Davis would be alive today and he wouldn't have been shot.

Slowly, he typed a response.

Ryder: *See you then.*

Dropping the phone by his side on the bed, Ryder looked forward to her visit, realizing he wanted to see Margot very much. Yeah, she'd hold his hand and tell him he was a dumbass. But the anticipation of seeing her was all he had left to hold onto right now. It helped him into a heavy, dreamless sleep.

* * *

Margot

By the time Margot made it to the door of the Hounds of Hell clubhouse, she'd showered and changed into her street clothes, though she really couldn't remember doing any of it. She'd been on autopilot, going through the motions with an open sore in her chest where her heart had been. She'd arranged to visit Mabry's Funeral Home tomorrow because mentally she couldn't do it today. She wouldn't be able to visit Ryder long because grief threatened to crash in on her at any time.

Nerves got the better of her because she'd never actually been to the biker hangout before even though it had been in Mercy all her life. Before that, it had been the old sheriff's station. Were the jail cells still in there? Oh, she'd heard wild stories about parties and happenings in the clubhouse when she was younger. Parties with drugs, women, and violent fights were whispered about by other kids in their high school. She didn't know if any of it was true. It was still enough for her to have viewed both Ryder and his twin a little differently when they joined as prospects.

She assumed when she went to police academy that she'd learn the entire motorcycle club deal was far worse than she imagined. What it did reveal was that the Mercy charter of the Hounds of Hell wasn't so controversial after all. Yeah, they traded on the wrong side of the law, and they were damn good at not getting caught. They ran guns mostly from what she'd heard.

Her first job had been as a police officer in Oak Grove, the next county over. The Cottonmouths had a club chartered there and they were everything bad she'd ever heard about motorcycle gangs. The fights were violent, even within ranks, and they made money off guns like the Hounds but also from drugs and prostitution. It made her see red thinking about it.

Unlike the Hounds in Mercy, none of the Cottonmouths had old ladies. They kept "club sluts" in their clubhouse, and both used and sold them on a whim, not having a lot of respect for her gender at all. She'd only been in a couple of situations with the notoriously violent club, and it had been enough to make her wary of the entire lifestyle, even though her crush was a card-carrying MC member.

Standing on the porch of the Hounds' clubhouse, even though she'd been invited by Ryder, she felt hesitant. But after a beat, before she could talk herself out of it, she knocked loud enough to draw attention.

When Clayton Martin -- Beast, they called him -- opened the door, Margot glanced up. The man towered over her, a fringe of black hair swept just above his dark eyes. Before she said anything, the huge, muscular biker before her bellowed, "She's here!"

"Come on in," he said after a moment.

Beast had just closed the door behind her when she saw Wade Gabriel approaching her, hands shoved into his pockets and his gaze fastened on her. He went by Razor, the president of the MC, and Margot steeled herself when the tall, imposing man came to a stop in front of her.

After a minute, the handsome older man smiled, showing off the deep lines around his hazel eyes. "You've got nothing to worry about," Razor said. He scrubbed a hand through the shiny, silver locks of his longer hair. "You look like a lamb walking to the slaughter."

His smile put her at ease. Her shoulders dropped from ear level, and she blew out a nervous breath. "Sorry," she said. "I've never been in here before."

Razor nodded. "At least you're not in uniform."

His smile faded and his voice dropped. "I was real sorry to hear about Clyde. Your father was a good man. Hard-working. He didn't deserve what happened to him."

The wave of sorrow she was barely holding back threatened to break over her, stinging the backs of her eyes at his kind words. "Thank you."

"Anyway, Margot, we sure could use a favor right now." Razor's gaze held hers.

Given her position in the town and his, the words pushed her anxiety a little higher. But she didn't know what he would say so she nodded, encouraging him to continue.

"Ryder's not doing so well," Razor explained. "We had to pull him out of the hospital. Signed one of those against doctor's orders forms. Those Mafia fellas we've been dealing with? We were afraid they would come to the hospital to try and finish him off."

"I understand why you did it," Margot said. They'd saved his life.

Approval bled into the biker's gaze. "We need to get his ass back to the hospital and he's being a stubborn ass about it. We thought maybe you could help convince him."

Margot didn't hear a lot past the need to get him back to the hospital. She said, "Take me to him."

Razor was all too happy to oblige. Margot followed him out of the dark room just inside the clubhouse, down a narrow hallway to a room on the left. It was a normal bedroom, and Ryder lay on the bed at its center. It was jarring to see him like that. He was way too pale, his gaze seeming a little unfocused, like he had just woken up.

Concern for his welfare pushed everything else aside as she moved past Razor to Ryder's bedside.

Ryder's gaze focused on her when she reached him. "Margot. Glad you're here."

Beads of sweat dotted his forehead, his pallor scary. Glancing back at Razor, she saw her concern reflected on his face. They needed to return him to the hospital. *Now.*

"It figures you'd pull this shit," Margot told him, smiling. "I finally come to the big bad biker clubhouse, and you fuck it up."

Ryder seemed confused. Something was wrong. "You're not leaving already, are you?"

"No, *we're* leaving," she explained. "We're heading back to the hospital, Ryder. Right now. You and me."

"Okay," he said without hesitation.

Something was *very* wrong. He wasn't fighting her or trying to charm her.

"Razor," she addressed his club president. "Can you ask the big fella out there to carry him to my car?"

Razor nodded. "I can."

He marched back the way he came while Margot looked Ryder over. The sweatpants he wore had seen better days. The old flannel shirt wasn't a lot better, unbuttoned down the front to show the muscle and abs she always knew were under there. And she would have appreciated it so much more if not for the bandages covering his bullet wounds.

"Where we going?" Ryder asked her, looking disoriented.

"Back to the hospital," Margot told him with a smile. She was scared to death for him, but she wasn't going to show him that. "They're going to fix you up."

"I thought you were going to visit with me."

Margot's heart squeezed in her chest at the sad way he said that. But he likely didn't know what he was saying right now. Still, she wanted to be reassuring. "I'm going to stay as long as you want me to, okay?"

Ryder nodded, trying to pull himself into a sitting position and falling back. His weakness had her panicking. She'd never seen that before.

When Beast walked in, with Razor on his heels, she knew a moment's relief. Razor nodded toward Ryder and Beast moved to the other side of the bed.

Edging past her, Razor said, "Step back."

Margot winced as they managed to lift him off the bed, not too delicate about it. She hoped moving him wouldn't make anything worse or do any damage. By the time they made it out to her SUV and had Ryder situated in the front seat, she felt better. Razor tapped on the driver's side window, and she lowered it.

"Will you have any trouble getting him back in?" Razor asked.

"No, I won't."

"We'll let Axel know," he said. "And we'll be by in a little while. Take care of him."

"I will," she assured him.

Margot had never been so grateful that the hospital was a five-minute drive. Pulling up to the emergency room doors at Mercy Community Hospital, she parked and fished her phone out of her pocket. She had the ER desk number saved and hit the button. When old Yale Thomas answered, Margot disregarded his pleasantries.

"Yale, I've got an emergency on my hands," she said. "I'm just outside. I need a stretcher ASAP."

The kind older man must have recognized the urgency in her tone. "We'll be right out."

Ryder's gaze met hers and she feared he would pass out. "What's happening?"

Covering his hand with her own, Margot smiled. "They're coming out to help us get you back in the hospital. Beast and Razor aren't here yet and I'm not strong enough to pull your ass out of this car."

When he chuckled, she felt a small measure of relief. "No, you're not."

Her gaze moved past him to the small team with a stretcher swiftly making their way toward her vehicle. "Here they are."

Climbing out of the SUV, Margot walked around to open the passenger door for them. With way more finesse than his biker friends, the medical team carefully extracted Ryder from her vehicle and got him on the stretcher.

Ryder's gaze searched for her as they prepared to race him back into the hospital. "Margot?"

Reaching for his hand, she smiled. "I'm here."

"You're not leaving, are you?"

It was the second time he asked that question. She really didn't like the strange, sad tone he used. "No. I'm going to park the car and then I'll find you. Promise."

Grateful for their help, Margot watched until they made their way through two sets of sliding glass doors as they rushed Ryder into the ER. Driving her SUV way too fast to find a parking space, Margot rushed to follow them. She had no intention of leaving Ryder until he was out of danger.

Chapter Three
Margot

"Margot?"

The voice that pulled her out of sleep sounded like Ryder, so she shifted in the uncomfortable hospital chair. Her eyes squinted open to see someone leaning down in front of her. There was a cut on his cheek and his left eye was bruised. Her foggy mind thought it was Ryder for a second, but it didn't take long for her to realize it was his twin, Axel.

Scrambling to her feet, she looked from him to the young woman behind him. Margot recognized the brunette from *Austins' Nursery and Greenhouse*.

"I'm so sorry, honey." Axel pulled Margot into him for a solid hug. Margot clung to him while he rubbed small circles into her back. "Clyde was good people. The best."

Tears pricked her eyes as she eased back, swiping at her tears with the backs of her hands. "Thank you," she murmured.

"I don't know what you said to my idiot brother," Axel went on. "But thank you for getting him back here. Razor was having a time with him before you showed up. Pride and all I guess."

"Glad to do it."

"This is Sadie." Ryder introduced her to the woman with him and Margot shook her trembling hand.

Something about Sadie's demeanor felt off. Why was Sadie looking at her like that? Fear and apprehension were easy to read on her young face. Did she know Margot was a deputy? Was she in some sort of trouble?

"The conquering hero." Ryder's voice was raspy

from the bed, but he was awake now. His steely blue eyes were slits, and he still looked way too pale. But as his gaze moved from his brother to her, Margot sent up a prayer of thanks that he was still with them.

"Hey, brother." Axel approached the bed, hugging his twin carefully. "You look like hammered shit."

"Feel like it too," Ryder said. "Margot dragged my ass back here."

"Technically, I drove," she said. "But Razor and Beast *did* drag your ass out to my car."

Axel glanced from Sadie to Margot, blowing out a sigh. "Ladies, can you give us a minute?" Axel asked. "We just need to talk about a couple of things real quick."

"Sure." Margot headed for the door. Sadie was behind her, looking like she'd rather be walking across an acre of broken glass barefoot. But she closed the door behind them to give the twins privacy. Shoving her hands in the pockets of her jeans, she leaned against the wall by the door, sniffling.

Margot studied her, saw her pretty green eyes were filling with tears.

"Are you okay?" she asked. Was the young woman upset to be left with her? Was it something else?

Bravely, Sadie met her gaze. "Was Clyde Donner your father?" Sadie asked after a long, tense moment. "The man from Cowboy Pete's?"

"Yes, he was."

"I'm so, so sorry." Tears spilled from Sadie's eyes now.

Margot was puzzled. Why on earth was *she* so upset?

"It's okay." She didn't know what else to say. It

didn't lessen the devastation she read on Sadie's face.

"It's not." Sadie looked miserable. "It's my fault he's dead."

"Come again?" How was it her fault?

"I came here to Mercy back in February," Sadie explained. "Maybe you heard I ran from a bad relationship and my car broke down here. At Cowboy Pete's. The lady who worked there called Axel to come tow my car to his garage and I just... ended up staying. And the Hounds helped me. They did. Especially Axel. But... my ex found me here. It was him and his men who shot Ryder and killed that woman. It was him who shot and killed that lady and your father."

Margot hadn't been expecting any of that. All she could do was stare at Sadie while her mind struggled to keep up. Those Mafia members who came to Mercy to launch a one-week killing spree were there because of Sadie?

If what Sadie said was true, they'd be seeing more of them. Her ex was in custody and unless something went terribly wrong in the courts, he'd be going to jail. His cohorts would be looking for payback. They'd be coming after the Hounds. They'd be coming after Ryder.

The young woman curling in on herself in front of Margot had real pain etched in her face. The sincerity of her words echoed in the misery she read in Sadie's green eyes. It was probably more her training than anything that had her wanting to comfort the younger woman.

"Hey." Margot tried to hold her own pain at bay. When Sadie's gaze was back on her, she said, "What happened to my father isn't your fault. I need you to know that. Okay?"

Her young face crumpled, and Margot moved to

hug her. To comfort her. Sadie's entire body was shaking, and Margot could only imagine what she'd been through. In her short time as a deputy, she'd worked more than a few domestic violence cases. The victim trying to shoulder the blame for everything her partner did was common.

When they parted, Sadie swiped at her tears with her fingers. The fear in her eyes only slightly diminished as her gaze returned to the door to Ryder's hospital room. "Is he going to be okay?"

"I hope so," Margot replied. "Now that we've got him back here, he has a fighting chance."

Axel opened the door, stepping out into the hallway with them. The look he exchanged with Sadie answered one of Margot's questions. Sadie was with Axel and from the concern in his blue eyes, she wasn't a casual girlfriend.

"Margot, if there's anything we can do for you right now," he said, "name it. If Ryder wasn't here in the shape he's in, he'd be there for anything you needed. Since he can't, you have me. You have all his brothers."

The declaration had tears stinging the backs of her eyes. "Thank you."

"We're going to be keeping someone here from the Hounds until he's well enough to be released," Axel said. "But you're welcome here whenever you want."

Margot also appreciated that more than words could express. Ryder just might need the protection, and the fact that they were acknowledging her friendship with him given her new job meant a lot to her. Especially now.

"I'm taking Sadie home," Axel went on. "Snow is heading up here in an hour or so. You mind staying until he gets here?"

Margot shook her head. There was nowhere else she wanted to be right now.

Sadie glanced back at Margot, still in tears, as Axel led her away.

* * *

Ryder

It rained the day Clyde Donner was laid to rest.

It nearly took an act of Congress to get Ryder discharged from the hospital in time. But this time, he was deemed stable enough to be discharged and Razor got it done the evening before. They hauled his ass back to the clubhouse and no sooner had he reached his room when he saw the suit draped over the foot of his bed. Black with a crisp white shirt and silver tie. On the floor by the bed were glossy black dress shoes that looked to be his size.

Turning to face Axel, Ryder just stared at him in wonder. "Where did you get this?"

"Bought it." Axel walked into his room behind him, closing the door. "Neither of us own a suit, but I figured you'd want to go to the funeral tomorrow. I just need to go pick up some nice socks."

Yes, he very much did want to go. The gesture just about moved him to tears.

"It will probably fit," Axel said. "They tailored it to me. You've dropped a little weight, but it will work. It was Sadie's idea."

Shrugging, Ryder moved to sit on the bed, inspecting the simple black suit that was now the nicest piece of clothing he owned. "At least we can share it for shit like this."

Axel's sigh drew his attention. "I got one for myself. Just hoping when I wear mine and the next time you wear yours, it will be for a happier occasion."

Ryder hoped for the same thing.

He slept like the dead, relieved to be away from the hospital where he'd barely gotten any rest. The funeral started at noon and his phone told him it was half past ten. At least he'd woken up in time to get ready.

Ryder managed to climb out of bed, but it was a struggle. He felt weak as a kitten, dazed and sweating by the time he reached the bathroom to take a piss. He vaguely heard his twin follow him, stopping in the doorway behind him.

"You okay?"

At the sound of Axel's voice, Ryder nodded. "I will be."

"Let's get you in the shower."

His twin got him cleaned up and dressed with the efficiency of a SWAT team, and it was just after eleven when they walked out into the clubhouse main room where Sadie waited. She wore a simple black dress, handing Axel a clothing bag.

"I'll just be a minute," his twin explained, navigating Ryder into a chair before rushing off to change into his suit. He was more than a little relieved his twin and his old lady were going with him.

Sure enough, Axel's suit matched Ryder's own, his blue tie being the only difference.

Sadie's face lit up to see her man all dressed up. She kissed his cheek when he returned. "You look so handsome."

They reached the funeral home just a few minutes before the service. They waited in line to greet Margot.

Bravely, she stood alone, trying to smile through tears as she greeted each guest. So many people turned out, but she was holding up through it. When the three of them neared the front of the line, he was happy to see she wasn't completely alone. Sheriff Sawyer sat stoically in a chair behind her, his quiet support appreciated by Ryder who found it hard to swallow the rising anger at himself, growing by the minute.

If he hadn't been such a useless asshole, he could have been standing by her side. Supporting her. But no, he had to fuck around and get shot. And now, when his friend needed him the most, he wasn't much use.

Still, when it was their turn, Margot's gaze met his and she flew into his arms, hugging him tightly. Yeah, it hurt but he wasn't about to let on. He wrapped his arms around her too, trying to absorb some of the grief she was drowning in. He held her as long as she needed it and everyone else in line be damned.

When she finally let him go, her big dark eyes were glossy with tears. "You shouldn't be here. But I'm really grateful you are."

"I'm here," he told her, pressing a kiss to her forehead. "For you, I'll always be here."

"Stay with me," she whispered, her gaze begging far more than her words.

Ryder nodded and Axel helped him over to where Sawyer sat. The sheriff instantly rose from the chair, offering it to Ryder. His twin and Sadie stood on one side of the chair, the sheriff on the other. And they silently watched as Margot greeted the rest of the folks who'd come to say goodbye to her father.

When the service was about to start, Razor walked in with Hero and Jade. Hero looked like a damn movie star in his suit, blond hair slicked back, with Jade in her gray dress, looking picture perfect on his arm. Razor wore a nice shirt and tie with his jeans and boots. His long hair was tied back, and his expression was appropriately somber. He came up to Ryder as Axel helped him out of the chair.

"How're you holding up?" Razor asked.

"I'm making it," Ryder said. "Thank you, guys, for coming out."

"Yes, thank you," Margot said as she approached. She looked close to losing her composure, blinking back tears, her chin trembling. "I don't know what the funeral director was thinking. They saved two whole pews for my family… It's *just* me."

Ryder found his strength in that moment, taking her small cold hand in his. "Your family *is* here."

The gratitude and love in her eyes just about finished him off where the bullets couldn't.

"Yes, we are," Razor said. "Y'all come on."

Snow and Emily arrived just then. Snow was dressed like Razor, his tie the same shade of black as Emily's dress. Razor watched as the small blonde walked up to give Margot a hug. Margot loved visiting Emily's bakery, and it was clear the two women had a positive connection.

Between the Hounds of Hell and the three other deputies that arrived, those front family pews were filled and Ryder sent up a small prayer of thanks it worked out that way. Yeah, some tongues would be wagging about the MC sitting with the cops at the funeral, but anyone who had a problem with it could fuck off.

The service was beautiful with the young reverend in town asking everyone in attendance if they had anything they wanted to add about Margot's father when it was done. So many people spoke. One after another, the people who knew Clyde Donner in Mercy told of his countless acts of kindness over the years. Margot quietly cried at Ryder's side. He kept her hand in his, supporting her the best he could.

Margot rode with him in Sadie's car to the cemetery and the burial was far shorter than the service, but just as filled with tears. Slowly, people started drifting back to their cars when it was over. Sheriff Sawyer told Margot to take all the time she needed before he left, nodding to Razor as he walked away.

"We'll be in the car," Axel finally told them as Sadie hugged Margot one more time.

Then it was him and Margot standing by her father's grave. Clyde Donner was buried next to his wife. The rain was now a cold drizzle, and Margot shivered. With surprising grace, given the state he was in, Ryder shrugged off his suit coat and draped it around her shoulders. She seemed so lost in her grief that he wasn't sure she noticed.

"They're both gone," she said. "I thought I'd be a lot older when I lost them. I regret so many things."

"Don't."

"How?" She blew out a long sigh. "They never got to see me get married, Ryder. They never had a grandchild, and I know my mom really wanted at least one."

"Don't think like that." Ryder knew such thoughts all too well, having lost both his parents before he was twenty.

"I have to," she went on, tears in her voice. "I was so set on what I wanted. I was just so laser-focused on becoming a deputy, maybe sheriff one day. I should have... spent more time with them. With *him*. He was so lonely once my mother was gone, Ryder."

"Honey, you *did* spend time with him," Ryder pointed out. "I can't tell you how many times I saw you two over at the diner. He was so proud of you. He loved you. You know that. Chasing your dreams is what you're supposed to do. That's what a parent should want for their children. That's what he wanted for you. Clyde may have left this life way too soon, but he knew you'd be okay when his time came. And you *will* be."

Her little chin inched up slightly at that. "I will be."

"And when all of those things happen in your life," he went on, "they'll be there. You might not be able to see them anymore, but they'll be there."

It was at that moment the dam broke. Margot couldn't hold the tears back any longer. Her sobs were raw sounds of anguish as she let him pull her into his arms. All Ryder could do was hold her as she cried, as she tried to burrow into him for comfort and her tears soaked into his shirt.

Ryder was so grateful to be there for her, when she needed him the most.

Chapter Four

Ryder

Today was the first day he felt something close to normal. Stretching on the front porch of the house he shared with his twin, Ryder's gaze moved over the expanse of land his parents had left to them. Well, that their father had left to them. Their mother…

To this day, he couldn't linger in the living room of the house. That's where he'd found their mother that night over half his life ago, after she'd taken her own life. And he'd been all alone.

Now he was alone again because Axel rarely stayed home, electing to be at the Hound clubhouse to spend more time with Sadie.

Ryder was okay in the house if his brother was there, and Axel came at least once a day to check on him. When Axel was gone, which was most of the time now, the past preyed on his mind. It all came back, dragging along guilt, blame, and the last words his mother ever said to him. Her belief that he wouldn't accomplish anything in his life, that he'd end up broken and alone, could either be a prophecy or the battle of his life.

Shaking it off, Ryder blew out a breath. He couldn't think about that. He *wouldn't*.

He sure as shit had felt better than he did right now. But that didn't stop him from striding out to the garage, looking over his Jeep, his El Camino, and his Harley. He hadn't really been in a vehicle for weeks aside from Margot driving him home from the hospital a few weeks ago. He hadn't driven anything since the night he got shot.

Do you have to go this week?

Ryder smiled with Margot's words in his head. If

she had her way, he'd sit out another month while she fretted over him. Now that his strength was returning, he was about to lose his fucking mind laid up in bed all day, watching endless documentaries and YouTube videos. Plus, he wasn't exactly helping financially. His absence from the garage left Axel and Hero to take up the slack and he knew they were getting slammed. His groceries weren't cheap and with him laid up that bill fell on Axel too, though he never complained.

Without another thought, Ryder fished his keys from the pocket of his cut and climbed onto his bike. The roar of the engine was satisfying as he started it up. It felt good. It wasn't totally without effort but after a moment, he got on the road, heading into town to the garage.

The cool air he rushed through felt exhilarating in the hot summer morning. He got to *Three Guys Garage* a little after seven. Just like old times. Parking in his spot behind the garage, Ryder slowly climbed off the bike. His body still hurt, and he wasn't back to full strength yet. But he had to start somewhere.

"Hey," a sweet voice came from behind him.

Vickie Hale headed in his direction, her glossy red lips curved up into a smile. He'd had her a few times. With her painted-on jeans and skimpy little top, she looked fine. There were green streaks in her dark hair, the shade almost matching her low-cut top. He wondered if the matching was deliberate when she stopped in front of him.

Ryder hoped she didn't notice he shook a little from his efforts in getting there.

"Ryder, I'm so glad to see you," Vickie said, taking another bold step closer. "We've all been worried sick about you."

Worried sick, huh? Funny, he hadn't seen her at

the hospital or his house.

"Thanks." Ryder walked toward the front of the garage. And there were a shit-ton of vehicles parked all around, waiting for repairs.

Vickie kept up with him with her long, long legs. Ryder had to admit, he liked the way they'd wrapped around him. She was a good fuck. He just wasn't in the mood.

"So, you going to be around *Sackett's* any time this week?" Vickie asked, walking along with him until he reached the garage entrance. "We could play some pool. Mess around."

The little wink and the saucy grin that went with it were meant to be enticing. Out of habit, Ryder smiled before heading on into the garage without her. That he wasn't feeling it probably had a lot to do with it being his first day out and about.

A quick glance around the shop showed him even more vehicles waiting for repairs. Damn.

"Look who's here," Hero's voice boomed in the garage area.

Axel peered over the hood of the SUV he worked on, smiling. Wiping his hands on his jeans, he dashed over, grabbing Ryder in a careful hug. "Good to see you up, brother," Axel said. "I was afraid Margot wasn't going to let you come back."

That had Ryder chuckling. "Same."

Hero came over, gave him a quick hug. "How are you?"

Ryder nodded. "I'll live. I've got to get back at it. Looks like I came back just in time."

"Yeah." Axel agreed. "You did."

For all his brother's virtues, Ryder *was* a better mechanic. It wasn't a case of Hero and Axel not being good. Hero did body work and painting on top of it.

But auto mechanics was one thing Ryder excelled at and was valued for in the MC.

"Where you want me to start?" he asked.

Ryder ended up working on a whole-ass engine rebuild for a half-ton truck. It wouldn't have been his choice where to start. But once he got into it, it went fine. He'd been so focused on it that he hadn't realized it was lunchtime until he heard Axel telling someone, "He's back there."

He smiled. Was Margot here to see him?

"Ryder!"

It wasn't Margot who tackle-hugged him from behind, making him wince at the slight pain from where she squeezed him. Anita Anderson had a bright smile, a big ass, and a bigger laugh that echoed through the garage around them. The little tank top and short shorts she wore didn't hide a lot. Her dark curls danced around her head as she stood there grinning at him.

"How are you feeling, handsome?" she asked when he didn't say anything.

"I'm making it," he said. "What are *you* up to?"

"Waiting for you to get better. You promised to take me dancing soon. Remember?"

He had, huh? Ryder didn't remember that promise. Then again, it wasn't uncommon for him to be drunk off his ass half the time.

"Going to be a while before I'm up for anything like dancing, darlin'." He turned his attention back to the engine. "But I appreciate you stopping by to see me."

"Oh, well, I could come over to your house." Anita pressed herself to his side as he tried to work. "I could make you some dinner. Make you *feel* better."

It would make him feel better not to have to deal

with her, but he didn't say as much. "Let me get back on my feet. And then we'll talk. Okay?"

It took a little of the wind out of her sails but didn't completely deter her. "Okay, Ryder," Anita said after a minute. Like many of the girls he went around with, she wasn't used to getting a no from him. "I'll catch you around."

Anita's ass was round and firm. He'd enjoyed it a few times. But the urge to watch her walk away wasn't there today. The energy to do much of anything was waning so he decided some lunch was in order. He'd just finished washing his hands in the bathroom when he ran right into Margot, standing outside the door and talking to Hero.

Ryder grinned. Margot wore her uniform, her dark auburn hair twisted up in a bun. Somehow Margot managed to look feminine despite the uniform, and with the tiniest hint of makeup on her face. She didn't even try to cover up the sprinkling of freckles across her nose and cheeks. He'd always loved her big brown eyes and the slightly crooked smile that she'd gotten from her father.

"Hey," Ryder said when her conversation with Hero came to a stopping point. "Hit your quota for speeding tickets already?"

"You're funny." That had her smiling at him. "How are *you* doing today? I didn't know you were planning to return to work already."

Ryder smiled back. "I've binge-watched the hell out of everything out there on streaming. I needed to get out of bed."

"This from a man whose goal is usually to get back to bed as soon as possible," she chided him.

It wasn't lost on him that Hero stood there listening, arms folded across his chest and grinning.

"Well, now, that depends on who I'm trying to take with me." Ryder winked at her, enjoying the color emerging beneath those freckles. "If you're offering…"

Margot laughed, shaking her head. "Seriously, how are you feeling?"

Shrugging, he said, "Fine."

That dark-eyed gaze studied him, concern causing her smile to fade. She was trying to decide if he was telling her the truth.

"Besides," he went on. "We're all backed up here. They can't hold down the garage without me."

Hero smiled, rolling his eyes. "Sounds like his dumb ass is getting back to normal to me."

Axel shook his head, approaching them. "How are *you*, Margot? You finally sell Clyde's place? I saw the 'for sale' sign is gone."

Ryder looked at her in question. He knew she'd put the home up for sale, but she hadn't said a lot to him about it.

"I decided to keep it," she explained. "Looks like I'm doing a pretty good job of writing tickets and such." Her gaze cut to Ryder and back, a teasing grin on her lips. "I'm going to sublease my apartment and move into my parents' house. It's paid for. It's home."

The tone she used when she said the word "home" was softer, sad. Like him, both her parents were gone now. Maybe like him, she hated to be alone?

"You going to need help moving?" Ryder said without thinking about it first.

"You're in no shape to help me if I do," Margot pointed out. "But I've been moving things out a little at a time. I doubt I'll take the furniture. The house is already furnished. Maybe that will help me find a taker for the apartment faster."

"You need help moving anything," Axel said,

"let us know."

"Thank you both," Margot said after a moment. "I appreciate it."

"What are you doing over here?" Ryder asked the minute the others were out of earshot. "Making sure I don't pick up a wrench?"

"I wanted to check on you," she admitted. "I saw your bike. Somehow I knew you would show up here today."

"I was going to go get lunch," he said. "Want to go with?"

"I'm buying." Margot led him out of the garage and to the diner across the street.

With scary efficiency, she ordered them lunch, paid for it, and had them tucked away at a small table in the corner, enjoying burgers and fries. She got a soda for him, a huge pink milkshake for herself.

"What's that?" Ryder pointed at her tall, covered cup.

"Strawberry shake. You want one?"

"Nah," Ryder said. "Just a little concerned is all. You start with milkshakes. Milkshakes lead to donuts. Next thing you know, you lose your girlish figure and you're stuck running radar out by the interstate."

Margot laughed, a high, lovely sound. "Don't worry about my girlish figure."

"I like your girlish figure," Ryder said, grinning.

"Since when?" A little of the humor faded from her expression at that. "I'm probably the only female you haven't slept with in a hundred-mile radius."

"More like fifty," Ryder said.

But he hadn't been lying when he said he liked her figure. Why hadn't he noticed before? Margot was just about perfect. Nice rack. Great ass. A killer smile made all the more adorable for her dark eyes and the freckles across the bridge of her nose.

Margot had a good head on her shoulders too. He enjoyed talking to her, their playful banter. He couldn't imagine a world where he couldn't have these light-hearted conversations with Mercy's newest deputy sheriff. "It doesn't bother you to be having lunch with a biker?" he couldn't resist asking.

"It doesn't bother you that you're having lunch with a cop?" Margot eyed him. "How did you get to town?"

"Rode my bike," Ryder said. "Might not have been my best idea. I mean, I was okay getting here. Not sure how getting back is going to go."

"How long are you going to stay?" Margot's dark-eyed gaze stayed on him.

Shrugging a shoulder, Ryder finished off a French fry. "I'd like to finish the day out," he admitted. "But now that I'm sitting here, I'm feeling pretty fucking tired."

It was the truth and he'd never been good at keeping that from her. His friend's gaze was knowing.

"Why don't we take you home after lunch? I'd be glad to drive you back."

Ryder knew she would. But he would disappoint himself if he left after lunch to go home and climb back into bed in that lonely, quiet house. Shaking his head, he ate another fry, thought it over. "I'm tired. Just not sure I'm tired enough to go back to the house and hang out by myself."

More concern bled into her expression. "At least take a nap in the lounge or something. No one's going to give you shit for it. You almost died."

He had. Axel and Hero both had kept cutting him worried looks the entire time he'd been working on that engine. Margot had a point.

"Well, now that I'm getting back on my feet, let me know if you need help with anything at the house." He meant it. "Clyde was as bad as you about never wanting to bother anyone. If you need help with anything, I'm right here."

Margot nodded, eating her burger. After a moment, her gaze met his. Her dark eyes were glossy. "I still can't believe he's gone, Ryder," she said quietly. "No warning. Just gone."

Reaching across the table, he covered her hand with his. Some emotion flashed in her eyes, but it was gone as quickly as it came.

"He loved you more than anything," he said. "Clyde was so proud of you."

A tear spilled down her cheek at the words. "I know he was. It's just... I worked so hard to find a job back over here in Mercy so I could be with him, help him as he got older. And now he's gone. Shot by some Mafia asshole like he was nothing."

Swiping at her tears with her free hand, Margot tried to regain her composure.

"Clyde didn't deserve that. And I wish my brother had been able to take that asshole out. *Slow*. But Sawyer was there and now the bastard's in jail."

That stopped her cold. Carefully, she moved her hand out from under his, shaking her head. "Don't say that. He'll pay for what he did in the system. He'll think about what he did."

"Will he?" Ryder asked. "He's part of a criminal organization, Margot. They have a lot of resources. Maybe he'll go to jail, but he won't think a second about your father. He won't be sitting up in some jail cell regretting his crimes either."

He didn't like the way her confidence waned, but he had to say it. "He'll be trying to find a way out of there. And when he does, he'll be looking for some payback and he'll have his entire crime family at his back."

Margot's spine straightened where she sat, meeting his gaze squarely. "I have faith in the system. That man will pay for what he's done."

Ryder wasn't so sure about that. He didn't give a shit about the system. "He *will* pay," Ryder said, hoping that he'd be the one to administer that retribution. What he wouldn't give to have a shot at the sons-of-bitches who killed Clyde Donner and Morgan Davis. Who tried to kill *him*.

He had faith in Margot. She'd been through the training, worked in the next county over. Margot knew what she was doing. But she was new enough that she still thought the criminal justice system infallible. Had she ever had dealings with big crime families? Did she understand what she was getting into? Or worse. He worried that the loss of her father would cause her to make a decision that would put her in harm's way.

"Okay," she said, her dark-eyed gaze on him. "If you won't let me drive you back home and you insist on staying at the garage, I'll make you an offer. If you're too tired to ride back to the country, you can crash at the house. I don't have a spare key on me. But I have one. I'll leave it under that old stone squirrel my dad loved."

Always looking after him. What would he have done all those long weeks after he'd gotten out of the hospital without her? Axel had been the one to help him change his bandages, got him in the shower. Margot took care of most everything else from changing his bedding and keeping up the house, to bringing him meals he could warm up and eat. Her daily visits were something he looked forward to.

What he'd done to deserve her, he didn't know. Maybe she needed to stay busy to deal with her own loss.

"Sounds good," Ryder said after a moment. "In case I haven't told you, thank you. For everything. I'm not sure why you took it upon yourself to take care of me but I'm grateful."

Soft pink darkened her face. "You're welcome."

Something occurred to him. "Wait. You're working day shift," he pointed out. "Where are you going to be later that you need to leave me a key?"

"Tonight's my first class," Margot reminded him.

"That's right," he said. "Your self-defense class." She'd been so excited about it, telling him about what she had planned over the last few weeks. "I think Sadie signed up for it."

"She did," Margot said, smiling. "It'll be good for her after everything she's been through. And I was surprised. You know, the day we got you back into the hospital, she came with Axel. We had a minute in the hall, and she was just... apologizing to me for my dad. She was blaming herself because it was her ex that killed him. But it wasn't her fault."

"No, it wasn't," Ryder said. "I think your class will help her." Something about the smile she gave him had his heart skipping a beat. Was it because he hadn't fucked in weeks? Just talking to his friend had his cock hardening under the table. Shaking his head to clear it, he grinned. "Thanks for the offer of a place to stay," he said. "Might take you up on it."

Margot smiled. "Please do." The flirty little way she said that had him thinking thoughts he had no business thinking about his best friend.

Chapter Five

Margot

Despite how tired and frazzled she was at the end of her first self-defense class, Margot was happy. Seven students showed up, a better start than she'd expected. Two of them were around her age, a couple others were middle-aged and really into it. They were eager to learn and practice.

One woman Margot knew wasn't coming back. Her expressions straddled the line between confusion and worry the entire time. The older lady next to her seemed unsure too but Margot was hoping *she'd* be interested enough to give it another try.

Then there was Sadie.

Axel's girlfriend was young, somewhere in her mid-twenties. Her normally dark hair was now bright red curls that framed a beautiful, heart-shaped face. The new color suited her better. Her green-eyed gaze never left Margot, and she really concentrated on the basic lessons Margot started with. Sadie didn't volunteer to try anything, preferring to stay in study mode. But she gave Margot her full attention.

Margot had predicted to herself that Sadie would be the first one out the door tonight, but she lingered. After everyone had their chance to ask questions and chat once the class ended, it was only Sadie left in the room with her. Axel's girlfriend patiently waited for her turn to talk to Margot.

"How are you doing?" Margot asked.

"I'm fine," Sadie said quietly. But she moved closer, meeting Margot's gaze. "It was a good class. I'm sorry I didn't… participate. It's just…"

"You're fine." Margot wanted to be reassuring. Ryder explained a little of what Axel had told him she'd gone through in her previous relationship.

"I'm not sure I can learn any of this," Sadie said. "I want to, but I don't think I could. I mean…"

Margot smiled. "It's okay. It seems intimidating at first. But all you need is a little know-how and a little practice."

The other woman's gaze swept over her. Margot could guess what she was thinking. She was five seven, not much taller than Sadie.

"Yeah, I'm not that big either," Margot assured her. "But I can hold my own. Most of the time."

"Can I ask you something? Why did you learn all this?" Sadie's gaze was steady. "Why did you want to become a cop?"

"That's fair." Margot leaned back against the table with her flyers and instruction sheets, crossing her arms across her chest. "I was a tall kid. Early on, I mean. I shot up in elementary school and I was the tallest kid in my class. I was taller than even the boys."

Some of the tension faded from the redhead's pretty face.

"Including Ryder and Axel," she threw in. "Well, they were Alex and Randall back then."

Sadie laughed.

"I loved being the tallest. I took up for weaker kids, cut off bullies." Margot dropped her arms, relaxing her stance. "A year or two later, most everyone caught up with me. Many of them kept growing. I ended up being average height by high school, no taller than I am now. But I guess I never got over how empowering it felt to be able to protect others. It seemed like a good direction for me."

"You're not afraid?"

"I've been afraid on the job many times. But it gets a little less as time goes on. Panic fades to fear.

Courage conquers fear. I stop and think about the situation, who I might be saving, and I'm ready to go."

Sadie stared at her in wonder. "I don't think I could be that brave."

"You've survived quite a lot already," Margot said.

Dropping her gaze, Sadie nodded.

"You're brave too."

"I'm not though." Sadie didn't look up. "A dog with an abusive owner who gets kicked every day survives. Doesn't make it brave."

"Doesn't it?"

Now the other woman's gaze was back on her. She knew Sadie was trying to determine if Margot was serious or having fun at her expense.

"Why would you want to help me?" Sadie asked. "After…"

"Sadie, your ex killed my father," Margot said. "You were in no way responsible for his decision."

"If I hadn't run away," Sadie replied, "your father would still be alive."

The mention of her father's cold-blooded murder sent a spike of pain through her heart. Fighting it, she pressed on with the point she wanted to make. "That's the programming talking. He trained you to think everything bad was your fault. He taught you that you deserved every hateful, awful thing he did to you. That's how he kept control of you."

Shame at the truth in those words darkened Sadie's pretty face. But it wasn't Margot's intention to tear her down now.

"And yet you were brave. You made it out. It took him months to find you."

Sadie's green eyes widened in surprise.

"How many times had you tried to leave him?"

Margot asked, hoping to earn her trust.

Sadie just stared at her, trying to find words to answer the question. Margot waited, letting her put together the words she wanted to say.

The redhead's sigh was a deep, tired sound. "I'd thought about it plenty of times. But I *knew* if he caught me, he'd kill me. He'd --"

"But you made it out." Margot needed her to understand. "That's extraordinary. Most of us will only move out of our comfort zones to protect someone else. Someone we love. You made the move to save yourself. I'd call that brave."

When Sadie had nothing to say, Margot went on.

"If the moment ever arrives when you need to be brave for someone else," Margot said slowly, "you'll be amazed at how brave you can be."

Shaking her head, Sadie said, "I'm not sure I could be as brave as you. But I want to learn."

That's what Margot wanted to hear. "You can."

"It's just..." Sadie huffed a dry laugh, swiping at the tears pooling in her big green eyes. "He's in jail right now. He won't be there long."

"He'll go on trial." Margot guessed the MC put the idea in her head that her ex wouldn't face consequences. "The law will handle him."

Sadie shook her head, her curls bouncing with the movement. "He'll get out. The law won't stop him. He'll find a way. He always does. And once he's out, he's coming back here."

"We're not going to let anything happen to you, Sadie." Margot meant the comment to be comforting. "He'll have to go through the law to get to you. And the Hounds."

That got Sadie's attention.

"I'm not worried about *me*," Sadie explained. "I

don't want him hurting the people I care about. Axel...
I'd gladly hand myself over to him to protect Axel or
any of you."

"What if you didn't have to?" Margot asked.
"What if you could handle your ex?"

What little color in the redhead's face drained
quickly. Her green eyes widened. "What?"

"What if you could handle him? Have you ever
considered that?"

Her red curls bounced as she shook her head.
"No. Oh, God, no. I mean... No way I could stand up
to him."

"I'll bet there was a time you would have given
me the same answer if I asked if you could ever leave
him."

The thought stopped Sadie cold. Mutely, she
stared at Margot for a moment before slowly nodding.
"Yeah, I would have told you that I couldn't possibly."

"But you *did*. If you can do that, you can learn to
stand up to him or anyone."

Seeming to consider Margot's words, she met her
gaze. "I can learn all that in this class?"

"Some." Margot sized up Axel's girlfriend,
watching hope bloom in her expression. "I'd be glad to
work with you beyond the class too."

"I wouldn't want to take up your time," Sadie
said.

"Well, maybe we'll make a trade," Margot
offered.

"I don't know what I have to offer you." Sadie's
expression showed concern.

Margot grinned. "You can teach me how to do
my hair or makeup like yours sometime," she said
shyly. "I never did learn how to do all the important
girl stuff."

It likely wasn't what the younger woman expected her to say. Sadie's gaze swept over Margot as if she was considering. After a moment, she slowly nodded.

"I can do that," Sadie told her in a way that left Margot feeling oddly relieved.

Yeah, she'd never been any sort of beauty like Sadie. The few girlfriends she had weren't any better at being girlish than she was. She'd been firmly in the nerd camp. At least Sadie didn't think she was a lost cause.

"Then we have a deal," Margot said, offering her hand to Sadie. And Sadie shook it. "Want to start tonight?"

Sadie laughed, a nervous sound. "No!"

Margot chuckled. "Fair enough. How about this? I've worked things out with my day job to have this class each Wednesday night for the next three months. We can meet for half an hour after class each week. If that works for you."

"Okay. I'd like that." After a moment, the younger woman said, "Thank you."

And as she watched Sadie make her way out of the small room Margot had rented at the gym for the class, she realized she liked Sadie. Whatever the girl had been through had negatively impacted her. But she'd survived and she was kind. Margot dealt every day with the rage aimed at Sadie's abusive ex, who had been the one to execute her father. Margot couldn't summon an ounce of anger at Sadie even if she'd wanted to.

Still, Ryder's words echoed in her mind. Sadie's ex was part of the Mafia, and should he get out of jail, he *would* come looking for payback. What would he do to Sadie if given the chance?

As she gathered her things so she could lock up and head back to her house, Margot decided she'd do her best to prepare Sadie for whatever the future held. And even if her brutal ex never returned to threaten her, she'd learn to handle herself.

* * *

The sight of Ryder's Harley parked off to the side in her driveway had Margot smiling as she pulled in. He'd been struggling earlier, working all morning, not to mention driving into the garage and working on his feet all day. He still likely needed a couple more weeks to rest. It had only been a week since he'd started getting around in his house. By the time they went to lunch, he'd looked washed out and tired. Despite all Ryder's protests, pride motivated him. That and his need to get out of his house.

Throwing off her seatbelt and gathering her things, she thought about his place as she climbed out of her truck. Until he'd been shot, she'd never been to the house he shared with his twin. The first time she entered, it felt like a rental unit. It was too neat for two single men and there were no photographs anywhere. Axel wasn't there often.

Margot was grateful Ryder had heeded her advice and decided not to drive back home on his own.

Quietly, because he was probably sleeping, she let herself into her house. Sure enough, Ryder was sprawled over her couch, making himself at home. The T-shirt he'd been wearing earlier was dropped to the floor, his boots and socks not far from it. Her guest had pulled the zigzag afghan her mother crocheted when Margot was little over himself because her air conditioner was powerful. The sight of him asleep on her couch in just jeans stopped her cold.

Ryder was muscular, his arms and chest marked

up with scars and tattoos. One long arm was shoved under one of her throw pillows, sandwiching it between his bicep and head. The other rested along his body, twitching slightly as he slept. What would it be like to stretch out next to him and drape that arm around herself, snuggling into his warmth?

When she spotted one the scars from one of the bullets that almost killed him, she snapped out of it. *Stop staring at the man like a creep. You're his* friend.

An opened beer sat on the coffee table before him, half-drunk without any condensation on the glass. He'd been there a while then. Next to it were the pain pills he was almost out of and what looked like the crust of a sandwich on a plate. At least he'd eaten with his medication -- something he wasn't always mindful of.

Ryder was safe and resting in her home so she could watch over him. Margot couldn't ask for more.

Since she had tomorrow off, Margot decided she didn't need to be in such a hurry to go to sleep. She showered, changing into the one cute pair of pajamas she owned on the off-chance Ryder would see her. After that, she headed to the kitchen. In her rush to get changed after work and get ready for her self-defense class, she hadn't bothered to eat. In the quiet of her kitchen, she warmed up the leftovers of the Chinese food she ordered a couple of days ago. Sitting at her kitchen table, she read the news on her phone while she ate.

Margot didn't notice Ryder at first, lurking in the entrance of the kitchen in the dim light. When she did, she gasped in fright and her heart lurched in her chest. Dropping her fork onto her plate with a loud *clank*, she just stared at him.

Ryder chuckled. "Didn't mean to scare you."

Taking a deep breath, she smiled. "I didn't mean to wake you up."

"You didn't," he said, as he wandered into the kitchen and pulled out the chair next to her. Settling in with his elbows on the table, he grinned at her. "How did your first class go?"

Yeah, he remembered. Friends were supposed to remember important things like that. Still, it made her heart skip a beat that he asked. It also wasn't making things better that he was sitting next to her shirtless. She could feel the heat coming off him since he had sat so close to her.

"It went well." She didn't sound convincing to her own ears. Ryder cut her his *really?* look and she laughed. "Okay, it was chaos. But after the first twenty minutes or so, I got a handle on it. It turned out well in the end I think."

"How many did you have?"

"Only seven. One of the older ladies probably isn't coming back. Maybe not her friend either. But I think the rest will stick it out."

Ryder reached over to grab her fork and spear a steamed dumpling for himself, chewing while he seemed to consider her story. "Was Sadie there?"

Margot nodded. "She was. And she didn't run out the door screaming the minute class was over. I'll count that as a win."

Ryder smiled, returning her fork to the plate in front of her. "That's good. Axel was afraid she'd lose her nerve. Glad she made it."

Margot thought about having Sadie in the class tonight, and their talk afterward. "She was hesitant. I mean, most people are when they start learning self-defense techniques. On top of that is everything she's been through. But she's willing to learn. I told her I'd stay after class each week so I can have some one-on-one time with her, build up her confidence."

Ryder's blue-eyed gaze met with hers. "I appreciate you doing that. Axel will too."

"She's worried," Margot said. "She thinks one day she'll have to face her ex again. And she likely will face him in the courtroom. But I want to empower her. To make her realize if that day ever comes, she can hold her own." Margot wasn't sure what to do with the speculative gaze Ryder shot her then. "What?"

Ryder sighed. "That day *will* come. The fucker considers Sadie his property. He'll come back for her. My brother? That's the man he'll be gunning for. So putting the idea in Sadie's head of standing her ground with her ex isn't a good one. You might be better off teaching her to avoid her ex at all costs. Let us handle him."

Margot scoffed, both annoyed and offended. "Why would I teach her that when that's not how it'll go down?" She stared him down. "The Hounds will *not* be handling him if he comes back to Mercy. The law will."

His handsome face split into a grin and it fanned the flames of her growing anger. "Like the law handled him last time? Sawyer was a little late to the game. It would have been better if your boss had stayed out of it. We could have completely removed the problem that day and there would have been nothing more to worry about."

"You're lucky Sawyer chooses to coexist with you guys," Margot warned. "In other towns, that's not exactly the way it works with MCs."

"Not exactly?"

She didn't appreciate the grin or the way he thought he was toying with her. "Let us handle it,

Ryder. Sawyer's a good man and he has a lot of years of experience in keeping Mercy safe. That should be good enough for you and the Hounds."

"It's personal now, darlin'," Ryder continued. "Sadie is my brother's old lady. That makes her one of us. And a Hound will never allow anyone from the outside to fuck with one of us. Club business."

"Club business doesn't circumvent the law, Ryder."

Again, he grabbed her fork. Spearing her last dumpling with it, he popped it into his mouth as he considered her words.

"The law needs to keep up," Ryder said. "By the time your boss got to Bianchi, it was mostly said and done."

Margot remembered the day in very vivid, painful detail although she hadn't been on duty. She'd been reeling from her father's murder.

Immediately, Ryder's expression shifted, filled with concern. "I didn't mean that *you* should have been there. Fuck, I'm sorry. That's the last thing I would have meant to imply. I know how much the law and doing the right thing means to you is all," he finished awkwardly.

"The law isn't some hobby I took up," she said. "It's the *law*. It's the rules that keep us all safe, protect our freedoms. I get that we're on opposite sides of the fence here but what would really be great is if we could work together."

Of course he pulled a face at that. Margot laughed.

"You can pretend you're a big bad outlaw all you want," Margot said. "But you're friends with a deputy. I've even been inside the clubhouse."

Ryder studied her seriously for a moment, his

blue eyes flashing some emotion that was gone the second she noticed it. Did he catch hell from his brothers for being friends with a cop? Did it bother *him* what she did for a living?

"Okay, let me rephrase," she tried. "Can *we* work together? You and me? I only want to keep Sadie and anyone else caught in the crosshairs safe. I'm not doubting you or anyone else from the club, all right?"

That got his attention, and he nodded as he considered her words. "We can. I'm sure you can handle yourself. I'd like to see you in action. But I also worry about *your* safety."

"Because I'm a woman?" Margot wanted to know.

"Because I care about you," he said, looking her in the eye.

Her heart squeezed in her chest at his words. She knew he cared about her. It just played with her emotions because she wanted so badly to give those words a different meaning.

"Those Mafia fuckers are bad news. I want you to be careful is all. They're like coyotes. They rarely come at you alone because they're fucking cowards. They come at you in a group. We'll take care of the problem."

Blowing out a breath, Margot said, "We'll see."

Scrubbing a hand through his dark hair, Ryder rose from his seat and went to her refrigerator, pulling out another bottle of beer.

"You had one already open in the living room," she reminded him with a grin.

"I know," he said as he twisted off the cap of the one in his hand. "I finished it before I came in here."

When he gulped down about half of the fresh one, she shook her head. "Should you be drinking that with your pain meds?"

"Absolutely. The meds work better like this." His return grin was pure mischief.

Margot rose, dumped her plate and rinsed it off in the sink. She felt Ryder's gaze on her while she did.

"You work tomorrow?" he asked.

"No, I'm off."

"There's a new horror movie on Hulu. Want to watch it?"

Ryder knew she wasn't a horror movie person. She only watched them with him. "Do you mean hide behind the afghan in there while you enjoy all the unadulterated gore and violence?"

"Basically," he said, smiling.

"Fine," Margot told him. "But if I can't sleep after the movie, I'm going to keep you up too." She passed by him to head for her living room.

Chapter Six

Ryder

Stretching out on Margot's couch, Ryder grabbed the remote for her TV and looked through channels, trying to find something new to watch. In the last couple of weeks since he'd been staying at her house, he'd binged three new series and watched a slew of bad movies.

The best part? He slept well. Sleep had eluded him for weeks after returning to his lonely little house in the country.

Margot had a much better air conditioner to battle the hot August nights. Did it also have anything to do with the fact that he could be at Margot's house after work in less than five minutes? Sure. It also had helped with the bad memories that haunted him in the house where he grew up. Ryder didn't like to be alone there. He *hated* to sleep alone.

Ryder didn't feel alone at Margot's though. Even when she wasn't with him.

Margot worked second shift this week, but she'd be back not long after midnight. While he didn't always wake up, somehow he always became aware when she arrived.

When he got up each morning for work at the garage, no matter what shift she worked, she got up with him. If she worked days, she milled around her kitchen making coffee and getting ready for her day, dressed in her uniform with her game face on. When she worked second shift? Well, those were his favorite mornings. She drifted around her kitchen, sleepy and cute in pink pajamas. He'd only ever seen her wear the one set, but the T-shirt and pant set didn't do a lot to hide the body underneath. And the mechanic in him very much wanted to see how that machine ran.

Margot was physically fit and made regular visits to the gym. He never minded a curvy girl with some softness to her but something about Margot's muscular figure messed with him. He could bounce a quarter off her ass. Hell, that wasn't *all* he wanted to do with her ass.

Scrubbing a hand over his face as he sat up on her couch, Ryder admitted to himself that his X-rated thoughts about his *friend* were becoming a problem. Yeah, it had been a while since he'd gotten laid. Easy enough to fix. But he didn't want to fix it. He didn't want to go back to picking up a different girl each night at the bar to scratch an itch. It was more than that.

Margot was more than that. Ryder just didn't know what to do about it.

Currently, he lived on her couch, and she let him. Now that he'd worked his way up to full days back at the garage, he made good money again. He wanted to help. He'd stopped by the grocery store after work. Yeah, he got stuff he liked. But he also got her fancy coffee creamer, the yogurt she ate, the little granola bars she packed for her lunch. Hell, he even cleaned up the kitchen.

His twin had asked him today since he felt better if he would head back to their house. *No.*

It bothered him a little to read the concern in Axel's face when he asked the question. His twin worried about Margot, worried Ryder would hurt her. He worried about that himself. Because Margot wasn't just someone he wanted a night of fun with. She was the best friend outside the Hounds he'd ever had.

His heart whispered that wasn't the truth either. Most of the time he elected to ignore the nagging little voice.

Finishing his beer and settling on a true-crime documentary, Ryder drifted off to sleep. When he woke up some time later, the TV screen was dark. The soft chorus of crickets played in the darkness as he got up to head to the bathroom. Peeking through the living room curtains while he scratched his bare chest, he saw Margot's truck in the driveway.

Still half-asleep, he stumbled down the hall to the bathroom. His sleepy brain became aware of the soft music coming from Margot's room. She didn't usually play music at night. Was she up?

No light was under her bedroom door but it was slightly open. At a glance, she appeared asleep with her back to the door. Soft beams of moonlight showcased her sensual form underneath the thin blanket that covered her to the waist.

Wait. Blinking, he took a closer look. Her back was bare, and she shifted, the movement of her hips consistent and circular. Then he heard the delicate humming sound.

His heart sped up, pumping blood south in a hurry. *Holy shit!* Was Margot busy in there with a vibrator? Was she thinking about him? He hoped so. Without thinking, his hand slid down to his painfully hard cock, squeezing. *Fuck me, that's hot.*

Ryder knew he needed to walk away. *Now.* If she caught him ogling her through the crack in her door like a fucking pervert, he'd be out on the street minus one friend. Just one more minute. Then he'd --

That soft little moan had his cock jerking in his boxers. It wasn't easy but he managed to drag himself away to the safety of the bathroom. Locking the door, he masturbated like a teenage boy after his first kiss. Working his cock frantically, Ryder couldn't unsee her lying on her bed, the erotic sight and sound of her bringing herself off. No, he really hadn't "seen" anything, but he imagined quite a bit. How did Margot tease her pussy with that little power tool? How wet was she right now? From the sound of that desperate little moan, he'd be willing to bet his cock could slide right into her, take her for a proper ride.

Fuck.

It didn't take much imagining how tight Margot's pussy would feel around him. Was she a screamer? Would she carve tracks down his back with her nails? How sweet would her pussy taste?

Gasping, he kept mostly quiet in the bathroom as he came in thick white spurts. A good thing with her room across the hall. Ryder stood shaking, draining his balls that ached in the best way. It had been a while for him and his cock kept jerking, sending pulses of pleasure through every fiber of his being until his balls were emptied.

"Ryder?"

His heart flew in his chest as he scrambled to clean up, hoping with everything he had she didn't know what he'd just been doing in her bathroom.

"Are you okay?" She sounded worried.

Relief flooded him. "Yeah." It worked out well that his voice shook. "Sorry. Didn't mean to wake you up."

"It's okay." She sounded out of breath herself. "I'm... just worried about you. Are you sure you're okay?"

It was nothing for Ryder to think up a quick story. Opening the door, wearing just his black boxers, he found her standing in the dark hallway, now in those little pink pajamas. Leaning against the doorframe like he was struggling, he sighed. "Yeah,

I'm sorry. I had to piss. I got up off the couch... and I just felt dizzy."

Immediately, concern bled into those big brown eyes, and she moved closer to wrap an arm around his waist. "Let's get you back to the couch," she said, gently urging him to walk with her.

Any other time he would have protested. But her softness against him felt enticing. Ryder smelled her, the slightest whiff of sex, as they walked. Maybe just his fucking imagination -- the scent of her excitement. But Ryder went with it, in no hurry to get back.

Once she had him safely back on the couch, she urged him to lie down. Situating the pillow under his head, she covered him with the blue throw she'd left him so she could wash the afghan he usually used. Guilt poked at him. She was in full-on nurse mode while he tried to imagine what her breasts looked like, how they'd feel in his hands. How hard had her nipples been when she used the vibrator?

"Can I get you a glass of water?" she offered. "Maybe take one of your pain pills?"

Ryder shook his head. "Nothing hurts. Damn pills probably made me dizzy."

"I'm getting you a glass of water anyway."

Right. Because he needed to watch her walk to the kitchen, her round little ass swaying in the pool of light from the windows.

Blowing out his frustration, he stared at the ceiling, waiting for her to bring his water. Then he had no idea how he would fucking sleep with what he just saw playing on repeat in his head. *Goddamn it.*

* * *

Margot

Sinking onto the edge of her bed, Margot sighed.

She'd never be able to sleep.

Not long after her shift started, a federal agent called the station. As a courtesy, they told Randy they were coming to town to question Sadie about the case they were building against Robert Bianchi. Randy'd told her about the visit, and she was grateful. She'd give Sadie a head's up because given her past trauma from her relationship, it wouldn't be easy for her. She'd also tell Ryder, advise him and the Hounds to stay out of it. The sooner they talked to Sadie, the better.

The rest of the shift had been business as usual until around ten. Then a huge fight broke out at *Sackett's*. Dawson and Noll showed up, but called for backup when it turned into a free-for-all. They'd arrested seven and sent one man to the hospital for a stab wound. It looked like he'd recover. Margot had talked Emery Phillips down after the mess made in his bar. The frustrated older man just kept saying he was "getting too old for all the shit."

By the time she'd clocked out, it was almost two.

Ryder had fallen asleep sprawled over her couch as he always did, shirtless in just his boxers. He'd left the lamp on this time, so all those muscles and tattoos were on perfect display for her. Usually, she just moved along. She'd have a snack and get ready for bed. But tonight, no, she took a good long look.

Fucking beautiful bastard.

Was it wrong to want what so many other women got to enjoy? If she'd never gone to school with him, never got to know him, could she have slapped on some lipstick and skimpy clothes and got on that ride? *Jesus.* It was the most she'd ever seen of him when he wasn't fighting for his life, and she still wanted more. His cock had to be as beautiful as the rest of him. How would it feel in her mouth? In her pussy?

Her nipples tightened to achy little points. The tight-fitting vest she wore under her uniform made it worse. A delicate ache began between her legs, making her entire evening more frustrating.

And Margot had her snack, got ready for bed, and... Deciding she was a masochist to have the man she'd wanted for so long staying under her roof, she turned on one of the playlists on her phone. She dug her magic wand out of the drawer of her bedside table. It had been a while since she used it, but she needed it tonight.

With the music just loud enough to mask the noise, Margot got into bed and got comfortable. Peeling off her pajama bottoms and panties, Margot got comfortable, first on her back. Then on her side. After a minute, she pulled her top off too. Naked as the day she was born, she settled in under the blanket to work some magic with her wand.

Imagining sex with Ryder was so easy. She'd done it so many times with her vibrator or fingers that he just might be impressed. Using her wand in all the ways she liked, she envisioned his hands and mouth on her body. How good would those rough mechanic's hands feel against the softness of her skin? Margot could almost see his head between her thighs, blue eyes lit up in mischief as he took her apart. Sliding up and down on his cock would be heaven, filling her up...

Margot had just managed to bring herself off when she heard something in the hallway. The final spasms of her release shook her as she glanced over the shoulder to see she'd left her door open. Fuck. *Fuck*! Was Ryder out there? Did he know what she'd been doing?

Mortified, she hid her wand back in its drawer -- she'd clean it later -- and scrambled back into her pajamas. Her heart flew in her chest. It was quiet now. Ryder was in her bathroom. *Oh God*! Had he seen anything? Her door had been open!

When she didn't hear anything else, worry bled into her panic. Was he okay? She reached the door. "Ryder?"

It was too quiet.

"Are you okay?"

"Yeah." Ryder's voice sounded weak. "Sorry. Didn't mean to wake you up."

"It's okay," she lied, feeling like a huge selfish asshole. "I'm... just worried about you. Are you sure you're okay?"

He opened the door, and she did her damnedest not to ogle the man. He leaned against the doorframe looking disoriented and sighed. "Yeah, I'm sorry. I had to piss. I got up off the couch... and I just felt dizzy."

What the fuck was the matter with her? Her friend was still struggling, and she'd selfishly masturbated and wondered if he heard. Shaking her head at herself, she said, "Let's get you back to the couch."

Chapter Seven

Ryder

The next night, Ryder had just settled on *Jay Leno's Garage* on YouTube when the piercing wail of sirens shattered the silence. Police cars. Just one, maybe, at first. More joined in, the distinct blare of firetrucks mingling with the urgent screech of multiple police vehicles. What was happening in town? The heart of Mercy and the small cluster of businesses that comprised it were only a block away from Margot's house.

Instinct had him grabbing his T-shirt off the floor. He pulled it on, along with his boots. Whatever was happening in town, his mind went right to Bobby Fuckface and his minions.

Yeah, and with Margot because she'd be there.

Ryder had just reached the main street when he spotted the smoke. *What the fuck*? Running in its direction, he realized how out of shape he'd become during his recovery. Pausing, he caught his breath. The first thing he thought of was Liza Austin's place but when he reached the edge of their yard, he didn't see anything out of order. Besides, they would have known right off since Snow installed the security system there.

No, the smoke came from across the road. Carmen's, the small clothing store, and the pharmacy next to it, were both okay. His gaze followed the smoke past those two shops to the end of the street, *Whisk and Whimsy. Holy shit*! Emily's bakery.

Ryder moved closer. The front of the bakery was consumed by a raging inferno. The small, dedicated group of Mercy firefighters worked with determination to battle the blaze. The acrid smell of smoke filled the air, making his eyes sting.

Anger boiled beneath the surface as he watched the firefighters in their heavy protective gear work. Someone didn't randomly decide to torch a fucking bakery. Hoses snaked across the pavement; powerful streams of water were aimed at the core of the fire. The flames roared in defiance, licking at the brick walls and threatening to spread to the other shops. A small group of people gathered, their faces mirroring the alarm Ryder felt.

The bakery belonged to Snow's old lady, and he didn't believe for a fucking minute it was anything but deliberate. *Arson.*

Pulling out his phone, Ryder moved back, away from the smoke filling the air. His call must have woken Snow up. It was almost one in the morning.

"Yeah?" Snow's voice was scratchy from sleep.

"Brother, you need to get to town," Ryder said without preamble. "Someone's lit up Emily's bakery."

For a moment, it was silent. Had Snow heard him? But before he could say anything else, Snow said, "On my way."

Thoughts raced through Ryder's mind at lightning speed. He'd only talked to Emily Frost a couple of times. Everything about the woman was warm and precise. She didn't strike him as someone who would carelessly lock up for the day and forget to turn something off or check anything that would be a fire hazard.

Somehow, he *knew* it was those Mafia fucks. The feds had just come to town yesterday to question Sadie. Bianchi and his men had tracked her to Mercy. Who knew how many days they'd been there, quietly watching? They might know everything about each member of the Hounds by now. Where they lived and who they loved. A man's family was some powerful fucking collateral to damage.

Rapid footsteps came up behind him as he slid his phone back into his pocket.

Margot marched in front of him. "What are you doing here?"

"I saw the smoke and came to see what was going on." Ryder hooked a thumb behind him. "Like them."

Impatience was stamped across Margot's face. "They'll have the fire under control soon. Why don't you head back to the house?"

"I'm waiting for Snow." Ryder folded his arms across his chest, not planning to go anywhere until his brother arrived.

Margot blew out a breath. "No need. We'll talk to them when they get here, Ryder. Why don't you --"

"Why are you trying so hard to get my ass out of here?" Ryder asked, a little pissed. "You think it's *them*?"

"Them?"

Margot would suck at cards because she had a terrible poker face. Playing dumb with him wasn't going to work. She knew exactly who he was talking about.

"You *know* who did this."

"No, I'm trying to get you and everyone else back home so we can do our jobs and investigate, Ryder." Oh, she was mad now. "Go home."

The low wail got everyone's attention. Emily Frost ran full speed in the direction of her burning bakery in a shiny pink robe. It took Ryder and Margot both to stop her from running right into the burning building. Her pretty face was streaked with tears. She struggled in their grip until Snow caught up, taking her in his arms.

"Why?" Emily cried.

Snow held her tight, pressing kisses into her hair and whispering words of comfort.

The bakery was Emily's livelihood. Ryder's heart sank thinking about what the future held for her. Snow did his best to comfort his old lady. But when Ryder's gaze caught his, he saw his brother's cold fury.

The bakery was under the MC's protection. Someone was going to pay for this.

Margot caught the exchange of looks. Grabbing Ryder's upper arm, she steered him away from the couple and the growing group of onlookers. "Ryder, we'll handle this," she said in a lowered voice. "Just head back, okay?"

"We'll handle it too," he said, needing her to understand how this had to go.

"We don't know what exactly happened here." Margot glared up at him. "It's too early to tell if this is connected in any way to the murders."

Ryder couldn't have that conversation with her now. He had to let the MC know what was happening. "Right," was all he said.

Walking back over to Snow, Ryder said, "I'll go tell Razor."

"Do it, brother," Snow said holding onto his girl.

Margot shot Ryder a warning look as he marched back toward her house.

* * *

Margot

When she returned to her house, Ryder wasn't there -- a good thing. They were going to have a talk he wouldn't enjoy when he got there.

Margot paced, practicing what she'd say to

Ryder when he arrived. When she got tired of that, she went to the kitchen for a glass of wine. She could have changed out of her uniform into her comforting pajamas. But she needed the uniform. She wanted to wear it to drive home her point that he shouldn't, under *any* circumstance, interfere with her job or the law. Period. He and his entire club needed to accept that.

After the second glass of wine, Margot's anger began to wear off. What if Ryder didn't come back to her house? What if she'd been too harsh? What if he decided it was time he moved back to his own place?

When headlights flashed outside her living room windows, she jumped in her seat on the couch. A truck pulled into her driveway. It was likely Ryder. Placing her empty wineglass on the coffee table, she angled herself on the couch with a perfect view of the door. Still, she kept a hand on her firearm, in case it wasn't him.

When the doorknob turned, whoever was on the other side of the door found it locked. The truck backed out of the driveway and then she heard a key in the lock of her front door. A beat later, Ryder walked in, looking as tired as she felt. Scrubbing a hand through the short locks of his hair, his gaze moved over her.

Margot froze, buzzed from the triple threat of fatigue, alcohol, and adrenaline.

"You planning on shooting me?" Ryder's tone was meant to sound lighthearted, but he missed it by a mile.

Margot took her hand off her piece, blowing out a deep sigh. "Ryder, we need to talk."

He didn't look surprised. Shoving his hands in the front pockets of his jeans, he walked into the living room with an expression that was hard to read. Nodding, he took a seat in the armchair next to the couch where she sat.

"Is this how it's going to be, Ryder?" It was all she remembered of what she rehearsed. "Every time something happens in Mercy the Hounds are going to be up in arms?"

Ryder's brows lowered as he stared her down. "Don't do that."

"I *am* doing that." She met his gaze, watching anger flare in those steely-blue eyes. "We don't know yet who was behind the fire at the bakery. But there will be an investigation."

"I don't give a fuck about your investigation or the law, Margot," Ryder told her, looking her in the eye. "Tonight, whether you want to admit it or not, was a hit against our club. That can't be ignored."

"How was that a hit against the Hounds?" she asked. "Yes, Emily is seeing Snow. That doesn't automatically mean it's a hit against your club. How would they even make that connection?"

"Margot, those assholes tracked Sadie here to Mercy," Ryder said, still glaring. "They could have been here for weeks, watching and waiting before they made a move."

Ryder had a point.

"Maybe," Margot said. "But there's someone with a stronger motive to go after Emily than our Mafia friends."

It was satisfying to watch the color creep up from the collar of his tight T-shirt.

"Her ex is a much stronger possibility," she explained. "There have been a few reports filed about him. He was arrested for DWI and urinating in public three years ago. Complaints were filed about him the year after that. Now she's dating Snow. It's possible it's him."

Ryder's smile didn't reach his eyes. "No. He showed his ass this past Christmas at the kid's charity party that Emily coordinates."

"No one filed a report."

"No, there wasn't because we dealt with him," Ryder said.

Margot froze. What did he mean they *dealt* with him?

"And he'd be stupid to come back to Mercy."

Okay, he wasn't dead.

Margot shook her head. "That's what I mean, Ryder. That's vigilante justice you guys live by. It's not going to work here."

"Why not?"

"No offense," Margot said, "but your club and those men have some things in common. You take matters into your own hands, unchecked. It escalates, grows more violent. People get hurt. People die. The law, on the other hand, provides a finite end to the conflict. It stops there."

"That's naive, Margot," Ryder said.

"Is it? Or maybe you've been trading on the other side of the law for so long you don't realize what the law can do."

That earned her a look. "Oh, I've seen what the law can do."

Margot elected to ignore his sarcasm. "What will it take to convince you guys to step back?"

"What will it take to make *you* realize what you're dealing with?" Ryder said. "These aren't store robberies or random shootings. They're a crime family, Margot," he explained. "You piss them off or wrong them, they'll hit back hard. And believe me, they're good at it."

"We brought Robert Bianchi in, didn't we?" Margot countered.

Ryder threw up his hands. "Yes. But he's got money. And lawyers. What are the odds he'll stay in jail? Even if the Feds bring their own charges. And being locked up doesn't really change anything. Those fuckers can still order hits from prison. His men, his family, they're going to keep coming -- because you brought him in. The feds showed up this week to question Sadie. A couple of days later, Emily's bakery gets torched. Seems like an awfully big fucking coincidence."

Before she could respond to that, Ryder sighed, pointing at the firearm at her hip. "And if you really thought that these incidents weren't related at all, why were you ready for anything when I walked in the door?"

"I was just being cautious," she said. But it was a lie, and his expression told her he knew it.

"No, you did it because if they can hit Emily's place, and she's with our VP," he said slowly, "they can come after you."

"That doesn't make any sense, Ryder. I'm not dating one of the Hounds. I'm just letting you crash on my couch."

Ryder glared at her. "Makes sense to me."

"I appreciate that you care about me," she said slowly, "but I'm a big girl. And I don't want you to feel you owe me anything for the last few weeks. You don't. You're my friend."

Why was he looking at her like *that*?

"Are we going to be at odds with each other until all this gets resolved, Ryder? I need you to understand, I have a job to do. If you ever interfere, and I have to arrest you, I'll do it."

She didn't appreciate the shit-eating grin that formed on his handsome face. "Well, if you want to put me in handcuffs, you could just ask. I'm pretty game for most anything."

That stopped Margot cold. Ryder had never said anything like *that* to her before. A flash of desire sped through her at his words. "Excuse me?"

"You're still wearing the uniform," he pointed out. "Usually, you're in pjs by now."

Margot's anger flared. "I kept the uniform on to make a point. That's *all*."

That grin didn't go anywhere, and she wanted to slap it off his face. Damn him. She didn't need images right now of riding his cock while he was handcuffed to her bed.

"Whatever." She was tired of the conversation. "Look, I needed to make things clear about my job. It would be complicated if you *weren't* a Hound. Since you are, that makes things worse. And yeah, I get that I'm a woman, but I can handle myself. Okay?"

The smile faded. "Hey, had nothing to do with the fact that you're a woman. You're badass."

The sincerity in his face and voice had her ire fading. But it didn't do a damn thing for the ache that started in her clit. Margot nodded. "I appreciate that. I'm going to bed. Goodnight."

His gaze was still on her as she moved to leave the room. "So, no handcuffs tonight?"

Where was this coming from? Margot turned back to him. "No, we're not doing handcuffs tonight." She put her hands on her hips. "Since when do you hit on *me*?"

Ryder shrugged. "I've been thinking about you a lot lately."

"About me handcuffing you?" Margot shook her head. "We're not doing this."

"Doing what?" Ryder asked feigning innocence.

"Ruining our friendship." Margot stumbled over her words because she was in unfamiliar territory. "I'm not going to be Miss Right Now for you because we're both here and I'm convenient."

Blowing out a breath, Ryder studied her for a minute. Her heart skipped a beat because he was looking at her the way she always wanted him to. Now, she realized she didn't want it at all. Not *that* way.

Dropping his gaze, Ryder slowly rose from the chair. "Sorry. I'm so fucking bad at this. I really am."

"Judging from the parade of women I've seen come and go from your life, I'd call you successful," Margot pointed out.

Ryder shrugged. "That's different."

"How?" Margot's mind spun. Her body warmed, pulses of desire that her magic wand couldn't dispel racing through her.

"I'm good at flirting," he said slowly. "But this?"

This? Had he been drinking? Was it his pain meds?

"I'm tired," she said, wanting to cut this off. "We'll talk tomorrow."

He moved closer. "*This* is different. You and me."

Margot snorted. "Yeah, we're friends. That's different from your usual dealings with women."

"We don't *have* to be just friends." Ryder moved closer.

Her heart hammered in her chest with the intensity she wanted him to hammer *her*. Her brain screamed at her to put the brakes on.

Margot sighed. "Yes, we do. I care about you too.

You know that. But I don't want to be your casual booty call for six weeks until someone else catches your eye. I deserve more than that. So, thank you. But no."

Ryder wasn't backing down. "What if that's not what I'm looking for?"

Margot had to put a stop to this. *Now.* "Randall Harper, I've known you since kindergarten. You've never had a different type of relationship with women. Not once. You wouldn't know how."

"And you know that how?" Now he moved closer, into her personal space. She was staring up into his blue eyes, lost for the moment. "You've been paying attention. You wouldn't have been if you didn't think about me that way."

Oh, he nailed it. For a moment she froze, caught. Yeah, what he said was true. But she wasn't going to play the moon-eyed girl here. "I once did," Margot said. "But I figured out that wasn't happening after high school."

Ryder's look said, "Really?"

"I'm tired," she tried again. "Can we not do this?"

"What if I *want* to do this?"

He captured her face in his hands in the span of a heartbeat, his touch so gentle he could have been cradling a baby bird. When his lips touched hers, a careful caress, Margot let him. His kiss was soft, seeking. It wasn't the lusty, passionate exchange she would have expected and that her body craved. He took his time until her heart was flying in her chest, until she couldn't breathe.

It would have been so easy to convince herself the kiss meant something to him. Yet she questioned his intent. Did he have some misguided notion he owed her something? Was he curious? Was he playing her now like he had so many others over the years?

When he ended the kiss, he peered deeply into her eyes, one hand lingering to cup the side of her face. A smile played about his lips. Slowly, he stepped back. "Goodnight," he whispered.

Margot spun to escape, losing her balance and tripping on the way to her bedroom. Her heart pounded in a fierce rhythm as embarrassment warmed her face.

Yeah, it was just one kiss. But how would she ever recover from it?

Chapter Eight

Ryder

Margot was still on second shift. He had to be at the garage early the next morning, so he didn't see her. But he sure as shit was thinking about her. That *kiss*.

The impulse came out of nowhere. At first, he hadn't understood the need. He just had to do it. The fact that she didn't cut him off or try to kick his ass, told him what he'd always suspected. Margot still had feelings for him.

Ryder knew. From the time they were in elementary school, and she would navigate things to be on the same kickball team as him, to the time they were in high school and she'd pretend to do homework in the stands during his football practices, he always suspected she had a thing for him.

She was right about what she'd told him earlier. They'd always been good friends. He trusted Margot as much as he did his brothers in the MC. And she had a valid point. Was he really thinking about tossing away the friend he counted on because he liked the way she tasted? The way she trembled in his arms?

Margot had seen him go around with so many women over the years. Hell, she even joked about it with him.

Margot herself? Well, he recalled maybe one or two guys she'd gotten involved with. If she'd been with someone when she lived in Oak Grove for a time, he didn't want to know about it.

From what he remembered; he hadn't really liked the two guys she'd been with. What had she seen in either of them? For the longest time, he wrote it off. Margot handled herself well. She was a badass who looked fucking adorable in her deputy uniform.

When did things change? Why had his feelings for Margot changed? Why now?

"Deep thinking?" Axel walked up to where he stood staring blankly at the engine of the Cadillac he was working on.

It was impossible to hide anything from his twin. "Something like that."

"I get it," Axel said after a minute. "Sadie's upset about what happened last night too."

Ryder had been so lost in replaying that one tender kiss in his head, it took him a moment to even remember what Axel was talking about. Right. The fire.

"Razor called a meeting this evening at the clubhouse," Ryder said.

"What time?" Axel asked.

"Six."

The Hounds needed to come up with a plan. Sadie's ex was in prison. *For now.* It didn't mean the fucker wouldn't get out before too long. In the meantime, his men were going to keep coming to Mercy to stir up shit just because they could. The Hounds couldn't allow that to continue. The Mafia fuckers' beef was with the Hounds, not the citizens of Mercy. They had to be protected.

And then there was Margot. The MC preferred to handle things under the radar to avoid attention from the law. Hell, they had to. The club made a lot of its money outside the law, and it wasn't likely to change.

Margot could be a problem. Sadie's ex had no way of knowing who he killed that night in Cowboy Pete's. And Bobby Fuckface wouldn't care if he did. Elsie and Clyde were collateral damage to them. But Clyde was Margot's father. She'd be watching right along with Sawyer, proactively trying to keep the town safe.

Shaking his head at himself, Ryder's emotions were a double-edged sword. Yeah, he was confident in Margot's ability to handle herself and do her job. She was proud of her position, and unlike a lot of lawmen he'd encountered over the years, she was honest-to-God in the job for all the right reasons. It was admirable as hell.

But Clyde's murder at the hands of Sadie's Mafia ex was very personal. What if her emotions clouded her judgment? Got her killed? Ryder wanted to do everything in his power to keep her safe. To keep her out of it.

To keep her?

Thoughts of her filled his head through the rest of the day. When it was time to close the shop, Axel ordered takeout for the meeting from the diner across the street. Ryder waited for his brother to pick up the order and rode over to the clubhouse with his twin for the meeting.

People were gathered at the table in the conference room, and he helped Axel hand out burgers and fries to their MC brothers. Everyone started eating aside from Razor. Their Prez's expression was grim.

"Last night," Razor said, "some shit went down at the bakery. Someone deliberately torched the place."

Snow looked furious across the table from Ryder, his jaw locked.

"Do we think it's the same fuckers who shot Ryder?" Hero asked.

"We do." Razor's gaze landed on Ryder. "Margot tell you anything?"

Snow stared at him intently.

Ryder shook his head. "She claims they don't know anything yet. That was at two this morning. I haven't talked to her since. She tried really hard to convince me that this may not have been Bianchi and his men. She's claiming it's more likely to be Emily's ex."

"The fuck?" Snow looked really pissed off now. "I'd be really surprised if the little weasel dick ever comes anywhere near this town again."

Ryder remembered. He'd been there with Hero and Axel.

"I told her," Ryder explained. "I ended up getting a whole lecture about respecting her job and the law. And how our friendship wouldn't prevent her from arresting my ass if she felt like it."

Razor tried not to laugh. Hero did a better job of containing his amusement.

Most of the MC knew he'd been staying at her house for the last couple of weeks. If they didn't, they were about to. "Yeah, I caught hell when I got back to her place last night," Ryder explained. "She might still be pissed at me." *And I fucking kissed her after watching her masturbate.*

"So are you and Margot…" Hero hedged.

Axel shot him a look. "It's not our business if they are."

But as Ryder glanced around the room, he saw the curiosity in their faces. And why wouldn't they think that? It pissed him off that any of them would think that way about Margot. She was nothing like the women he usually went around with. And he didn't like them trying to drag her into his need to be a womanizer either. "Margot offered me a couch so I don't have to drive back every night," he explained. "I'm not a hundred percent just yet and it's closer to work."

Razor looked skeptical, his sharp gaze assessing.

"Should you be fucking a deputy, Ryder?"

"Not fucking her." Ryder met his Prez's gaze steadily. "We're friends." But he *wanted* to fuck Margot. "Thought we were here to come up with a plan," Ryder challenged. "Not to talk about who I'm fucking. Or not fucking."

Axel grinned. "That would be a long conversation."

"Fuck you," Ryder said.

"Since when are you defensive about fucking anyone?" Hero asked.

"We're not here to talk about Ryder and his shit!" Snow's shout got everyone's attention. "Emily's place got fucking scorched last night. Fucking bakery wasn't even paid off yet. I want to know what we plan to do about this."

Razor leaned forward in his seat. "We *do* need a plan. These Mafia fuckers are going to keep showing up until they're given a good reason not to anymore."

Ryder nodded.

"First, we're going to need to get vigilant fucking fast," Razor said. "I want our prospects posted all over town by morning. Beast, make assignments. I want anything out of the ordinary reported to me ASA-fucking-P. *Anything.*"

Beast nodded.

"What about us?" Hero asked.

"Maybe they figured out the owner of the bakery is Snow's old lady," Razor explained. "Maybe they didn't make the connection. Either way, the feds are building a case against Sadie's ex, and they'll call on her to testify. His men can't take her out without making things worse for him. So, they're going to try to scare the living shit out of that little lady and the whole fucking town to keep her from saying anything."

Razor was right, and it filled him with dread. Axel sat by his side, and his twin's tension was palpable. They had to keep Sadie safe. He'd do everything in his power to help his twin protect her, to protect Mercy.

And to protect Margot, even though she didn't realize she might need it.

"Also need eyes on Liza and Henry," Razor went on. "They harbored Sadie. They're just now getting the greenhouse back up and running. How's the security system looking?"

Snow was still agitated, his color high. "It's state-of-the-art. Anyone tries anything, they'll be notified and so will I."

Razor nodded his approval.

"We need to protect Emily," Snow said. "I don't give a shit what Margot thinks." Snow shot a glare at Ryder. "It ain't her fucking ex. They went after Emily because of all this shit. Because of *me*."

"Emily's your old lady. She's one of us. Period," Razor said.

Snow nodded. The entire situation had him rattled. "Yes, she is."

"She have insurance on the place?" Razor asked.

"It wasn't paid off," Snow replied. "She *had* to have it insured out the ass. Now her business is gone. I don't want her to lose her house."

"You still have your place," Beast pointed out.

Snow shrugged. "Her place is better. I'm putting mine on the market. If I can sell it, we can use the money to get her business back up and running."

"Might be a good time to reach out to Eli," Hero said. "They had a whole-ass civil war in their club last year after Eli took out Babyface. Now they got demands for guns but not the manpower to run them. Maybe we make a deal with them and expand our operations."

Razor nodded, leaning forward to place his elbows on the table as he did when he liked what he was hearing.

"Seriously?" Snow glared at him. "You want to kiss Cottonmouth ass?"

"No." Hero stayed calm. "I want to siphon off some of their business. They help us, we help them."

Razor scrubbed a hand over his beard. "The extra money can go to the bakery. Show of hands. All in favor?"

All of them raised their hands.

"We do it then," Razor said. "And we keep a sharp eye out. I want these assholes taken down. They drew the blood of one of ours. They killed citizens here in Mercy. Our territory. *Our town*. No forgiveness."

Glancing around the table, Ryder didn't see any hesitation in any of their faces. It raised his spirits. Not only would they be doing something to help Emily, they'd be on the lookout for the fuckers who posed a threat to the entire town. Yeah, they'd drawn blood. *His* blood. They'd murdered three innocent people. And with any luck, the Hounds would get some payback.

For Clyde.

The fact that Clyde had been killed in all of this had dread pooling in the pit of his stomach. Because of Clyde, Margot wouldn't avoid this entire affair even if he asked her to. It put her in the line of fire.

Yes, Margot was a deputy sheriff in Mercy. She was trained, good at her job. She'd been his friend for many years now. But he would personally destroy anyone who touched a hair on her head. He'd fight *anyone* to keep her safe. Even her if he had to.

Ryder was proud of the way the Hounds handled the rest of the week, all the while balancing their own busy lives. Hell, they were still backed up at the garage, mostly due to his absence. Still, they found the time to get work done and manage many assignments in posting prospects and club members in strategic areas around town. By the weekend, they had a good system in place. The prospects were willing to do anything to earn a coveted space as a full member.

It wasn't all good though. The fire inspector determined the cause of the fire at *Whisk and Whimsy* to be faulty wiring and not arson. It was bullshit. No one else believed that. Emily told Snow the fire marshal came once a year to check everything, just as he did for Langer before she bought that portion of the building from him. He'd cleared the building back in February, only six months before. And *now* there was faulty wiring?

Beast and Crash were assigned to that part of town, and it made sense since they both worked in construction. Beast had combed every charred inch of the bakery, trying to find anything to prove the fire inspector wrong. So far nothing.

Hero told them they *wouldn't* find anything, and he was right. The Mafia fuckers knew exactly what they were doing. They had experience doing the worst things imaginable and making it look like an accident or freak occurrence.

And all the while, the Hounds kept watch. They'd struck twice. They'd do it again unless they were stopped. The MC's under-the-radar presence in Mercy wouldn't deter them much.

This time, the Hounds would be ready. Axel stayed with Sadie at the Austins' for the time being.

Two prospects were staying on the property each night with them in camping tents they set up.

It was too fucking bad Margot didn't see it that way. Late Saturday evening, Ryder stopped at the store, bought a six pack, and headed for her house. They hadn't talked a lot since the night he kissed her. Tonight was her last night of second shift. She was off Sunday and Monday, then she was back on day shift.

How would things be between them?

As he flipped through TV channels, he grinned. Would she want to talk about the kiss? Ryder hoped so, because he couldn't get it or her out of his head.

What made Margot different? What would a relationship with her be like? A *real* relationship. Worse yet, how would he ever convince her he was serious? Margot knew all the worst things about him.

Three beers in, Ryder fell asleep on the couch. He woke up when Margot made it in from her shift, his eyes slitting open but not finding her. After a moment, he heard her shuffling around in the kitchen. He thought she might go on to bed, but she returned to the living room, carrying one of his beer cans. Popping the top, she dropped onto the armchair next to the couch where he'd been sleeping.

Margot chugged half of the beer before slowly placing the can on the coffee table in front of her, looking like she was carrying the weight of the world. Had something else happened?

"I'm sorry," she said quietly. "I didn't mean to wake you."

Scrubbing his hands over his face, he sat up on the couch. At first, he didn't realize why she was looking so hard at him but then he realized it was because he'd peeled off his shirt before he fell asleep. Her gaze was fixed on the tattoo the Hound members bore, the face of a hound wreathed in flames above the words "Hounds of Hell MC," in black ink. Ryder had been falling-on-his-ass drunk the night Outcast started it, so he wasn't sure it had been his best decision to put it on his left pectoral, above his heart. At least Outcast did the damn thing and it was a fucking beautiful tattoo.

"Do all of you have to get that tattoo?" Margot pointing to it.

He nodded, hoping she liked what she saw. "It's an honor. You earn a membership in the MC and it's one of the first things you do."

"What happens if they kick you out?"

Ryder grinned. She didn't want to know the answer to that one. It looked like she'd had a bad enough day.

"How was *your* day?" Ryder asked.

Shaking her head, she dropped her gaze. "I've worked on the fire at Emily's bakery all week and I found nothing. I shouldn't even be talking to you about any of this. You can't say anything."

Using his index finger, he drew an X on his bare chest, right above his Hound tattoo and his heart.

"I talked to Emily about the fire and asked if she'd heard from her ex lately. I just wanted to see if she thought he could be behind it. But she doesn't think so. Considering she'd filed several complaints about him, I don't think she'd lie. You all think it's Bobby Bianchi and his men. What if that composed story was clouding her vision? It was worth a try. I went back to the station and did some digging. I was about to go talk to Ian Savage's father at the bank."

Her expression darkened. Ryder listened, letting her tell it her way.

"Imagine my surprise when I was told the police

had already spoken with him, before my shift started. Randy had fucking Dawson go around me."

Dawson was a useless prick. Always had been. He'd been a deputy for a few years and was one of those in law enforcement who gave the rest of them a bad name. The man was arrogant, all-knowing, and wouldn't give a pass to anyone. One of the prospects' girlfriends slid on the ice in her car back in January on her way to work. No other vehicles had been involved and she'd skated into a telephone pole and totaled her car. The fucker slapped her with a reckless driving charge. The judge threw it out in court, but it told him what type of man Dawson was.

And why had Sawyer gone around Margot and put Dawson on hunting down Emily's ex? Was it because they felt it best to keep Margot away because of her personal loss at the hands of Bianchi? Was it because Ryder was staying with her? Did they think he or the Hounds could change her opinion?

If so, Sawyer didn't know his newest deputy as well as he thought.

"Did Dawson find anything?" Ryder asked.

"Yeah." Margot's gaze was still on the beer can in her hand. "Ian Savage lives in Connecticut now. He was at a concert that night with his girlfriend and friends. The concert has been verified and they took pictures all night, posted on social media. Solid alibi. But it's a moot point because the fire inspector determined the cause of the fire at the bakery to be faulty wiring."

Ryder watched her sulk. "Do you agree with that?"

Her gaze locked with his. "No. Emily had the fire marshal inspect it a little over six months ago. He inspects her bakery each year. There have never been any concerns or suggestions noted in any of the reports. Not one. And it's hard for me to believe Emily Frost would be capable of overlooking anything."

Ryder completely agreed.

"It's not Ian Savage," she went on. "Which brings me back around to your theory."

It wasn't a fucking theory. Bianchi and his men were behind the fire.

"Why are you working so hard to prove it's *not* them?" Sitting forward, he planted his elbows on his knees.

"It's not that," she said slowly. "I understand why you're all up in arms about them. Sadie's your brother's girlfriend, not to mention they almost killed *you*."

"They also killed your father, Margot."

"Have you stopped to consider that if you continue with this plan someone else might end up hurt? Or killed?"

"From our point of view, if we leave it to the law, someone else *is* going to end up hurt or killed. All I'm saying is the law moves a little too slow for us."

"And the Hounds are going to do what, exactly?"

"Eliminate the problem," Ryder said. "These fuckers have terrorized Mercy, hurt and killed people we care about. Don't you want them to answer for that?"

"It doesn't matter what I want. The law matters. I'm asking you to let the law handle this. Okay?"

"Sure." Then something occurred to him. "Did Sawyer have you come talk to me?"

"No, he hasn't said anything. But it's only a matter of time before he sees the situation the way I do. And then he'll get involved."

"Not really seeing a reason to put the brakes on, Margot." Ryder was being honest. "The sheriff can get involved all he wants. He's never been able to stop us before and he's not going to be able to now."

He watched the color drain from her pretty face.

"Wait. Why would you think Randy would send me to talk to you about all this?"

He couldn't help grinning. "I'm staying at your place right now."

"It doesn't mean anything," Margot replied. "I'm letting you sleep on my couch so you're closer to work until you're fully recovered. That's all."

"We're *just* friends?" He didn't want to be just friends anymore. "That kiss wasn't so bad, was it?"

Ryder could have laughed at the face she pulled. "That's not what I wanted to talk to you about."

"Wasn't it?" Ryder stared her down.

"What are you doing? I'm not going to be like every other woman on the planet and have a fling with you. Just so we're on the same page."

No, she wasn't. Because she wasn't like any other woman on the planet, and he wanted much more than a fling.

"What makes you think I want a fling?"

"Because that's what you do." Margot looked more uncomfortable by the minute. Even though she was still stealing glimpses at his chest, his arms. "You hook up with a new girl and after a few weeks, you end it and move on. Sometimes after a night. I'm not going to be one of those women, Ryder."

"You never could be one of those women."

"Then why are you playing with me like this?" she asked, dead serious. "You and I both know we're never going to be more. And as you pointed out the other night, yes, I have -- have had -- feelings for you.

So doing what you're doing isn't nice, Ryder. No good can come from this. Me and you."

"How do you know that?"

"Because I want a *real* relationship with someone. And that's something you've never had. I'm not sure you would even know how."

Her words pissed him off but only because they were true. "Do *you*? You've had what? Two serious boyfriends. What happened?"

Margot was slightly stunned, struggling with an answer. "They didn't work out."

"That's right," Ryder said. "And that's the gamble you take on any relationship, isn't it? So why would it be so hard to give *me* a chance?"

He had her and he knew it.

"How would I even trust you? How do I know the minute you got bored with things you wouldn't be back to your old tricks with a different woman each week?"

"You trust me as a friend," Ryder pointed out.

"That's not the same thing."

"It *is* the same thing, Margot." Why was she fighting him on this?

Just as Margot was about to reply, Ryder's phone lit up and hummed on the coffee table in front of him. It was almost one in the morning, the call from Sadie. Ryder grabbed it and answered quickly.

"They're at the garage." Sadie's voice on the other end was filled with tears. "Axel ran right over."

"Call Jade," he said. "Have her get word to Hero and Razor."

"Okay," she said, and he ended the call.

"Fuck!" Grabbing his T-shirt from the end of the couch, he rushed to pull it on along with his boots.

Margot looked startled at his hurried

movements. "What's happening?"

"Something's going on at the garage," was all he said, and he was out the door. Margot ran out as his bike roared to life and he raced off.

Chapter Nine

Ryder

Reaching the garage in record time, Ryder was off the bike the minute he arrived at his co-owned shop. He saw no sign of the fuckers now. Just Hero and Axel's bikes. The two prospects assigned to keep an eye on the garage had hidden theirs.

On closer inspection, Ryder saw one of the side windows of the garage was smashed. The bright floodlight on that side of the building revealed that wasn't the full extent of the damage. He saw the cars parked on that side of the garage for repairs. Windshields and windows were smashed to hell, the roof and hood of Derrick Mottley's irreplaceable El Camino had been bashed in and the side of it was keyed. Almost every client car on that side of the garage was fucking damaged.

Scrubbing a hand over his face, Ryder marched in the direction of the garage and walked in, headed to the office. The lights were on.

Back in the office, he found Axel, Hero, and one of the prospects. Stinger was a skinny, tattoo-covered kid who wasn't twenty yet and played a hell of a game of pool. He looked scared shitless, dirty and shaking, where he stood. Ryder heard the roar of other motorcycles coming, the sirens of a squad car in the distance.

"Where's Chance?" Ryder asked.

Axel tipped his head in the direction of the road. "Took off after them."

The kid nodded, trying to put a brave face on it.

"What the fuck happened?"

"They fucking came out of nowhere." The kid's eyes were wide in alarm. "They jumped out and started smashing shit with metal baseball bats. They threw a fucking brick through the window." He pointed to the window at the side door. "We came out shooting. They started shooting back. Chance popped one of them in the leg."

"How many?" Hero asked.

"There was five." Stinger was struggling to breathe as he talked. "In two cars. One was a big black sedan, and the other was a dark SUV. They were all wearing ski masks."

"Chance was tailing them?" Axel asked.

"Yeah, he told me to stay and get the word out," the kid explained.

"They got most of our fucking customers' vehicles on this side." Ryder hooked his thumb in that direction. "What else did they get?"

"Not sure," Stinger muttered.

Ryder marched back out with Hero and Axel on his heels. Razor and Snow ran up as they walked out. Margot pulled up in her squad car then, killing the lights and sirens.

Axel recounted everything for their Prez and VP as Ryder watched Margot exit the car and head in their direction.

Razor took in the situation as Margot approached. She stopped to speak into the portable transceiver on her shoulder, requesting backup. Razor held up a hand to cut Ryder off before he said anything.

"Evening, Margot," Razor said.

Her dark-eyed gaze met Ryder's before returning to Razor. "What happened?"

Razor allowed Stinger to recount everything and while he talked, another sheriff's department car pulled up. Ryder half-expected it to be Sheriff Sawyer, but it was Dawson.

"Is everyone okay?" Margot asked them. But her gaze was on Stinger who stood shaking like a leaf.

"Everyone is okay," Axel told her.

Margot directed Dawson to survey the garage and the yard around it, to rope it off so they could gather evidence. While he did that, Margot approached Ryder. "Can I take a look inside the garage?"

Ryder followed her in. All the lights were already on as Margot took in the scene. "Did anyone move anything?"

"Don't think so. Stinger said they threw a brick in through the side door window."

She stopped and pinned him with the oddest look. Pulling latex gloves from a pouch at her belt, Margot had them on before she moved closer to where broken glass littered the concrete floor at the side door. Its window was a huge, jagged hole trimmed with shards of glass. The brick was a couple of feet away from the pool of broken glass, swallowed by shadows.

Carefully walking over the broken glass, Margot fished the brick off the floor. Spotting him out of the corner of her eye, she held up a hand. "Stay where you are."

Margot rose with the brick. Like a scene out of a movie, it had a white piece of paper held to it with rubber bands. Carefully, Margot pulled off the bands to see what message might be on that paper. And there was one. Her dark eyes scanned it before she held it up for Ryder to see.

"What's it say?" he asked.

Margot's gaze met his as Axel walked up and stopped behind him. Her voice was calm and professional when she said, "It says, talk to the feds and you're all dead."

Ryder and his twin exchanged a glance. They knew this was coming. Just because Bobby Fuckface was in prison now, it wouldn't stop his cohorts from continuing their terror campaign as punishment.

Ryder got it. The MC would do the same thing if they were worried someone was going to rat. These were warning signs. It was the sort of hit-and-run that was hard to do anything with and the fuckers knew it. The problem was, if the Hounds didn't put a stop to it soon, they *would* kill someone next.

More cops arrived. Ryder talked to his MC brothers while the police went over everything.

"Axel and I are staying," he told Razor, who nodded.

"Hero is staying too," Razor said. "We're meeting tomorrow morning about this shit. Eight sharp."

The ire in Razor's eyes mirrored what he felt. Ryder was sick of this shit.

These fuckers needed to be dealt with yesterday. Their prospects could have been killed. Chance was still out there chasing after them.

What a fucking night.

* * *

Margot

It was nearly five in the morning when she found herself sitting across from the sheriff at his desk. She was tired and her nerves were shot. Between the fire at Emily's bakery and the latest attack at Ryder's garage, Margot was growing more concerned by the day about the situation with Sadie's ex and his Mafia associates. They weren't going to stop until the situation was resolved. If the MC had their way, the resolution would be bloody and violent.

Finishing his phone call, the sheriff's gaze met hers. The sheriff was normally the epitome of calm and professional. But this morning, the deepened lines of his forehead gave away the fact that he was as anxious about the entire situation. Hell, he was just starting his day and hers was supposed to have ended a few hours ago.

Yet here they sat.

"What time did the attack at Three Guys happen?" he asked.

"I got home at quarter to one. I'd been sitting there talking to Ryder for a few minutes when he got the phone call about the incident."

"Who called?"

Margot didn't know exactly. She assumed it was his brother. "I didn't get a chance to ask."

Sawyer nodded. "The chances that these two events, tonight and the bakery fire, are linked to Bobby Bianchi are pretty strong. I don't need to tell you that."

"No, you don't."

"And it's going to be pretty damn hard to keep Razor and his Hounds out of this," Sawyer went on.

She knew that too. There was no chance they could keep them out of it. Most especially Axel and Ryder.

"But we're going to have to do our best," Sawyer said. "You're off today. I'll send Dawson back to the scene and see what he can find out."

Fuck. Of course she was off the day after this happened.

"I was hoping I wouldn't have to say anything, Donner." Randy's gaze locked with hers. "But I'm very concerned about the fact that Ryder is staying at your house."

That got her attention.

"Sir, I don't discuss our work with Ryder or anyone for that matter." That hadn't been a lie before tonight.

Holding up a hand to cut her off, he said, "I know."

"Then why are you bringing this up?"

"I'm just going to be blunt. It's no secret to anyone who's been in Mercy for any length of time that you've got a thing for Ryder. Always have."

Margot froze, listening.

"I'm not saying I think you'd consciously do anything to undermine this department or your position," he explained. "But I'm concerned that you will be put in a situation somewhere down the line that will put you in a compromising position."

Now she was pissed. "Excuse me?"

At least the sheriff looked a little contrite. "You're an outstanding deputy in this department, Donner. I'm just looking out for you and your future."

"If I were Dawson, would we be having this conversation?" she asked. "Yes, Ryder is staying at my place for a while. Until he gets back on his feet. Yes, in the past I had a thing for him. I've grown past it."

She really didn't appreciate the look her boss gave her.

"We're friends, sir." Her voice shook as she got the words out. "Not that that is anyone else's business."

"It *is* my business. One of my deputies has a close *friendship* with one of the Hounds."

Margot didn't like what he was insinuating.

"You're worried about how it looks? How it will play out for you? The election is next year," she pointed out, knowing she was going a little far.

His countenance never changed; he was still

infuriatingly calm.

"No, I'm worried about *you*." His gaze held hers. "I know how much this job means to you and how hard you've worked to be here."

The fact that he'd noticed took the edge off her ire.

"I've also been in law enforcement long enough to know how interpersonal relationships can cloud your mind," he said. "I want you to think carefully before you act on anything to do with this particular case. We're called upon to make quick decisions, ones that can have life and death consequences. I'm worried your friendship with Ryder and the Hounds might lead you to make the wrong call somewhere down the line. And it only takes one wrong call to end a career in law enforcement. Or to end someone's life. That's all I'm saying."

Margot didn't know if it was the fatigue or the constant worry about the situation developing between the Hounds and the Mafia and how it would affect their town, but she felt numb in that moment. Frozen. She knew what the sheriff was saying was correct.

Margot was too afraid that what he was concerned about would happen.

Chapter Ten

Ryder

Tensions were high around the table at the clubhouse the next morning. Ryder was the last one to arrive. It was ten past eight, but it was better than his normal arrival times for important meetings. Normally, the meeting would already be in progress.

But not today.

Snow smirked at him from where he sat to Razor's right. "You're early."

Ryder flipped him off, but it was lighthearted.

Their Prez shook his head. "And he's not hung over and smelling like cooch. That's something."

"Being Margot's housemate is working for you, brother," Axel said, smiling.

Ryder didn't miss the look Razor shot his twin for the remark. Did Razor have a problem with him staying with Margot? Half the MC assumed they were fucking.

"Let's get to business," Razor said, drawing everyone's attention. "These Mafia assholes are doubling down on us. The feds showed up to talk to Sadie and then Emily's bakery burned. Then they pulled the stunt last night at the garage and smashed the shit out of a bunch of their customers' vehicles."

"We let them keep coming," Hero said, "it's going to get worse."

"Anyone seen Chance?" Razor asked. "I'm going to beat his little ass for taking off like that. He checks in and I want to know about it ASAP."

No one had heard from Chance, and it had Ryder wondering what became of him. Had he found something? Had something happened to him?

Snow shook his head. "Stinger was pretty shaken

up."

"He handled it," Razor replied, pinning Ryder with a look. "It would have been so much better if we could have dealt with this Bianchi asshole without the police."

Axel dropped his gaze then. From what he'd told Ryder, the police were on the scene fast the day Bobby Bianchi had been taken in, leaving them no time to deal with things the way the MC wanted to. Axel had wanted to end the fucker that day.

But like the MC, the Mafia was a brotherhood. A slight to one was a slight to all. They would keep coming.

"Probably wouldn't matter," Ryder said. "Even if we'd managed to take him out ourselves, they'd still be coming after us. Might even be worse."

Axel's expression shifted and he nodded. Razor seemed to consider his words.

"But the fucker would be dead," Razor pointed out. "It would die down. Instead, he's alive and sitting pretty up in Bland right now, awaiting trial. Since the feds are involved, I can only guess that murdering three people here in Mercy is one of his *minor* offenses."

Ryder nodded. "We found a note strapped to the brick they threw into one of our windows. It said, 'Talk to the feds and you're all dead.'"

Razor's hard gaze met his. "Did it now?" Blowing out a sigh, the older man looked at each of them in turn. "We need to end this, and we need to end it meaningfully. I want these fuckers out of Mercy."

"What's the plan?" Snow asked. "We can't sit here and wait for them to hit us again."

Razor studied him for a moment, thinking. "No,

we can't." Then his steely-eyed gaze landed on Ryder. "We need to set up an ambush."

That got everyone's attention.

"What do you have in mind?" Ryder asked.

"Best way to shake a man down is by showing he can't protect what he loves." Razor looked at each of them in turn. "*Shame him.*"

It was true.

"They just burned down Emily's bakery. A fundraiser to raise money for the rebuild might grab their attention."

"A fundraiser?" Beast asked, beefy arms crossed over his chest.

Razor nodded. "We can put collection jars all over town. It sets the stage. We put up posters for a charity pool event, like the ones Stinger's always competing in. All proceeds go to restore the bakery. These jars and posters include the sweetest picture of Emily and Sadie, with Sadie being the organizer of the event."

"That's throwing down a challenge," Hero said.

"You want to use Sadie as bait?" Axel spoke loudly. "No. No fucking way."

"She's their primary target." Razor held up a hand before Axel could say more. "Hear me out."

They listened to their Prez explain how they could use the event to draw the fuckers in. Yes, they'd use Sadie and Emily as bait, which was a risk. But when he explained how the event would go, it had all of them fired up and ready. After the hell Bobby Bianchi and his men had put them through this summer, a plan to turn the tables on them was what all of them had been itching for. It would be dangerous, and blood would be spilled.

"Where we going to stage this?" Snow asked.

Razor considered that for a minute. "I was thinking *Sackett's* might work."

"*Sackett's?*" Hero asked. "Just one problem. Old man Phillips. He loves MCs about as much as he does hemorrhoids. He's never going to let us have it there."

"Big Billy's?" Beast offered.

Razor shook his head. "I know we're talking to the Cottonmouths about some gun-running business for extra money." "Not sure we need to get *that* involved with them. Maybe Jade can talk Emery into letting us use *Sackett's.*"

Hero's old lady, Jade, who also happened to be Razor's daughter, could be very persuasive. But Ryder wasn't sure Emery would agree to that. Even for Jade, whose grandmother Mina had been the older man's girlfriend for at least a decade.

"I'll make assignments," Razor said. "I'll also reach out to our Kentucky and North Carolina brothers and see if they want to come up and give us a hand."

Their Prez wasn't playing. Axel tensed up, silent at his side since Razor mentioned using his old lady as bait. But even he seemed a little geared up about the direction it was heading in.

Razor left all of them with a lot to think about with the promise that he'd be making assignments for the charity event by day's end. With that decided and a few other business items visited, the meeting was dismissed. Axel made a beeline for the exit and Ryder knew he was pissed. As everyone else started wandering out of the main room, Razor's gaze caught Ryder's. "Come talk to me for a minute."

He followed his Prez back to his office, taking a seat on the other side of Razor's desk. Ryder could guess what the man was going to say to him.

"You've been staying at Margot's place." Razor

cut to the chase.

There it was. "Is that a problem?"

The sound of the man's deep sigh told him he wouldn't like what was coming next.

"It could be," Razor told him. "I've never involved myself in your personal business. Hell, most of my life, I was just like you. I enjoyed pleasurable company, but I never got too involved except once... I went around with all types of women. But a cop? Never did one of those."

Ryder rolled his eyes. "We're not fucking." *Not yet anyway.*

"No, it's worse," Razor said. "I guess you think of her as a friend. You're a *lot* more than that to her. I think you know that."

Things were changing. But it was to his advantage to let Razor keep to his assumption for now.

"That close proximity might bite us in the ass," Razor explained. "She's still in that phase where she thinks the justice system works for everyone."

"You're worried about the charity event." It wasn't a question. "You're worried she's going to figure out what we're up to through me."

"You live in the same house," Razor pointed out. "Some distance would be helpful."

Ryder got what he was saying. "But if I stay with her," he countered, "I have an inside angle. It gives us a way to monitor to the law, make adjustments if we have to so we can keep them the fuck out."

His Prez nodded, conceding the point. But it wasn't over. There was something else.

"What?" Ryder asked.

"How long do you plan on staying?" Razor asked. "Not asking because of this situation. I'm asking because... Well, it's going to hurt her worse the longer you stay. You get that, right?"

He did. But hurting her wasn't what he wanted or intended. Leaving her wasn't what he wanted either. He realized over the past few weeks that he just wanted *her*.

"Give it some thought," Razor said.

As Ryder rose to leave the office and headed back to Margot's house, hoping she wasn't up yet, he realized he needed to decide what he was going to do. He knew what he wanted.

Yeah, Margot was a cop. She was way more than his friend now. Lately, she was the star of all the pornos that constantly played in his head.

Most important of all, his heart *craved* her.

The last thing Ryder wanted was to lose her. Worse, he was afraid he'd *hurt* her.

* * *

Margot

The sunlight lit up one edge of her blackout curtain, telling her it was morning. When she grabbed her phone off her bedside table, she squinted at the digital display to see it was almost eleven.

Fuck!

Yeah, she had the day off and last night had been challenging, but she never slept that late. After a quick trip to the bathroom, she pulled her hair back from her face with a scrunchie and stumbled to the kitchen to make coffee. She'd made it maybe halfway up the hallway when she smelled coffee and something else. Was that bacon?

Her stomach growled in hope.

It was a little bit of a shock to see Ryder tooling around in her kitchen. And he wasn't wearing a shirt. Margot paused, watching the rippling display of muscles as he worked, admiring his physique. So many tattoos and scars littered his skin. Three of those scars were from the bullet wounds but were almost healed now. Most of the older ones looked like old knife wounds, faded to thin, silvery lines.

What she wouldn't give to be able to trace each one with her fingers.

"Margot?"

Fuck, had he said something?

"What?" she asked, only feeling half-awake.

"I asked how you liked your eggs?" One-handed, Ryder cracked an egg and allowed its contents to slide into one of her metal bowls on the counter.

"Over easy," she said. The man was *cooking* for her. She got a show and a meal?

Ryder nodded, going back to his work. "How about your bacon?"

"Crispy, please."

"You and Axel," he said, cracking another egg into the bowl before he prepped his skillet. "He's the same way. Even though the minute you take a bite, it disintegrates."

"But it's good," she said, smiling.

Ryder stared at her for a moment. Why was he looking at her like that?

"I'll take your word for it," he said. "I prefer chewy bacon myself."

It was a nice day outside and the sound of birds calling in the yard made her happy. It gave her somewhere to focus her attention besides the handsome, shirtless biker making her breakfast.

"How is everything?" she asked. "Dealing with all the damage to those vehicles is going to suck."

Nodding, he went about his work at the stove. "Yeah, an insurance agent is coming in tomorrow morning. We'll see what he has to say. And dealing with the insurance company's one thing. Dealing with our customers whose vehicles were collateral damage is another."

Margot had to wonder what the MC would do now. She knew they wouldn't just stand down after everything Bianchi and his men had done to Mercy this summer. The Hounds wouldn't ignore the burning of *Whisk and Whimsy* any more than they were going to tolerate the vandalism at *Three Guys Garage*. The plans they might be making for their next hit filled Margot with dread.

But on the heels of this morning's conversation with the sheriff, Margot wanted to forget about all of it. At least for a moment. After all, she'd never had a man cook for her before. And it was Ryder. That deserved some attention.

In a matter of minutes, he sat across from her at her kitchen table, still shirtless. Her over easy eggs were perfect; the bacon was too. Her toast was just the way she liked it. What was he up to? "Thank you for breakfast," Margot said. "It's really good."

That saucy smile again. "Well, I'm glad you like it." Gnawing thoughtfully on a chewy strip of bacon he'd cooked for himself, Ryder studied her. "You're off today."

It wasn't a question. "I am."

"Any plans?"

"Catch up around the house," she said. "Do some laundry."

"I did the shopping," Ryder told her. "I think we'll hold until next weekend anyway."

Margot couldn't take it anymore. "What do you *want*?" She grinned at him. "For the shopping and breakfast?"

"I'd tell you, but you'd probably throw me out," Ryder said with a shit-eating grin.

Her heart skipped a beat and the rest of her interpreted that statement exactly the way it wanted to. Her breath came faster.

"You don't owe me anything for taking care of you." She wanted him to know it. "Or for letting you couch surf here until you feel better." But then, he didn't appear to be struggling physically. He shifted in his seat less these days and the old swagger was back in his walk. Ryder seemed his normal self again. Especially if the little flirty glances and that killer grin were any indication.

He'd just never unleashed them on her before. Something was up.

"You're not trying to distract me for some reason, are you? Keep the deputy busy while the Hounds are out doing God only knows what?"

Ryder laughed. "I get why you think that. Hell, Razor and the guys think --"

He caught himself before he could say anything else. Margot stared at him. "They think *what*?"

Ryder pinned her with an assessing gaze before he said, "They think I'm staying here because we're fucking."

It was Margot's turn to laugh. "Right."

She'd almost finished her eggs when she noticed he was quiet. And he wasn't laughing. His expression was dead serious.

"What's so hard to believe about that?" he asked.

Margot shook her head. "If I were the last woman on earth. *Maybe*."

The intensity of his gaze didn't dim at her words, nor did he look away awkwardly. He was laser-focused on her.

"Why do you say things like that?" Ryder asked. "You act like it's impossible for anyone to find you attractive, Margot. You act like it's impossible for *me* to find you attractive."

He didn't just say what she thought he said, right?

"Ryder, we both know you don't find me attractive like *that*." She needed to change the subject. Her anxiety was rising, and her heart felt like it would beat its way out of her chest. "Stop it."

"What if I don't want to?"

The intensity of his gaze forced hers to the nearly empty plate on the table in front of her. "Please stop this."

"But I mean it," Ryder said.

Her gaze flew back to his, looking for the lie in his expression. The punch line. Because she knew it was there somewhere. "You might think you do," Margot said. "Out of some subconscious, misguided need to repay me? Because you're bored and I'm here? Only you can answer that. But I'm not about to throw away my friendship with you for whatever you're thinking is going to happen here. It's not happening."

"Can you look me in the eye and tell me you just want to be my friend?" Ryder stared her down.

Not without lying. And Margot had always been a terrible liar.

A subtle shift in Ryder's expression told her he could see right through her.

Nerves got the better of her. Margot rose awkwardly from her seat and kept her gaze on her plate. "I'm going to get a shower."

Picking up her coffee cup, she took it with her as she fled the room, hating that he'd made her a coward in her own home.

Chapter Eleven

Ryder

Monitoring his texts, Ryder kept busy while Margot tried to avoid him.

It bothered him ever since he'd been staying there that she didn't have a deadbolt on her door. She was a deputy sheriff for fuck's sake. That would put a target on her head all by itself.

Ryder stopped by the garage after the meeting, picking up the tools he'd need to install the deadbolt he bought at the hardware store. He grinned, knowing that the sound of the drill and other noises he'd be making while installing the safety measure would get her attention.

He was halfway done when he heard her heavy tread approaching. She walked on her heels when she was pissed off. It was like she wanted whoever she was pissed at to know she was coming to raise hell. And he liked her mad.

"What are you doing?" She used the terse little tone she used on the job sometimes.

"Installing a deadbolt," Ryder replied without pausing in his work.

Ryder caught sight of her out of the corner of his eye. He wanted to laugh at the way she blew out a frustrated breath and folded her arms across her chest.

"You could ask."

"Ask what?"

"If I wanted a deadbolt since it's my house instead of just fucking doing it," Margot grumbled.

Ryder knew.

"You've got to knock this off." Margot sounded a little more reasonable. "It's not winning you any points. I can take care of myself, Ryder. I've been doing it for a long time."

He kept on the task, just listening.

"What's gotten into you?" She was frustrated, moving closer. "I don't know what you think you're doing, but I'm not changing my mind."

"About what?" He continued working.

Margot hated gaps in conversations. He was using that because if she kept talking, maybe he'd learn something.

"Seriously, are you a diversion of some kind for whatever the Hounds are up to?" Margot asked.

"No," was all he said. Okay, he was lying a little bit. But once they got into making all the preparations for the charity event, he would tell her as much as he could under the circumstances.

"Then why are you doing all of this?" There was a note of desperation in her voice. "I'm just trying to understand."

On a sigh, Ryder stopped, turning to face her. "I don't want to be just your friend anymore, Margot." Ryder met her gaze squarely. "I think you and me could be good together, despite the fact we trade on different sides of the law."

He didn't think she realized her jaw had dropped a little as he just stared her down. It didn't take her long to get herself together though. "For how long? Do I get the standard week or two?"

With a screwdriver still in his hand, Ryder put his hands on his hips. He wasn't backing down. "It's not like that. I know my past with women better than anyone, including you. It is what it is. I didn't promise any of them anything beyond what they got. If they had a good time along the way? Cool. But all of them knew what they were getting into, Margot. I don't lead anyone on."

Margot waited, trying to keep that false bravado going. The trouble was he knew her as well as she knew him. He didn't like the cracks around the facade. He couldn't fight the feeling that if he said the wrong thing he'd break her. It was the last thing he wanted. Making himself go slow, Ryder considered his words carefully.

"I'm going to have a hell of a time convincing you of this, but that's not what I want with you. I want to have a chance at something special."

When she didn't say anything, he went back to working on the door. He'd let her take her time, wrap her mind around everything.

"What changed?"

"What do you mean?"

"I didn't change, Ryder," Margot said. "Not that I'm aware of. The only conclusion I can reach is that I took care of you after you were shot, and you feel a need to --"

"Don't psychoanalyze me," he warned, turning and throwing the screwdriver into the toolbox at his feet with force. "I know what I'm after. And I'm not playing."

Marching up to her, Ryder got in her face. Margot did what he expected and held her ground, but he hoped the slight tremble wasn't from fear.

"You don't want this?" he asked. "Now's the fucking time to say it. Tell me you don't want me and to fuck off and I will."

All the fight bled out of her at that point as she gazed up at him. So many emotions swirled in those warm, chocolate brown eyes. Need? Love? Fear?

"I... I'm afraid, Ryder," she admitted, taking a small step back.

Ryder took another step closer. "I'm afraid too.

You're the best friend I've got outside of the MC."

"If this goes wrong," Margot whispered, "we can't go back. We can't come back to this friendship. You know that, right?"

Ryder did. It was a huge gamble. But one his heart demanded. "What's it going to be? You willing to give me a try? Or you want me to move on out of here?"

"My boss would love that," she said, holding his gaze.

Sawyer had brought it up to her, huh? "So would my MC," Ryder said. "But right now, I really don't give a fuck what they think, Margot. It just matters what we think. Me and you. So, tell me. What's it going to be?"

He'd never seen her look so emotionally defenseless. He couldn't breathe, standing there so close to her, waiting for her to make a move. Would she reject him?

Her trembling hand moved slowly, so slowly, to press over his heart. Her touch on the bare skin of his chest had him closing his eyes. He wanted that small gesture to burn into his memory. He wanted to keep it to revisit it whenever he needed to smile, to feel good about life.

The hope in her gaze had his heart shifting in his chest. It wasn't going to be easy, and she'd doubt him for a while. But it would be worth it. Margot was worth everything.

Ryder covered her hand with his own, holding it in place. "This isn't going to be a picnic for you at first," he said softly. "But please just give me a chance." It wasn't just her job on the line if it all went to shit. Somehow, he didn't think that would be the outcome. He was surprised when she took another step back. He moved closer, until her back met the wall. Now that he had her right where he wanted her, Ryder cradled her face carefully in his hands, his lips meeting hers with a soft entreaty. He kept his movements slow, gentle. His Margot wasn't just a rough tumble here and there. She was so much more than that to him.

Margot surrendered to that simple kiss, and he didn't need more encouragement than that. He deepened this kiss, crowding her against the wall as his lips danced with hers.

And there it was. The way she tasted, the way she shook in anticipation in his arms, pushed his need higher. Ryder reveled in wanting to kiss a woman sober, no fumbling drunk in the shadows. They were pressing into one another on a Sunday afternoon with the sun lighting up the room around them. He loved the way she fit right against him, the way her hands smoothed up his chest to wind around his neck and pull him closer.

Pressing her back into the wall, he trapped her between it and him. Sliding a thigh between hers, he nudged gently against her. If she thought he was moving too fast, he'd put the brakes on even if he didn't want to. But the way her muscular thighs tightened around his had him thinking she wanted him too. Ryder held her closer, enjoying the kiss.

When Ryder broke that kiss, his lips trailed across her face to her neck. She gasped when he nipped at the lobe of her ear with his teeth. When he went to work on the tender flesh at her throat, her thighs were squeezing him, demanding more.

"Ryder?" her voice was breathy, sensual. "Want to go to my room?"

"Thought you'd never ask," he said with a grin.

* * *

Margot

Margot felt lost in a dream. Ryder swept her into his arms, working hard at kissing her while he guided her back through the hallway to her bedroom.

And of course, once she finally got him in her bedroom, it was as much of a mess as her life right now. Normally her bed was made, her clothes weren't strewn all over the floor. If she'd known... Who was she kidding? She'd never expected to be in her bedroom with Ryder. Ever. When her legs met the edge of the bed, Ryder pushed her back, sent her sprawling onto the mattress. Then he was stalking her up the bed while she scrambled backward toward the headboard.

With a laugh, Ryder grabbed one of her ankles and yanked her playfully back in his direction. When she was flat on her back with the sexy-as-sin biker who'd starred in all her late-night X-rated dreams hovering over her, her heart pounded like it would explode any minute.

"I can't believe this is happening." She said the thought out loud.

Ryder stole a kiss from her as he dropped some of his weight on her. Margot wound her limbs around him as he proceeded to kiss her senseless, taking his time. He wasn't busy trying to peel her clothes off. No, he was chaining heated kisses over her throat, up the sensitive hollow just below her ear.

"You've been all I could think about," Ryder whispered in her ear.

When his lips returned to hers, she didn't miss the opportunity to slide her hands up into the thick locks of his hair. Unlike his twin, Ryder wore his hair short, always wore that sexy stubble of a beard. What would that feel like against her skin?

Carefully, he removed the plastic clip holding her hair up, tossing it aside. Ryder broke the kiss long enough to get his fingers into the thick mass of her hair, spreading it around her head. His gaze was almost reverent as he took her in.

"Why don't you ever wear your hair down?" he asked while she lay panting beneath him.

That he'd noticed took her completely off guard.

"Your hair is beautiful," Ryder said, gazing into her eyes now. "*You* are beautiful."

Another kiss, and damn could he kiss. Their hearts were beating together as they clung to each other. Lost as she was lying in her bed with the man she always wanted and never expected to get, she had one last rational thought.

"I've seen the girls you've gone around with," she said. "None of them look like me."

Ryder smiled. "I noticed that too. And I never wanted anything lasting with any of them. I'm thinking there was a reason for that now."

He dropped kisses over her face, down her neck. She barely noticed that he'd grabbed the hem of her T-shirt until he was roughly pulling it over her head. Then heated kisses rained over her chest and shoulders, every uncovered inch of her skin, until she was squirming in need, wanting him so badly. Her nipples were tight, burning points. The throbbing in her clit only gained in intensity.

When his hand slid under her, she arched her back to give him access to the hooks of her bra. Ryder peeled it away, and the fear he'd find her lacking had her frozen beneath him.

Ryder didn't give her time to think about anything else. One of his rough hands palmed her breast and she gasped. When his lips covered the center of her other breast, she thought she'd lose her mind. Her hands clutched in his hair as he teased her breasts mercilessly. He had her writhing mindlessly beneath him, and he'd just gotten started.

"You like that?" The beautiful bastard grinned at her as he moved down her body. Faster than she could process, he'd yanked her comfy sweatpants and panties down and off, leaving her bared to him completely. His gaze darkened as it roamed over every inch of her.

"Look at you." His head dipped to plant a hot kiss on her upper thigh. "Your body is…"

Margot's hands flew to cover her face. Depending on what he said, she could melt or shatter into a million pieces of humiliation. When she thought about some of the flashy women he'd gone around with…

"Stop," he said, moving back up to pull her hands away from her face. Those steely-blue eyes were lit up with sincerity as he got nose to nose with her. "You're gorgeous. All of you. I should have known." He claimed her mouth with a long slow kiss, burning down her insecurities.

As soon as he released her, she realized that she couldn't keep the tears from sliding out of the corners of her eyes. Tears that blended fear and insecurity with gratitude and relief.

"Hey," Ryder said, brushing away one of her tears with a thumb as one hand cradled her face. "You're beautiful, Margot. You always have been."

Sniffling, she tried to halt the tears, but they choked her voice. "I'm not, Ryder. I don't look like the women you've been with over the years. All dressed up and gorgeous…"

"Were they?" Ryder was so still above her. "I don't remember a lot of them, to be honest. They were warm bodies to ground me after a night of drinking and fighting. Pleasurable company, I guess. The reason they came and went from my life was their convenience. I'd wake up next to any of them the next morning, beat up and hung over. And some of them were okay in the light of day. A lot of them were all paint and hair extensions and fancy clothes. Most of them were actually pretty average."

Ryder's honesty about his womanizing ways had her heart squeezing in her chest.

"You're different," he whispered, pressing a kiss to the tip of her nose. "You've never worn a lot of makeup and that makes me happy because I love all those freckles." He pressed another kiss to her cheek. "You are who you are. In your uniform. In your sneakers and jeans. And I figured you had to have a nice body under there, but damn..."

"I'm... muscular," Margot said awkwardly.

"You are," Ryder said, trailing a careful hand over her breast, down over her tummy. His careful touch left gooseflesh in its wake and she shivered. "But I think you're badass."

He drugged her with more kisses, sweet and slow until the trembling stopped. The care he took pushed most of her insecurities to the back of her mind as his lips blazed a trail over her chin, down her neck, and back to her breasts. Her hands clutched at the bedding beneath her as she watched him chain kisses over her tummy, stopping when he reached the apex of her thighs.

Margot knew she was staring hard at him. She couldn't help it. It was better than every porno her mind had ever conjured about him. When his rough hands slid over her thighs, she shivered. When he pushed her thighs open, all of her was revealed to him. His kisses felt like warm rain, slowly moving closer to her wet, aching center.

Now her thighs were trembling, just as he pressed a light kiss over her neatly trimmed pussy. That blue-eyed gaze locked with hers and a smirk played around his lips. "You've had this before, right?"

Margot scoffed. "I have."

"You have?"

She wasn't sure she appreciated what he was insinuating. "I don't have the body count I'm sure you do," she said, and chuckled nervously. "But I'm not a virgin either, Ryder."

"Any of them any good at eating you out?" he asked, his finger sliding between her pussy lips to tease her clit delicately.

She didn't want to know what color she was turning at that. Worse, how did she even answer?

Ryder interpreted her lack of response the way he wanted to. "Then get ready for me to rock your world."

Margot rolled her eyes at him, wanting to come across as playful.

But he wasn't playing when he went down on her. He'd been closer than he realized when asking about her experience. She was prepared to awkwardly endure it as she had the few times someone had tried to do that for her.

But Ryder made good on his promise. He easily held her in place on the bed, his muscular arms wrapped around her thighs. The view of his head between her thighs was surreal. When he got started, all thoughts went out of her head. As he took her apart with his lips and tongue, Margot pawed at the bedding, his head. She moaned and begged with no idea what she was pleading for. Ryder had her dancing on the tip of his tongue, leaving her a writhing mess in his thrall.

Margot may not have been a virgin, but she'd never orgasmed unless she was alone. When release slammed through her, she didn't expect it, gasping like a drowning woman on her own bed. And he didn't let up. Ryder doubled down before the spasm of that release faded, pushing her off the ledge a second time while her hands gripped his hair desperately.

Swiping at his mouth with the back of his hand, Ryder's smirk was unapologetically cocky. Pride lit up his eyes as he took in the wreck he'd made of her. Margot was just struggling to catch her breath, feeling as if she'd been struck by lightning.

"Not bad, huh?" he asked, moving back up to her on the bed.

Margot grinned at him, shaking her head. "Not sure... I want to think about how... you got those skills."

"Never been more grateful for them," he said, kissing her with her own juices shining on his lips, on the sexy stubble he wore. He deepened the kiss, giving her a taste of her own excitement. They wound around each other, rolling until Ryder was flat on his back and she was hovering over him. When she ended the kiss to breathe, Ryder got his hands on her breasts, giving them a playful squeeze. "Want to take me for a ride, Sheriff?"

Damn, he looked so good beneath her, and she took a moment to smooth her hands over his scarred, muscular chest. She knew what he wanted. His heated length beneath his jeans nudged up into her aching flesh. Her hands flew to the button of his jeans, popping it and yanking down the zipper. In a rush, she was shoving his jeans down over his slim hips and he was quick to help her. He wore nothing underneath.

As she pulled the denim free of him, he took himself in hand. Quick strokes of his hand showed off his cock, swollen and red. He caught Margot staring at it, needing that.

"Hop on," he said with a wink.

He didn't need to tell her twice. Lining him up with her aching pussy, Margot carefully slid down on him, taking him slow and enjoying the burn as he split her open. It had been a while since she'd been with anyone. But this wasn't just anyone. This was Ryder and a situation she never expected to be in. What if she never got another chance?

His hands gripped her hips, urging her to move faster but she wasn't going to be rushed. Not right now. She was enjoying the moment, wanting to burn it into her memory. Planting her hands on the warm wall of his chest, Margot slid down until she'd completely taken him in. Her inner walls squeezed him, appreciating how he filled her.

"Darlin', you've gotta move." There was a hint of desperation in his expression. "Or I'm going to lose my mind here."

Happy to oblige, Margot began fucking him, moving with ease up and down that heated flesh. She loved the way he hit so many sensitive spaces inside her. She loved the way his mouth fell open as he watched her, trying to guide her movements with his hands. To rush her. Margot kept her own pace, gasping as she used him to fill herself again and again. Her thighs burned as she moved on him and it felt so good, making her shiver with how he felt inside her, how he looked beneath her.

"Love the way you're taking me," he said with something like reverence as she rode him. And the sincerity in his eyes had her heart swelling as her movements sped up. "Need you to come for me."

When his fingers slid between their bodies, teasing her clit as she fucked him, Margot cried out. Sensation coursed through her veins like electrical current as she moved faster, harder. Ryder's hips were bucking up under her, moving with her until she came, screaming. Her vision blacked out around the edges as he continued pumping his cock up into her, drawing out the orgasm until she couldn't stay upright.

When she was about to collapse, Ryder took over. Rolling her under him, he began fucking her hard. Chasing his own release, Ryder moved in a frenzy. All she could do was hang on with her legs wrapped tightly around his waist, her hands skimming over the slick, warm flesh of his back. His thrusts brought the slightest sting of pain as he came, growling as he pulled free of her body, allowing his release to spurt over her tummy and thighs. Watching him work himself over her, lost in sensation, had her heart flying. She wished the moment never had to end.

Ryder collapsed on the bed next to her, his breathing a rough chorus with her own. He patted his chest with a hand, and she took the hint, curling into his side and laying her head on his chest. The drum of his heart in her ear was a comforting sound as he held her there.

"Why haven't we done that before?" he asked breathlessly. Then he laughed. "Don't answer that."

That had her giggling too. Because yeah, she'd just give him shit if she did answer.

"I'm so glad we did though," he said after a moment. "I love the way you feel, Margot. I love how easy it is to be with you."

Nothing he could say could diminish her happiness in that moment. Her mind recorded that last remark, and she knew it would haunt her in the days to come, fueled by her insecurities. But for now, she was happy, held in the arms of the man she'd always been in love with.

Chapter Twelve

Margot

Ryder kissed the breath out of her the minute she made it through her own front door. The door was slammed, and she was pushed back into the wall. When he finally let her up for air, she had to smile.

"I can't right now." Playfully he held her in place, nibbling at her earlobe. It had taken him exactly three days to hunt down all her weaknesses and use them against her.

"Why?" His heated breath pelted her neck.

"Self-defense class," she whispered, momentarily forgetting why it was important.

But as Ryder attempted to burn her down, logic broke in. People paid her for the classes. And Sadie…

"I can't." Margot gently pushed him away. "I have half an hour to change, get there, and set up."

"I don't need much time," he said. "Just need you."

He tried to navigate her uniform, her utility belt. After a moment, he gave up and laughed. "You needed to change clothes, right?"

"Is this Ryder Harper, famous ladies' man, admitting he finally found a woman he can't undress?" Margot couldn't keep a straight face.

"Fuck you," he said, grinning.

"If you can get a move on, maybe." Margot winked at him.

What she didn't expect was for Ryder to sling her over his shoulder and race back to her bedroom. The world spun for her, and she half expected him to sling her across her own bed. Carefully, he lowered her to her feet instead, taking a seat on the edge of the bed.

"Strip." Ryder pulled off the T-shirt he wore,

showing off his powerful upper body.

Margot shook her head. "There is nothing sexy about stripping off my uniform and gear, Ryder."

She didn't realize how efficient she was at disrobing until then, with his heated gaze on every move she made. She made quick work of stripping down to her bra and panties. And at least today she'd had the foresight to wear a nicer set in black. She was about to say something clever when he impatiently got off the bed, pinning her to the wall. His hands and mouth were everywhere, working her into a frenzy.

With an ease she didn't expect, he gripped her ass and pushed her up the wall, making her wrap her arms and legs around him. His lips burned paths into her neck and chest. The hard length of him straining the front of his jeans nudged up into her until he couldn't take it anymore. The sound of a zipper sent pulses of excitement running through her. Pulling her panties to the side in his impatience, he pressed himself to her entrance and started pushing in.

The frenzy and desperation of it had her trembling in his arms. As soon as he slid home, he started fucking her into the wall with everything he had. His mouth claimed hers as his cock powered into her and all she could do was hang on as they worked together in the quiet of her bedroom, the slapping of flesh and their labored breaths an obscene chorus. She was right on the edge when she decided to help herself along, sliding one hand down to work her clit. Ryder broke their kiss, his gaze darting to the movement of her hand.

"Oh, fuck, yeah." Ryder struggled to breathe. "Come for me, darlin'. I'm not going to last long with you doing that. Need you to come."

When he shifted the angle of his thrusts, he hit a

space that lit her up. Then he kept hitting the mark, the sensation combined with the efforts of her fingers to push her off the ledge. Margot screamed as she came, barely aware Ryder was thrusting into her with abandon as he came too, growling as he thrust one last time and held.

After the fury of their coupling, he stilled, kissed her tenderly. For a long moment, he held her like he didn't want the moment to end any more than she did.

Blowing out a sigh, he said, "This is a shit time to be asking this but…"

Margot laughed. "We're covered. I got an IUD a couple of years ago."

When her gaze met his, she didn't find the relief she expected to find in that moment. He kissed her forehead before carefully pulling free of her and helping her to stand. "So, self-defense class?"

"If I can still walk to get there," she chided him. Stretching up to kiss him, she dashed to her dresser to pull out what she'd wear to her class. A glance at her watch showed she had fifteen minutes left to get to class. Their tryst had still been totally worth it.

"Want me to make dinner?" Ryder sprawled across her bed with just his jeans on. If only she didn't have her class…

"Yeah." She liked this. Incredible sex *and* he was willing to cook? "That would be nice. I'll be home by eight."

"Late dinner," Ryder said. "I'll whip something up."

She didn't have time to get into a conversation at the moment, but she was surprised he was in such a good mood. Everything at the garage was such a mess right now between cleanup, meeting with clients about how their vehicles had been vandalized while waiting for repairs, and the pervasive threat from Bianchi and his men.

As soon as she was dressed, she found him and stole another kiss, grinning because she could. Ryder smiled back, letting her take anything she wanted as she finally pulled herself together enough to get out the door.

Something felt off. Margot made a mental note of it. With ten minutes to go, she was going to be late now for sure.

* * *

"I'm sorry I'm late," Margot called out to her class as she marched in.

Doing a head count, she realized all seven students were there. No. *Eight*. One young woman had her back to Margot, busy stuffing something in a tote bag at the back of the room. When she straightened and stopped next to Sadie, Margot smiled. It was Jade Dock.

"Jade, will you be joining us tonight?" Margot asked.

The pretty brunette smiled and nodded. She and Hero had been an item since not too long after Jade's grandmother passed last year. It was no secret Mina never approved of motorcycle clubs. After she died, it made waves when word got out that her granddaughter's father was none other than Razor himself, president of the Hounds of Hell. She didn't know Jade's reason for signing up, but Margot would take it. Maybe Sadie had even liked her class enough to recommend it.

"Let's get started," Margot said, leading them through warm-ups before getting into this week's defense maneuvers.

When it came time to find a partner, normally

Margot was Sadie's, and over the last few weeks, the redhead became less timid. Sadie had even gotten to the point where she didn't mind being at the front of the class, letting Margot use her as an example.

"Tonight, we're talking about what to do if someone grabs you by the hair," Margot explained. "Sadie, would you be willing to help me with this one?"

Sadie nodded. It had become her habit to pull her thick red curls back into a ponytail for class each week. When she looked ready to pull the band from her hair, Margot said, "Leave it."

Sadie walked up to the front of the class to stand with Margot, looking ready. Looking stronger. Margot explained when someone grabbed a person's hair, the way to make it less painful and to keep from having their hair ripped out was to gain control of the attacker's arm. The idea was to pull their hand and arm *closer*, not try to pull away. She first demonstrated the technique by grabbing the hair at the top of Sadie's head. Then she demonstrated what to do if someone grabbed a person's ponytail.

After demonstrating how to manipulate the attacker's arm in a way to make them let go or experience pain themselves, she asked Sadie to try it on her. Sadie grabbed Margot's hair, working against her to try and maintain her grip. Sadie was a quick study, eager to learn. It made Margot so proud to see her taking back her own power after what she'd been through at the hands of her sadistic ex.

When Margot urged everyone to pair up, Sadie ran back to partner with Jade and the two of them enthusiastically went at it. Margot went around the room, assessing each pair of women to make adjustments and offer suggestions. They were all doing a great job and getting better by the week. For her first time teaching self-defense to women, well, it exceeded Margot's expectations.

When class ended, Sadie and Jade waited until the other students left. Margot smiled as they approached her.

"Thank you for letting me join in," Jade said. "I'd like to officially sign up, pay for my first month."

"Glad to have you." Margot pulled signup forms from her bag.

As Jade filled out her paperwork, Sadie looked to Margot expectantly. "Will we see you next Saturday night for the pool tournament?"

Margot paused. "What pool tournament?"

Sadie and Jade exchanged a look. What was this?

With a sigh, Jade paused in filling out her form and walked over to the tote bag she left in the back of the classroom. Pulling a paper from it, she walked back to Margot and handed her a flyer.

"You're going to see it anyway," Jade added.

The flyer announced a pool tournament being held next Saturday night at *Sackett's*. It was sponsored by the Hounds of Hell and *Three Guys Garage*. The proceeds were going to the rebuilding fund for *Whisk and Whimsy*, Emily's bakery. Toward the bottom was a photo of Emily and Sadie, arm in arm, smiling for the camera. It listed prices for tickets, enticements like door prize drawings, and special prices on refreshments.

At the very bottom, if someone had questions, they could reach Sadie Downing, the coordinator, via email and phone. It also clearly stated attendance was RSVP only. *Interesting.*

Now she knew why Ryder had been acting funny when she got home today. This was some sort of plan by the Hounds to take action against the men who'd been attacking Mercy. Were Jade and Sadie aware? Or did they think it was a real event?

Margot made note of the way Sadie twisted her hands in front of her. The way Jade hadn't yet gone back to finishing her signup for class. She made eye contact with each of them.

"What is this?" Margot asked. "I'll support any event to raise money for Emily's bakery or anything to help our citizens out. You know that."

Another guilty look passed between the two women.

"But this? It feels like there's something more to it." Margot folded the form and slipped it into her own bag.

Sadie looked scared but she was still holding her own. Jade's back straightened. One more glance at Sadie, and Jade's mind was made up about whatever she was going to say.

"There *is* more to this," Jade said. "We can't wait for these men to cause more trouble, more damage. We have to do something about it before more people get seriously hurt or killed."

"And I'm not supposed to know because of my job, right?"

"Razor thought it would be a good idea for you know as little as possible because he knows Sheriff Sawyer is watching us." Jade held her gaze, not holding back. "Ryder said you'd figure it out. I take it he hasn't talked to you about it yet."

Margot shook her head. "What does Razor not want me to find out?"

Jade shrugged her shoulder. "Aren't you with Ryder now?"

"Who thinks I am?"

"All of us," Jade replied.

Sadie grinned. "We all kind of knew but…"

Ryder had told the MC they were together. Now that she and Ryder had taken their relationship to another level, what did it mean? Were they friends with benefits? Were they more? Was the club pissed at him being with a cop?

How would it affect *her* job when the sheriff found out?

Hell, she'd been so blinded by all the sex and bliss the last few days those questions hadn't really occurred to her until now.

"I can see why Razor thinks it's a bad idea for me to know," Margot said.

"No disrespect to the sheriff or you," Jade said. "But I hope you understand why this needs to happen. We need to run these men out of Mercy for good."

"And you don't think the law can accomplish that?"

"The law can't do a lot until something happens," Sadie spoke up. "This is proactive."

"Right. They're coming back." Jade folded her arms across her chest. "This is concerned citizens doing something about it."

It wasn't going to be that easy. Margot had so many questions. "Is that why Sadie's in the picture? Her email and phone number are on the flyer?" Margot's gaze shifted to Sadie. "You're bait."

Sadie nodded. "The number is for a burner phone, but yeah."

"And you're okay with all this?" she asked Sadie, a little pissed the MC would even consider using her like that.

"I agreed to it," Sadie said after a moment.

"Why?"

"I'm tired of being afraid. I've spent most of my life either being rejected or abused by those who are supposed to love me. I can't run for the rest of my life. I'm not defenseless. I finally figured that out thanks to your lessons."

Margot was proud. Maybe she wasn't happy with this particular situation. But the determination in the younger woman's face? It had her heart swelling with pride in her chest.

"I understand," Margot said. "But you also don't have to be used as bait to draw these people out. They're Mafia. They're dangerous."

"So are the Hounds," Jade told her.

Margot shook her head. "Now that I'm aware of this, what am I supposed to do? The right thing to do is to let my boss know, to have the sheriff try to reason with Razor and the rest of them."

"The rest of *us*," Jade said.

It took her off guard. Jade's grandmother had been anti *anything* to do with MCs, just like her boyfriend Emery Phillips who owned *Sackett's*. Was Emery in on it? And was he okay with letting them do this at *Sackett's*?

Now Jade was involved, dating Hero. Her father was the president of the MC. Margot understood her. Sadie? She understood her reasons too. Sadie blamed herself for everything that had happened in Mercy, including the murder of Margot's father. None of it was *her* fault but Margot got why she felt she needed to make amends in some way.

And yet, here she was, so bravely putting herself out there to force a confrontation that could put people in danger. Most especially herself. Margot had to try and cut this off.

"This is going to be a public event?" Margot

asked. "I noticed your RSVP requirement."

"It is," Jade replied. "With a very exclusive guest list."

Meaning it would appear to be a public event. But everyone attending would understand what it really was. A trap for Bianchi's men. *Jesus*. What were they planning?

Margot's anxiety was rising. "Why are you two telling me this? Why aren't you leaving it to Ryder? You know the position I'm in."

"Yeah, we do." Jade looked unfazed. "You're a deputy. But if it's true you're with Ryder, then you're also one of us, right?"

Her words hit her hard. *Hard.* Margot had worked so diligently to carefully define herself. She was an instrument of the law. A teacher. A good friend.

It had been a while since she'd been in a relationship, and unlike many other women, she didn't define herself by her relationships. Not that she had a problem with it. She'd just never had much of an opportunity to do so.

Now she was with Ryder, and that still seemed surreal to her. Thinking about defining herself by that relationship she'd always wanted so badly stopped her cold. She *was* with Ryder. Did that make her his girlfriend? Old lady one day? Did it really make her part of the Hounds by that connection?

Her mind was spinning for answers. But as she gazed from Sadie to Jade and back, she realized both meant what they were saying. If she was with Ryder, wasn't she with the Hounds too? Wasn't she with *them*?

Deep in her heart, she loved the idea. With no siblings and both parents gone, she craved connection and sense of belonging.

"And what is it you want me to do if I go?" Margot asked.

"You said it yourself," Jade answered. "Sadie is bait. Emily might as well be. Help us keep them safe. Help me protect Sadie. The men can't be in charge of everything."

Fear blended with hope in Sadie's big green eyes. The younger woman had come so far since she arrived in Mercy. She mustered the courage to go back to wearing her natural red hair. Then she'd signed up for self-defense classes. Margot knew no matter what Sadie said, she still tried to shoulder all responsibility for what had happened in Mercy since her arrival in it.

Now she was brave enough to try and stare down her biggest fears. What kind of person would Margot be if she didn't try to help her? But what consequences would Margot face if she did as they were asking?

Chapter Thirteen

Margot

After a quick shower and change into pajamas, Margot took a seat at the kitchen table. Ryder served her dinner, looking proud of himself. The burger was thick and juicy, perfectly assembled next to a small mountain of French fries. Passing her the ketchup bottle, he took a seat across from her with his own plate.

"What do you think?" Ryder asked, watching her expression.

"The burger looks amazing." It really did. "But I really don't appreciate the fact that I had to learn about the 'pool tournament' from someone besides you."

Ryder blew out a deep sigh.

"Did you think I wouldn't understand what it *really* is?" Margot asked, taking a bite of her burger. It was amazingly good.

"It's a pool tournament, Margot." Ryder gnawed on a fry. "It's to raise money for Emily's bakery."

Taking her time while she ate, Margot watched Ryder from beneath her lashes. "I'm sure."

Now he was staring her down. "Margot, everything is going to be fine."

Margot knew better. "RSVP only means you'll have control over anyone who attends. A benefit for Emily's bakery with a photo of Emily and Sadie on the flyer. Sadie, the original target of Robert Bianchi and his men. Oh, and she's coordinating the event with an email and phone number for any questions."

Ryder didn't say anything. But she could tell from his expression he knew he was caught.

"I'm so confused about a few things, Ryder." Margot shook her head. "You think you're what?

Setting a trap for Bianchi's men?"

"Yes."

Well, he finally said the quiet part out loud. "What the hell are you -- all of you -- thinking?" Margot had to say it. "This has the potential to go very badly."

His dark brows rose and lowered.

"That's bad enough," Margot went on. "But using Sadie as bait? How did Axel even allow that?"

Taking his time with a bite of his burger, Ryder seemed to be thinking about what he'd say next. "Axel wasn't happy about it, honestly."

Margot wouldn't have believed it before today's class. Sadie bravely talked about the tournament and her part in it. But she had no idea what was coming. Staging a battle with the Mafia, even on Hound turf, was a serious risk.

"How did you get Emery Phillips to allow you to have this pool tournament in *Sackett's*?" Margot was still trying to wrap her mind around that one. "Did he lose a bet?"

"That wasn't easy either," Ryder said. "It took Jade a while to convince him but... he finally agreed."

"Is he about to retire?" she asked. "And he's letting you destroy the place?"

The question earned her a look. "Emery understands what needs to happen here, Margot."

"Right. The Hounds need to find a way to hit back at Bianchi's men."

"It's our only choice," he said with feeling.

"It's not, but you don't want to hear anything about letting *us* handle things so --" She grabbed another fry.

"About letting *you* handle things?" Frustration darkened his face. "So far, our town's bakery burned down. They hit our garage next and that's a bad situation. We had roughly fifteen vehicles on the lot waiting for repairs. They beat the fuck out of all but two and those were locked inside the garage. We have to explain to folks the bodies of their vehicles are smashed to shit, windows busted out. It will take a lot longer to repair them now. Do you think they're bringing their cars back to us next time they need something fixed?"

Margot didn't realize the situation at that garage would be that bad.

"What's the sheriff's plan then? Try to hit them the next time they strike? Will they hit the construction site where Beast and Crash work? The school because Jade works there? What happens when they come back into town and shoot someone else in cold blood the way that fucker did your father? What's stopping them?"

It struck a nerve. While she was trying to do her job, to do the right thing, the mention of her father had her guilt spiking. She didn't want anyone else to suffer a loss like she did. A senseless, crushing loss where a loved one was taken in the blink of an eye in a random act of violence. She also didn't want to give the impression that her father's murder didn't matter to her. She *did* want to see Robert Bianchi pay for his crimes. Seeing him brought to justice would help her get closure. But Ryder and the rest of the Hounds seemed to be working under the assumption nothing would happen to Bianchi and their way of justice was the only way to truly resolve the entire affair. It was vigilantism.

Margot shook her head. "You all act as if we're doing nothing but watching and waiting, Ryder. That's not true. We're working with the state police and the

FBI since Bianchi is wanted for a lot more than what he did here in Mercy. I know they're trying to scare Sadie away from talking to the feds. But all we need is the right lead at the right time and we can stop this. Maybe you guys could even help on that front if you weren't so busy taking matters into your own hands."

"Anyone on your end seen or heard anything out of Chance?" Ryder asked, changing the subject. "We haven't."

No, they hadn't. Chad Teel was a prospect for the Hounds of Hell who went by the name of Chance. According to the other prospect who'd been staying at the garage that night, Chance took off on his bike to follow the men who vandalized *Three Guys Garage*. They expected him to turn around and come right back. No one had seen or heard from him since. Thinking about it now under Ryder's stare made her stomach drop.

"That's what I thought." Ryder was looking at her as if she'd lost her mind. "If you don't want to help, don't. We weren't counting on your involvement anyway."

"Jade and Sadie sure seem to be counting on me," she said.

"Yeah?"

"I didn't just find out about this plan of yours at self-defense class. Jade showed up with Sadie. She signed up for class. They waited until class was over and told me what was going on."

Margot could tell the way his brows gathered he didn't realize they were going to talk to her. "Did they say why?"

She nodded. "Sadie says my self-defense class is helping her overcome her fears. She's tired of running. They both wanted me to be there, to help keep Sadie safe. To help keep Emily safe because apparently, she's involved in this too."

"Her whole damn business burned down," Ryder shot back.

"And my father was killed, Ryder. You were shot. Nothing we do or don't do is going to change any of it."

"So, you don't even want to try?" Ryder had stopped eating. "I realize you don't have a lot of experience yet in your career. Like how clubs like ours operate. We trade outside the law, and we always have. We handle our business. We're going to handle *this*. You do what you've got to do."

Margot stared right back at him. "I have no idea what I'm going to do," she admitted. "I know what I *should* do. I should go talk to the sheriff. He should know what's about to happen in his town."

When Ryder didn't say anything, she continued. "If I don't help, I'm going to feel responsible now for whatever goes down. If I help, I'm betraying my profession and my promise to myself to always do the right thing, no matter how hard it is."

"How can you say our plan isn't the right thing to do, Margot?" Ryder gathered his plate and utensils. Apparently, he was finished with his meal. "At the end of the day, we have the same goal. We're protecting Mercy and her people."

Leaving his dishes in the sink, he marched out of the kitchen. Only a couple of minutes later she heard him ride off on his bike into the night.

Margot sat with her plate for quite a while. Ryder had left her a lot to think about.

* * *

Margot clocked out on Friday and made it home around sunset. The nights were arriving earlier now that it was September, and they were cooler.

She'd barely seen Ryder the day after their argument. He came home after their disagreement Wednesday night but was up and gone before she ever made it to the kitchen the last two mornings. Last night, he hadn't gotten home until after she was in bed, lying there feeling like her stomach was one huge knot.

The entire situation made her feel paralyzed. Her mind had been running through every scenario for the last two days. She couldn't keep going on like that. She had to decide what she was going to do.

Margot really only had a couple options. She could act as if she wasn't aware of what was going to happen next Saturday night with the "pool tournament" at *Sackett's*. Which was bullshit because she *did* know, and Ryder, his Hounds, and the ladies all knew it. If she even tried to convince Sheriff Sawyer she had no idea, he'd never believe her. By now, her boss probably figured out she and Ryder were together. She was expecting *that* talk any day.

She could tell her boss everything. But he'd have no choice but to get involved. Where would that leave her with the Hounds? Did she want bad blood with the MC for the rest of her career because she "ratted"? That was how they'd take it. She wouldn't be forgiven. And she didn't even want to think about how Ryder would handle that.

Ryder. Yeah, it would be the end of their new relationship and another level of misery entirely. She finally got what she'd always wanted, a chance with the man she'd been in love with forever. Could she really throw it all away now? Had she already? Could her heart handle that? Margot had exactly one week to decide.

When her phone hummed in her bag, she fished

it out and answered without seeing who the call was from. Her heart pounded, hoping it was Ryder.

"Margot?" Sadie asked.

"Yes." Margot had given her number to all the students in her self-defense class, but it was the first time one of them had used it.

"We're having a cookout," Sadie said. "It's going to be me, Jade, and Emily. We'd love to have you come over if you're free."

Margot couldn't have been more of a mess if she tried. She was grinning like a fool at the invite. She was shaking because of the entire situation involving these ladies and the Hounds. Ryder wasn't home, she didn't know where he was. Maybe an evening out would be a good thing.

"When?"

"At six."

According to Margot's phone, it was almost five thirty. "Where?"

"Axel and Ryder's house," Sadie said. "We've got food covered already. If you wanted to bring a bottle of wine or something, that would be great."

"Okay, thank you," Margot said. "I may drop by later."

If she went out to hang out with Sadie and the others, would Ryder be there? Or maybe it would just be a girls' night, and she hadn't had one of those since college.

Margot made it to the house where Axel and Ryder grew up by six thirty, smiling to see the other three women hanging out on the porch. They waved to her as she pulled up in her truck. Margot had a wine bottle in each hand as she walked up to the porch to join them, smiling at how excited they were to see her.

"She brought wine," Emily said, grinning.

"Finally!"

"No," Jade said. "Not yet. We can do wine later."

Margot wasn't sure what that meant, but she pulled up a chair. It looked like everything was set up for a cookout, and from the looks of everything, just maybe some others would be joining them. Like the guys.

Hope lifted her spirits a little. She'd feel so much better talking to Ryder, just to see where things stood.

They all chatted over nachos, listening to Emily talking about taking baking orders out of her house for the time being. Snow was apparently trying to sell his house to help.

"I think that's great." Sadie grinned at the blonde. "You made your own deliveries at the bakery anyway."

"That's how my biggest competition has gotten by all these years," Emily said.

"Corrine Martens, right?" Jade shook her head. "Grams didn't like her stuff. She said she took a cake decorating class years ago and thought she was a world-class baker ever since."

"I've heard that too." Emily laughed.

"Are you from Mercy, Emily?" Sadie asked.

The blonde shook her head. "I've been here almost six years though. Jade grew up here."

"So did Margot." Jade's gaze landed on her. "I'm sorry if I caused a problem between you and Ryder. I really am. We didn't tell the guys we were going to talk to you."

"I figured that out," Margot said. "It's okay. I'm sure we'll talk about it at some point."

"You don't have to be involved in this," Sadie said. "I know what we said after class, but you've already done so much for me. Don't feel obligated to go."

And that made Margot feel ten times worse. Anxiety mixed with guilt.

"She's right," Jade said. "Neither of us meant to put you in a bad situation. With your job and everything."

Margot nodded. "The fact that I work with the sheriff does put me in a bit of a situation. And Ryder..."

"So, you *are* together?" Emily asked. "You and Ryder?"

She couldn't keep the smile off her face. "I was. When I confronted him about all this Wednesday night, we kind of got into it. So..."

"More reason for you to just forget about getting involved in this," Sadie said.

Margot was feeling a little better about her situation. At least Sadie wasn't going to be angry at her for not showing up, cowardly as that thought felt.

"But you *could* help us with something," Jade said.

"Name it," Margot said.

"Will you teach us to shoot?"

She couldn't have heard Jade right. "What?"

"Just in case," Jade said. "Can you teach us how to shoot?"

Reaching under the table, Jade picked up a good-sized metal box and placed it on the table before her. When she opened it, she pulled out two Glocks, both 9 mm from the look of it. Then she pulled out four boxes of ammunition.

"Are those yours?" Margot asked.

Jade grinned. "They belong to the twins. Though I'm not sure if they belong to both. Or just one of them." She pulled another from a bag at her feet.

"Hero got me this."

She held up a petite Smith & Wesson revolver. It was cute.

Their request had her pausing. It had her reconsidering. Was she making the wrong choice in agreeing to teach them? Then again, if they didn't know how to properly handle a gun, they could hurt the wrong person. Or themselves.

Excitement flashed in Jade's face. "What do you think?"

If Margot refused to teach them, they'd try to use them anyway. Reluctantly, Margot nodded. "Okay."

An old voice in her head said they'd only invited her to their get-together to have her teach them to shoot. That voice was eventually forced to shut up as Margot went over the basics of the 9 mm Glock, the same gun she used at her job.

They ended up at the old fence post a few hundred yards from the house and so they could fire off into the empty field. Ryder's family had a good twenty-five acres of land around the house which was probably why they chose that location. Margot took some of the cans Jade pulled out of recycling and placed them along the fence as targets. There was a gun for each of them, but they were still not ready.

Going back to the box Jade pulled the Glocks from, Margot found what she was looking for. At least for two of them. There were two sets of protective eye gear and two sets of earmuffs. She dug out her own set of earmuffs and eye gear from her truck along with her own gun, strapping on a holster for it. Once her three students were all geared up, Margot reviewed what they were doing one more time before she gave the signal to shoot.

Sadie handled a gun more confidently than

Margot would have expected. Jade struggled, trying to teacup the gun she used. Slowly, she got the hang of it. The surprising star of the class, however, was Emily the baker. She got her stance down quickly and had great hand-eye coordination. She leaned into firing the shots instead of leaning away from them.

They reloaded. Margot worked with Jade one-on-one, explaining she needed to bring the gun up to her eye not her eye down to the gun. Jade's confidence slowly improved. Her shots became more accurate.

The roar of motorcycles approaching got Margot's attention, though her students stayed focused on what they were doing. When Jade grinned over her shoulder, she understood they wanted their guys to see what they were doing. Margot stepped back as the four riders reached the yard. The twins led the way followed by Hero and Snow.

Margot was nervous too, but for a different reason. She didn't know how Ryder would take her being there.

Ryder was the first off his bike, strutting in her direction with a grin on his face. Before Margot even had a chance to wonder what the hell was going on, Ryder kissed her soundly in front of the rest, drawing a couple of eager shouts from Jade and Sadie. When he finally let her up for air, Margot just stared at him in wonder.

"I told them they weren't going to get you over here for this," Ryder said, tipping his head in the direction of the other three women. "Happy to be wrong."

"Doesn't mean I'm going to *Sackett's* next week," Margot said in a low voice.

"I know." Ryder wrapped a possessive arm around her and pulled her to his side. "How's the class coming?"

Emily picked that moment to hit three cans in a row she'd set up for herself. They all laughed at the look on Snow's face. Walking up, he stole a kiss from Emily as she reloaded.

"Remind me not to piss you off, Emmy," Snow said.

More shooting skills were shown off before the cookout started. Axel pulled out a huge grill and the rest of them worked together to get food ready for grilling, to get drinks. The twins apparently had a liquor cabinet that was well-stocked, and they did damage to it. The group of them had a good meal, had fun talking. As evening blended into night, they drank, they dragged out the cornhole boards and played for a while in the work lights Ryder set up.

By eleven, Axel decided he and Sadie would stay at the house tonight. Emily climbed on the back of Snow's bike and headed back to town with him. Jade drove her SUV back up the road while Hero followed on his bike.

"Want to stay over?" Ryder asked, wrapping his arms around Margot from behind.

She didn't have to be at work the next day. Why not?

They ended up in his room with the world spinning for both from all the drinks they had. With a little courage from the alcohol, Margot pushed him back onto his bed and climbed up after him, straddling him. This time, she wanted to take the lead. She wanted to show the ladies' man she wasn't that much of an amateur.

Before he could do anything, Margot pulled the tank top she wore up and off, reaching to unhook the strapless bra while she was at it. Ryder's gaze was riveted to her breasts, lifting his hands to catch them. The ache in her tight nipples turned to hurt against the rough hands that kneaded them.

"What are we doing?" he asked, grinning.

Margot let him take a good long look. "I have an idea."

When she ground down on him, he rotated his hips and pushed up into her core. At that angle, he felt iron hard against her. And her panties were already soaked under her jeans. When he reached behind him to grab the collar of his T-shirt and pull it off for her, it only pushed Margot's need higher. *Damn.*

Ryder got his hands in her hair, dragging off the band that held her ponytail. Then he pulled her down for a kiss, tasting her lips in a restless, greedy way that only made her want him more. Ryder kept grinding up into her. He used enough pressure to drive her insane but not enough to give any satisfaction.

Margot stripped him bare, and he let her, watching as she moved back up his body, smoothing her hands up over his thighs as she went. His cock was swollen and red, lying on his abdomen and all ready for whatever she wanted. She pressed a soft kiss to the shaft just above his balls, and he hissed lightly. It did wonders for her ego to see his fingers clutching at the comforter as he fought to hold still. Ryder's junk was everything a woman could want, and *big*. All shaved so neatly. Margot grinned.

"Oh, fuck, yeah." Ryder's voice was low, gritty.

Margot got her hands on him, then her mouth. One hand gently stroked up and down his shaft while the other caressed his balls. She rolled them lightly, trying to learn what he liked. When her lips spread over the crown of his dick, she used her tongue to tease the smooth, sensitive flesh. Margot tasted the light, salty drops there, soothing him carefully with her lips and tongue as he started writhing on the bed.

"That's so fucking good." His voice was breathy, his gaze never leaving her.

Pulling his dick into her mouth, Margot moaned. The anticipation of what she hoped would come next had her pussy weeping in anticipation, her clit aching. Tightening one hand around his shaft, she pulled a sexy sound from him. When she tugged on his balls with gentle pressure, he sucked in a breath.

"Yes," he said, panting.

"Yeah?" she asked, tucking her hair behind her ears to keep it out of the way. Tugging gently on his balls again, she watched in delight as his eyes rolled back. His breath came faster now, which had Margot's libido growing fangs.

Making herself smaller between his powerful thighs, Margot chained kisses and licks down his cock. She got her mouth on his balls, working them with careful licks and nips. His thighs tightened on her and his hips started moving in need. Margot sucked one ball carefully between her lips, teasing it with her tongue.

Moving back up, Margot pulled him into her mouth to meet the back of her throat, encouraged by the sexy chorus of sounds he made, one hand sinking into her hair and clutching hard. The slight pain only pushed her on. Faster and faster, she worked, hollowing out her cheeks and keeping her tongue busy around him the entire time.

When Margot moaned around his cock, working him into her throat, his other hand landed on her head, and he wasn't gentle about it. Letting him guide her motions, letting him move her faster, deeper. Ryder fucked her face, and it was heaven to watch pleasure swamp him.

"Oh, darlin', I'm..." Ryder's breathing was harsh, his hips pumping.

Teasing his balls with her hand, she brought him off. Ryder yelled above her as release tore through him. It was a beautiful sight, all those muscles flexing in a dazzling display as the orgasm rocked him. Working him through it, Margot swallowed him down, using gentle touches, kisses.

Taking him apart like that had her heart welling in her chest with pride. She just hoped he wasn't done for the night.

Moving to his side, Margot smiled to see him lying there, eyes closed and trying to regain his breath. Her gaze moved over all those gorgeous muscles as she worked off her jeans.

One blue eye slit open to watch, then both, even though he was still recovering. Margot took her time. Once she had them off, the black lace thong she wore was revealed.

"Wow," he mouthed, just watching.

"We going to sleep now?" she asked, winking at him.

"Fuck no," Ryder huffed. "Just need a couple of minutes..."

Smiling, Margot moved closer to run her hands over his body. "We could do morning sex," she offered, teasing him.

Rolling on his side to face her, he propped his head up on one hand. Margot appreciated the view of his beefy arms and chest. His other hand pulled her in for a kiss.

It was slow and deep. Margot knew he could taste himself on her tongue. His hand slid over her shoulder, making her shiver. His fingers trailed down to brush over one tight nipple. Leaning forward, he wrapped his lips around it, teasing it lightly with lips and tongue as his hand slid down her body. He hooked his thumb at the side of her thong.

"Take these off," he whispered hotly.

She barely had time to do that when Ryder grabbed her by the hips, easily pulling her up as he rolled onto his back. When he situated her over his face, Margot's breath caught. It was something she hadn't done before but her body's need overruled any objections in her head.

Margot learned just how strong he was as he wrapped those powerful arms around her and made her ride his face. Ryder started by working her in crazy patterns with his tongue, leaving her gasping above him. When he unleashed his other tricks, he had her hanging onto the headboard with one hand, pawing at his head with the other.

"Ryder," she whispered, feeling her body go up in flames. Margot writhed on his tongue as he teased her clit and opening in turns until she thought she'd lose her mind. There was no give to his hold and when she ground down on him, wanting more, Ryder doubled his efforts. Margot struggled to breathe against the waves of pleasure rising within her.

"Ryder." His name came out as a low sob.

"Come, darlin'," he muttered against her slick, aching flesh.

Margot's cries filled the room, her heart thundering in her chest. He kept at her until the room was spinning around them.

Dimly aware she had collapsed over him, Margot couldn't fight him when he rolled her under him. With a firm grip on her thighs, he pulled her down the bed until he loomed over her. The scent of her excitement drifted on the air around them as his mouth painted her torso with sloppy, wet kisses. Traces of her stained his lips when his mouth claimed hers.

"My Margot," he whispered.

His powerful thighs pushed hers wide, his cock pressing at her opening before she'd completely come around. Ryder whispered her name again.

He sank into her, stretching her open just the way she needed him to. This time he wasn't slow and careful. His kisses became dirty and heated as he pushed inside, and Margot wrapped herself around his hard muscular body.

When Ryder began to move, pure pleasure coursed through her veins. Ryder gave her enough of his weight to make her feel it, trapping her between him and the mattress as his hips powered into her. Her legs wrapped around his powerful thighs, her hands sliding over his slick, flexing back.

Caging her to the top of his bed, Ryder filled her hard and fast, hitting spaces inside that took her breath away. The entire time he stole fevered kisses from her lips, dropped kisses over her hair and face. The harsh rush of her breath and his blended with the cries and moans he drew from her with little effort.

One huge hand slid between their bodies, carefully teasing her clit in a way that had her tightening around him like a vise.

"Give it to me. Want you to come on my cock," he whispered hotly in her ear.

Margot really had no choice, writhing wildly beneath him as his thrusts gained in speed and strength. His hold on her tightened. Release blew her apart, sending wave after wave of heat and searing pleasure radiating from her lower body through every fiber of her being.

Margot clamped around him tightly and Ryder shouted as he managed to pull free of her, shooting thick white ropes over her thighs. Margot twisted beneath him, loving the view of him working himself over her, the sound of his pleasured grunts.

Somehow, they ended up with Ryder draped over her, the weight and heat of him feeling so good in the cool night air that drifted in from the window. Wrapped up in Ryder's arms, they fell asleep in the quiet of the country.

He wasn't mad at her. She wasn't upset with him. It was a gentle truce.

And a wonderful night.

Chapter Fourteen

Ryder

The evening was heavy with tension, the scents of paint, gasoline, and determination in the air. The setting sun cast long shadows on the garage floor. Razor walked into the garage, his gaze cold as steel, thirty minutes before closing time on Tuesday.

Axel climbed out from under the sedan he repaired as Razor approached, joining Ryder to see if there had been any news. Their gazes met Razor's, searching for answers, for reassurance that they weren't facing this alone.

Razor didn't mince words. He never did.

"Aside from a handful of brothers from the Carolinas coming up to help us out," Razor began, his voice a low growl that echoed through the silence, "we're on our own. The Kentucky Hounds, despite owing us many favors, are tied up in their own wars. Our brothers to the north have apparently taken some hits against this Mafia. They think we're already dead men."

Ryder shook his head.

A pause, thick with the weight of the unsaid, settled over all three of them. Razor looked at each of his men, his stare unwavering. "But we aren't dead. Not yet anyway."

His words struck a match in a powder keg, igniting a fire in the hearts of the two men before him. They weren't just bikers -- they were fucking warriors, forged in the crucible of the roads they ruled and battles they won. They'd faced death dozens of times, walking away every time with blood on their hands and victory in their hearts.

"Mercy is *ours*," Razor continued, his voice

rising, "and we're the only thing standing between those bastards and everything we've built in this town. Sawyer isn't going to help us."

Ryder's heart clenched in his chest. Sawyer could try to shut them down, make everything worse. And Margot? She'd have to decide which side she was on. Once Margot had something in her heart and mind to do, no one was convincing her otherwise. Not even the sheriff.

"Those Mafia fuckers think they can come in here, threaten us and our people for a war they started, and walk away unscathed? They better fucking think again. We don't need anyone else. We don't need numbers. And we will dispatch these fuckers to hell."

Their Prez stepped closer, the weight of his presence bearing down like a storm. "Saturday night, we show them what it means to cross *us*. We're the nightmare they'll never wake up from."

Axel's eyes burned with the same intensity as Razor's. The determination he read on his birth brother's face fueled the fire burning within him. No fear here, no hesitation. Just the cold, lethal resolve of men with nothing left to lose and everything to fight for. Mercy, Sadie, Emily... They'd avenge Morgan Davis and Elsie Damron. And as for Clyde Donner...

Ryder hoped he personally got to take fucking Bobby Bianchi down himself. Axel wanted the man because of what he'd done to Sadie. Ryder wanted him for killing Margot's father.

Anyone but Margot... Her job would demand she try to take him alive. But was she even capable of that? Ryder would rather pull the trigger than force her into that decision.

"We should check in with our brothers in Mississippi," Ryder said. "I was there a few weeks ago.

Hell, they'll come."

"Call them *today*, brother," Razor told him.

Ryder nodded. He planned to call them the minute Razor walked out of the garage.

"Still nothing from Chance." Razor ran a hand over his silvery beard. "At this point, I think we have to assume the worst."

"We'll fucking make them bleed for him too." Axel fumed. All of them were drowning in anticipation, the rage of the coming confrontation.

"Keep your eyes and ears open," Razor told them.

Turning, Razor headed back the way he came, leaving the twins watching.

Hero returned from the stockroom. He'd been doing inventory, planning his order for paint and other supplies he'd need.

Bobby Fuckface's men had done a number on several of the cars on the lot, waiting for repairs. Hero would be working night and day on the body stuff while all the other repairs fell on Ryder and Axel. It would take working many long hours just to catch up and to bring in money for new repairs to help recover their losses.

Who were they kidding? People weren't exactly beating down their door for help with their vehicles now that word got out about the vandalism at *Three Guys Garage*. Ryder didn't know what the fuck they could do about it.

"What did I miss?" Hero asked, looking from Ryder to Axel.

"Catch him up," Ryder said. "I'm going to go call Mississippi."

With any luck, Mississippi would answer the call. They needed some hard-hitting motherfuckers for

Saturday. Especially with their old ladies present.

An image of Margot flashed in his mind as he hustled for the office. She wasn't his old lady. Yet. He was hoping she would want to be down the road, if they made it through Saturday night.

And they *would* make it through Saturday night. Razor was right. Fuck the numbers. Every last fucking one of the Hounds in Mercy were killers. They'd set up this trap for Bianchi's men and they weren't going to back down now. No matter who had to die. But they needed to move fast.

There was a lot to do, and time was running out.

* * *

Margot

"You wanted to see me?" she asked Sheriff Sawyer, standing in the doorway of his office.

Looking up from his laptop, the sheriff nodded. "I did. Come in. Shut the door behind you."

Here we go. Margot had wondered all day Monday when her boss would ask to speak with her. Now it was Tuesday, and she just wanted to get it out of the way. Closing the door as he requested, she approached the desk and took a seat across from him. "What's up?" Margot asked.

Closing his laptop, the sheriff regarded her speculatively. The sheriff of Mercy had a nick just under his chin from shaving. A food stain of some sort littered the front of his shirt. Little things like that the sheriff seemed oblivious to. When it came to his job, however, the sheriff missed nothing. Absolutely nothing.

"I wanted to talk to you about an event coming up this weekend," he said. Grabbing a folded paper from under his laptop, he opened it and handed it to her.

She already knew what was on that paper. She'd seen the flyer before. Still, she took it from him, read it again.

"You're aware," he said. The sheriff stared at her hard.

"I'm aware." Margot was no good at lying.

The sheriff pushed the paper back down on the desk, keeping her from using it as a thin wall between them. "There's more than meets the eye with this pool tournament," Randy said. "Don't you think?"

Margot fought back panic. The urge to tell him everything she knew, everything she *thought*, was intense. She'd worked so hard to do a good job from the moment she accepted the position as deputy. Margot made herself a student of the law, a student of her sheriff. And in the months since she'd come to work in her hometown, she'd tried hard to earn her boss's trust. To demonstrate her loyalty. She allowed nothing to hold her back from her goal of being the best deputy possible, a protector of the people.

She'd never seen the situation with Ryder coming. Wouldn't have expected it in a million years. And yet, here she sat across from the sheriff, her boss, feeling like an imposter. When had that happened? Margot still did her job to the best of her ability. She hadn't done anything wrong. *Yet*. And she didn't like being put on the defensive. "It's just a pool tournament," Margot replied with her heart flying in her chest.

Randy wasn't buying it. She read it in his face. "Margot, I'm just going to come out and say it. Ryder Harper's been supposedly sleeping on your couch for weeks. Now I'm hearing you two are a thing."

People were finding out about them. It felt

surreal to even think it but -- Ryder was hers. For the moment anyway. Her heart whispered that it probably wouldn't last long. In time, he'd probably move on. She hoped he wouldn't, but she needed to be prepared, right? Why couldn't the fucking universe just let her have this time with him, pitifully short though it may be?

It also irked the shit out of her that she'd finally found a couple of minutes of happiness, and someone made an issue out of it. "My relationship doesn't affect how I do my job, sir. I've kept my personal life separate from my duties as a deputy and you know that," she said. "I've always been dedicated to this department. So why am I being called into question now?"

"Because your boyfriend is a Hound," Randy said. "Margot, you're all too aware of the line we have to walk in this job. Your relationship with one of the Hounds -- someone who's on the wrong side of the law -- puts you in a very difficult position. I'm just concerned that your personal life will at some point compromise your duties as a deputy."

"I get where you're coming from," Margot said. "I do. But I still can't help but wonder if I were a male deputy whether we'd even be having this conversation."

The sheriff appeared unmoved. "If you were a male deputy dating a woman in an MC, it wouldn't be that big a deal. At least right now, it's a boys' club. But you're not a male deputy and Ryder Harper ain't no saint."

"Okay, he's not. And you're still dragging my personal life out into the light without cause." Margot's anger kept her grounded, logical. "My professionalism and loyalty to this department is being called into question because my boyfriend is a biker and you're worried about a pool tournament they're hosting on Saturday."

Blowing out an irritated sigh, Sheriff Sawyer shook his head. "Professionally, yes, I'm concerned that your relationship might put you in a compromising position. Especially since you have access to sensitive information about investigations or ongoing operations here in Mercy. And I've been in this job for a couple decades now. I know that's not just a pool tournament we're dealing with here, Margot. I've been hearing whispers about something big going down Saturday night. I think it's a trap they're setting up for Bianchi's men. You know it too. And if this goes sideways, it could turn our town into a war zone. If this goes bad for the Hounds or escalates out of control, what's the fallout for us?"

"I'm on duty Saturday night. If you're correct, since I *am* in a relationship with Ryder, then I would be closer to this situation than anyone else. Wouldn't that put me in a position to keep things from getting out of hand?"

It was her one advantage. Through Ryder, she knew what was going on in the MC. Through her job, she knew what was going on from the vantage point of the law. Surely, something good could come from such a position.

"I've always trusted you, Margot. You've got good instincts. But this situation... it's making me question your loyalties. I'm not going to lie. Are you still fully committed to your badge? Or is your heart pulling you in another direction?"

"How can you ask me that?" Margot fought back anger.

"I have to ask you that," the sheriff said.

"Because I know if your loyalties are divided, it could undermine the mission and effectiveness of this department. And that I just can't have."

Margot recognized the truth in his words. Taking a deep breath, she realized she needed to be careful here. Yes, she wanted to help Ryder and the Hounds in their quest to rid Mercy of Bianchi's men. But her career was on the line and her future with Ryder wasn't guaranteed. If she didn't tread lightly, she'd find herself without a job and a relationship.

"Look," he said in a gentler tone. "If what you've got going on with Ryder is real then --"

"Real?" What was he trying to say?

"It's crossed my mind a couple of times that this thing with you and Ryder might be... staged. I mean no insult toward *you*. I just wouldn't put it past the Hounds to find a way to use that to benefit the club."

"Are you serious? You think if I were to have a relationship with Ryder, it's impossible that it's real. You think it's just because I'm a deputy?"

Regret bled into his expression. "There's no good way to word that. I'm sorry. But you have to consider --"

"No, I don't." She didn't want to hear that. Maybe it was because she'd known Ryder since elementary school, and he was many things. But someone who would fake a relationship to benefit the MC? Ryder wasn't that person.

Still, since her boss introduced the fear, it seeped into her bloodstream like a slow-acting poison. Trying to keep calm, to stay in her head, Margot elected to push aside that train of thought. "I know the ethical implications of my situation with Ryder," she said slowly. "I need you to *trust* me."

Because at the end of the day she knew it was a

trap, but she didn't plan to say anything to the sheriff. It was a huge risk that loomed larger every day. But there really was no way to stop them.

If everything worked out as the Hounds wanted it to, just maybe they'd run Bianchi's men out of town for good. The men from the New Jersey crime family had caused so much chaos and damage, going beyond the people they were targeting like Sadie to terrorize the citizens of Mercy. They'd destroyed the Austin greenhouse and intimidated the sweet older couple who owned it. They'd killed three innocent people. Shot Ryder. They burned down the bakery and vandalized the garage. Chance had followed them the night at the garage, and the young man hadn't been seen or heard from since. And Bianchi's men weren't likely to stop, especially knowing the feds were counting on Sadie's testimony when their boss went to trial.

"Margot, if anything illegal happens, and you know about it beforehand, that puts you in a dangerous position -- both legally and career-wise. You wouldn't want to be seen as complicit."

She didn't need him to tell her that. If the Hounds' ambush backfired, or escalated out of control as her boss feared, it could be more than just her job and relationship on the line. What if she ended up facing criminal charges herself? And if more innocent people ended up injured or killed, how would she live with that?

"I know what position I'd be in," she said. It had plagued her thoughts for the past couple of weeks, kept her from sleeping.

What the Hounds were planning was dangerous. But something had to be done to protect the town and prevent a larger conflict. As much as she'd lectured

Ryder about letting the law handle it, the law's hands were tied.

"I'm not turning a blind eye to anything illegal," she said, rising from the chair. "I'll be on duty Saturday night and sincerely hope nothing happens at the pool tournament. I'll do my job no matter what happens. And I hope that's good enough."

Walking to the door, she opened it to head back to her desk to get her things for the day and clock out.

"Me too," he said quietly as she walked away.

* * *

Friday Night

When she arrived at her house, she saw Ryder's bike already in her driveway. She felt so tired as she climbed out of her truck and walked into the house. Margot wanted a night of peace. It'd been a hell of a week. She didn't want to talk about Saturday or hear the latest plans. She still hadn't talked to Ryder about her talk with the sheriff. She just wanted to eat dinner, curl up on the couch, and watch some bad television. Nothing more.

The TV was on when she closed the door behind her. It was just after six. The local news would be on. "Hey!" Ryder called from the kitchen. "I'm working on dinner."

Margot smiled because hearing that was always going to make her smile. Pulling off her boots as she always did, she noticed a breaking news announcement when the broadcast came back from commercial break. She saw a view of the Bland Correctional Facility on the screen with the words "Prison Break" flashing on the screen. The well-groomed blonde anchor's expression was suitably grim as she reported a jail break only an hour ago and

Robert Bianchi, the notorious murderer from a New Jersey crime family, had escaped with two other inmates.

Staring at the screen in horror, she listened as they showed a mug shot of Bianchi and read his description. They announced he was armed and dangerous and that if spotted, to call the law immediately. The anchor stressed that people shouldn't confront him.

"Did you hear me?" Ryder asked, walking up to her with a smile.

Margot swallowed hard but didn't look away from the television. When Ryder followed the line of her gaze, catching the tail end of the announcement, he stood by her in stunned silence. Because they both knew exactly where Robert Bianchi would be headed first. To Mercy.

Chapter Fifteen

Margot

She felt frozen, staring at the TV screen as they talked about Robert "Bobby" Bianchi's escape on the newscast. The reality of their situation hit her hard at that moment. The pool tournament was tomorrow. With Bianchi now on the loose, the Hounds needed to call off the event. *Now*.

"Oh, my God," she said. "This changes everything."

Ryder raked a hand through his short hair as he listened. "It certainly fucking does."

"You have to call this off." Walking around him, she dropped heavily on the couch. "With Bianchi out now it's too dangerous."

Ryder turned to face her, looking at her like she was a crazy person. "What?"

"You have to call it off." The look of sheer determination on his face had her heart clenching in her chest but she had to try. "He's a fugitive now and it raises the stakes here significantly, Ryder. The plan from the beginning was to lure lower-level Mafia members out. Now you're facing Bianchi himself."

"And you don't think we can handle him?" Ryder asked, his color high.

"That's not the point, Ryder. The risk of people being hurt or killed is much higher with him out of prison."

"We're having this at *Sackett's*." Ryder joined her on the couch. "It's on the outskirts of town and we're holding it there for a reason. We're not putting innocent people in the line of fire here, Margot. That Bianchi is out of jail makes this even better. This is our best chance to catch Bianchi and his men off guard. The event's already in motion and I can guaran-damn-tee you they still think they have the upper hand right now. If we cancel, they have time to regroup, and fucking disappear. We won't get another shot like this."

Ryder wasn't listening to her. With Bianchi out, they had no idea how many men he might bring with him. The Hounds had a few brothers coming from Mississippi from what he told her, but that was it. They'd likely be outnumbered. How hard was it for him to understand she was worried about the Hounds getting taken down? Ryder could end up dead.

"This isn't going to be the planned takedown you wanted, Ryder." Margot was fighting back panic. "Bianchi has nothing left to lose, all right? There are too many unknowns now with him in play. You can't predict how this is going to go."

Frustration colored his face. "We've faced worse than him before, Margot. Yeah, he's got nothing left to lose and he's looking for payback. But so are we. Don't you want him to pay for Clyde?"

Yes. "I'm not answering that," she said.

"Because you do, Margot." Ryder wasn't backing off. "We can't cancel this without looking weak. The fucker has already done enough damage to Mercy. Not taking him on will make this so much worse. Bianchi would hit us even harder."

"How can you possibly know that?" Margot asked.

"It's what *we* would do," he said.

Now she was afraid. And she likely wasn't the only one. "What about Sadie? When she hears this, it might change her mind about things. There's a target on her head, and when she came up with this idea Bianchi was in prison. Now he's not. She may not be able to go through with it, Ryder. Did you think about that?"

That stopped him and he seemed to consider it. "Even if she can't, we have to carry on. If we do this right, the Hounds can end this on our terms and prevent these fuckers from hitting Mercy whenever they fucking feel like it. I'm sorry, but I don't see the law doing anything about it."

"I've told you why." Margot grew more frustrated by the second. "The Hounds are taking the law into their own hands. You're undermining the authority of the sheriff's department with this plan. And it could backfire on you. If this goes badly, things might spiral out of control. It might start a war with the Mafia and Mercy would be caught in the crossfire. Is that what you want? Are you willing to sacrifice Mercy for your need for revenge?"

"What do you think they're going to do to Mercy if we back down, huh? We protect this town every bit as much as the law does. Whether you like it or not, Mercy is our home turf, and we defend what's ours all the way up to heaven and all the way down to hell. And they're coming either way."

Margot understood that, admired it. But she didn't know anything else to say between trying to make her point and the dark thoughts tumbling around in her head.

"If all of you think so little of the law," Margot said slowly, "why get involved with me?"

"What?" He stared at her in confusion.

"Sheriff Sawyer said... he thinks maybe you got involved with me because..." Margot couldn't bring herself to finish the sentence.

"He said what?" Ryder tensed on the couch next to her. "He thinks I got involved with you because you're a deputy. For information or something?"

Dropping her head, Margot nodded.

With gentle fingers, he tipped her chin up to make her look at him. "Think about how it sounds, Margot. I don't give a shit about the law. Never really have. That's not why I'm with you."

"Why are you with me then?" She had to ask the question. "And for how long?"

It took some of the wind out of his sails. When he reached for her hand and captured it between both of his, she didn't fight him.

"I guess I've earned that," he said. "I understand why you'd think that, at least based on my past. I don't have any secrets from you, Margot. And I sincerely fucking hope I haven't given you any reason to doubt my intentions toward you."

Margot shook her head.

"Sawyer needs to mind his own goddamn business." Ryder squeezed her hand. "What happens between us is just that, between *us*."

"I'll be ready." Margot was shaking. Her insecurities were out in the open now. "I'll be ready when you end this. It's selfish and stupid but I've wanted this -- wanted *you* -- for so long I don't care how long this lasts. I'm going to enjoy it while I have it."

The stricken look on his face made her pause. She didn't understand.

Her heart jerked in alarm when he dropped her hand and rose from the couch. He started to pace, agitated.

"God, why *wouldn't* you think that?" Ryder stopped to stare at her. "You've seen me go around with so many women over the years. Hell, we've joked about it. But I never told you why, did I?"

"Why what?"

"Why I've lived my life like I have." Sadness crept into the steely-blue eyes. "Why I went from one woman to another, from one fight to another. Why I went from one bottle to the next."

Margot waited patiently for him to gather his words, figure out what he wanted to say. After a moment, he sat next to her on the couch again.

"Do you remember me telling you about how my parents died?"

Margot nodded. He told her the story years ago, after her own mother died, to comfort her.

"My father? It was the widow-maker that killed him. Just one of those things." Ryder took a deep breath, his gaze locked with hers. "My mother? Yeah, she took herself off the board. Axel would tell you she lost interest in life after our father died. Depression got the best of her. Maybe that's true. But I left out a key part of the story."

Margot listened, waiting for him to tell her at his own pace. Dread at what she was about to hear welled up within her.

"In those last few months before our mother died," he said, "she and I fought a lot. A *lot*. Axel tried to step up because that's how he coped. He got a job before we graduated. He tried to take up all our father's duties around the house to make life easier for her. Me? I didn't know what to do. It was a fucking funeral parlor in those last months. I tried to stay out of the way."

Margot didn't know Axel as well as Ryder. Had their mother compared them because of Axel's actions and found Ryder lacking?

"I also got out of the house when I could," he admitted. "It was fucking depressing, and I didn't know what to do to make it better. Axel was already doing everything perfectly. I was ashamed, resentful. When I'd come home at night, she'd still be sitting in the living room in the dark, watching the TV screen. She'd say… all these awful things."

Her heart dropped as she listened. "What did she say?"

Ryder's eyes were shiny as he spoke. "She told me… She said I wouldn't amount to much. Said me and my brother wore the same face but we couldn't have been more different. Didn't I notice how hard Axel worked to keep our family together and looked after? I wasn't doing a damn thing to help. And, honestly, it wasn't a lie. She told me I was such a disappointment to her."

His hands shook and Margot took them in hers. "Ryder, I'm so sorry."

"Me too. The first time she said those things, it leveled me. I didn't leave the house for a week. Hell, I didn't leave my room."

"Did she look for you? Apologize?"

"No." Swallowing hard, he continued. "She stayed in that chair and smoked and watched the television screen. But she really wasn't watching, you know?"

It sounded like their mother had been lost to depression after the loss of her husband. And her two young sons were left with her, not equipped to deal with the situation.

"The first night I went out with my friends after that incident, she didn't say anything to me before I left. Usually, she got in some smartass remark about going out to forget about my family or how she hoped I enjoyed my night out with the only people I really cared about. That night? Nothing. I stayed out way later than I should have. I just didn't want to go back home."

Her heart ached for him.

"When I got home, she was in the living room floor in a puddle of her own vomit." Pain bled into his expression as he went on. "Ice cold. She'd been dead for a while. And my brother was upstairs sleeping in his bed. He had no idea. She didn't even care about him and all he tried to do was make things better for her."

One tear spilled from his eye. "It took me a long time to get over that. If I ever really did. She'd never approved of my spending so much time with friends, girls. But she didn't turn mean about it until my father died. She let me know nothing I did was good enough. Nothing I did mattered. I guess I took it to heart. Somewhere along the way, I decided maybe it would be best to avoid getting too serious with anyone. I'd just let them down like I let her down."

"Ryder, it wasn't your fault. It was her decision."

"I could have done *something*."

"You were eighteen." Margot's heart cracked and she pulled him to her, holding him.

"I want to try this, Margot." He pressed a kiss into her hair. "I want to be with you. Doesn't mean I know what the hell I'm doing, but I love you."

Tightening her arms around him, she said, "I love you too."

Ryder eased back from her like he wanted to search her face, look for any lie. It was heartbreaking because here was the man she'd always longed for, and he was looking at her like she could break him with a single word.

When she leaned in to kiss him, she didn't intend to start something. But he kissed her back, and she tasted desperation and raw need. Hanging onto him, she let him pull her onto the floor. She helped him with her uniform, belt, and the vest she wore each day for protection. When she was bare beneath him, she scrambled to undress him. She wanted to feel his skin against hers, nothing between them. And once they were both freed of their clothes, they went after each other in a frenzy.

Ryder's hands worshipped her. Her hands smoothed over the map of scars and tattoos on his skin. Their lips danced together, gently at first. Then the kisses grew more demanding. By the time Ryder had her worked up with his hands and mouth, Margot was begging for him, needing to feel him inside her.

"Fucking love how you feel," he whispered as he pushed inside her, sliding home in a single, slick movement.

The way his cock filled her stole her breath, hitting all the right places as he took her slowly. Margot's legs wrapped around his slim waist, her hands sliding on the damp muscled wall of his back. The two of them moved together, joined as one in lust and longing.

Ryder brought her off screaming on his cock. As she rode out the orgasm, he pulled free of her and got his mouth on her. His deep moan pushed her back up on that wave, left her gasping in his grip. She was too sensitive, too breathless and she tried to push his head away, but he wasn't having it. Ryder ate her out until she was begging him to stop, begging for... she wasn't sure what. He didn't let up until she came again on his tongue.

When the edges of her world faded to black and she fought to catch her breath, Ryder rolled her onto her stomach and slid back in, fucking her hard.

Dropping his weight on her, he pinned her to the floor, driving hard enough to bring a tinge of pain in her pussy. One hand slid beneath her, and when his fingers started teasing her clit, he drove his cock into her mercilessly. She screamed the house down when she came one last time.

Chasing his own release, Ryder came with her. Growling out into the quiet of her living room, it was a deep possessive sound, and she felt it everywhere. Between her thighs. She felt it in her heart most of all.

Margot didn't want to move, lying beneath him with her cheek buried in the carpet. Ryder felt so good on her, in her. Contentment left her drowsy. They stayed there, hearts beating in unison.

Until an acrid smell stung her nose. "Is something burning?"

"Fuck," Ryder muttered, pulling himself off her and scrambling naked to the kitchen. Oh yeah. He'd been making dinner when she got home.

Smiling, she pulled herself off the floor and pulled on her panties, his T-shirt. On shaking legs, she followed him to the kitchen to see smoke rolling out of her oven and laughed at how frantically he pulled the smoking pan out, dropping it into the sink and turning on the water to extinguish the charred dinner he'd made.

"Sorry," he said with a sheepish grin.

Before she could retort, his phone chimed on the kitchen counter, and he answered it. All the happiness of the last few minutes evaporated as reality came crashing back in.

"Yeah, I saw it on the news," he said to whoever called.

And that brought her back to earth, to the current situation with Bobby Bianchi running around free somewhere. The trap they were setting for Bianchi and his men tomorrow night.

"Wait. What?" Ryder's gaze found hers, his eyes rounded by some horror. "I'll be right there."

"What happened?" Margot asked as he ended the call, dreading the answer to her question.

"I'm not sure. Razor needs me at the clubhouse as soon as I can get there."

Watching him throw on his clothes and boots, all she could say was "Be careful!" as he raced for the door.

* * *

Ryder

The rumble of Ryder's Harley quieted as he pulled into the clubhouse lot. Tension had his heart flying, adrenaline racing through his veins. Killing the engine, he parked the bike, his trepidation growing. Something was wrong. *Very wrong.*

He spotted Snow standing near the back of the lot, his shoulders stiff and his face unreadable. Ryder pulled off his helmet and swung his leg off the bike. The smell of engine oil and smoke lingered in the air, but Ryder sensed something else -- something darker.

Snow gave a curt nod toward the tree line behind the clubhouse. "It's bad, brother."

Without a word, Ryder followed him toward the back of the property, his pulse pounding in his ears. As they moved past the clubhouse, the setting sun cast long shadows over the dirt. And then he saw it -- just beyond the edge of the woods.

Three crosses. *What the fuck?*

The air froze in his lungs. Stopping in his tracks, Ryder stared in disbelief at the macabre display. The first cross, on the left, held Chance, the missing prospect. Blood ran down his arms from where he'd been nailed to it, his head slumped forward. The grayish cast of his skin made him realize Chance had likely been dead a few days.

"Jesus Christ," Ryder whispered, unable to take his eyes off Chance -- what was left of him.

The second cross on the right held another prospect. Ryder barely knew Perry, a young kid just starting to prove himself. He was in slightly better shape than Chance but also dead, nailed up there to send a sick message.

But it was the empty cross in the middle that made Ryder's blood run cold. It wasn't the fact that it was empty. *No.* It was the name carved into the wood, jagged and uneven, like someone had scratched it in a hurry.

Sadie.

Ryder's fists clenched as he stepped closer to the center cross. The wood was rough, the cross poorly made, and barely standing upright. But the name -- the way it was carved -- there was no mistaking the message. They were coming. Tomorrow. Bianchi was coming for Sadie.

Rage boiled in Ryder's gut, thick and violent. He turned to find Axel, his twin and the man Sadie belonged to, had come up behind them, his face hard, jaw tight.

"Bianchi," Axel muttered, his voice barely restrained.

Ryder's vision blurred with fury, his breathing ragged. The Mafia fuckers had already taken so much from Mercy -- Elsie, Clyde, Morgan Davis, Chance, Perry, and now this. It was more than a fucking message. They were out for blood.

"He wants Sadie," Axel said, his voice low and

cold. "But he's not getting her. Not now. *Not ever*." He stepped toward the crosses, his boots kicking up dirt, his eyes shining in the dying sunlight. "This ends tomorrow."

"They want a war," Razor said, stepping up beside him, his voice a dangerous growl. "We'll give them one."

All of them stood silent before the crosses. Ryder's heart pounded with a mix of rage, fear, and determination. This wasn't over.

Not by a long shot.

Chapter Sixteen

Margot

She didn't sleep at all Friday night and Ryder didn't return to the house. He sent her texts through the night, telling her that they were handling preparations for tomorrow -- which she didn't want to think about and was largely the reason she couldn't sleep. Eventually, she *did* fall asleep; the humming of her phone pulled her out of sleep late the next morning. It was Ryder.

Instantly, she was awake. "Are you okay?"

"Everything's fine, darlin'," Ryder said, sounding tired. "I just wanted to hear your voice before everything goes down tonight."

Why did he have to put it that way? "Please be careful," was all she could think to say.

"Always am." Then a deep sigh. "I know all this has put you through hell the last couple of weeks and I'm sorry. I really just called to tell you that if I don't see you tonight, I will understand and so will everyone else."

Why did those kind words make her feel even worse?

"You've helped Sadie and Jade out a lot and it's appreciated," he went on. "I appreciate *you*. And I meant what I said last night. I love you. As soon as we make it past this mess, I'll spend some time proving to you that I'm not going anywhere. Okay?"

Tears stung the backs of her eyes. Why did it sound like he was also saying goodbye?

"I'm holding you to that," she said, hoping he didn't notice her voice breaking.

"I know you will." She heard the smile in his voice. "You're on second shift?"

"I am." Which put her on duty during the pool tournament.

"You be careful too, Margot." Another deep sigh on his end. "If you're off tomorrow, maybe we just spend the whole day in bed."

That had her smiling. "I am off. Sounds like a plan."

When he didn't say anything else, she just said, "I love you."

"Love you too," Ryder said, ending the call.

Sending up every prayer she knew that things would turn out that way for them, she got out of bed to get ready for work.

* * *

Ryder

The roar of engines filled the parking lot as the Hounds rolled up to *Sackett's*, the familiar flicker of its neon sign casting red light over their bikes. The bar looked like it always did -- rough around the edges but alive with the kind of energy that only a small-town bar could create. Inside, the muffled sounds of music and conversation drifted out into the cool night air.

Tonight, though, the mood inside *Sackett's* would be very different. Beneath the usual noise, tension simmered, with every Hound on edge, waiting for the storm to break. Ryder felt the weight of the night and everything they had planned pressing in on him.

The interior of *Sackett's* was warm and smoky, the air thick with a mix of cigarette smoke and grilled food. The bar area was packed, couples and small groups gathered around tables, laughing over shots and beers. The jukebox pumped out classic rock, and the dance floor at the center was alive with motion. Young women swayed under colorful lights, the music masking the seriousness that was about to unfold.

Ryder took a quick glance around. If someone walked into the bar right now, they wouldn't think anything out of the ordinary would happen tonight. There were a few familiar faces -- mostly locals and a scattering of bikers. Emery would have told anyone not directly related to the Hounds to start drifting out around seven when the "tournament" began. Tickets were "sold out." But the crowd wasn't what held his attention now. It was the sense that every Hound in the room was on alert, watching, waiting.

Snow led the way, weaving through the crowd, nodding toward a couple of brothers already posted by the bar. Ryder followed, his eyes scanning for any sign of Bianchi's men. They hadn't arrived yet, but they would. They'd left a grisly RSVP behind the Hound clubhouse. Two of their brothers dead and a direct threat aimed at Sadie. They'd pay for that. Perry was Crash's little brother. He was going to take that shit hard.

But they couldn't call the police because that would have ruined their plans for tonight. And tonight was important. Tonight, they'd deal with Bianchi and his men and get them out of Mercy once and for fucking all.

At the back of the main room, Snow opened a door and led Ryder into the adjoining room, quieter but just as crowded. This room had better lighting, less smoke, and was dominated by the pool table at its center, with tables pushed around the edges. It was here that the tournament would take place -- the perfect setup for what was about to go down.

The Hounds had already spread themselves out, most of them blending into the crowd, casually leaning against the walls or sitting at tables. At first glance, it looked like just another busy night at *Sackett's*, with a few pool players racking up their shots, drinks being served at the small counter nearby, and bikers talking in low voices. But Ryder knew better.

Tension rolled off his brothers, their muscles coiled and ready for whatever was coming. He glanced at Axel, who was leaning against a wall, arms crossed, his face a mask of cold focus. Ryder gave him a quick nod. Everything was set. The "tournament" officially started at seven, ten minutes from now.

"Ryder?" Crash hustled in his direction. A couple of years younger than him and Axel, Crash had blond hair that just touched his shoulders, bright blue eyes, and enough swagger for three brothers. Yeah, he was a cocky bastard, but he was a fucking force to be reckoned with in a fight. The sleeves of the red flannel he wore under his cut were rolled up to his elbows, revealing an intricate, creepy skull tattoo on his forearm. It was new.

Crash stopped next to him, concern easy to read on his face. "Where's Perry? Has he gotten his sorry ass here yet?"

"Haven't seen him." Guilt hit Ryder like a gut punch for lying to his brother. To make it even worse, they'd had to move all of that away from the clubhouse to keep word from getting out across the MC about the murders. They moved the crosses with their fallen brothers and the one meant for Sadie to the barn in the field a couple hundred yards behind *Sackett's* in the dead of night. "I'm sure he'll turn up."

A flash of red hair drew his attention to Sadie who just walked into the room to find Axel. Tugging on his arm, she seemed to be trying to get him to go back with her to the main room at the door. Ryder followed them out the front door. Emily and Jade were out front with Hero. Razor had just arrived. The riders who came with him were *not* expected.

What were the fucking Cottonmouths doing there?

Eli Crizer climbed off his bike to approach their president. Their Prez had a wild, unkempt look about him -- nearly white hair, cold eyes. Lines from the kind of hard years that came from a life spent in back alleys and bar brawls marked his face.

Hero, tensed and angry, marched in their direction but Razor held up a hand to cut him off.

"What the fuck is this?" Hero demanded, a murderous scowl on his face.

"It's partially thanks to *you* we have some backup." Razor hooked a thumb over his shoulder to indicate the dozen or so bikers that arrived with him. "Eli's been having trouble with our friend Bobby."

The Cottonmouths weren't friends. Bad blood ran deep between the two MCs. The Cottonmouths were known for being unpredictable, brutal, and unapologetic. They operated outside the lines, not just with the law, but with the unwritten codes between biker clubs.

Behind him, the rest of the Cottonmouths followed, peeling off their bikes one by one, their movements slow and deliberate, predators sizing up their prey. They didn't care that they were on enemy turf. If anything, they seemed to enjoy it -- the thrill of pushing boundaries.

The Hounds stood their ground, every muscle coiled in readiness. There was no trust here, just a fragile truce born out of necessity. The Cottonmouths might have come as allies for now, but hostility was thick in the air, the kind that could turn violent in a heartbeat if one wrong word was spoken. Crizer sauntered forward, his boots crunching on the gravel, stopping just shy of Axel and Ryder. He gave them a slow, humorless grin, like he realized he wasn't welcome and didn't give a shit.

"The fuckers you're dealing with have all but shut down two of our contacts in Jersey," Crizer drawled, his voice rough as gravel. Amusement lit up his eyes like this was all some twisted game to him. His gaze moved over each of the Hounds, like he was daring someone to make a move. "We want in on this."

Hero wasn't happy and neither was Jade. But apparently the deal had been struck and that did boost their numbers. Snow came up from behind them, talking with Razor and Crizer about assignments.

As the group made their way into *Sackett's*, others began making their way out. Old man Phillips had a list of who was supposed to be there -- the Hounds, their friends, a few old ladies, a few sweet butts. Now, the fucking Cottonmouths too. They just had to wait.

The tournament was already in progress, Stinger and a couple of his friends playing pool. Ryder's eyes followed the game for a moment. One of the prospects was at the table, chalking up his cue, while a couple of locals cheered him on. It was all part of the act. A distraction for when things turned. And now that Sadie was here, he imagined things would start pretty fucking soon.

His thoughts shifted to Margot then. Ryder had no idea if she'd show up or not. Part of him hoped she'd stay away. He'd catch her up tomorrow if they could just make it through the night.

* * *

Margot

It was nearly eight that evening and Margot drove by Emery Phillips' bar on the outskirts of town. There were a ton of bikes outside *Sackett's*, scattered around with the other vehicles in the parking lot. It looked like a busy night at the bar.

It was probably the fourth time she'd driven by, and everything seemed okay as she passed. But in the side mirror to her left, a black sedan, an old Crown Vic turned into *Sackett's* with a couple of other SUVs following it.

Instinct had restless energy coursing through her. Was it Bianchi's men? Was Bianchi himself coming now that he'd escaped prison? A widespread manhunt for the man was underway. Mercy would be one of the first places they'd be looking for him.

Should she have told the sheriff about the trap the Hounds set? Would her decision cost lives?

With a heart full of dread, she drove up the road until she found a place to turn around. Then she headed back to *Sackett's*, thinking about where to hide her squad car. Her heart raced in her chest, hoping the Hounds' plan didn't backfire on them spectacularly. Hoping Ryder and the rest of her friends, Sadie, Jade, and Emily would be safe.

* * *

Ryder

When the first one stepped through the door, the tension in *Sackett's* snapped like a wire pulled too tight. The music seemed to fade into the background, swallowed by a tense, electric silence. Two more men entered -- looking like regular guys at a glance. And then several more over the next few minutes. The determination on their faces gave them away, expressions as cold as the steel they carried.

Then it started. A bottle shattered on the floor, followed by a shove, and the entire bar erupted into chaos. There was no way to use guns without possibly hurting a friend. But there were plenty of other ways to only hurt the enemy.

The first punch was thrown in the blink of an eye, and suddenly, fists were flying everywhere; tables were overturned. The bar devolved into a violent frenzy. The Hounds were on their feet in an instant, slamming into the Mafia soldiers like a tidal wave. The Cottonmouths, unpredictable and wild as ever, jumped into the fight with reckless abandon. *Sackett's* wasn't nearly big enough to contain the brawl, and within seconds, the melee spilled outside into the parking lot, where floodlights cast long, menacing shadows over the scene.

Ryder's blood pounded in his ears as he ducked a wild punch from one of Bianchi's thugs, driving his fist into the man's gut before sending him sprawling across the hood of a car. Axel fought close by, fighting like a man possessed just like Snow, Razor, Hero, and the rest of their MC brothers.

But something gnawed at Ryder -- Bianchi. He wasn't there. Ryder had never seen him face to face, but he'd studied the fucker's photos from the papers and online.

"Where the fuck is he?" Ryder growled under his breath. Scanning the fight, he searched for any sign of the man who had caused so much pain.

The parking lot was a blur of motion. The Hounds held their own, trading brutal blows with Bianchi's men while the Cottonmouths, true to their nature, fought with no thought for strategy, just raw aggression. Fists and boots connected with sickening thuds, a grim soundtrack for the battle.

Ryder spotted Axel just a few feet away, grappling with a Mafia soldier, both locked in a brutal struggle. Before he could go help his birth brother, he caught sight of Sadie, Jade, and Emily, slipping out of the back of the bar. They were supposed to get in Jade's SUV and leave. The chaos in the parking lot had blocked their exit.

Ryder's chest tightened. Their women couldn't be out here. Not with Bianchi still unaccounted for.

"Axel!" Ryder shoved his way through the brawling bodies. Axel broke free of his opponent, his eyes flashing toward his brother, understanding instantly.

Without a word, the two of them moved like a unit. Ryder pushed through the tangle of men, his only focus on getting the women out. Emily spotted them first, her eyes wide with fear, clutching Jade's arm as they tried to stay low. Sadie, to her credit, was holding up. She was scared, but she wasn't panicking. Not yet.

Ryder reached them first, grabbing Sadie by the arm, Axel close behind.

"You need to get out of here, now." Ryder glanced between the women and the ongoing brawl. "Bianchi's not here. We don't know where he is."

Sadie's face paled, but she nodded. "Where do we go?"

"There's a storage shed behind *Sackett's*," Axel said quickly, his voice low but urgent. "Find it. Hide. Don't stop until you're out of sight." Anything to keep them away from the barn and the horror it contained.

Jade opened her mouth to protest -- she wasn't the kind of woman who liked running -- but Emily grabbed her arm, already pulling her in the direction of the field. "Come on," Emily urged, her voice tense. "Let's go."

Axel locked eyes with Sadie for a brief second, his gaze intense. "Go. We'll find you. Just stay hidden." Axel kissed her quickly.

Sadie hesitated, then nodded, squeezing his hand briefly before turning and following Emily and Jade into the shadows beyond the parking lot.

Ryder's stomach churned as they disappeared into the darkness. It wasn't just Bianchi and his men that had him on edge -- it was the unpredictability of the Cottonmouths, the wildness of the brawl, and the feeling that everything could spiral out of control in seconds.

"Where the hell is Bianchi?" Axel muttered beside him, frustration lacing his words as they moved back toward the fight.

* * *

Margot

All hell had broken loose at *Sackett's* by the time she hid her squad car.

A huge fight was in progress, and it took everything she had to battle her instinct to call it in, ask for backup. The Hounds violently fought a group of men she had to assume were Bianchi's. After a moment, she realized that not all the bikers were Hounds. She could have sworn she spotted a Cottonmouth patch on one huge man who wore a black mask over the lower half of his face.

Bodies littered the ground, bikes overturned. And that was just what she could see in the flood lamps attached to the bar. A lot of the fighting was concealed by the shadows.

Her heart flew as she watched from behind the huge oak tree to the left of the bar. Where were Sadie, Jade, and Emily? Were they still inside?

Margot spotted Ryder fighting; the ferocity of his attack on one man after another took her breath away. He'd always shown her a man that was sarcastic and charming. She wouldn't have guessed he could beat people down like *that*. He could take a hit too.

When he stopped and fought his way through the fight to the side of the bar, she saw him, then Axel, head that way. She couldn't make out who they were talking to, but Margot's gut told her it was Sadie, Emily, and Jade. Now Margot had a mission.

Keeping to the shadows, listening to the grunts and punches and muttered threats, she edged her way around *Sackett's*, moving quietly. Sure enough, she spotted her friends at a metal storage shed just behind the bar. Jade tried the door, but it was locked. The three of them lingered, looking unsure what they should do.

Margot made it to them. Sadie froze before turning to see who approached. Jade raised her handgun, pointing it in her direction. Margot froze.

"Easy, Jade," Margot said. "It's me, Margot."

Jade huffed out a shuddering breath, lowering her gun. "Thank God."

"What's going on?" Margot asked.

"The plan was for us to make our way out of the bar as soon as the fight began," Jade said. "But then the fight ended up in the damn parking lot."

"And this is locked," Emily said, pointing to the shed.

"There's an old barn in the field." Margot pointed in that direction. "Let's try that instead."

Sending them ahead of her, Margot kept an eye out for anyone else as they scrambled across the field, the moon lighting their way.

The barn was a forgotten relic, half-swallowed by

shadows in the moonlight. Its paint was faded to a dull, peeling gray, the wood weathered and cracked from decades of neglect. The roof sagged in the middle, patches of rusted tin hanging loosely over the frame, making it seem like the whole structure could collapse any time.

A single broken window, high up near the loft, let in a sliver of moonlight to slip through, casting eerie, angular shadows across the dirt floor. Margot turned on her flashlight, just to check things out when she entered. Inside, the space was vast but mostly empty, the ceiling looming high above like a cavern. The darkness inside was thick -- almost claustrophobic.

A sharp cry had them all turning in alarm.

"I'm okay," Emily said. "I tripped and --"

"What happened?" Jade asked.

"Oh, my God," Emily said.

Margot headed in that direction, pulling out her flashlight and turning it on. When she reached Emily, her light moved to the floor where it illuminated a macabre scene. Three crude wooden crosses laid on the dirt floor, with figures on two of them like Halloween decorations. It took her a moment to realize those weren't Halloween props on two of those crosses. They were actual human bodies and they'd been nailed to the crosses. As she moved closer to examine the scene, she was guessing they died before being crucified.

Jade rushed around to join them with Sadie. "It's Chance!"

"And Perry," Emily said, tears in her voice.

Margot moved her light over the third cross. It was bare. All except for something carved into the wood at the top. Moving around her friends, Margot got closer until she noticed the name "Sadie" had been crudely carved into the wood. The threat was unmistakable.

Margot immediately turned off her flashlight, but it was too late. Sadie stood next to her and her terror was palpable. Her breath was coming too fast, and Margot was afraid she was having a panic attack.

"Breathe." Margot wrapped an arm around her. "Deep breaths."

Some movement in the corner of her eye got Margot's attention. The shadows shifted at the barn's entrance, barely noticeable at first, like a ripple in the darkness. But then, one by one, four figures emerged, moving with a deliberate, deadly silence. Their footsteps were soft against the dirt floor, barely whispers, but the weight of their presence was impossible to miss.

The first man stepped into a sliver of moonlight; his features still half-concealed in shadow. He was tall with broad shoulders, wearing a dark leather jacket. His hand rested easily on the grip of a gun holstered at his side, fingers twitching, ready. His expression was amusement mixed with fury on a face accustomed to violence.

Behind him, the second man moved like a shadow, shorter but no less terrifying. His pistol had a silencer screwed on, his eyes sharp and alert, scanning the room like a predator. His lips curled into a faint smirk, as if he enjoyed the fear in the air. The other two hung back slightly, features hidden by the darkness.

Like a vision from a nightmare, Margot stared as the four men walked into the barn. Instinct told her it wasn't any of the Hounds. Slowly, she shifted her flashlight to her left hand. Her right reached for her firearm and --

"Draw on me and I'll put a fucking bullet in your brain," a deep voice said from the shadows.

Sadie moved behind her, trembling, and those men approached, backing them further into the barn. Something told her the voice belonged to Robert Bianchi himself.

"You like my present, baby?" Bobby smiled. "I didn't leave it here for you but hey, this works out."

"You sick fuck." Jade's voice was low in the darkness.

"*I'm* sick?" the leader asked. The man next to him turned on a flashlight and the men were revealed. The leader was Robert Bianchi himself.

Margot took a deep breath. She needed to draw on her training and experience now. If she panicked, all four of them would be dead.

"I know Sadie here has filled your ears with lies about me," Bobby said. "That's what she does. She lies. Don't you, baby?"

"Leave them alone," Sadie said behind her.

A spike of fear went through Margot. "Don't say anything," she whispered.

"Nah," Bianchi went on. "Let her talk. We're all interested in what the little cunt's last words will be. Aren't we, fellas?"

Stepping out from behind Margot, Sadie put herself in the line of fire. Her body shook but her hands were curled into fists, her stance defiant. "Let them go," she said as calming as she could. "Kill me if that's what needs to happen."

Margot was afraid now. Proud as she was of her friend's bravery, it wasn't the time or place for it. Not if any of them were going to make it out alive.

"Oh, I'm going to kill you," Bobby warned with a smile that didn't reach his eyes. "But let them go? Where's the fun in that?"

Slowly, they moved closer. Sadie didn't budge

and Margot stayed with her.

"No, I'm going to take out each one of your friends first so you can see them die," he said. "Then I'm going to kill you. Then I'm going to kill the asshole biker you've been fucking around with because... well, I owe him."

"I wish he'd killed you," Sadie's voice was resigned but still defiant.

"I'll bet you do." Bianchi laughed, looking Margot up and down, sneering. "Too bad our time is limited. I'd love to live out my female cop gang bang fantasy. That would be so much fun."

The words were meant to terrify Margot, the only one they considered a possible threat.

"You know what happens when you kill a cop," Margot warned.

"I know what's supposed to happen." Bianchi stared her down. "But you're not the first cop I ever killed."

Rushing forward, Bianchi tried to grab Margot, but she dodged him. The flashlight she carried was enough to double as a small club. With her left hand, she hit his torso hard with it, hoping she cracked a rib or two. The man's grunt of pain was satisfying but he caught her arm when she swung again. Twisting her arm behind her, he jerked up on it until the pain was excruciating, until she dropped the flashlight.

Margot refused to cry out, unable to do anything about it when he kicked the backs of her knees, forcing her down until she was kneeling before him, facing away.

"No!" Sadie cried out.

"Marty, come shoot this bitch in the head," Bianchi ordered as Margot's heart lurched in fear. The same man who killed her father was going to kill her.

* * *

Ryder

"You see him?" Axel hit the man who charged him hard in the balls, dropping him into the gravel.

"No, he's not here." Ryder scanned the floodlit parking lot again, looking for any sign of the Mafia boss. The chaos continued to rage around them -- fists flying, men shouting, and the screech of metal as someone slammed into a parked bike.

Something was off.

The Mafia soldiers kept coming, and there were a fucking lot of them, but they seemed almost... unfocused. Like they were buying time. That's when it hit him.

"They're stalling," Ryder said, his voice tight with realization. "Bianchi's not coming here."

Axel's eyes flashed toward him. "Then where --"

Ryder's breath caught in his throat, and he turned, his gaze darting toward the distant outline of the barn. Then he saw lights flashing wildly from within it. Ryder's gut knotted in dread, and for a moment, the sounds of the fight outside *Sackett's* faded into the background.

He exchanged a quick glance with Axel. "The barn."

Axel didn't hesitate. Without a word, they broke from the melee, dodging bodies as they sprinted toward the back of the bar. Ryder's focus was on the distant outline of the old barn, barely visible in the darkness. His heart hammered in his chest as they picked up speed, legs pumping over the uneven field.

They reached the edge of the barn just as a sharp cry cut through the night.

"Sadie." Alarm lit up Axel's eyes and they kicked

into overdrive, their boots thudding against the ground as they slammed into the barn doors.

The scene that greeted them was a nightmare. Bianchi had his Margot on her knees in front of him, cruelly twisting her arm behind her to keep her immobile. One of his men was closing in on her, his gun pointed at the back of her head. The other two men had Sadie, Jade, and Emily cornered, fear etched into their faces.

The twins didn't think -- they acted.

Ryder charged forward, his fist connecting with the jaw of the man with his gun on Margot. The impact sent him sprawling backward, crashing into the wall with a sickening *thud*. Axel was right beside him, barreling into the man threatening Sadie, knocking the gun from his hand and sending him reeling.

Ryder thought before pulling his gun. In the dark of the barn, he didn't want to start a gunfight with the women there.

Snow and Hero stormed in behind them, all muscle and fury. Hero tackled the guy who came at him with the shotgun, both crashing into the dirt floor, fists flying. Snow took on the last man, expertly disarming him with a swift kick to the face. The man yelled in pain as he fell to the ground hard, blood spraying from his face.

The quiet of the ancient barn erupted into chaos then, the confined space amplifying every grunt, every crack of bone against bone. Ryder's focus was on Bianchi now, his pulse a steady drumbeat of rage and adrenaline as he squared off with the man who had caused them so much pain. Axel, at his side, was a mirror of his intensity. The twins moved in sync as they closed in on their enemy.

Bianchi laughed, looking from one to the other.

"There are *two* of you fuckers. How did we miss that?"

Bianchi lunged first, swinging a heavy fist at Ryder's face. Ducking, Ryder countered with a brutal punch to his ribs. The Mafia boss hardly flinched. His dark eyes gleamed with malice.

Margot was holding her own behind them, fighting with techniques Ryder had seen her practice. Taking down one of Bianchi's men with a swift, calculated strike to his throat, Margot was fierce. Even as she fought, he saw the exhaustion setting in, her body running on mostly adrenaline. The sounds of flesh pounding flesh echoed through the old barn with Hero and Snow deep in their own battles, dirt kicking up all around them.

"Which one of you did I fight before?" Bianchi asked, looking from one twin to the other.

"Me!" Axel moved in, landing a punishing blow to the bastard's jaw. The Mafia boss spun on his heel, catching Axel with a savage elbow to the ribs. His twin was only distracted for a second, but it was enough time for Bianchi to kick Axel in the face, send him flying.

It was brutal, neither side giving an inch, but Ryder knew they had to end it -- fast.

Fueled by their rage and the need to get the Mafia out of Mercy forever, the twins launched a final coordinated attack on Bianchi. Axel caught him in the side with a punishing kick, sending the Mafia boss staggering into Ryder's waiting fists. With one last powerful blow, Ryder sent the bastard flying back at Axel who, with one swift motion, snapped the man's neck. Bianchi dropped to the dirt hard at Axel's feet.

When the barn doors slammed open again, Sheriff Sawyer and his deputies strode in, flashlights cutting through the gloom. Deputy Dawson, gun drawn, stopped as Margot landed the final blow on the last standing Mafia thug. The man landed at her feet as her gaze moved to her boss and coworkers.

It was all Ryder could do not to laugh as Dawson actually took a small step back.

"Dawson," the sheriff said. "Radio the state police and the feds. We also need medical, please."

"On it," he said, ducking back out of the barn like he couldn't get out fast enough.

"Donner." The sheriff motioned her to him. "I told you to stay out of this."

The barn fell into an eerie silence, broken only by the heavy breathing of the Hounds and the three men they just pummeled who lay motionless on the ground. Their boss was dead, his reign of terror over.

"We've got a lot to unpack here," the sheriff announced to all of them. "Stay put."

When the sheriff marched out of the barn, taking Margot with him, the rest of them breathed a sigh of relief as Bianchi's men were handcuffed and led back up to *Sackett's*. Hero and Jade were talking quietly. Snow and Emily stood with them.

Axel held Sadie, who looked destroyed, crying into his chest. She'd be dealing with everything for a while. Bobby was dead; she had nothing left to fear from him. But the guilt she'd always shouldered, even though the fucker's actions weren't her fault, would be heavy. Especially since the women had ended up in the barn with the bodies of their fallen brothers.

There would be a lot of explaining to do. Two Hounds were dead. Bobby Bianchi was dead. The Cottonmouths had done God only knew what.

When Margot returned to the barn, Ryder's heart pounded in pride as his gaze took her in. She was still standing, bruised but fierce, her dark eyes locking with his. Relief flooded through him as he stepped toward her, pulling her into his arms.

"Are you okay?" he asked.

With a small nod, she surrendered to his hold.

"It's over," he whispered, though the words felt hollow. He knew it wasn't really over -- at least not for the Hounds, not yet.

They'd mourn Chance and Perry and do right by their families. They'd figure out where things were with the Cottonmouths. But for now, he had his Margot in his arms.

They'd won.

Epilogue

Margot

She woke up just before noon the next day. She was off work. It was a blessing because she felt like she'd gotten hit by a truck. Her bladder was screaming at her. Somehow, she extricated herself from Ryder's octopus grip and made it to the bathroom.

Within minutes, she had a steamy bath running, added Epsom salts. She luxuriated in the water when the bathroom door opened. Ryder wandered in, not a stitch on, grinning at her.

"Got room for one more?"

Ryder ended up lying back in the tub with Margot leaning back against him. She didn't miss the way his hands skimmed over all the bruises on her body.

"How are you feeling, darlin'?" he purred as his hands moved lightly up her thighs.

Margot smiled. "Not sure I'm up for the fun stuff this morning."

Ryder laughed. "Yeah, I feel like a mile of bad road myself."

"I still have a job." She was grateful for that. "We're going to be dealing with the fallout from all of this for months but... Sadie is safe now."

"She is." Ryder sighed, a contented sound. "If they know what's good for them, those Mafia fuckers will stay the fuck out of Mercy."

"How are Chance and Perry's families?"

Ryder tensed around her. "Bad as you'd expect. Crash is taking it hard. He was the reason Perry signed on as a prospect."

Perry had just been nineteen years old. The bodies had been sent for autopsies. The sheriff was fit to be tied over the fact that the bodies had been moved from the location where they were found without calling the police.

"What are you thinking about?" Ryder pressed a kiss to the top of her head.

Blowing out a breath, Margot said, "I'm okay. I'm happy right now."

"Okay. For a minute there I was afraid you were going to tell me I'm too much trouble," he said.

It made her laugh.

"Reminds me," he said. "You know all that land we have at our place? Axel wants to buy me out of half of it. Wants to build a place for him and Sadie."

"Are you going to do it?"

"Depends."

"On what?" Where was he going with this?

"Do you want to stay *here*?" Ryder asked. "I mean, we are close to work. Or how would you feel about the house out in the country?"

That got her attention. "The house you grew up in?"

"That's the one."

Her heart sped up listening to him. "I thought you didn't like being there because…"

Margot remembered well the story he told.

"I don't," he said. "But I got to thinking when you came out there all those weeks ago, it didn't feel the same."

"You mean because I was bringing you cheeseburgers?"

Ryder's laugh was a deep rich sound that temporarily made her forget all her aches and pains.

"Okay, yeah," he said. "I love those fucking cheeseburgers… I let the ghosts of the past haunt me in that house when I was alone. Even when Axel was there, I just felt… I brought women back to the house, but it didn't really change anything."

"But when I was there it was different?" Margot's tone came across a little more sarcastic than she intended.

Catching her chin carefully in his fingers, he gently urged her to look at him. "I realize that it really wasn't about that house or my mother at all. It was about home. It feels like home when you're there."

The tears came on with frightening speed from the emotion in his words.

"I guess what I'm trying to say, is… you, Margot." Ryder kissed her mouth carefully. "I love you. I spent years looking for happiness and… you were with me all the while."

Margot let the tears come on. They were happy tears. "I love you too."

"Maybe we could build a life together," he whispered against her lips. "Even though you're a cop."

"Do I get more than a few weeks?" Her tone sounded more afraid than playful.

"You can have every minute I've got left, darlin'." Ryder claimed her mouth again in a gentle kiss, silently pledging his heart to her.

Jamie Targaet

Jamie Targaet is the author of the Hounds of Hell MC. She's anxious to introduce you to this club of gorgeous, dominant men and the lucky women who surrender to them. The ride is going to get wild at times, not going to lie. But there's thrilling action, scorching hot sex scenes, and all the feels.

Jamie writes erotic romance for Changeling Press, a little fanfiction on the side, and she's an aspiring horror writer in another life. She enjoys time with her family (including the fur babies). She likes good horror movies and shows, emo metal and classic rock, and time spent in other worlds writing and reading. She loves hearing from readers and is looking forward to hearing from you.

Hounds of Hell MC is part of the Hounds of Hell MC Multiverse.

Jamie at Changeling: changelingpress.com/ jamie-targaet-a-227

Changeling Press LLC

Contemporary Action Adventure, Sci-Fi, Steampunk, Dark Fantasy, Urban Fantasy, Paranormal, and BDSM Romance available in e-book, audio, and print format at ChangelingPress.com -- MC Romance, Werewolves, Vampires, Dragons, Shapeshifters and Horror -- Tales from the edge of your imagination.

Where can I get Changeling Press Books?

Changeling Press e-books are available at ChangelingPress.com, Amazon, Apple Books, Barnes & Noble, Kobo, Smashwords, and other online retailers, including Everand Subscription and Kobo Subscription Services. Print books are available at Amazon, Barnes and Noble, and by ISBN special order through your local bookstores.

Changeling Press, LLC

ChangelingPress.com